THE MECHANICS' INSTITUTE REVIEW
ISSUE 6 AUTUMN 2009

The first Mechanics' Institute in London was founded in 1823 by George Birkbeck. "Mechanics" then meant skilled artisans, and the purpose of the Institute was to instruct them in the principles behind their craft. The Institute became Birkbeck College, part of London University, in 1920 but still maintains one foot in the academy and one in the outside world.

The Mechanics' Institute Review
Issue 6 Autumn 2009

The Mechanics' Institute Review is published by MA Creative Writing, School of English and Humanities, Birkbeck, Malet Street, Bloomsbury, London WC1E 7HX

ISBN 978-0-9547933-6-4

Project Director: Julia Bell

Editorial Team: S. J. Ahmed, Ingrid Glienke, Jacqueline Haskell, Caroline Macaulay, Tamara Pollock, Deirdre Shanahan, Sarah Walcott

The Editorial Team would like to thank Russell Celyn Jones, Julia Bell, Sue Tyley and Anne-Marie Taylor for making this project possible.

For further copies or information, please contact Anne-Marie Taylor, MA Creative Writing, School of English and Humanities, Birkbeck, Malet Street, Bloomsbury, London WC1E 7HX. Tel: 020 7079 0689. Email: a.taylor@english.bbk.ac.uk

Website: www.bbk.ac.uk/mir

Printed and bound by
CPI Antony Rowe, Bumpers Farm, Chippenham, Wiltshire

Cover design and typesetting by Raffaele Teo

The Mechanics' Institute Review is typeset in Book Antiqua

TABLE OF CONTENTS

FOREWORD Jean McNeil 1

FREE COUNTRY David Savill 9

NOTES OF EXPERIMENTS ON MICE AND OTHER MAMMALS M. L. Stedman 19

MY AMERICAN JON Chimamanda Ngozi Adichie 27

THE MOTHERFUCKING PAPERBACK QUEEN OF ANADARKO Anna Baggaley 39

MR BONNER'S DREAM THE NIGHT BEFORE HIS EXECUTION Emily Cleaver 49

CONFESSIONS OF A FUZZY MAN Maggie Womersley . . . 55

THE ACCIDENT Anna Ackland 65

LAST BUS TO ELSINORE Sue Gedge 69

WHAT YOU KNOW Peter Ho Davies 83

YOU'RE LISTENING TO PAUL POWER Graham Hodge . . . 97

IN A DARK PLACE Richard English 105

LOVING RELATIVES Mary Irene Masaba 115

EL SALVADOR DEL REY Josh Raymond 129

REVOLUTIONARY COLOURS Moira Sharpe 139

THE TREE OF THE DEAD David Quéva 145

LORD OF DYFED Russell Celyn Jones 155

HOPE AND THE STAG Joanna Ingham 169

PICTURE THIS Chris Lilly 175

PRELUDES AND ELUSIONS Kavita Jindal 183

JAMES' JAM SANDWICH STAND-OFF Richard Milward . . 197

FOUR CORNERS Margi Williams 209

THE OTHER SIDE OF ANYTHING Jon Elsom 219

THE COUSINS Carol Wong 227

PEARLS OF WISDOM Lesley Saunders 241

EMBER Thea Bennett 255

THE FAREWELL TOUR K. K. Dayal 265

NOTES ON CONTRIBUTORS 271

FOREWORD
Jean McNeil

What's to be done about the short story? Writers want to write them, readers very likely want to read them, but publishers (at least in the UK) don't want to publish them. Because publishers think we don't buy collections, which means that writers don't write them – your ordinary vicious circle, folks. What is certain is that the short story has not flourished in this culture to the extent it has in Canada and the States, or in certain European countries. This matters for writers in Britain, because those literary forms that find success have much to do with how writers themselves flourish, and in particular with how they learn to write.

Every writer has an apprenticeship. Mine happened to take place in Canada, where I grew up and went to university. As an aspiring writer I had access to many quality literary magazines, most of them funded by provincial or federal governments and hosted by a university English literature department. In them I published poems, short stories and essays before attempting my first novel, aged twenty-two. Canada is friendly to the short story, in both its reading and writing culture. For a new writer to début with a collection of short stories is expected and lauded. They even win prizes – in 2006 Vincent Lam, a medical doctor and writer, won the country's pre-eminent literary prize for his collection of short stories, *Bloodletting & Miraculous Cures*.

For the last few years I have taught a seminar course on the

1

short story and the novella on the MA in Creative Writing at the University of East Anglia. The pressing questions my students want answered are: what is involved in writing a truly good short story? What is a short story in the first place? And why is it not valued here?

A short story is very often defined by what it is not, namely a novel. What separates the two has less to do with length than structure, and with what I call emotional intent. The Italian writer Alberto Moravia wrote a little-known but very helpful short essay, "The Short Story and the Novel". In distinguishing between the two, Moravia writes that "The principal and fundamental difference lies in the ground-plan or structure of the narrative . . . what we could call ideology, that is the skeleton of the theme from which the flesh of the story takes its form. The novel has a bone structure holding it together from top to toe, whereas the story is, so to speak, boneless."

Moravia goes on to observe that in the novel, the plot "is made up of not only intuitions and feelings (as in the short story) but primarily of ideas expressed poetically but well defined." Short-story writers, he states, have more variety, and paradoxically a broader world view than novelists. He cites the examples of two hyper-prolific writers, Guy de Maupassant (who wrote over 800 short stories) and Anton Chekhov: "while Maupassant and Chekhov . . . exhaust the variety of situations and characters of the society of their time, Flaubert and Dostoevsky are rather like those solitary birds that restlessly and loyally repeat the same significant cry."

William Faulkner regarded the short story as harder to write than a novel. Having written a few novels now myself, I'm not so sure that's true, but there is one old adage I do believe: only exceptional short-story collections will get published, whereas there are plenty of middling novels out there.

Not that this tells us very much about the short story's essential mystery. As Moravia cautions, "all this has little to do with the principal qualities of the short story – I mean that indefinable and inexpressible charm of narration experienced both by the writer and the reader. An exceedingly complex charm, deriving from a literary art which is unquestionably purer, more essential, more lyrical, more concentrated and more absolute than that of the novel."

Where does this "charm" come from? As a genre, the short story has been remarkably little theorised; the reams of opaque literary criticism studded with terms like *parole* and *récit* simply haven't been written. This means you can do what you want with it. Here's what I foreground in my class: in short stories, images, curtailed thoughts, fragments, glimpses, often make the point that explicit commentary or extended set-pieces would make in a long novel. In the short form you have to be deft, precise, observant – the magpie with the beady eye. To write short stories well, a writer must have a feel for the delicacy of the moment, which is the kernel of life, an understanding that what is left out is at least as important as what is left in, and finally a furtive quality, which I can't really put my finger on.

So why does Britain remain largely immune to its charms? The anthropologist in me takes a cultural approach to literature, meaning I see literature as a reflection of a society, an era, its concerns and desires. I detect a strong streak of philistinism in British culture, as well as a vaguely masochistic desire to be instructed. Big novels – big social novels in particular – might not have a single real person or emotion in them, but if they are intellectually ambitious and seek to "tell us how the world works" (to quote Zadie Smith), then we love them. We are impressed by novels that reflect the "society we live in", stocked with hyperbolic personnel and plotted across large swathes of space and time. In contrast, the short story almost never seeks to instruct. It's far too subtle for that.

In 2004 a unique report on the issue was published. The report, "The Short Story in the UK", was funded by Arts Council England and other writing bodies. The data is a bit old now, but I think its findings are still worth consideration.

The report found that most short-story collections are bought on impulse, so visibility in shops and promotions like three for two were deemed very important. Around 25 per cent of short-story collections were bought as gifts. Virtually all of the top hundred short-story bestsellers for 2002 were from mainstream publishers, and most were written by novelists. (In 2002 the bestselling short-story writers were Frederick Forsyth and Catherine Cookson.) Advances for short-story collections were (and remain) significantly lower, on average, than for novels. The report found that short-story writers increasingly had to turn to independent publishers to get published.

The report's more qualitative findings are illuminating. The researchers talked to readers, writers, publishers and booksellers and found that "Most readers prefer novels, partly because they can become 'lost' in the world of the novel but partly because they are 'afraid' to tackle a short story, feel they won't 'get it' and need to be reassured that it's not such a difficult form"; "the best way of all to support the prestige and profile of the short story would be to assist writers to write them"; "Mainstream . . . publishers are likely to buy a writer's short stories in order to secure a novel. The implication is that, without a novel, short story writers will find it very difficult to be published by a mainstream or independent publisher"; and "There's no point marketing something that isn't there." Among the report's conclusions were the need to develop a reading culture for stories, starting in schools; the need to "rebrand" the short story; the need for an annual anthology of best UK short stories and to establish "a new high-profile prize for short story collections".

What I notice is that this is all about the market, rather than literature. In Britain we have a highly commercialised attitude to literature; the only way to solve the problem of the short story is prizes, money, and notoriety. (You could conclude the only things anyone in Britain values are money and fame.) In Canada, I was brought up to consider literature an art form. But that's me the sackcloth-and-ashes purist, wandering in my own private desert.

The good news is that judging from the reviews pages of the broadsheets, and from the literary anthologies coming out of creative writing programmes (of which *The Mechanics' Institute Review* is a shining example), the short-story form remains much admired by critics, by teachers of literature, and most importantly by writers themselves. Many writers thrill to the "high-wire act" (according to one national-broadsheet review of recent collections) of writing a good short story: Will it work? Can I do what I want to do? Where is this all going?

That thrill, and the desire to try out new ways of telling stories, are what drove me to write my collection *Nights in a Foreign Country*, published in Britain in 2001 and in Canada a year later. At the time, I had just published my first novel. I didn't know what to write next, and feared that whatever it was, it would lack the freshness and resolve of my first book. The collection was born out of an episodic period in my life, when I was changing countries and jobs often, living in Brazil, in Central America, Mexico, encountering an array of people and situations. The story seemed the only form that could offer me the variety to test out ideas and settings. Then, as now, what thrilled me about the short story was its intensity, which does not come solely from the incident depicted, the story, or the theme, but from a tight patterning of drama, symbol, motif in such a way that its dramatic tension is exposed; how everything within it is directed at a single emotional effect.

Also, by my mid-twenties, when I started *Nights*, it was beginning to dawn on me that in life we don't encounter people and situations locked in the vast web of occurrence and happenstance, as in grand social-panorama novels. People in short stories are very often portrayed caught in isolated moments. If the novel's natural territory is "how the world works", and the novella's of memory and desire, the short story's is, I think, the turning point: fulcrum moments, or short timeframes, which represent a change.

Because or in spite of these qualities, the isolation and the brevity and attack of the form – Raymond Carver's advice for writing short stories was: "Get in, get out. Don't linger." – a writer's sensibility is more apparent in short stories. The short form requires more control of story, and better emotional judgement, than the novel because its very brevity forces the meaning of such moments beneath the surface, where, as one critic writes, "by the nature of its indistinctness, it gives the impression of being inexplicable." Stories are often like photographs, blurry and indistinct, as if seen through myopic eyes, or in the developing tray, gradually becoming more distinct. This sharpening of focus mirrors the process of understanding, often aided by epiphany – the moment of revelation – and of the simultaneous realisation that a moment of enlightenment is perhaps all you're going to get. The novel promises understanding. The short story generally eludes it, although somehow – and this is part of its genius – in its very evasion points to a more expansive and more honest truth.

Then there are those furtive aspects of the story I can't quite explain: my suspicion that it is an elegiac form, an unannounced elegy for what is lost or missing, not only in the characters' existences, but in all our lives. Nadine Gordimer has written that short-story writers deal with the only thing we can be sure of – the present moment. There is a loneliness to this, I think. We are stranded in the moment with our awareness that life is not that grand narrative, but more like the flash of fireflies, off and on, now here, now there, flitting through the darkness.

Like every literary form, the short story has its limitations and its weaknesses – coyness, a tendency to miniaturism, a breathy portent that calls attention to its every manoeuvre. Writers themselves tend to fall into the trap, when writing them, of an over-emphasis on craft, and on perfection. Often this results in a story-by-numbers approach; we end up writing the same story over and over again. Creative writing students love the short story because it seems to proffer the beguiling possibility that there is a "way" to write, that the craft can be learned and perfected, and you don't need to spend ten years at your desk sawing away at some six-hundred-page monster to do it. But the truth is the story's power lies not in craft, nor in perfection, but in the emotion that drives it.

When teaching story-focused workshop classes, there is an exercise I use wherein I ask my students to write *what your character dreamt the night before the story started*. The result is writing that displays anticipation, energies and forces gathering to enact what will be an intense and concentrated effect, even if what students write will not appear in the story, like figures just outside the frame of the photograph. Dreams are of course mysterious, and at the heart of short stories is a mystique. Joyce Carol Oates has written that "the root of all stories is in the Brothers Grimm, in dreams; not in cameras and tape recorders." The short story, Oates writes, is "the dream realised."

I find short stories harder to write now than I did when I started out as a writer. Perhaps because I am too aware – of the conventions of the genre, of the tasks it sets the writer. I lack the reckless clarity I had as a young writer. Or maybe all my ideas are simply novel-length and novel-breadth these days. I don't know.

What I do know is that I benefited from knowing virtually nothing about the form when I wrote my stories. I broke many of the rules, not entirely successfully. Now I counsel my students to read widely and consider what we discuss in class about the history, conventions and expectations of the story; but when writing their own stories I say: take risks, make the story work for you, not the other way around. The short story is a flexible, intelligent, subversive form. Dream the dream of the night before the story started. Make it yours. Make it new.

A scrupulous writer, in every sentence that he writes, will ask himself at least four questions, thus: What am I trying to say? What words will express it? What image or idiom will make it clearer? Is this image fresh enough to have an effect?

George Orwell

FREE COUNTRY
David Savill

I am twelve and certain that pineapples come from palm trees. Kemel is nearly fourteen and creases up when I tell him. For a few months of the year I will be thirteen and Kemel will still be fourteen. But we haven't got there yet. We are underneath the palms of the Riva in Split and when Kemel laughs I am no longer so sorry his dad is dead.

It was Kemel's idea to come fish for girls on the harbour wall. Kemel's idea to go to bed in our jeans and wait for my grandmother to fall asleep before sneaking out of her apartment. None of this was me. It wasn't even my idea for Kemel to be here. My older brother is never coming back from Düsseldorf and my mother works with Kemel's mother. Apparently Kemel's mother cries a lot. Enough tears in any case for me to end up looking at the unfamiliar shape of her son's body in the springs of Edin's holiday bunk.

Beneath the summer sheets we lay in our jeans, the smell of fried *ćevapi* meat filling the air; the clatter of cutlery and the sound of Macedonian songs playing outside the restaurant on a narrow street three floors below. Grandma fell asleep in front of *Knots Landing* and we were waiting for her to wake with the music at the end. She would put her head round the door to check on us. Then the tinkle and drip of her pee through the wall, the sound of false teeth swilling in a glass and finally, *finally* the shaft of yellow light across the parquet floor of the hall would close like the door of the spaceship swallowing ET.

I follow Kemel's commando crawl. We are bare-chested and our T-shirts are stuffed into the back pockets of our jeans. I am Chuck Norris creeping through the jungle in *MIA3* and the enemy won't know what hit them. Not until my left nipple gets trapped in a piece of loose parquet and my squealing nearly blows the entire operation. In the aftershock we lie long enough for the darkness to turn blue and reveal not two special operatives in the camouflage of night, but two half-dressed boys, spreadeagled on the hall floor in bright moonlight. The musicians on the street outside finish another song. A sad trickle of hands clapping. Then Kemel gets to his feet and tiptoes to the key hook and my heart is in my mouth because for just one second the coats are like a huddle of people turning their backs to us.

I hear the key in the lock and then the chain and standing up next to the wall find myself eye to eye with the picture of Colonel Tito – who is black and white, bushy-browed and stiff-jawed and would never betray his grandmother.

"Come on!" Kemel whispers.

The stairwell is cool and when the door closes this is all a thing we can't put back.

I wait on the cobbled street in the green light of Beko's shop where Kemel queues to buy cigarettes from a man who knows my face too well. A man who sells me Grandmother's bread and yoghurt and always tells of how he knew my mother when she was a little girl.

German pornography aside, the best thing about Beko's is in the window: a tourist map of Yugoslavia. Kidney-shaped towns and plastic mountains crinkled like the dashboard of my father's Fico when it melted in the summer heat. That was the year we went to Korčula island, when Edin still came on holiday with us and the car smelled of burning rubber and the fumes of the petrol tank leaked from the rear engine. Behind the handbrake there was a jagged, rusting hole in the chassis floor where we dropped chewed gum, sweet wrappers, matches and stones, watching from the back window to see if we could spot them on the road. Then Edin thought of eggs and Dad taped up the hole. Eventually we got a Golf. The first in our neighbourhood. Then Dad got a better job and we moved into a new apartment.

Korčula is too small for the map. I keep my back to the restaurant and its laughter and loud voices. I am safer in the company of a blind man who sits on a wicker stool and plays a stringed instrument on his lap. The blind man has a dog but not a homely one – a street dog with one pearly, grey eye like its owner's and a lump on its jaw like coral stone. The dog watches his master's hands float over the strings and I think of my grandmother knitting and how she will feign a heart attack if she ever finds out about any of this.

There is a blind man back home in Tuzla called Jefer. He wears dark glasses so we know he is blind. Looking at the cloudy marbles of the man in Split I realise Jefer doesn't wear the glasses because all blind men do. He wears them to cover his ugly eyes. It gives me a headache the way the blind man's eyes roll into his brow, bouncing with the notes. So I stare at the map and practise finding Tuzla and follow the winding line of the Drina. I have also learned to tell the Neretva and the Vrbas and the Sava – which I trace from the point where it runs alongside the Danube and into another river called the Morava. And where the Morava splits in two there is a town I have not heard of until the girl on the beach said its name today: Niš.

She seems important somehow. Though we only saw her once. Important then because just being near a girl was as close as we got to interplanetary space travel. Important now, just because I remember.

She turns up when it is reaching midday and we have been in the sea and watched our pee fizz and now we are looking for something new to do.

"Where are you going?" she says.

"Over by the boats," Kemel says.

"Can I come?"

"Free country," I say because it is something I have heard Kemel say.

(Months later I will be visiting Kemel's house and his mother will scold Kemel's uncle for putting the best chairs outside the front door so he can drink Tuzlanski with the neighbour. "Free country," Kemel's uncle will say, and feeling cheated I will never use the phrase again.)

"How old are you?" the girl says.

"Fourteen," I lie.

"My brother's fourteen."

"Congratulations," I say.

In bare feet we pick our way over the needling rocks and I want to look back to where the girl is scrambling behind us in yellow bikini bottoms and no top. But something between Kemel and me forbids it.

"What's your name?" she says.

"Lolek," I say.

"Bolek," Kemel says.

"Lolek . . . ?" Then she gets it and says, "No, your *real* names!"

"I'm Chuck."

"He's Norris."

"I'm Bruce."

"He's Lee."

I pull myself up onto the barnacled ridge where a seagull kicks off with a cracking flap. Kemel is jumping ahead, down into the next gully of rock pools. When he is out of sight I turn to offer my hand to the girl.

She is looking for places to put her feet and when she reaches for my hand her fingers are warm and small and it occurs to me how easily I could crush them. Then she springs onto the rock with a strength I don't expect and in that moment I have an urge to lift her by the waist, high into the air, turning a circle of the sun.

Instead I chicken out and begin to climb down, rock by rock. She has blonde hair dried dirty like bleached kelp. Her body is bony. Her arms are burned and peeling-papery like the skin falling off hazelnuts. Her ribs show and there are two brown nipples desperate to be breasts. I steal this information in glances but can't work up the courage to look in her face.

"My name's Dragan," I say.

"My brother's best friend is called Dragan. I'm Csilla."

"What sort of name is that?"

"C-S-I-L-L-A," she spells. "Csilla. Bulgarian. My daddy's daddy is Bulgarian but we live in Niš."

"Why do gorillas have big nostrils?" I say.

"What?"

"It's a joke. Why do gorillas have big nostrils?"

"I don't know. Why *do* gorillas have big nostrils?"

"Because they have big fingers."

Csilla doesn't laugh. She says, "Yes, that's funny," then "Your friend, what's his real name?"

"How do you know Dragan's *my* real name?"

"Because you told me."

"I might have lied."

"Why would you tell a lie?"

The last person to ask me this was a teacher and even then I had no answer.

"He's not my friend so much," I say. "I mean, he is. He's this boy I'm on holiday with."

The girl wrinkles her nose.

Kemel has made the harbour wall and climbs a rusting ladder. The muscles in his back are like the older boys' in the judo team at home and his shoulders are broad and where his legs are wet I see for the first time dark hairs plastered over the back of his thighs.

I am as bare and pale as the girl from Niš.

"Are you really fourteen?" she says.

"Two cows are standing in a field," I say, "and one turns to the other and says, 'Moo-oo-oo.'"

"And the other one says, '*I* was just about to say that.'"

The rocks are gulping the sea somewhere beneath us. I don't want Csilla to see I'm upset she knows the cow joke so I let her climb the ladder first. Her toes curl over the rungs double-jointed and as I follow I watch the half moons of goose-pimpled flesh trapped in her bikini bottoms. Water drips from her skin and onto my face and when I get to the top the stone of the wall is hot beneath my feet.

Kemel carries Csilla over his shoulder. She beats his back with her fists and laughs and he is singing *Rock Me Baby*, by Riva. At school we have our own chorus which goes "Fuck me, baby . . . fuck me!" We sing it from the playground wall because this is 1989. The year Riva won the Eurovision Song Contest for Yugoslavia.

When Csilla finally wriggles free of Kemel she runs down the harbour wall and the last I see of the girl from Niš are the bleached soles of her feet, scratched and cut by the barnacled rocks.

*

On the Riva that night we share a concrete bollard. Kemel lights me a cigarette from the end of his own and I notice for the first time his nails bitten to nothing, the cuticles ripped and chewed. My first drag takes me up into the fairy lights of the palm tree, into the music of a gypsy band playing a gypsy version of *Rock Me Baby* over the road. It is just possible that Csilla will be one of the sunburned girls who passes by with her parents. It is just possible she will see us sitting here, smoking, and she will shoot me a look and just that look and the feeling of her hand in mine and her legs on the ladder will be enough to keep me going for months.

"Maybe we can get a moped," Kemel says.

"How old do you have to be?"

Kemel doesn't answer. He is too busy biting a piece of dry skin from his knuckle and watching where a man sells ice creams from a refrigerator beneath an umbrella printed with faces of Eskimos. Then without saying anything he hops down, sidles over and asks for a Milka.

"If you pay like everyone else," the man says.

Kemel sucks on his cigarette. "Pay you later, when we've got some money."

"Money where?"

Kemel nods at the restaurants over the road. "Singing."

The man shakes his head and attends to a pensioner in a railway engineer's cap. I feel sorry the ice-cream man has to smile the whole time. He drops the smile when the customer has gone, suddenly a different person. Like my dad when my mum isn't looking. Adults want you to think they are adults all the time. But I've seen them when they are not.

"Here's an opportunity, Pavarotti," the ice-cream man tells Kemel. "Sing for me now and it's a deal."

Kemel looks at his feet and I actually wonder whether he's going to sing.

Though of course he doesn't.

"Thought not," the man shouts at Kemel's back.

On the bollard Kemel sulks, stubbing his cigarette on the broken shells embedded in the concrete and shredding the tobacco, making a fat black spot.

"These Drina taste like shit," he says.

I have never smoked any other kind of cigarette. I know there are different colours on the packets but it has never occurred to me that one kind would taste any different to the other.

"Like shit," I say. Because I don't have a brain of my own. Then I flick the shit cigarette onto the pavement – afterwards having to hide the fact that it has burned the tip of my finger.

"Well, don't fucking waste them," says Kemel.

But he isn't looking at me. He is looking past me, still staring at the ice-cream man, and suddenly I feel too close to Kemel's face. His eyebrows are thick and dark and lighter hairs bridge the gap between them, covering a yellow pimple. It makes me think of the back of his legs on the ladder that afternoon and how there is a smell when he takes his clothes off at night.

Then Kemel is gone. I don't know whether I notice this first or the fact that he is running towards the ice-cream man. Kemel runs and the ice-cream man bends into the refrigerator and when Kemel gets there he pushes down on the man's back and grabs a handful of stuff.

Man. Kemel. Shove. Stash.

Ball. Window. Smash. Glass.

There are times when everything stops. The ice-cream man, the woman about to run after Kemel before he disappears into a crowd, and the child limp at her hand like a doll being dragged by a girl.

Then first the ice-cream man, and next the startled woman, and then even the child imitating its mother; they all turn to look at me – three open mouths.

And I know I can run. I know there are crowds to run into and I have a good chance. I even spring to my toes. But there is something in me won't run like Kemel. Something won't make the decision. There is thinking. Always this *thinking* in me. Thinking about my grandmother when we crawled along the hall floor, about the chances of being spotted by the people in the restaurant outside the shop, about the map in the window, and all night thinking about the girl on the beach.

Now I'm thinking about tripping over my own feet, about an arm grabbing me in the crowd. About a policeman who clubs me round the ear and walks me to the door of my grandmother's house. Thinking about my grandmother on the telephone to my parents and my parents meeting me off the coach in Tuzla where I will feel sick from not eating.

Thinking has me reaching into my pocket for the money Kemel didn't know about. I hold it out to the ice-cream man as he walks towards me, a look on his face that says *you won't run*. A look on his face that knows me. There is sweat on his nose and he smells of beer and rotten like melted ice cream. He wipes the sweat off then takes the notes without saying anything and to my surprise starts to count them in his sticky fingers, saying the words on his breath. One, two, three, four, five. And he could take the lot for all I care. But he doesn't. Instead he counts them and folds five of the notes into his apron before giving one lonely note back to me.

Which is all the worse. Worse like the way he keeps quiet instead of shouting. Worse like me suddenly opening my mouth to find myself saying, "His dad died . . ." like it will mean something.

"His dad died," like it will excuse Kemel and get us out of trouble.

"His dad died," like the man will suddenly reach out and pat my shoulder and comfort me. As if it's really my own father who died. Because at that moment I feel like it is.

But the man doesn't even blink at the death of a boy's father. He just shakes his head and returns to the customer and his smile is sadder than ever.

In the end Kemel hasn't gone far. He is behind the toilet cabins, sitting on a low wall, surrounded by the melting Milka, puddles of creamy paper and the smell of piss. He puts his hands on my shoulders and shakes me and asks me if I saw the man's face and did I see how he jumped over that child? I tell him I did. I laugh until it hurts my stomach and I tell him how fucking great it all was. And then Kemel asks how I got away and I tell him some complete mountain of shit about pushing a bike in the way of the man and running along the harbour wall, jumping over the break where the jetty cuts through. Jumping high over someone's head like T. J. Hooker on the bad streets of LA. I tell him lies that will get bigger and bigger; a story I will repeat on the football pitch in Slatina, lies that will fill the judo club and the playground when we are back at school and Kemel is my new best friend. A story I will repeat until I believe it is true. A story like this one, full of half-remembered things and the rest just my wish for a country we used to call free.

If
writing
is not an
argument
with the

قارئ

then it is
nothing.

Salman Rushdie

NOTES OF EXPERIMENTS ON MICE AND OTHER MAMMALS
M. L. Stedman

The mouse on the treadmill is going round and round and round. His name's Graham. His whiskers shiver and his little pink nose is soft as a new mushroom. The wheel chatters on, ricketa-ricketa-ricketa, rhythmic as a beat box, so you wouldn't know just from the sound that he's missing a leg. Scuttling like a devil, he is.

His eyes are red like raspberries but I don't think that makes him look evil – more angry, and I wonder if he sees the world through a red mist of rage about his missing leg. But he's only a mouse – how angry can he get? I mean really? And what difference does it make to the world if he does?

Graham lives in his cage in my bedroom. He lost his leg on account of I bit it off when Dad and Mum went out and I hit the crème de menthe. Wicked stuff. *Really* messes with your head. Used to be banned completely. (Or maybe that was the other one, absinthe?) Anyway, it's what they're least likely to miss. So, after a bottle of crème de menthe and a couple of tabs of some shit I scored at school, I got to wondering what it would be like to be Hannibal Lecter. I decided to do an experiment. On my little brother, Jakey. Just a toe, say. A single bite would do it – he's barely a year old. But he was out with Mum and Dad. Graham was the only one home, so I just bit his little leg off: the right back one. To see if I could. You know. And I could.

I let Graham limp around the empty bath while I chewed the

19

tiny leg. It was a bit crunchy, like chewing a toenail or the end of a chicken wing, only with fur. Salty, too, from the blood, and warm. Then I went down the park to sleep off the tabs.

He's my half-brother really, is Jakey-Jake. And "Mum"'s my stepmum. She still hasn't worked out I'm taking the piss when I call her that. Dad didn't pick her for her brains.

When I got home from the park she gave me this really strange look and said: "Barny, I have to talk to you."

Fair enough, I thought. She'd probably send me off to the school counsellor again, who'd say it was a "cry for help" or some other crap about gifted children or maternal rejection. But she said, "Barny, something awful's happened." I thought Dad must be dead. Then I heard him coughing in Jakey's bedroom. She said, "It's about Graham . . ."

"What about Graham?"

She said, "Oh, poor Barny. Graham's . . . Graham's at the vet's."

"Why?"

"Because he . . . something happened to him." She put her hands together like for a prayer. "I don't know how he got out of his cage. I found him in the bath when I got home. I'm *so* sorry! – Princess bit him . . ."

I almost laughed, but managed to hold it in. I pursed my lips just a touch. Princess was her cat, and came to live with us when she moved in with Dad.

"I know you're upset, but it'll be all right," she said. "The vet's operated on him. He says he'll make a good recovery. And that a mouse – well, a *pet* mouse – can live a full life with three legs . . ."

"*Three legs?*" I gave her my zombie stare of horror.

"Should have finished it off with a shovel!" That was Dad, coming back from putting Jakey to bed.

"Oh, Alan! For goodness sake! Not in front of Barny."

"Well, it's a bloody mouse! They cost about 10p at the pet shop, or they're free if you hang around the garden shed."

"Alan!" She was torn between paying attention to me and making eye contact with him, to warn him off. "Alan, *please* try and be a bit more sensitive. He's upset. Say sorry!"

"Oh, for God's sake!" He opened the fridge and pulled out a jar of pickled onions. He fished for one with his fingers and shoved it in his mouth. "Sorry," he said to the jar.

"Waaaaaaah." Jakey started to wail.

"I'll go," said Dad, stuffing in another couple of onions as he left.

I waited a bit, then looked at the floor as I said, "I think you should have it put down."

"Barny! But I thought you were so fond of Graham! I thought you'd want us to do everything to save him." She sounded like a TV drama.

"No . . ." I turned to her. "I mean *Princess*. I think you should have Princess put down."

She didn't move. She just looked at me, angry, but frightened too. "But . . . But she's so old. I've had her for fifteen years."

"Exactly."

"Well, why would I have her put down?"

"If she can whip Graham out of his cage when he's just minding his own business, what else might she do? I mean, what if she was to hurt Jakey or something?"

"She wouldn't hurt Jacob!" she snapped, like Princess was Mother Teresa.

"Are you sure? How would you feel if, next time, you came home and it was *Jakey* had been bitten?"

"That's horrible! And it's . . . it's impossible nonsense! Graham's a mouse!"

"I'd have to tell Social Services about this attack on Graham, if that happened . . ."

She stared at me.

"Well, think about it. I'd have to tell them because it would be *relevant*, wouldn't it? In our class on Social and Legal Structures they were teaching us about liability – about how it makes all the difference if you know there's a risk and don't do anything about it. It's like why all them tobacco companies got sued. So when one of your pets has gone feral . . ."

She started to laugh but I just kept staring at her until her lip began to quiver and she was in tears. She sat down on the yellow chair like a little girl on the naughty step. "Oh, God . . . God give me strength . . ." But I could see I'd managed to plant just the tiniest doubt.

I went and put my arm around her shoulder and wiped a dribble of snot from her nose, and I patted her head and said, "It's OK, Mum. But you know I'm right, don't you?" and I watched how the snot from my fingers clumped together a few bits of her blonde hair.

After I'd gone to bed I heard Dad in the kitchen shouting, "Have you gone bloody mad, woman?"

And she said, "It'll be worth it, Alan. It'll be worth it just to get him to trust me. It'll be worth it to be a proper family. I really want this to work, Al. Imagine how hard it's been for him since I moved in. Then here barely two minutes and Jacob's born. He's fifteen. He's at a very delicate stage –"

"He's a bloody pain in the arse and quite frankly if I had to choose between *him* and the cat I know who I'd choose, let alone between the cat and the bloody mouse!"

"Alan! You're his father! Is this how you'll be talking about *Jacob* when he's a teenager?"

"I'm telling you, he's nothing but trouble! Janet'd had enough of him by the time he was three, and *she* gave birth to him. No wonder she pissed off! I've lost one woman because of him and I'll not lose another!"

"Shhh! He'll hear you!"

That was my cue to stumble down to the kitchen. "I've been having nightmares," I whined. "About Graham. In the nightmare there's lots of blood. And I can *feel* his tiny leg in my mouth, like it was *me* bit it off. And Princess is *huge* and she's looking at Jakey, drooling."

"Oh, poor kid!" She hugs me, and she's wearing her white cotton nightie and I can feel her nipple against my cheek so I snuggle my head more against her chest to get it harder and I say, "I'm scared," and she says, "It's OK, it's OK." And with her nipple practically in my mouth I look up at Dad and he looks at me. And he doesn't smile. And she doesn't notice the looking. And finally he blinks first and says, "All right, let's get you to bed," and he adds, "young man," just to show her how fatherly he is.

Two days later I helped Jakey put the cat's collar with its little tinkly bell around the neck of his teddy bear. Well – shame to throw it out.

Charles Darwin used to eat loads of the species he discovered – he was well known for it. Our biology teacher, Mr Sargeant, says the difference between an ordinary scientist and a world-class one is an "unflinching lust for knowledge". "You don't have to go to Mars to do an experiment," he says. "Just look in your everyday environment and you'll find a thousand questions that need answering – a thousand things worth observing. There's no substitute for first-hand experience. Be bold!" I bet if I told him about my experiment on Graham he'd give me a distinction. Dad wouldn't. When they put me into the class for "gifted children" Dad snorted, "Twisted children, more like." Then he pretended he was joking.

There are other kinds of "unflinching lust". Dad fancies the pants off my stepmum. Literally. All the time. Dirty old bastard. No one over forty should be allowed to have sex – it's too gross to imagine. Especially with a woman that much younger. Her body's not half bad. Not porn standard, but her skin's got this soft, almost invisible hair all over it that makes it shimmer.

She's spent the whole afternoon in her room, sniffling. I can hear her down the corridor, and the fffffft of another tissue coming out of the box. And Graham's little wheel goes ricketa-ricketa-ricketa. Round and round it goes. Round and round.

I saw her other bloke come here twice, after she moved in. I saw from my observation platform in the top of the old chestnut tree in the back garden. I spend hours there. She knows that *now*, but she didn't *then*. From the platform (it's basically two planks nailed onto a branch) I can see everything that goes on in our house – like it's a doll's house and I could just take the back wall off and move all the furniture around.

So I saw him. Young. Good-looking. Why she'd choose Dad instead of him though . . . Well – financial security, I suppose. Biologists say it happens all the time – some females choose one partner for the mating bit and another for raising the young. It's the same from mice to macaque monkeys. I could see right into the bedroom – see every little thing they were doing, and with the binoculars I could even make out some of the words she was saying. Like porn with the sound down.

I didn't tell anyone. I just logged the data.

Later, Jakey was born, and I've never seen my dad so happy. Never. "My *son!*" he kept saying. "Meet my *new son* Jacob," like he'd just traded up for a better car.

When we did Greek tragedy at school, you could always tell when someone was heading for trouble. It was just after they stood up and said, "Now I'm finally happy. Life's perfect." Last week, after Princess went, I was watching Mum and Dad and Jakey-Jake from the top of my tree. I heard her say, "Alan, it was all worth it, wasn't it? I can't believe how lucky we are . . ."

The Graham experiment was about breaking taboos. But I couldn't be sure how much of its success was down to the crème de menthe and that. How "unflinching" would I have been if I hadn't been shit-faced? So that's what today's experiment was for, seeing as Dad's away for a few days.

I went into the kitchen. She was busy feeding Jakey-Jake. Yoghurt or peach vomit or something. He was grizzling and she looked hassled. I sat on the table and said, "We're doing this really cool project at school."

"What's it about?" she asked, trying to shovel stuff into his mouth even though it was shut tight.

"Genetics and that . . ."

"Jacob, sweetie, open your mouth for goodness sake."

I pretended to be put off because she wasn't listening. "You're busy. Forget it."

That got her. She loves it if she thinks I'm "talking to her". As in "I mean, really *talking*, Alan . . ." sort of talking.

"No, please, Barny. I'd love to hear more. I can feed Jacob and listen too."

So I started to tell her a little story, about how we were studying DNA at school and how Mr Sargeant had arranged for some mate of his from Imperial College to come and show us how DNA tests were done and how when he'd asked for volunteers I'd offered.

"That's great, Barny. So," she asked, wiping Jakey's face, "what'll they do: make a picture of your DNA or something?"

"*Our* DNA."

"What do you mean?"

"Well, it's the whole family. We're ideal, you see." She let a gobbet of yoghurt fall down the gap between Jakey's neck and his bib. "Because apparently it'll be really interesting to demonstrate the effect of Dad's genes on his two sons because of the two different mothers."

She went white as a sheet. She tried to smile as she asked, "What's your dad said about it?"

"I haven't told him yet. I think he'll like it, though, don't you reckon?"

It was one of those chess moments – you know those times when you just *see*, all at once, how every move's going to play out until checkmate. Like time's suspended, and the strategy's so perfect it's actually beautiful. I think that's how God would see things. If he existed.

She said some crap about not wanting Jakey to have a needle.

"It's only a mouth swab," I said.

Then she wasn't happy about what they might do with the DNA: "They use it for fraud these days. I saw a documentary on it."

I said, "I don't think Mr Sargeant does fraud, only crimes against fashion."

The excuses got more and more pathetic until she said, "I've got to put Jacob down for his nap," and yanked him out of the high chair. When she came back she said, "I've been thinking, Barny, and I just don't want to do it. Actually. No. I'm Jacob's mother and I'm just saying no. I don't have to justify myself. Now," and she took off her apron, "how about Chinese for dinner, as a treat while Dad's away?"

I was quite pleased at how easily I'd got her to confirm my hypothesis. That was the first part of the experiment. So I said, "Ah, 'adverse inference' . . ." She looked blankly and I said, "That's what it's called in courts and stuff when they decide that, if someone doesn't want to answer a question, it's because their answer would show their guilt." I put my finger into the peach vomit on Jakey-Jake's high-chair tray and spread it out more evenly. "So here, for example, if you don't want little Jakey-Jake's DNA tested, the adverse inference is that it's because –" But before I could finish she slapped me, hard. Right across the face.

"For Christ's sake, stop calling him that! His name's Jacob!" Then she got that look in her eye you get when you realise you've just fucked up in a *big* way.

But I said, "It's OK." And she looked relieved for a moment, then a bit confused. I held one of her hands between mine. "I saw him, you know. After you first moved in. I saw your other boyfriend."

She clenched her free hand into a fist, and closed her eyes. "I love your dad so much, Barny. So much."

I said, "I know."

"Sometimes the things grown-ups do are . . . are complicated. And sometimes we make stupid mistakes. But I love your dad more than anything in the world. And he loves Jacob. And you. Everything would fall apart . . ."

"Don't worry. I won't tell, Mum," I said. "Look, I can get out of the experiment . . . I'll have to make an excuse to Mr Sargeant, though – tell him a lie. Is that what you want me to do? Lie? Would that help?"

She gave a tiny nod of her chin. I slid her hand onto my thigh. Even then it took her a few seconds to twig, until she tried to pull it away and I forced it onto my fly. I looked into her eyes. No other squares for her to move to. And she started shaking, just like Graham.

She could be put on the sex offenders register. I reminded her of that, after.

Ricketa-ricketa-ricketa. Round and round on the wheel goes little Graham. Like he knows he can never get away from me, no matter how far he runs.

MY AMERICAN JON
Chimamanda Ngozi Adichie

There is something forlorn about Baltimore; I thought of this every Thursday when my taxi sped down Charles Street on my way to the train station to visit Jon in New York City. The buildings were connected to one another in faded slumping rows, but what really held my attention was the people: hunched in puffy jackets, waiting for buses, slouching in corners, making me wonder again and again why the dankest, drabbest parts of all the American cities I knew were full of black people. My taxi drivers were mostly Punjabi or Ethiopian. It was an Ethiopian who asked where my accent was from and then said, "You don't look African at all," when I told him Nigeria.

"Why don't I look African?" I asked.

"Because your blouse is too tight."

"It is not too tight," I said.

"I thought you were from Jamaica or one of those places," he said, looking in the rear-view with both disapproval and concern. "You have to be very careful or America will corrupt you."

Later, I told Jon about this conversation and how the driver's sincerity had infuriated me and how I had gone to the station bathroom to see if my pink blouse *was* too tight. Jon laughed. But I was sure he understood; this was during the early months, the good months of our relationship.

We met at a poetry reading. I had come up to New York to hear

27

the new Nigerian poet Chioma Ekemma read from her *Love Economies*. During the Q&A, the questions were not about why she chose to write poems without active verbs, or which poets she admired, but what could be done about poverty in Nigeria and would women ever achieve equality there and wasn't she lucky that she could come to America and find her voice? She was gracious – too gracious, I thought. Then Jon raised his hand from two rows ahead of me and said tourism was the easiest way to fix the Nigerian economy and it was a shame Nigeria was not tourist friendly. No hostels. No good roads. No backpackers. He spoke with absolute authority. Chioma Ekemma nodded enthusiastically. I raised my hand and said one could fix an economy in other ways that did not involve richer people going to gawk at the lives of poorer people who could never gawk back. There was some scattered clapping; I noticed the most vigorous came from the black people. Chioma Ekemma said something conciliatory and moved on to the next question. She was clearly thinking of keeping the peace so that as many people as possible would buy her book.

Jon was staring at me; a white man wearing a metal wristband who thought he could pontificate about my country irritated me. I stared back. I imagined him taking in my Afro-shaped twists, my severe black frames, with distaste. But there was something else between us, between the chairs and people separating us: a sparkle, a star, a spark. His face was solemn when he came over after the reading and said I had really felt strongly back there and did I want to get coffee and have a little bit more of a debate? It amused me, the way he said "debate". But we did debate, about devaluation and deregulation and debt, and later, when we kissed at Penn station in a sudden press of our bodies before I got on the train, it was as if the debate was continuing, the way our tongues darted around inside our mouths without meeting.

He had never been with a black woman; he told me this the following weekend with a self-mocking toss of his head, as if this were something he should have done long ago but had somehow neglected. I laughed and he laughed and in the morning sunlight that streamed in through the windows of his apartment, his skin took on a bright and foreign translucence. After we broke up two years later, I would tell people that race was the reason, that he was too white and I was too black and the midway too skewed in his favour. In truth, we broke up after I cheated. The cheating was very good, me on top gliding and moaning and grasping the hair on the chest of the other man. But I told Jon that it had meant nothing. I told him that I had hated myself although I was filled with well-being, with a sublime sense not just of satisfaction but of accomplishment.

At first, Jon was disbelieving. "No, you didn't have a one-night stand. You're such a liar."

I did lie to him sometimes, playful little lies like calling to say I could not come that weekend when I was just outside his door. But I did not lie about the big things.

"It's true," I said.

He got up and turned down the volume of the stereo and paced and looked through the tall windows at the cars and people below. *Unknown Soldier* was playing. Jon loved Fela Kuti; it was the reason he'd visited Nigeria and attended Nigerian events, perhaps the reason he thought he knew how to save Nigeria.

"Why?" he asked finally.

I should not have been pleased by the prospect of telling Jon why I had cheated. I sat down on the sofa and said, "It was desire."

It *was* desire. It felt as though gentle peppers had been squirted at the bottom of my stomach, a surge of pure aching desire that I was grateful for feeling and was determined not to waste.

"Desire?" Jon was watching me. Maybe he was thinking that it had always been good between us. So I got up and held him close and said that even though it had been a physical desire, the act itself had meant nothing because my self-loathing made pleasure impossible. Jon did not push me away. He said, "The sin is not the sex, Amaka, the sin is the betrayal. So it doesn't matter whether or not you enjoyed it."

That all-knowing tone of Jon's had always made me stiffen. If the circumstances were different, I would have asked him – Did the people at Yale teach you how to talk with such authority about things you know nothing about? I had often asked him this in the past. Such as when, two or so months into our relationship, I arrived at his apartment and he kissed me and gestured to the table and said, "Surprise. Tickets to Paris for three days. We leave tonight. You'll be back in time to teach Tuesday."

"Jon, I cannot just jet off to Paris. I have a Nigerian passport and I have to apply for a visa."

"Come on, you're an American resident. You don't need a visa to go to Paris."

"I do."

"No you don't."

After I showed him on the Internet that Nigerian citizens who were resident in America did in fact need a visa to get into Europe – a process that required bank statements, health insurance, all sorts of proof that you would not stay back and become a burden to Europe – Jon muttered "Ridiculous" as though it was the French embassy and not he who had been wrong. We did go to Paris, though. Jon changed the ticket dates. We went together to the French embassy but I went alone to the window where a woman wearing silver eyeshadow glanced at me, at my passport, back at me, and said she would not approve the visa because Nigerian passport-holders were high risk and it seemed suspicious to her that I was going to Paris for just three days. "But . . ." I started to say and she made an impatient gesture and pushed my documents across under the glass. Jon got up then, tall and sinewy and angry, and told her I was going to Paris as his guest and my documents included his bank statements and my employment letter and insurance and everything else, if only she'd look at them. "We're together," he added, as if it was necessary to make it clear. The woman smirked. She said I should have explained myself better. She made a show of looking through the documents and said the visa would be ready for pick-up in two days.

It filled me with a dizzying pride, how Jon would often stand up for me, speak for me, protect me, make me omelettes, give me pedicures in the bubbling foot bath, slip his hand into mine as we walked, speak in the first-person plural. "*O na-eji gi ka akwa*: he holds you like an egg," Aunty Adanna said admiringly when she finally accepted that I was serious with a white man and asked me to bring him to lunch. Aunty Adanna was one of those Nigerian immigrants who, when they spoke to white people, adopted a risible American accent. I took Jon to her seven-room home in

Columbia, outside Baltimore, and suddenly she was calling her son "Mek", my bewildered teenage cousin whom we had always called Nnaemeka, and talking about how good he was at golf. She spoke of fufu and soup, which Jon had eaten many times before in New York, as if Nigerian food could not be worthy unless it was like something American. This is like your mashed potatoes, she told him, this is just like your clam chowder. She spoke of her swimming pool needing to be drained. She told anecdotes about the patients at her medical practice. Jon asked when last she had been back in Nigeria and she said it had been six years; she could not bear the dirt and chaos and she did not know what the matter was with all of those corrupt people in government. "Matter" came out sounding like "marah". Even though Jon had not asked, she proudly told him she had lived in America for eighteen years, that she had sponsored my trip here eight years ago after my Nigerian university kept going on strike after strike. I stabbed the chicken in my soup and said nothing. I was ashamed. I was ashamed that she did not have books in her house and that when Jon brought up Zimbabwe, she had no idea what was going on there and so to cover my shame I muttered "Philistine" as we drove away. "Nigerian doctors and engineers and lawyers don't read anything unless it has the possibility of leading them to bigger paycheques," I said. Jon laughed and said it had nothing to do with Nigeria, it was the same for the American bourgeoisie and, leaning over to kiss me, said that Aunty Adanna had been sweet, the way she was so keen to make him comfortable. It wasn't sweet, it was pathetic, but I liked that Jon said that and I liked that he wanted to be liked by my family.

I had never felt that love I read about in books, that inexorable thing that made characters take all sorts of unlikely decisions. By the time I met Jon, I had convinced myself that the feeling was like an orgasm; a certain percentage of women would never have one after all. At first, each long weekend with Jon in New York was a pleasant break to look forward to after teaching three days a week at the Shipley school. Soon, each weekend became something I longed for, and then something I needed. I realised that what I felt for Jon was becoming an inexorable thing when I saw the flyer advertising a teaching position in a New York City private academy on a board outside the general office and immediately went in to ask the secretary Nakeya if she knew more. She shook her head and said it wasn't a good idea. "They like you here and you'll rise quickly if you stay, Amaka," she said. I persisted. She said the academy was a good place although the pay at Shipley was better; the student body there was richer, though, and the class size smaller. She added in a lower voice that they were a little conservative and it was best if I took my twists out for the interview. "You know how our hair can make them feel threatened?" Nakeya asked with a smile. I knew. Why adults would feel threatened by hair has never ceased to amaze me but, after I called the academy and was asked to come in for an interview, I removed my twists and straightened my hair with a hot comb that burned my scalp. I was even willing to buy blonde dye. I wanted the job. I wanted to be in New York City with Jon. I had been rashly honest at my Shipley school interview, telling them that I had just graduated from Johns Hopkins graduate creative writing programme, had published only a few poems in journals, was struggling to complete a collection, and was unsure how to make a living. For the academy interview, I decided I would be more circumspect. I told the two white men and one Hispanic woman that teaching was my first love and poetry my second. They were attentive, they nodded often as if to show approval. I didn't tell Jon about it because I wanted to surprise him but after I got the email only three days later, thanking me and telling me they had selected a better-qualified applicant, I told Jon. He smiled, his big generous smile. He asked me to resign from the Shipley school, to move in with him and take some time off and focus on my poetry and, if I was worried about not paying rent, I could do so in kind. We laughed. We laughed so often during the early months. I put up an advertisement for subletting my Baltimore apartment, put my furniture in storage, and moved in with Jon.

Later, almost two years later, on the day I told Jon that I had cheated, I wondered whether my moving in had contributed in some way; perhaps things would have been different if I had stayed in Baltimore, visiting for long weekends. That day, it took hours of sidestepping each other, of drinking tea, of Jon lying face up on the couch, before he asked, "Who is he?"

I told him the man's name: Ifeanyi. We had met years ago at the wedding of a friend of Aunty Adanna's. He had called me a few times and then, recently, he moved from Atlanta to Harlem and we met for coffee and the desire happened and we took the train to his place.

Jon said, "You gave him what he wanted."

It was an odd thing for Jon to say, the sort of thing Aunty Adanna, who persisted in speaking about sex as if it were something a woman gave a man at a loss to herself, would say.

I corrected Jon gently. "I took what I wanted. If I gave him anything, then it was incidental."

"Listen to yourself, just fucking listen to yourself!" Jon's voice thickened and he got up and shook me and then stopped, but did not apologise. "Amaka, I would never have cheated on you. I didn't even think about it in the past two years, I didn't think about it," he said and I realised that he was already looking at us through the lens of the past tense. It puzzled me, the ability of romantic love to mutate so completely. Where did it go? Was the real thing somehow connected to blood since love for children and parents did not change or die in the way love for romantic partners did?

"You won't forgive me," I said.

"I don't think we should be talking about forgiveness right now."

Jon was the kind of man for whom fidelity came easily, the kind who did not turn to glance at pretty women on the street simply because it did not occur to him. He sat down on the couch and I felt a terrible loss because I had become used to knowing that he was undisputedly there, to the cultured ease in the life he gave me, to his upper-class tickets and his boat and house in Connecticut and the smiling uniformed doorman in his apartment building. Even though I had shrugged, non-committal, the two times he brought up marriage, I often thought of it. The first time I told him I was not sure I wanted to get married. The second time I said I was uncomfortable about bringing mixed-race children into the world. He laughed. How could I buy into the tragic mulatto cliché? It was so much bullshit. He recited the names of our – his, really – biracial friends who seemed perfectly fine with being as they were. His tone was arch, superior, and perhaps he was right and it was bullshit but this was truly how I felt and it did not help

33

that Jon approached my misgivings about race with an intellectual wave of his hand.

And who says that race did not play a role in our break-up? Who says we were not lying all those times we clung to the comforting idea of complexity? It wasn't about race, we would say, it was *complex* – Jon speaking first and me promptly agreeing. What if the reasons for most things didn't require blurred lines? What about the day we walked into a Maine restaurant with white-linen-covered tables, and the waiter looked at us and asked Jon, "Table for one?" Or when the new Indian girlfriend of Jon's golf partner Ashish said she had enjoyed her graduate experience at Yale but had disliked how close the ghetto was and then her hand flew to her mouth after "ghetto" and she turned to me and said, "Oh, I'm so sorry," and Jon nodded as if to accept the apology on my behalf. What about when he, Jon, said he hated the predatory way a black man had looked at me in Central Park, and I realised I had never heard him use the word predatory before? Or the long weekend in Montreal when the strawberry-haired owner of the bed and breakfast refused to acknowledge me and spoke and smiled at Jon and I was not sure whether she disliked black people or simply liked Jon and later in the room, for the first time, I did not agree that it was complex, at least not in the way I had agreed all the other times. I shouted at Jon – "The worst thing is never being sure when it is race and not race and you'll never have this baggage!" And he held me and said I was overreacting and tired. What about the evening we attended a reading at the Mercantile Library and afterwards Jon's friend Evan, who wrote travel books, told me he was sure it had to feel like shit when ignorant people suggested I had been published in the *Best American Poetry* because I was black and Jon merely shook his head when I told him that the ignorant people had to be Evan himself because nobody else had suggested this. And what about the first time I met Jon's mother? She talked about her Kenyan safari in the seventies, about Mandela's majestic grace, about her adoration for Harry Belafonte, and I worried that she would lapse into Ebonics or Swahili. As we left her rambling house in Vermont where she had an organic garden in her backyard, Jon said it was not really about race, it was more complex than that, it was that she was too hyper-aware of difference and consequently too eager to bridge it. "And she does that with me, too. She likes to talk about only the things she thinks I'm interested in," he said. This he did often: a constant equalising of our experiences, a refusal to see that what I experienced was different from his.

And what about Jon's wife? Jon was divorced from a woman who he described as brilliant and needy. She lived in Cambridge but was on sabbatical in Europe and so did not feature in our lives during the first months, the good months. Then she came back and began to call often. She was unhappy, she wasn't sure what she wanted to do, she wasn't tenure-track, she had given up on her book. Jon often put her on speaker and said soothing things to her about hanging in there and ended the conversation by mentioning me. I have to go, Amaka and I are late already. I have to go, I'm cooking Amaka dinner. On the evening we were to go and see *Thom Pain* off-Broadway, she called and hung up after only a minute or so and he said she was awfully drunk and had called to confess that she still loved him and felt bad that he was with someone else and worse that the someone else was black. He was laughing. I wanted to cry. I am tough, believe me, but that day, as I stared at the high-heeled sandals I was about to slip on, I wanted to cry. All I said was, "I can't go to the theatre." This woman whom I did not know had brought out in Jon something I loathed with a visceral lurch in my chest: an inability to show necessary outrage. For this new power of hers, I resented her. When, finally, we met, her unremarkably small breasts delighted me, the lines around her eyes and the saggy skin of her neck delighted me. It was at Ashish's garden party. She wore a pretty jersey dress and a limp string of green beads around her neck and smiled too brightly as we were introduced.

"Jon has told me so much about you," she said.

"You sound different," I said.

"What?"

"When you call Jon puts you on speaker so I can follow the conversation and you sound nothing like you do on the phone," I said, smiling.

She looked away and then back at me before she excused herself to go find a drink. When I went to the bathroom, I was not surprised that she had followed me. She was standing by the door when I came out.

"It's not real," she said.

"What's not real?" I asked. I was bored with her. I was a little disappointed that Jon had not been with a less predictable woman.

"What you're doing isn't real. If it was, he wouldn't be trying so hard."

I turned and walked back outside to the party, hoping she thought I was taking the high road when the truth was that I had no idea what to say in response. On the day that I told Jon I had cheated, about eight months after that garden party, I repeated her words to Jon and said I had never told him about it because a part of me had always suspected that it was true.

"That what was true?" Jon asked.

"You were trying too hard to prove that my being black didn't matter and it was as if it wasn't a good thing and so we had to pretend it wasn't there and sometimes I wanted it to matter because it does matter but we never really talked, truly talked, about any of this . . ."

Jon started to laugh. "This is rich," he said. "Now you blame it on race? What are you talking about? We've always talked about everything. And you told me you didn't even remember I was white!"

I had indeed said that and it was true, but only when we were alone, when we were silent, when we sat side by side and watched a film, or lay side by side and passed *New York Times* sections to each other. And yes, we did talk about race, either in the slippery way that admitted nothing and engaged nothing and ended with that word "complexity". Or as jokes that left me with a small and numb discomfort. Or as intellectual nuggets to be examined and then put aside because it was not about us (such as when he read somewhere that mainstream women's magazine sales fall with a light-skinned black on the cover and plummet with a dark-skinned black).

Jon was still laughing, his bitter laughter.

"I should leave," I said. "I'll go and stay with Aunty Adanna for a while."

"No, wait." Jon got up. "Will you see him again?"

I shook my head.

"Does he mean anything to you?"

Again, I shook my head.

"We can talk. Maybe we can work through this."

I nodded. He placed his hand on my chin and gently tilted my head up and looked into my eyes. "You don't want to, do you? You want to make this look like my decision but it's really yours. You don't want to be forgiven. You don't want to work through this," he said, with that all-knowing authority of his and I stood there and said nothing.

A week later, I was back in Baltimore, a little drunk and a little happy and a little lonely, speeding down Charles Street in a taxi with a Punjabi driver who was proudly telling me that his children did better than American children at school.

All you have
to do is write one
true sentence.

Write the
truest sentence
that you know.

Ernest Hemingway

THE MOTHERFUCKING PAPERBACK QUEEN OF ANADARKO
Anna Baggaley

So here's the thing about the job in the bookstore. Even though I bitched and moaned about it till Jay just about told me he'd bust my balls if I had any and even though it was in the tacky old mall out by the exit to Highway 44, I didn't hate it. I mean, being, like, real honest, I kinda freaking liked it.

When I go there for my "induction", as the employee manual calls it, the lady who interviews me gives me this fugly blue uniform thing and I kinda make a face about it coz that's what I'm supposed to do. I can tell by the way she gives me this real bored look – like she's seen far too many dumbass kids pass through this place.

"Everybody gets one and you don't got any choice about it. You wear it or you're out. Are. We. Clear?" she says like she thinks I'm from freaking China or something.

I just nod because even though I wasn't giving her any lip she seems to think I was so I figure it's best to just keep my mouth shut. Nanna Jo always said that. If you can't say nothing nice, don't say nothing at all. Although this lady clearly never grew up with anybody telling her that.

"I s'pose you'll be requiring a large?" she asks looking down at my belly, which is already beginning to get round even though I'm only four and a half months.

Least I'm pregnant, not fat like you, I want to say, but I hold my mouth. Mom would go apeshit if I lost this job and she had to borrow money for the utilities from Jennifer Mayberry, who lives in the apartment downstairs. Again. Not because Jennifer wouldn't give it, but because Mom'd have to ask. And I know how rat-like that feels.

So I say, "Yes, ma'am. Sounds 'bout right."

"Umhmm," she agrees, picking up various sweaters from the boxes under her desk and pulling the little bobbles off them. She looks like a monkey on one of those shows about African wildlife, picking at her mate instead of blue polyester uniforms that probably haven't been washed since, like, 1981 or whatever. She's got fat hulk arms like the wrestlers on *Friday Night SmackDown* and eyebrows that seem permanently knitted together.

She tosses me one of the sweaters and says, "That ought to do it," giving me this creepy weird-ass smile. I suppose the manager's manual told her to smile at me but I can tell she doesn't feel inclined. I get that I'm probably strange to her and that it looks like I'm trying to scam them for the social security money so I smile too, trying to look wholesome, putting my hands together between my knees and bowing my head a little so I look like a real God-fearing farm girl, but I doubt it works. So we're both sitting there grinning like retards until I say, "Thanks."

"Your shifts are Tuesday and Thursday after school from 4:30 till 8."

I just nod. Then she gives me a time card, which is kinda cool, and I play with it when she leaves me to find the delivery exit on my own, clocking in and out maybe four times over coz I love the sound those cards make, like the clocking-in machine is biting into a big cookie.

I start the next day and the hulk lady is the manager on the same shift as me. As it happens her name is Sandra, which makes her sound like something out of one of Mom's *Donna Reed Show* reruns. There's also a girl who I reckon's a few years older than me. She's called Abida because her dad's from Pakistan and she has this real long black hair, like a Girl's World doll that I just want to reach out and touch. But I reckon that might make me look like a greasy-pawed dyke so I don't.

Casey's hair used to be long like that, and when we were little I'd sit for hours just brushing it. I'm hoping the baby's hair will be the same because I'm gonna call her Casey too. Not just because when your sister's dead that seems like the right sort of thing to do, but because I want her to be just as beautiful and good as Case too.

Sandra gives me "a tour of the planograms" but as far as I can see she's just showing me different bookshelves with different sections. I feel quite in control of that bit as my memory's always been sharp.

Then she leaves me with this crazy heavy trolley full of books.

"These are the returns. You put these away."

"And then?"

"Then what? That's what you do. You don't talk to customers. *You don't touch the register.*"

"Oh. OK."

Sandra folds her arms across her chest like she's a bouncer outside an LA club or some shit.

"What if customers talk to me?"

She looks me in the eye then, like I've tried to slap her across the face.

"They won't."

When Sandra leaves I take hold of one end of the trolley and try to push it forward but as it happens those things ain't really built for a girl, let alone one carrying an extra person inside her.

Abida creeps over to my trolley, all slender and sly like the coyotes that patrol the dumpsters outside our apartment building, and starts pulling the other end.

"I do the register but whilst that witch isn't looking I figured it was the least I could do, especially as you're expecting."

Expecting.

She says it real soft, like she's got some fucking respect for the idea or something. It makes me blush because at school they only use words like knocked up and whore, and all look at me like a hippo just came in the room, walking upright on its stumpy little grey legs, and they don't even have the decency to act like they might be ashamed when they see me looking back.

Abida says her sister just had a little baby boy. Her third and she's still only twenty-four. But she's married. I guess when your family comes from another place it's OK and people are more likely to look the other way.

With Abida's help I'm pretty good at getting the returns organised on the right shelves. Like I said, I always remember shit like this. It's weird, I guess, because at school reading always kind of pissed me off, like when we all had to read the same chapters together, like books always mean the same thing to every single person. But that first day, with the books on my trolley all shiny and new, I could see they looked like maybe they were worth something, and I kind of got why Mom gets the bus all the way to the big county library in Norman to get her new murder mysteries even though there's still a little library here in Anadarko.

After that my shifts are kind of cool. It turns out that Sandra is about as dumb as the cows in the pasture down by the turnpike and that she doesn't notice much of anything. So sometimes, if I'm feeling like I'm due my five-finger employee discount, I hide books from the trolley down the back of my pants and go lurk in the World Religion section that's always empty and read them there. Abida's a college student so she tells me what books to pick. I start with *Frankenstein*, then *To Kill a Mockingbird*, and they're pretty weird and fucked up but I like them anyhow.

I tell Abida that I want to learn to do more than just the returns, so after hours she starts to show me how to work the register and it's like a computer screen but I do OK. Making the little bell noise that comes when someone buys shit makes me feel all accomplished, like I'm a proper shopgirl with a flat stomach who's allowed to talk to customers. It must excite the baby too because the first time she kicks is one night when I'm practising on the register. She really goes at it too, giving me a proper person kick like my insides just pissed her off. I must gasp or something real girly like that because Abida turns around, worry swimming about her big brown coffee-cup eyes, and she touches a hand to my arm.

"'m OK," I say and then I hesitate because I don't know how to do stuff like this. I take in a real big lungful of air and continue, "She just kicked."

Abida cracks out into this smile that seems to take up her whole face. She puts a hand to my belly and we wait for it to happen again but it doesn't. So instead, Abida shows me how to do the inventory.

When we're done she waits with me for Jay's car. Fall is starting to come in proper and the air feels cool. There ain't corn dust blowing in your face all the time so it's nice and the Wichita mountains stop looking like God just got bored and dropped them in the wrong place the way they do in summer. Oklahoma's always better when it's cold. At least, I think so but then I ain't ever left and Nanna Jo says I don't know from cold, so I guess my opinion doesn't count all that much. While we're waiting Abida and me don't really talk but it feels friendly, like we should be smoking green or something. Then Jay's Camero makes a racket coming into the mall's parking lot, the bumpers smacking the asphalt, just in case he needed to announce that a big man just arrived.

"You did really well today," Abida tells me and I smile properly for the first time in days.

Jay honks the horn so I haul ass and get in.

Jay's never been into small talk so I explain about my day as he drives me home.

"Sounds like a grade-A ass-fest to me," he says in that growly voice he gets when he's in a black mood or smoked too much bud. We stop at a crossroads and the street light pours through the windshield. He's got a new purple bruise, as wide as a baseball, across his forehead that's so obviously his dad's handiwork that it might as well have "Supplied by Wade & Sons Auto Parts" printed across it. I leave his comment the hell alone and pretend it's cool and we're still down like we used to be before I told him I was pregnant.

"Well, I had a good time," I say, trying to make my voice smile because my face won't.

"Mmm," Jay replies and I reckon I could have told him I was joining the circus at that moment and his response would have been the same.

On the radio Bob Dylan's telling us to take his gun away coz he can't use it any more. The kid kicks again then but I pretend it's nothing. Jay drops me off at Mom's and I don't say a word. I reckon I know how Bob feels.

Six weeks later when I get to the store Sandra takes me into her office and I'm real worried that I've got Abida into trouble. She motions for me to sit down on the chair opposite her desk but I kind of hesitate because it looks like it's made of that fabric that gives you those little electric shocks.

"It's OK," Sandra says and her voice is all kind this time. "I fear I may have underestimated you, Miss Morrison."

"H-how so?" I try and arrange my face into something that looks normal.

"I hear Miss Ahmed's been showing you the ropes."

"Yes." My hands are in my lap and I wanna get down on my knees like I'm in church with Nanna Jo.

"Well, Miss Ahmed is one of my top sellers and I trust her opinion."

"So?"

"So Stacy called in sick today. She's got mono, which means she could be out for at least a month. We're desperate for someone to take over the register and I'd like to give you a trial."

"Oh . . . Thank you."

When she first puts me behind the register I start to freak out because I've only done this with Abida pretending to be people before, not actual honest-to-God customers.

The first guy to approach my counter is old and bent almost all the way over, like the earth's preparing him for death already by starting to suck him back in. He wobbles when he walks and he's got the kind of glasses that mean there might as well be an actual fricking window between us.

"WelcometoMPSimonsMynameisKellyHowcanIhelpyoutoday?" comes out all in one word.

"I'm sorry, honey?"

I take a breath. "Welcome to M. P. Simons. My name is Kelly. How can I help you today?"

"I'm looking for a book."

I want to say, *No freaking kidding, what with this being a bookstore 'n' all,* but I hold myself back.

"Which book would you like to purchase today?" I follow the words from the manual.

"It's got cowboy boots on the front."

I freeze and look around for Abida, who should be at the register to the left of mine, and my hand's already started to shake but then I remember what the manual said.

"Do you know the name of the author?"

"I couldn't rightly say. But it's got cowboy boots on the front," he says and I quite want to smack his glasses off his face but I reckon assaulting a senior citizen would probably give Sandra cause to can my ass so I follow the manual phrases like I'm one of those freaky-ass talking-doll things that Casey used to love.

"Do you know the title, sir?"

"No 'm. But it did have a blue background, sweetheart," he says, placing one of his slithery hands on top of mine.

And here's the real funny part. It suddenly comes to me. All those hours stacking the books on my trolley weren't just for shit. I feel like I got the covers of some of them books burned onto my brain for the whole of eternity. I know which one he means.

I come out from behind my counter and he looks a little surprised I guess because not only did women not work in his day but especially not *in my condition*. I let him take my hand even though he grips too hard and he smells like he's wearing clothes he pissed in two days ago. Guiding him to the Travel section feels like it takes a century, but that's OK because if he's so slow that means he can be patient with my duck-waddle pace too.

Thankfully the book's on a low shelf so I can bend over without getting stuck, which is happening more and more, and pull it out real easy.

"*Road Tripping Through Dixieland* for you, sir," I say and he takes the book. Then he grabs my hand and kisses it like he's one of those cheesy guys on one of the Harlequin covers in the row behind us.

"God bless you, sweetheart."

"Th-that's OK, sir. Now let me take you back to the register."

I guide him over to the line at Abida's register and make it back to my station. The line is growing but Abida's not mad.

"How did you know the answer to that?"

"I just did," I shrug.

The next hour gets crazy busy and standing up for that long makes my back feel like someone's trying to saw right through it and by seven o'clock I've already taken six bathroom breaks. But somehow I can't wipe the smile off my face.

Stacy's off sick for five weeks in the end and by the last Friday it feels like I own that register. That evening Randy Varshan from Jay's bio class comes in. Randy's on the football team and he's got ears that stick so far off the sides of his head that you'd be able to pick him up by them if you were taller and stronger than him, which, of course, no one was. He was supposed to be a Senior this year but he'd failed two semesters last year, so was in the Junior class with us now.

"Hey Kel," he says in that way that popular guys always shorten your name without asking, or knowing that no one ever calls you that anyway. "I'm looking for a book for English class."

"Which one?"

"Some Dickerson dude or chick. I'm not real sure."

I don't even panic then because I already feel like I been doing this for years.

I take him over to the poetry and pretty swift I figure that it ain't Emily Dickinson, so then I take him to Classic Novels and hand him every Charles Dickens in the whole goddamned store.

When I get him back to the counter he says I'm amazing, which would totally kill half the girls in the Junior class.

Abida agrees with him. "Kelly's our little superhero," she says. "Seems like there isn't a book she can't find. It's like she's the paperback queen."

"Motherfucking paperback queen, huh?" Randy says because guys on the football team have this habit of repeating everything you say but turning it into a question and adding a "motherfucking" for good measure.

"I guess," I reply, ringing up his books, and I know I'd be twistin' one leg over the other, like I always used to do when I was nervous, if that were physically possible any more.

When Jay picks me up that night I tell him about the nickname, about how "paperback queen" seems to have stuck with Abida now and how she called me by it all afternoon.

"You wanna go for a smoke? I just picked up," Jay responds.

"No."

"Oh, guess I'll drive you home."

On the journey back we both do a real good job of pretending I'm not about to cry.

Of course, the next week Stacy's back and I'm reassigned to my old job with the returns. I act like I'm not sore about it but I bang my trolley up and down the aisles so loud I reckon I can probably be heard all the way over in the food court.

I'm only at the bookstore for three more weeks before the doctor says I need bed rest, and Mom says I ought to forget the place like I was supposed to and that we'll find me another job when the baby's good 'n' here.

One night when it's real near the end and I can't sleep because I need to go to the bathroom for the 98,889th time, I hear something clatter through the mailbox.

It's a thick brown envelope with the Oklahoma State University symbol on it and a neon-orange Post-it attached, covered in Abida's handwriting.

> You can always try, paperback queen!
> Love Abida.

I open the letter and it's a college application so I toss it in the trash.

But when I get back from the bathroom I still can't sleep. I pick up one of the books Abida gave me as a leaving present. *Huckleberry Finn* by Mark Twain. But that can't seem to make me sleep either.

I waddle back into the kitchen and start digging about in the trash can. Everything smells like Chinese takeout but the form is fairly clean so I shake it off a bit and take it into my room. I lay it out on my bed, slow and proper, the way explorers lay out maps in movies. It's real long and in that kind of font that lets you know it's important. The section for grades and previous experience is two whole pages and there's a small Kung Po Chicken stain in the bottom left corner of the second one. I turn them over in my hands a couple of times. I think about tearing the application up. I make a first tiny rip and then decide against it. I ball the application up and go back to the kitchen and return it to the trash.

The baby's kicking so I stroke my belly but that won't quiet her.

"Did you know that I'm the motherfuckin' paperback queen of Anadarko, huh, kid?" I ask her quietly so that I don't wake Mom.

That seems to make her kick less often.

But still neither of us can fucking sleep.

FICTION IS THE TRUTH INSIDE THE LIE.

STEPHEN KING

MR BONNER'S DREAM THE NIGHT BEFORE HIS EXECUTION
Emily Cleaver

The pictorial, which appeared in the *Illustrated Police News* the day after the execution, bore hardly any resemblance to what William Bonner actually dreamed about the night before he died. Even so, it was a fine piece of work. Given the notoriety of the case, the editor had devoted a double-page spread to it. Along the top in letters dripping with oozy water, suggestive of the canal where the body had been found, was the title. *William Bonner's Dream the Night Before His Execution.*

At the bottom of the illustration William Bonner slept on the narrow bed of a Newgate cell, his brow deeply furrowed. The artist, who had years of experience drawing murderers for the popular press, had given him a gaunt face and a weak chin overwhelmed by a moustache. His hands, grasping the prison blanket as he slept, were long-fingered and sinister. Above this, the tormented dreams of the condemned man were shown in a series of vignettes, each depicting a scene from the night of the crime. First, top left, Mr Bonner shouted at his wife. It was this argument, overheard by neighbours through the thin walls of the lodging-house room, that had convinced the jury to reach a guilty verdict.

In the next picture, Mr Bonner chased his wife from the house and into the night. In the murder scene his hands were at her neck, then he threw her body into the Limehouse Cut. The artist had skilfully captured the look of awful remorse as Mr Bonner saw what he had done. Next: the moment the night watchman found Mr Bonner on the ground in a faint, the discovery of the body, the arrest, trial and guilty verdict. In the final scene, the hood was pulled down over Mr Bonner's face, the rope already round his neck.

Since his arrest Mr Bonner had not slept at night, but in the daytime sleep would attack him like a dark blanket thrown over his head. It would take him suddenly in his cell, or even while walking in the exercise yard. He would wake minutes or hours later, feeling that he had been attacked by an assailant. No scenes of the murder troubled him when he slept. Instead he was haunted by the white dog.

The white dog had been in his dreams since the sleeping fits started in his childhood. As a boy, Mr Bonner believed that the white dog itself brought the sleep, because it was always there inside it waiting. It was a large brute with broad shoulders and a heavy muzzle. Its coat was a blank sheet of paper. One of its eyes was crushed shut by a scar, and the other was a cloudy white marble with no centre. Sometimes when sleep hit him the white dog would be on his chest, paws on his shoulders. Other times it would be behind him, and he would twist and turn to catch sight of the flicker of its coat.

What troubled Mr Bonner as he grew older was the dog's one white eye. It seemed to him that if he could only understand the message in that void gaze, something imperative and terrible would be revealed to him. He felt he had just to ask the right question, but in his dreams he could never think what it was.

When he married Mary, the dreams of the dog had stopped. They would lie in bed at night with their feet together for warmth, and Mary would place her hand on his thin chest. She had a mouth that broke easily into smiles, and her shape made Mr Bonner think of songs danced to a fiddle. They slept tangled up, her hair a black splash on the pillow.

But work was hard to get, and they moved to a Stepney lodging house. Mr Bonner had never been much good for anything but the lowest clerks' positions, copying ledgers or writing bills. He spent days at the agencies, shuffling up the hard benches as the queue moved. Often there was no work, and he would walk home, through streets crowded with carts and cattle and loud with the shouts from the markets, to Mary's silence. He would sit at the table with his head bowed while she clattered the pans on the stove, stirring the stew that would have to last another day.

That was when the dog had come back to his dreams. In them, he would be searching for his boots in the kitchen and the dog would appear at the window. Or, he would wait in the queue for work at the agency and when his turn was called the white dog would be sitting at the desk. In the worst dreams there would be nothing but the sudden gloom of dusk and the coat of the white dog gleaming.

There had been no work the day it happened. He had walked slowly back, planning his words. *No, nothing today.* He would say it lightly, as if it didn't much matter. *They say there'll be something tomorrow.* He opened the door to the rich smell of stewing meat. Too rich – they had had no meat that morning. Mary was at the table, her hair up around her rosy face and her hat still on. She was wearing a new red kerchief, bright against her drab brown dress. He looked around him, expecting a gap where some piece of furniture had been sold. Everything was in its place.

"Where did you get that?" he said, his voice sounding high in his ears.

"A present." She turned to him, her cheeks flushed.

"Who from?"

"Did you get work?" she said.

He was silent and she turned away. There were tears on his cheeks. "I would have got us money."

"I took care of it myself." She raised her hand to her hair where it had come loose under the rim of the hat.

The next part of the night had fallen out of his head.

Lying awake in the creaky prison bed, Mr Bonner often thought of his trial, and tried again to answer the prosecutor's key question.

"Your neighbours testify that your wife ran from the house, and that you went after her. What happened then?"

"I don't remember," Mr Bonner would whisper to the faint square of the barred window, turning in his bed to avoid the gaze of the jury.

"Ah yes, your lamentable lapses of memory," the prosecutor would say. "A common affliction in your household, it would seem. Your neighbours say your wife was sometimes inclined to forget she was married."

"That is a lie," Mr Bonner would shout, and the laughter of the court would mix with the howls and shouts of the men in the next cells.

As the weeks passed, Mr Bonner poked and probed that gap in his mind like a decayed tooth through every sleepless night, but though the ache hung over him each morning, he could not remember.

Then, on the night before his execution, Mr Bonner finally slept. He dreamed that he saw London spread out below him, murky in the dusk as if the city lay at the bottom of a blue-glass vase. He started to sink, plunked like a fizzing tablet into the watery sky. The streets and houses wheeled below him. He felt a sense of anticipation, of a date to keep down there in the darkening streets. Below him he saw the lodging house, and Mary leaving its door. He watched her out of view, and then he saw himself appear and follow behind her.

Then Mr Bonner was walking after his wife. She drew away, a dim smudge in the dark. And there was the white dog. It stood in a doorway and watched him with its one milky eye, its coat bone-coloured. The dog turned away and ran towards the canal. He could see it ahead of him like a hole in the night.

When Mr Bonner reached it, the whiteness seemed to be all around him.

"You are no man," said Mary, standing before him as the sky paled and drained.

He raised his white hands to her neck and a fierce shadow fell over him, a sleep within sleep.

In his dream, Mr Bonner stood on the towpath again and looked down into the water. Mary's face glimmered beneath the surface like a clean plate in a grimy sink. She called out to him silently, her mouth open, her throat bruised. Her hand waved, stirred by some current.

Mr Bonner's dream stayed with him, the dank water of the canal tainting his last breakfast. The priest arrived and asked for his confession. The secret of the empty eye of the dog was poised on Mr Bonner's tongue like a communion wafer. He remembered what his wife had taken from him, and what he had taken back from her. But these are my last possessions, thought Mr Bonner. To give or keep as I choose.

"May you find peace with God."

"I have already found it here," said Mr Bonner, laying his hand on his forehead.

The warder came. Mr Bonner held his hands behind him to be tied.

"They're waiting out there."

"I understand," said Mr Bonner.

The prisoners yelled and hooted from their cells and the chapel bell clanged. Mr Bonner raised his face to the sky as he was led to the wooden shed. He felt the anticipation of his dream again, the sense of a meeting to be attended out there in the gloom of the winter morning. He fell and the rope tightened. Somewhere at the edges of spluttering sleep, Mr Bonner was aware of the white dog waiting for him.

William Faulkner

66

Let the writer take up surgery or bricklaying if he is interested in technique. There is no mechanical way to get the writing done, no short cut ... The good artist believes that nobody is good enough to give him advice. He has supreme vanity. No matter how much he admires the old writer, he wants to beat him.

99

CONFESSIONS OF A FUZZY MAN
Maggie Womersley

I haven't always looked like this – a heat haze, a trick of the eye. Once upon a time before the war I was as crisply cut and definite as the next man. In fact in my youth I revelled in my physicality, excelling at tennis and cricket in the summer months and rugby in the winter. I swam for the school, ran for the county, and as I grew into a man I danced for the pleasure of seeing moonlight splash on a pretty girl's shoulder. In those days my limbs and profile were just as sharply fashioned as yours are now, even in that somewhat crumpled suit you're wearing. Yes, that's right. Though I cannot see you properly, hidden as we are in this gloom, I sense the solidity of your flesh and the contours of your form as you fill up that man-shaped space in the hallway. While you listen to me speak through the crack in this door, straining to catch my words, which I accept must sound very faint by now, I feel the determination of your outline. It is one of the stranger side effects of my disability, a bitter joke I sometimes think, that despite my own thin-edged and fraying carcass, I sense the denseness and physical consistency of others quite acutely.

It was very good of you to come all this way to see me, if you'll excuse my little pun, and to pander to these whims of mine which must appear morbidly eccentric to a twenty-first-century man such as yourself. I am sure like all good journalists you are a hound for truth, a sniffer-outer of fakery and falsities, but are you a cynic too perhaps? Well, why shouldn't you be? This assignment on me must feel like the short straw when all your scurrying colleagues are off covering the latest war or environmental disaster. Now that you're here though, I can only suppose that the urge to take just one peek around this door must be killing you. That picture of me you're thinking of was taken almost sixty years ago. No doubt you are wondering what I look like now? Well trust me, you're not ready to see the true extent of my deformity quite yet, not until you have grappled with something of its context.

I was born in 1893, which by anybody's account would make me one of the oldest citizens of the world today. No, I'm afraid I'm not at liberty to offer any further proof. You know my name of course and I am sure you will have done all the research you could to track me through the decades to this dark afternoon in this dimly lit place. You will just have to accept that I am indeed who I say I am. You'll know from my birth certificate that I was born in Norfolk and that my father was a vicar and my mother, as you might expect, his wife. Perhaps too you have whittled away at the rags and mags to discover that I grew up an only child and attended first a prep school in Norwich, and then one of the better public schools before making my way up to Cambridge on a scholarship for athletics. There I studied Classics somewhat haphazardly, and rowing and other sports with a much fonder application.

It was also there that I met the best three friends of my life. Men I can only describe as my bonded brothers; my shadows and my sunshine. Harry Flowbird, son of the right honourable member for Witton on Sticks, a tawny rangy fellow who made a solid right half and wouldn't let you down in a scuff; Walter Armitage, a poetic mischief with a taste for pranks whose mother was something notable at court; and closest of all to me, William Fishfidder-Meadows, the son of a bishop and, like me, a consummate oarsman.

For three years our opinions harmonised, and our youthful personalities were like second skins to one another. We became an accepted quartet at parties, and were written of in the smaller paragraphs of *The Times* as being exemplary among our generation. Certainly there was a picture of the four of us that appeared in the back pages of *Tatler* where you can see us standing arm in arm on the banks of the Cam with our straw boaters cocked at quite provocative angles. It is one of the last photographs that was taken of me, and one of the few that shows me as I might have been as a man, had I not succumbed to this weakness of physicality. That picture also marks the last time we four would lounge together amongst those dear old willows, for the very next day we enlisted for the war against Germany. Willy and I were to serve together with the King's White Devils, and happy and proud for me the day we passed out together under the joint gaze of our respective parents. As luck would have it Walter and Harry were on the same boat as us going over, and we had some laughs just like the old Cambridge days.

Though I believe each one of us secretly considered himself to be invincible, we said out loud that if it came to it, we would go to our deaths like men. How naïve we were. Little did I think then that there might be an outcome to that war worse than death.

Have you ever fought in a war? No, of course you haven't. Not that I mean to belittle you or the things you think you learnt of my war from any books you might have read. These are bloodthirsty times even now, I realise that. Though the battles are fought in deserts rather than trenches, young men will still discover too late that their training has not equipped them for the sight of their mate blown in half, still conscious but crying out for someone to finish the job. You reporters have shown us some of these atrocities through your newspapers and television, and I believe this to be a good thing. I sometimes wonder if the Somme might have had a different outcome if CNN had been there to go over the top with us live on the evening news. Perhaps.

Walter was the first of us to go. I saw it happen myself; a sniper's lucky hit. It was late March and we were resting between battles, trying to keep warm and maintain morale among the men. Walter, being always the clown, was midway through an impression of a private called Boggs who was doubly afflicted with a stutter and a nervous snorting laugh that resembled a pig snuffling for swill. As Walter reached the climax of his piece the performance grew more boisterous and he began playing to the gods as it were. The sound of his men's jaded laughter must have encouraged him because the next thing I knew he was standing up on a crate and attempting an encore. As I said, we were at that time enjoying a brief respite both from the enemy's attack and from the incessant rain that seemed to fall on us daily like God's own tears. A freak break in the clouds gave the sun its chance and as the light glinted off Walter's monocle the sniper took his potshot. The bullet travelled straight through the jelly of Walter's left eye and out again through his skull, leaving a fist-sized hole as it departed. It then pierced the backside of the cook who had been leaning over to break wind in the general direction of his oblivious commanding officer when the fatal shot was fired. We saved the cook but Walter was dead before he hit the ground.

Harry went a month later, but this time we were not there to see him go. His men heard him though, for two days after he was hit, calling out from some muddy foxhole. He assured them that although his legs were trapped in some wire he was otherwise tolerably fit and whole, and if a couple of the boys could just come out to him and cut him free, he really felt sure that a tight splint and a drop of brandy would set him quite to rights. Willy said it was superstition, a belief in evil spirits or ghosts, that kept Harry's men from going to his aid. Apparently the word went round like trench fever that Harry was in fact already dead and that this was just some clever ventriloquist's trick by the enemy, impersonating Harry to draw them into a trap. It was a rumour that was only quelled when on the third night Harry was heard screaming in agony as the rats began to eat him alive.

Willy and I tried not to think of our fallen friends, but we often spoke of the happier times we'd spent in Cambridge before the winter of war sucked the heat and humour from our blood. We clung together. Not literally of course but in a spiritual sense and mentally too. We slept in neighbouring bunks in our officers' dugout, and the still horizon of Willy's form picked out by the dirty yellow of the candlelight was the greatest comfort to me in those hellish, burrowing days.

Then one day, the war ended for both of us. It was a murky morning in late August and a party of wire-cutters had sneaked out under cover of a grey mist to crawl ahead and lay waste to the enemy's defences. Willy and I were to lead what was left of the regiment over the top at 0600 hours, just at the time we hoped most of the Hun would still be slumped in whatever sleep they could scrounge. The idea was to surprise them and take control of the machine-gun tower that from its sandbagged safety had been picking off our boys for the last couple of days. It was a foolhardy and desperate mission and Willy and I were under no illusions as to its possible outcome. We made the usual speeches, shook hands and held each other's eye. Later on I would remember with grief the bright intelligence in Willy's dear face as we talked of how we would return to Cambridge once this damn war was over. As the appointed time approached we drew our men together and gave them what you'd describe as a pep talk, telling them that God and his angels were on our side and that Britain and her king were proud and grateful for the sacrifice they were about to make. Then, just as the ever-present crows began their first rough calls of the day, we took ourselves up over the top. Within a few minutes our doom became apparent. The wire-cutters had failed in their mission, the Germans were not caught napping, and the mist we had depended on for cover vanished all too quickly to reveal a clear and sunny dawn. That morning the entire regiment except me and Willy Fishfidder-Meadows was wiped out, and what the crows were too faddy to touch soon became food for worms on that blood-fed Flanders field.

Somehow or another I must have half carried, half dragged Willy's unconscious body back to our lines that night. Apparently when they found me I was incoherent; raving and half blind from the flashes of cannon that had been going off all around me. Willy's right leg had been blown off at the knee and he had a nasty wound to his shoulder but somehow, miraculously – and I use that term with no sense of joy – I appeared to be physically unscathed. My manner though gave to all intents and purposes the impression that my mind had been lost, and so they shipped us back to Britain together, the last remnants of the King's White Devils, and what ragamuffins we were.

Three months later, at a sanatorium in Bexhill-on-Sea, I was pronounced as fit as a fiddle; the darling of the nurses and the bauble of the physicians. Whatever shellshock I had sustained during that fatal raid, the memory of which I have never to this day been able to retrieve, had gone. I appeared physically and mentally whole, a little older and wiser of course, but not an emotional wreck like all those poor wretches around us. Doctors cheerfully pronounced me a miracle of science and wrote articles about me to justify their research grants. Willy, however, was not so fortunate; his shoulder and leg mended well enough, but the delicate connections of his synapses had melted away. When I looked at his face now I saw only the ghost of the man I had once called my best friend. I stayed on at Bexhill, taking a little cottage in the town and visiting Willy every day, but the slowness of his progress began to take its toll on my spirits, especially on the days when he could do nothing but ramble about his childhood, a time long before I had known him. The nurses were kind enough, but I could tell that I was no better than a stranger to Willy and that our old friendship had perished on the battlefield the summer before.

As the months went by another niggling concern began to latch itself to my gloomy thoughts. The war was over now and I had returned to my parents' home where I attempted to adjust to civilian life teaching Latin and Greek to the sons of the local gentry. I couldn't quite put my finger on it at the time but a change had come over my appearance, a strange, hard to define shifting that at first would catch my eye in a mirror when I was least expecting it, but which went on to steadily engross my daily consciousness. Initially I thought it was something to do with my eyesight, a resurgence of that temporary blindness I'd sustained in Flanders. I'd be shaving myself and suddenly my reflection would seem to go wavy, like the ripples on a still pool when you throw a stone into it. I'd assume the glass had become fogged from the steam and go to wipe it with my sleeve, only to discover it was my reflection that was indistinct and misty, and not the glass at all. Or on other occasions it would be friends or family who drew attention to it. My mother was constantly accusing me of sneaking up on her and catching her unawares. She would hold her hand up to her eyes and squint at me as if I were as bright as the sun and blinding her, and then she would shake her head from side to side as though trying to shift a flea from her ear. Father experienced it differently; he was fairly near-sighted anyway, and suffered from migraines rather badly. He would self-medicate with whisky and water most evenings and was quite often a little unsteady on his feet. He got into the habit of saying he knew he'd had too much when he saw his son go fuzzy round the edges and we all used to laugh about it, but that was before things got worse.

The situation came to a head when I caught two of the boys to whom I was teaching *The Aeneid* giggling over their copybooks. To my chilled and sickening dismay I saw that one of them had drawn a cartoon that was unmistakably meant to be me, with a jagged outline that looked for all the world as though I had just been electrocuted. I scolded the boys as firmly as I could, given that my emotions were in shreds, and ended the lesson early.

The next day I took the first train to London and made my way to Harley Street where a friend of my father's had recommended a specialist. I will never forget that day, walking through the damp greasy streets of the capital, bunkered down in my great coat with an old college scarf of Willy's to keep me warm and cheer my low spirits. The crowds were quite overwhelming; the war had been finished a couple of years and business seemed to be getting back to normal. Women were wearing much shorter skirts and some had bobbed their hair, while the young men who weren't still in uniform looked sleeker, richer and dare I say almost insolent. Everybody was rushing somewhere and somehow I found that I was always travelling against the tide. Pavements became gauntlets to run; I found myself battered and bumped by elbows and umbrellas from every direction. An occasional "So sorry old chap," or "Excuse me, I didn't see you there," accompanied these collisions, but it soon became quite apparent to me that I was "apparent" to no one. In short, I had become an optical illusion to the casual observer, a blind spot on the collective field of vision. At home, around the few people who knew me, I had managed to ignore the obvious, but here among a sea of strangers the signs were all too evident.

I stopped in front of one of those large picture windows at Selfridges, pretending to watch two young women arrange a display of hats, but really to see what my own reflection could tell me about this malaise. What I saw confirmed my worst fears: if I tried to look directly at myself, the edges of my shoulders, arms and legs appeared to swim out of focus. My face was still recognisable, but the jaw-line was indefinite, blurring into the fluff of Willy's old scarf. It wasn't just my bodily flesh and hair that seemed to bleed into air either; clothes were affected too: my hat flickered like a desert mirage and the outline of my trousers appeared to tremble even though I felt nothing and there was no breeze to speak of. To make matters worse, as I stood transfixed but also *not* transfixed, the two girls in the shop window began squinting out at me. I could clearly see the quizzical, not quite believing expressions in their eyes as they tried to understand the shimmering figure looking back at them. This was the last straw. I turned on my heel and burrowed back into the crowd, keeping my head down and walking as quickly as I could towards my destination.

My visit to Doctor Bindfoot that day gave me some small comfort. He had not seen a case exactly like mine, but he had seen similar, he told me as he took the readings of my vital signs. Heart, blood pressure, pulse; all these were normal and I went on to inform him that generally my appetite was good, I had no bowel trouble and as far as I could tell no other symptoms apart from this general messiness of outline. I explained to him that I did not *feel* fuzzy and he confirmed that although I looked frayed I had managed to keep intact all three of my dimensions. Other cases he had seen since the war had not been so lucky. One man he knew was discernibly fading every day, his internal organs and digestive tracts clearly visible when he removed his clothes; another was slowly but unmistakably shrinking, losing a couple of inches every few months. These cases were all of course hushed up at the time. Britain had enough on its plate getting back to normal without being brought low and confused by the knowledge that some of its veterans were suffering from mysterious forms of battle sickness. He gave me something for my depression and bid me go back to Norfolk and take as much rest as I could. He recommended that I give up the teaching and I was relieved to oblige.

From that day on I pretty much led the life of a recluse. My parents had become quite elderly and I didn't bother to trouble them with a fuller explanation of what the doctor had told me, except to say that I would need to keep the curtains in the drawing room closed as much as possible, and that I would prefer no visitors. I went out for my walks in the countryside only very early in the morning or at dusk, so I didn't have to deal with meeting anyone. When occasionally I did, I made sure to give the immediate impression of a man blurring past in such a rush of urgency that nobody considered they had the time to stop and ask me questions about who, or what, I was. My parents both eventually passed away but I did not seem to age at all; a strange recompense for the lonely hermit's life I felt duty-bound to submit myself to.

Then the second war came along, and of course I was too blurry by then to fight. Doctor Bindfoot saw to it that I received a discreet waiver from service. Instead I grew vegetables in the vicarage garden to help the war effort, and took to wandering the streets quite freely during the blackouts.

After that war ended a change came over me. I grew restless; my fuzziness seemed to fizz a little more furiously than it had in the early years. I was angry that life had been passing me by and so I decided to "come out of the closet", as I believe the expression is, and show the world that I was fuzzy, but like them in every other way. I went to Paris and got a job as a foot messenger. My country walks had kept me fit, you see, and despite being in my fifties I looked no older than a young man of twenty-five – if, that is, you had the patience to try and focus on me. More importantly I fell in love for the first time. Her name was Babe, she was a dancer at the Folies and unrepentantly addicted to morphine. As life for her was always a little blurry at the edges she suited me perfectly. It was for Babe that I was running an errand in that picture the world purports to know so well. Babe had asked me to fetch her prescription from the chemist in the 4th *arrondissement* close to the Hôtel de Ville. I vaguely remember seeing Monsieur Doisneau there with his camera and all his young assistants, but I didn't see the famous kiss as a woman in a camel coat with a strangely preoccupied expression obscured my view. I found out afterwards of course that she was one of Monsieur Doisneau's assistants too, adding a bit of live background to the supposedly haphazard moment of passion. No, when that picture was taken I was too busy thinking about my Babe, eagerly awaiting my return in just her silk chemise and patched-over stockings, to worry about my smeary presence leaving its mark on history. So you see, that is my contribution to the myth behind the picture your readers have grown so fond of. I truly am the fuzzy man at the back of the frame, not a camera blur or a victim of perspective, but a frayed-edged guy out fetching his mistress a fix.

In the sixties the drugs improved but my shadowy, palpitating proportions deteriorated further. I left Paris when Babe passed away and took a bus to India with some hippy students who were so doped up most of the time they thought I was the straightest cat in their whole wacky circus. From there I moved around constantly, sometimes in the very dark places of the world and occasionally in the very bright ones – anywhere I could be with people who would accept me for the fuzziness I was. I never again had the confidence to live in the midst of people like those brief years in Paris, but then I was never in love again like I'd been with Babe. More recently though I've felt myself drawn back to Norfolk and to the place where I grew up and defined myself.

Doctor Bindfoot's son got in touch when he was going through his father's papers; I believe that is how you tracked me down. Apparently he wants to write a book that he hopes will clear his father's name of the insanity charges made against him in the 1950s. I'll do what I can to help of course, but I find myself shakier than ever in outline these days. Not fading away exactly, but flickering towards my maker.

So, does this answer your questions and ease your curiosity, or do you still insist on seeing me for yourself? Very well, I will not keep you waiting much longer. I am glad you followed my instructions and that no photographer has been present at this meeting; you can understand that I do not wish to be caught out on camera a second time. It has been enough to be a private freak to myself and those few people I've been close to, not now to become a public one.

It is too late for regrets, but if I do have one it's that I didn't leave poor dear Willy to die on that battlefield and thus save us both his painful potter into mental incontinency. For my part, I cannot wish I had died that day as well, for I rather feel it has been my duty to blur the edges and bleed the boundaries of the last one hundred and twenty years.

Perhaps you understand me and perhaps you don't . . .

Now, if you think you are ready, please open the door and turn on the light. I will stand as still for you as I am able.

THE ACCIDENT
Anna Ackland

When it happened, I saw not my whole life flashing before me, but a shower of Smarties – green, yellow, orange, pink and red, red, red – spilling from the upturned tube of the afternoon sky. In that instant, the steering wheel became chocolate melting between my fingers as one huge silver Smartie tore across the road and crunched into the metal shell of my rear door, sending my spine on a spiralling bounce of infinite pain – my arms, legs and head flopping after it – while I wondered where all the blue ones had got to, realised with a jolt it was too late to go looking for them now, and heard a snap like a sugar-coated sweetie bitten by the teeth of Death. Which, as you've since pointed out, was probably just that – knowing Death and her ways, as you do.

Listen, I'd love to help you, really I would. But I'm not sure I'm up to it, in my current state. And, actually, now I come to think about it, I'm also not sure I agree that angels deserve fag breaks and certainly not as an absolute right, like the human right to life, for instance. Still, I do appreciate that some of us are harder to guard than others and I'm quite prepared to believe I'm of their number, although – I would like to make it clear – this is *not* because I'm a frustrated Lewis Hamilton but because 1) there are far too many traffic lights in the centre of town for any reasonable person to get anywhere in a reasonable amount of time and 2) my daughter Felicity's Tuesday ballet class finishes at 4:45 p.m.

prompt, and I had to be there, this time; a good deal was hanging on it. I may drive a little recklessly but I am definitely the more responsible parent.

I do take your point about the driver of the silver Mercedes, that his behaviour after the crash indicated a singular disregard for the sanctity of life, which was doubtless also a not insignificant feature of his personality before the crash. This doesn't exonerate you exactly but it does shift some of the blame. As an insurance claims manager, I don't mind telling you, I've had my fair share of drivers who care more about their car than their victim. The same may well be true of angels during entanglements when learning to fly, worrying more, at the point of impact, about the gold trim of their robe than the welfare of their fellow celestial creature, but I can't help wondering if your mentioning this is a distraction from the crucial issue.

After all, you really should have been more alert, your hands and wings unencumbered, your mouth not all jammed up with a heavenly cancer stick but free enough to whisper in my ear, "Red light ahead! I'd stop here if I were you." And that's what the judge will conclude, isn't it? Now, I'm not saying I *won't* speak in your defence but, honestly, look at me. What future do I have? And what about my daughter's ballet shoes? Felicity's feet will grow, you know, and, I'm afraid, we just can't rely on her father to see to these things properly.

By the way, after Death took me by the hand and hauled me out of my crumpled body, I felt a certain amount of relief about that tube of Smarties not being the product of a deranged mind but a common feature of dying at an inconvenient moment: that last-minute search for the elusive blue one, as you call it; the quest for the sugar coating that's the colour of the sky – a quest that occupies some people for decades but occupied me just for the split second before it was way too late to look for anything at all.

To tell you the truth, the sweetness of Death was quite a surprise. After all those millennia of human culture, all that waxing literary and lyrical about its grandeur and momentousness, it was a genuine relief to see Death for the great Lollipop Lady that she is, a paper bag of pear drops always in her hand, along with a large red Stop sign that you can actually lick (without fear of infection), and her middle clad not in a luminous jacket but in a void that changes as she twirls from the blues of skies to the blues of oceans, always a blueness with a thousand reflections of everything you ever did that was seaworthy or soaring; and the place where her tummy button should be a white-rimmed hole, rumoured, by certain celestial beings with nothing better to do, to be a Polo mint.

No, I'm not making any promises about what I'll say when you come before the Great Court of Guardian Angels for neglect of duty. Nothing is guaranteed. Unless, of course, you can pull some strings in the mysterious circles you move in, and slip some blue Smarties into my daughter's hand.

"Ever tried.
Ever failed.
No matter.
TRY AGAIN. Fail again.
Fail better."
Samuel Beckett

LAST BUS TO ELSINORE
Sue Gedge

The day before my seventh birthday, my father appeared to me in the orchard. Enveloped in a thin mist, he was hovering some distance above the ground, to the left of the blighted pear tree, the crown of his Homburg hat brushing against an overhanging branch. I was so startled by this sudden manifestation that I dropped the bald, grey tennis ball with which I'd been playing and allowed it to roll away from me into the compost heap.

I had no doubt that this was my father. I recognised his cheeky, boyish smile, his thin, spiv moustache, and his lanky figure, clad in a baggy demob suit, from the photograph of my parents' wedding that Granny Delgardy kept face down in the left-hand drawer of the dresser. I'd often sneaked a look at that picture and the resemblance was unmistakable, even if his face did seem unnaturally pallid and there was a translucent shimmering around the edges of his person that might have unnerved a slightly more sensitive child than my pragmatic self. Had he brought me a present, I wondered?

"Hello, Junie-Moon," he said.

I was doing my best not to look at the hole, smack in the middle of his forehead. I'd been told, many times, that it was rude to stare. All the same, my eye kept being drawn back to that little red cavity. It was as neatly delineated as the rosebuds embroidered on the antimacassars in the sitting room. I knew something wasn't quite right, but I didn't know what it was. How could I? No one had even told me he was dead.

"Junie-Moon." He spoke the name as if he was tasting something delicate on his tongue. "Fancy seeing you, Junie-Moon."

So he *was* speaking to me! Here was another cause for astonishment. No one had ever called me Junie-Moon before. Granny, who was not given to endearments, always called me June Margaret, and at school I was taunted with playground nicknames like Gardy-Loo. I liked being called Junie-Moon. Somehow, the name reminded me of the dance-band music that Dymphna, our home help, used to listen to on the crackly old radio when Granny was out. Victor Silvester. *Music While You Work.* All the pleasures in the house took place when Granny was out.

My father held up his hand, apparently warning me to stay silent.

"I don't have much time," he said, "and I've forgotten some of what I had to say. Don't talk, Junie-Moon, or it'll all go out of me 'ead."

This was disappointing, as there were so many things I wanted to ask him. For example, where had he been for the past seven years and had he seen my mother lately?

"Listen, Junie-Moon" – his voice was soft, his accent redolent of South London – "I don't much care for the way your Granny's bringing you up. She tells you lies to make you behave. Half the things – no, *all* the things she tells you aren't true. A bull won't attack you just because you're wearing something red, eating orange pith won't make you ill, touching eggshells don't cause warts, picking dandelions won't make you wet the bed and when Granny Delgardy claims to be on intimate speaking terms with Catherine, Czarina of all the Russias, she's just showing herself up as a vain, deceitful old baggage."

This last revelation was shocking. Granny Delgardy was a respected medium and she always commanded a large and loyal audience at the Salutation Hall in Havelock Street. I'd been taken to my first séance when I was six, and I'd seen the way Aggie Simpson, a woman in her fifties who wore her greying hair in a chignon and kept a bottle of Scotch in her handbag, summoned the departed by playing *She'll Be Coming Round the Mountain When She*

Comes on the harmonium. Granny would sit on the big, plush chair on the podium, her head lowered in anticipation. The lights would be dim. Then Granny Delgardy would speak, her voice dropping a few registers, and becoming mysteriously croaky, even guttural.

"It is the Czarina," she would gasp. "She is leading others by the hand. Loved ones – they are coming forward to greet you . . ."

"I have to go now, Junie-Moon." My father kissed his fingertips and flattening his hands towards me blew his blessing in my direction. "You be a good girl, now, and remember what I've told you. Oh, and by the way" – he winked at me knowingly – "next time your granny mentions the Empress of Russia, ask her to get Catherine the Great to explain what *really* happened with that horse. That'll rattle her cage."

Then he was gone, and I might have doubted that I'd ever seen him at all had it not been for the heady, masculine scent of Bay Rum hair oil that he left behind him. It lingered by the pear tree for days, although I had the feeling that I was the only person who noticed.

It was typical of Granny Delgardy to insist on calling that ramshackle end of the garden "the orchard". Troubled by the stink from the gas works and full of rotting brown medlars, the only fruit that grew there in spiteful abundance, it was an unsatisfactory place. There were only two other trees, one that produced fewer than six pears a year and one where the apples were attacked by wasps even before they had left the branch. Dymphna would gather up the squashy harvest regularly, despite the fact that none of this fruit was remotely edible, especially not in Granny's bitter-tasting chutney which visitors would surreptitiously scrape to the edge of their plates. Just as I saw Mr Bolsover do, the following evening, when he came for supper.

"When the spirits speak to us, they often do so in riddles," he said, wiping his mouth on the starched linen napkin. "It is our mission to act as interpreters." He suppressed a belch.

"Exactly so." Granny Delgardy agreed.

I was sitting on a footstool by the piano, pretending to be absorbed in my book, *Rebecca of the Remove*, an old foxed volume with stiff, grey pasteboard covers which had belonged to my mother. Granny Delgardy appeared to hold Mr Bolsover in high esteem, despite his paunch, the shiny patches on the elbows of his jacket and the smell of whisky. She was decked out in her best dark-green velvet dress and black fringed shawl, and had put an ornamental diamanté-studded comb in her thick grey hair. Dymphna had been instructed to bring out the best china and a whole ham had been boiled. It was going to be a gala night at the Salutation Hall. Mr Bolsover had travelled all the way down from Manchester to lead the gathering.

It was January 25th, 1954. My seventh birthday, although there were no bright, cheerful cards ranged along the mantelpiece for me. Granny Delgardy disapproved of birthdays and my birth, as I'd overheard her reminding Dymphna during a chutney-boiling session in the back kitchen, had been nothing to celebrate: "She made her mother suffer, such a great lump of a baby, far too big right from the start. The pipes were frozen, so we had no hot water. She couldn't have chosen a worse time to be born. 1947, the coldest winter since 1814, and the doctor's car was stuck in a snowdrift so he didn't get here until it was all over. And that no-good father was nowhere to be seen. It was just as well it wasn't a stillbirth. The back garden was so frozen, we'd have never got the spade into the ground."

"The blessèd saints and Mary, Mother of God!" In her agitation, Dymphna had seized a scouring pad and begun scrubbing furiously at a burned-on mess at the base of the big, double-handled jam pan. "Mrs Delgardy, you can't be saying what I think you're saying! As if the poor child could choose the day of her delivery."

I knew that Dymphna would pay for that outburst and so she did. The very next time she asked for a rise in her wages, Granny retaliated by lowering them by sixpence.

"Has your granddaughter inherited your talent?" Mr Bolsover asked, casting a dubious glance in my direction.

"She has shown no sign of it," said Granny Delgardy. "She is an earthen child, I fear, not a single element of fire or air in her veins."

I turned the page of my book, looking studiously at a colour print of a girl in an old-fashioned gym slip holding a hockey stick. *It's absolutely beastly of you, Jemima,* the caption read, *to say you won't play this afternoon just because you want to sneak off to tea with*

Rupert! Good for Jemima, I thought. I'd do the same. Rebecca looked like an awful, self-righteous bully.

"I wonder," Mr Bolsover ventured, "if you have a drop of brandy in the house to guard against the cold before we sally forth?"

"I'm afraid not, Mr Bolsover." Granny Delgardy bared her yellowing teeth in what was supposed to be a smile. "This is a temperance house. It has been ever since my unfortunate daughter passed over."

"Ah, commiserations." He nodded. "And that was – how long ago, may I ask? How did it happen?"

I wondered why, if Mr Bolsover was a medium, he needed to ask. Had he no vision of my mother? I had. I could see her, at the moment she died. She was slim and her dark hair was styled in a permanent wave, and she had been wearing a clinging lemon silk evening gown, and she was sprawled on the rug before the fireplace, one silver-lamé sandal still on her foot, the other on its side by the coal scuttle. She'd fallen, something had dropped out of her hand and there had been music playing and the scent of rose water. And I knew it had happened right here, in this room.

"It was a tragedy." Granny Delgardy spoke sharply, rather too sharply perhaps, to such an important guest. "I blame that scoundrel, that cad. He broke her heart, deserting her. He went away without so much as leaving her a forwarding address. She should never have married him. But I do have one comfort. The Czarina has assured me that my daughter is happy now that she is on the other side. She is better off without him, even in death."

There was a crash as a sepia photograph of old Aberdeen fell off the wall and its ornately carved, burnt-wood frame landed in the fireplace with an emphatic splintering of glass. I had absolutely no doubt at all why that picture had fallen and whose unquiet spirit had tipped it from its hook.

"June Margaret, how many times have I told you to sit still!" Granny Delgardy glared at me. "And if you continue to read in that light, expect to be blind before you are twenty!"

"It was nothing to do with the child," said Mr Bolsover smoothly. "The string at the back of the picture must have been frayed and gravity has simply done its worst."

Granny Delgardy pulled the tasselled chord for Dymphna to come and clear up the mess. Ours must have been one of the last homes in London where it was possible to summon a maid in this way. The house was ugly and old-fashioned, so tall and narrow, with dark staircases and creaking doors, and chocolate-brown paint below the dado rails and tea-coloured wallpaper above, and the furniture was ancient and heavy, the table in this room covered by a thick, chenille cloth and the carpet smelling of dead mice.

"Granny," I said, "can I ask you a question?"

"If it is a sensible one." She looked at me with a forbidding expression.

"Then, Granny," I continued, "why doesn't the Czarina talk to you in Russian? Catherine the Great was a Russian, wasn't she?"

"When the spirits pass over," said Mr Bolsover, smiling at me, "such considerations become irrelevant. That is, they are not important, by which I mean, they do not apply."

"So you can ask the Czarina any question you like and she'll understand?" I looked at Granny.

"Naturally," said Granny Delgardy.

"Then could you ask her what *really* happened with that horse?"

"Horse? What on earth are you talking about, June Margaret?" With an impatient jerk, Granny Delgardy pulled the chord again for Dymphna.

I happened to know that this was a futile action, having seen Dymphna slip out through the back gate half an hour ago, on her way to see *The Glenn Miller Story* at the Odeon.

Mr Bolsover cleared his throat and leaned across the table, lowering his voice.

"I'm afraid your granddaughter is alluding to a scurrilous rumour concerning the death of Catherine the Great," he murmured.

"I can't think what story you mean." Granny Delgardy's lips tightened.

"I wouldn't dream of repeating it," said Mr Bolsover.

"I'm afraid I must ask you to do so." Granny Delgardy tapped her finger impatiently. "If the girl has learned an improper story, I need to know!"

"Very well." With a salacious glint in his eye, Mr Bolsover

cupped his hand and whispered a few words into her ear.

Granny Delgardy let out a snort of disgust and stood up so quickly that she knocked over the pink fringed standard lamp. Then she informed me that, as a punishment, I was to go out into the garden without my coat and stay out there until she had returned from the Salutation Hall.

It was freezing outside, with sleet falling, and I felt my fingertips tingling with the cold. My favourite part of the garden was between the wall and a bramble bush, just beyond the pear tree in the so-called orchard. This had often provided me with a hiding place and tonight, I crawled in and wrapped my arms round me, pulling the sleeves of my scratchy, old woollen cardigan down over my hands for warmth. After a while, I looked up and noticed several lush, ripe blackberries growing against the prickly leaves. I didn't realise there was something odd, that there shouldn't be any fruit here in January, nor did I worry about Granny Delgardy's warning that small insects which could make my tongue swell lurked in unwashed brambles. I started picking the fruit, cramming it into my mouth, letting the juice trickle down my throat. The berries had a strange flavour, sweet at first, but with an aftertaste that reminded me of the time I had grazed my knee badly in the playground and had put the wound to my mouth in order to suck out the grit. Blood, I thought, frowning.

"Happy birthday, Junie-Moon," a voice said close to my ear and I felt warm and comforted.

I saw him again just before my eleventh birthday. Once again, he was up by the pear tree, his Homburg hat tipped at a rakish angle, and he looked a little sadder than the first time I'd seen him.

"Oh, Junie," he said, "I think I might be dead."

"Yes," I said, sadly. "I'm afraid you are."

"That explains a lot." He shrugged. "Well, don't tell anyone you've seen me. Does your Granny ever mention me?"

"Yes. She said you left my mother and broke her heart."

"Lying cow!" my father exploded, then he grinned ruefully. "'Scuse my French. But it's not true. I was coming back – I was always going to come back. I loved your mother, Junie-Moon, and she loved me. What's happened to her? Where has she gone?"

"Don't you know?"

"No, I can't seem to find her," he admitted. "Can't you help me, Junie?"

"I don't know what to do . . ." I began, but he had gone.

Granny Delgardy was at the Salutation Hall and Dymphna was in the kitchen, and I could hear dance-band music playing in the sitting room even though the wireless wasn't kept in there. As I pushed the door open, the overpowering scent of rose water spilled into the dark hallway, and a woman laughed teasingly, as if flirting happily with a lover. In the dim light of the pink fringed standard lamp, I noticed that the little black-lacquered cabinet, which Granny Delgardy always kept locked, had been opened and there were two lead-crystal glasses on the table and a lighted cigarette in an ebony holder resting on the mantelpiece. I walked across the room and bent down to look inside the cabinet. There was a thick brown envelope stuffed full of papers lying at the back, tucked behind a decanter of rust-red liquid. I took the envelope out and closed the door of the cabinet carefully, smiling to myself at the thought of Granny Delgardy communing with the spirits at the Salutation Hall at this very moment, while all the time her house was haunted and she didn't even know it.

"Miss June!" As I walked into the kitchen, Dymphna looked up from her copy of *Picturegoer*. "Whatever have you got there? You surely haven't been poking around in your grandmother's things?"

"These aren't my grandmother's things. They belong to my mother." I sat down, emptying out the contents of the envelope on the table. "And she left them for me."

"And how do you know that?" Dymphna gawped at the papers spread out on the table.

"I know a lot of things," I said.

The letters were all on crinkly paper, written in a sprawling, undisciplined hand, the words difficult to decipher amongst all the crossings-out in thick blue pencil. *Chin up, sweetie, not long now . . . Cheerio for now and keep smiling through . . . Give the little sprog a kiss and cuddle for me . . .*

"These are from your father. Wandsworth Prison, that's where he was," Dymphna said. "You might as well know. They took him away in the Black Maria just before you were born. He got six years. And when they let him out, he never came home. Ran off with a floozie he'd known before the war. And when your poor mother found out, she killed herself with the poison. While the balance of her mind was disturbed, as they say. I heard your father was a bit of a charmer. That long green paper, there – it must be their marriage certificate."

I picked it up. Daniel Patrick Mooney, age 24; condition, bachelor; occupation, sales assistant. Dorothy Mavis Delgardy, age 20; condition, spinster. Oct 24th, 1946. Three months before I was born, almost to the day.

"Dymphna?" I frowned. "When my mother got married, she became Mrs Mooney, didn't she? So I ought to be called Mooney, too, not Delgardy at all."

"True enough, I suppose. And your mother called you June. Your grandmother thought the name June Mooney sounded silly, so she decided to call you June Margaret."

I felt overjoyed. I was going to Dalkeith Secondary Modern in the autumn. When I got there, I'd call myself June Mooney. No one would ever call me Gardy-Loo again.

"You change your name back and your granny will go mad," Dymphna warned me.

Good, I thought.

In 1960, Aggie Simpson collapsed at the organ during her playing of *She'll Be Coming Round the Mountains* and Granny Delgardy informed me that I was to take her place. While I would never be a medium, having no spiritual gifts whatsoever, I might have a future as an organist. I was not at all happy about this, especially since Mr Bolsover had returned. He had an unpleasant way of leaning over me to talk, and once he squeezed my upper arm rather too enthusiastically, his fingers brushing against my burgeoning breasts.

"You're getting to be a handsome girl, Junie-Moon," my father said, looking down at me from his position by the pear tree, on the eve of my fourteenth birthday. "Soon be time for you to find a sweetheart. Love is the best thing in the world, Junie-Moon, and don't let anyone tell you different."

"Dymphna says you ran off with another woman," I told him.

My father's eyes widened in horror and the cigarette he was smoking dropped out of his mouth.

"Jiminy Cricket!" he exclaimed indignantly. "'Course I never! Like I said before, I was coming home. I remember now . . . I was coming home for Christmas. Only I never got there. Because I died and I don't know how."

I looked at the mark in the middle of his forehead.

"I think," I said, "that someone shot you."

"Yeh?" He put his hand up to his head. "Blimey."

"Didn't you see who it was?"

"No." He shook his head. "It was too foggy. December '52, the great smog. I don't even know *where* I was. Anyone could have done it – you can make enemies in my line of work. And I was about to go straight – they wouldn't have liked that, not any of the old gang. Look, Junie-Moon, I never did anything really bad. It was just after the war, things were in short supply – nylons, good food, sweets . . . Well, it don't matter much now. Hey – do you want to really annoy that old bag? Whistle this tune, and if you can't whistle, hum it. This'll really rattle her cage."

He was fading fast, but I could hear him whistling *Perfidia*, quite tunefully as it happened. I knew that old dance-band number. I often heard it playing in our house.

When I was fifteen, Ted Delaney came to teach English at Dalkeith Road. He was a gentle, shambling man, with a mop of tousled brown curls and the most beautiful blue eyes I'd ever seen; he had a very slight stoop and walked with a limp, having been knocked down by a motorbike in Hammersmith Broadway a few years earlier. Some of the girls said his brain had been affected by the accident too, but I knew that he was thoughtful and open-minded and kind.

My class was reading *Hamlet*. I sat in the front row, making copious, conscientious notes as Ted Delaney talked and I listened awestruck as he read the iambic pentameter with the resonance of one who, given rather more classical looks, could have commanded the stage at the Old Vic. He was well into Act One, when I raised my hand.

"Sir?"

"Yes, June?"

"I don't understand. How can Hamlet's father possibly know that it was Claudius who poured the poison into his ear?"

"Well, June . . . I suppose that . . . as a spirit he knows everything. He's omniscient."

"But I don't believe ghosts are . . . omniscient, sir. I believe they say silly things and make jokes, and they can be just as confused as they were when they were alive. Hamlet's father was asleep in the orchard when Claudius killed him, so he never saw his murderer, and he might still be wondering who did it. And how would he even know it was the poison that killed him?"

There was a titter of laughter from the back row, but Mr Delaney didn't laugh.

"Thank you, Miss Mooney." He smiled. "That is a refreshingly original point, one I have never heard before. Why don't you write me an essay on the ghost in *Hamlet*? I'd very much enjoy reading your views."

It began snowing on Boxing Day, 1962, and the bad weather did not let up all through January. It was the coldest winter since 1740, colder even than '47. Granny Delgardy had informed me that once I was sixteen I could marry with my guardian's consent. Mr Bolsover was looking for a wife and helpmeet to accompany him on his forthcoming tour of the spiritualist halls of Canada. It was time, I decided, to take my destiny into my own hands.

"Mr Delaney?" I approached him as he was coming out of school, heading for the bus stop. "It's about that essay you asked me to write."

"Essay?" Ted looked at me kindly. He was wearing a Russian hat against the cold and a thick overcoat, his briefcase swinging from his gloved hand. He lived on his own, I knew that, because I'd seen him in the supermarket one Saturday, buying a small sliced loaf, a pint of milk and a rather nasty-looking frozen TV dinner for one.

"Yes," I said, "it's about the ghost in *Hamlet*. I've got a story I want to tell you. Would you like to hear it?"

"Well, yes, I'd like that very much."

"Could we go to my house, sir? I only live just round the corner."

"Well, I'm not entirely sure . . ." He looked down, shuffling his feet in the snow, suddenly abashed and awkward.

"Please, sir. It won't take long and you can meet Dymphna. She's looked after me since I was a baby. She'll be there. We won't be on our own."

Ted Delaney sat in Granny Delgardy's sitting room, looking at me with a bemused expression. He'd listened to me carefully, he hadn't tried to argue, and he'd appeared to be receptive as I'd described the hauntings of my childhood.

"Do you believe me, sir?" I asked.

"Well, June." He looked at me thoughtfully. "I'd say that there are more things in heaven and earth – of course, you know what Shakespeare says, don't you?"

Ted had dropped his coat over the back of the chair, and he looked cold, despite the thick, Aran sweater he was wearing. I'd have liked to offer him a drink, but the only alcohol in the house was that ancient stuff in the decanter in the black-lacquer cabinet.

"Hamlet's father comes back to seek revenge, doesn't he?" I said. "A ghost is a spirit with unfinished business. But my father doesn't *know* who shot him. And he's never mentioned revenge. All he does is tell me ways of upsetting Granny Delgardy. Humming tunes and asking what her spirit guide did with a horse."

"I'm sorry?" Ted looked at me quizzically.

"Catherine the Great. Granny claims she's her spirit guide," I explained, "only I don't know about the horse."

"Oh dear." Ted grinned. "Never mind about the horse."

I turned and looked out of the window. The snow was coming down thick and fast. It must have been just like this when I was born, when, as Granny Delgardy had said, all the pipes froze and it was so lucky I hadn't been a stillbirth or she'd never have got the spade into the – *Oh!* My stomach flipped over, as a thought struck me.

"Mr Delaney?" I turned back to him. "If a woman had a baby, and it was full term, and it was born dead, would it be all right to bury it in the garden?"

"Good grief, no!" He looked at me aghast. "Stillbirths have to be registered just like any death! What on earth made you think of such a thing?"

"My grandmother said –" I stopped, my thoughts racing. *My mother never knew my father was dead. She was expecting my father. She unlocked the cupboard and poured out a drink . . . Of course!*

"Oh, sir!" I had to tell Ted, the only person who would understand. "You know when Hamlet says Denmark is a prison? Well, this house is a prison. Not just for me, but for the ghosts. I've felt my mother's presence here. She's in this room, trapped, because this is where she died, where she *didn't* kill herself – it was an accident, the poison was in the decanter, Granny must have meant it for him – for my father . . . And my father . . . he's always in the orchard! That's it, he's *in the orchard*!"

It said a great deal for Ted's sympathy for me that he was prepared to go out and dig in all that snow behind the pear tree. The spade went in easily, almost as if the ground was welcoming us. And everything was just as I'd expected. The moment I saw the decaying, mulched-up Homburg hat, Ted stopped digging and I shouted for Dymphna, telling her to run to the telephone box on the corner and call the police. But in the end, Ted had to go, because Dymphna was hysterical.

"I didn't know." She wrung her hands. "I swear I didn't know anything. I heard the shot, yes, but she said she'd killed a fox that was coming over the garden wall. I believed her, I swear it. The evil, evil, old besom! She must have shot him with his own old service rifle that he'd kept back from the war."

It may seem extraordinary that anyone could have been shot so accurately in the head through that dense smog, but even if Granny Delgardy didn't see my father, she would have heard him, whistling my mother's favourite tune, *Perfidia*, as he climbed over the wall into the orchard. I just happen to know that.

It was a pity the police were unable to arrest Granny Delgardy, but when my father's body was found she was already laid out in the Parlour of Rest at the Co-op Undertakers in Meath Street. At her age, a fatal heart attack could have happened at any time, although it was odd that it should have coincided with the arrival of that card. The first birthday card I had ever received.

There was a picture of a cake with sixteen candles on it, and the card was so old and sun-bleached it looked as though it had been left in the window of a fly-blown backstreet shop for years. The message inside, written in a sprawling, undisciplined hand, read: "To Junie-Moon, Happy Birthday, Sweet Sixteen, from your loving father, Daniel Patrick Mooney. PS *Tell the old bag I'm coming.*"

I never saw my father again, after that.

WHAT YOU KNOW
Peter Ho Davies

People suddenly want to know all about my students, what they're like. What do I know? I want to say. I'm just a writer, a writer-in-the-schools. All I see is their writing.

So what are they like as writers?

They're shocking. Appalling, in fact. Indescribably awful (and when a writer, even one of my low self-esteem, says that, you know it's serious). The good ones are bad, and the bad ones are tragic.

When at the start of each class I ask them their favourite books their fifteen-year-old faces are as blank as paper. The better students struggle to offer a "right" answer: *Catcher*, *Gatsby*, the Bible (!). The honest ones, the stupid, arrogant, honest ones, tell me *For the Love of the Game* by Michael Jordan, or the latest Dean Koontz.

The most voracious readers among them are the science-fiction fans, the genre nerds, the heavy-duty bookworms (all those sequels and prequels; trilogies and tetralogies), but none of them is deterred for a nanosecond when I tell them that good science fiction is one of the hardest things to write. After all, they're thinking – I can see it in their eyes – it's just a matter of taste, isn't it?

As a matter of fact, no. I believe in the well-made story. Have your character want something, I tell them. Have a conflict. Have the character change. Learn these simple rules, and you can spend the rest of your life breaking them.

But most of the time I find myself telling them what not to write.

All the narrative clichés. No stories about suicide. No flashbacks longer than a page. No narrators from beyond the grave. No "and then I woke up" endings. No "I woke up and then . . ." beginnings. No psychedelic dream sequences. The list of boringly bad stories ("But it's supposed to be boring, life is boring") goes on and on.

"No suicides?" they say in their flat, whiny voices, as if there is nothing else, nothing better. "How can suicide be boring?"

Maybe not in life, I explain quickly, but in fiction? Sure. It's a cruel world of readers out there – callous, heartless, *commuting* readers, who've been there, seen that, read it all before. "I'm not saying you can't try to write about suicide," I console them. "I'm just saying it's hard to do well, that you owe it to the material to do it justice, to find a way of making it real and raw for readers again."

Writers aren't godlike, I tell them. Readers are. Writers only create; readers judge.

They nod in complete incomprehension. Yes, they're saying. Yes, we see now that there is absolutely no chance we'll understand a word you say. We're just here for the extra credit. It's the nod you give a crazy man, a lunatic with a gun.

What redeems it? My love of teaching? I do love teaching, but for all the wrong reasons. I love the sound of my own voice. I love to pontificate about writing, get excited about it, argue about it (and usually win) with people who have to listen to me, more or less (unlike my parents, my friends, my wife). But always, behind their acquiescence, behind the fact that however bad my taste I'm still the coolest teacher they have (the competition is not stiff), lie the awful, numbing questions: "What have you published? Why haven't we heard of you?"

What really redeems it are the laughs. The laughable badness of their prose. The moose frozen like a *dear* in the headlights. The cop slapping on the *cufflinks*. The *viscous* criminal. The *escape* goat.

It's as if they're hard of hearing, snatching up half-heard, half-comprehended phrases, trusting blindly in their spellcheckers to save them. (Think! Think who designs spellcheckers for a moment. Were these people ever good spellers?)

I once had a heated argument with a student about the death knoll.

"Knell," I said.

"Knoll," he insisted with vehemence, until finally we

determined that he was thinking of the *grassy* knoll. My way might be right, he conceded grudgingly, but his way made more sense. We took a vote in class (they love democracy) and the majority agreed. And perhaps this is the way that language, meaning, evolve before our very eyes and ears. "It's the death mole of literacy," I told them, but they didn't get it. Sometimes, I despair of language. If only there was some way for what I know to just appear, instantaneously, in their heads.

So *that*, if you really want to know, is what my students are like. Does any of it explain why one of them last week shot his father in the head across the breakfast nook, rode the bus to school with a pistol in his waistband, emptied it in his homeroom, killing two and wounding five, before putting the gun in his mouth and splashing his brains all over the whiteboard?

No stories about suicide? No viscous criminals?

In the moments after the crisis no one thinks to call me – as the other staff, the *full-time* staff are called – to warn me not to talk to the media. No one, in fact, thinks to call me *apart from* the media. "It's CNN," my wife says passing me the phone, then stepping back as if I hold a snake in my hands. But we're *watching* CNN, I want to say. I look at her and she mimes helplessness. It never occurs to me that all my fellow teachers have been asked to say nothing to the media, that this is why some bright spark in Atlanta, after trying five or six names and getting the same response, has slid his finger down the faxed list before him to "Other" and found me, not quite a teacher, but better than a janitor.

What he wants to know is if I had taught the killer, the dead boy, Clark, and when I admit (and it feels like an admission, nothing to be proud of) that yes I have, I have him – *had* him (watch those tense changes) – in a writing workshop, I can hear the reporter lean forward in his chair, cup his hand around the mouthpiece. I wonder for a second about him, this young journalist, probably around my age, looking for his big break. This could be it, I realise, and I feel an odd vertiginous jealousy, almost wanting to hold back. But later, listening to my voice over and over on national TV – a grainy photo from the latest yearbook, and a caption identifying me as a writer, floating over a live shot of the blank school buildings – I'm glad I talked to him, glad I didn't say anything stupid, that I come across as dignified and responsible. I answer all his questions in the first-person plural. "We're shocked and appalled. We'll all be doing our best to help our students through this awful period. Our hearts go out to the families in the tragedy." Later my mother will call from Arizona, then my colleagues, even the principal with a warning not to say anything else, but an off-the-record pat on the back for "our unofficial spokesman". "A way with words," my mother will say. "You always had a way with words." Even though she's never read a single one of my stories. I tell her it was easy and it was. It comes naturally. For months now I've been talking in the first-person plural. We're pregnant, my wife and I. We're expecting. We're about to be parents ourselves.

"CNN," my wife says, touching her stomach. "Something to tell the kid." It's not often she's proud of me, and I'm pleased, even though I despise the network, its incompetent staff. I heard one anchor a couple of years back talking about a first in the *anals* of country music. Another time I caught a piece in which the President was described as being *salt and peppered* with questions at a news conference. Someone wrote that, was paid to. "I suppose I should be grateful," I tell my wife. "My caption could have read 'waiter', not 'writer'." And she smiles uncertainly, not sure who this particular joke is on.

What I tell no one, though, not even my wife, is the reporter's last question, off air, quietly into my ear after he has thanked me and double-checked the spelling of my name. Only the tone alerted me, otherwise this could have been the same as any of the previous questions – "Was he a good student? What was he like?" This final shot: "Do you have anything he wrote for you? A poem or a story?"

I said, "No," but something in my voice must have made him wonder because he added softly, "It could be worth a great deal." So I said, "No," again, more forcefully, and then, "I'm sorry," and hung up.

Why was I sorry? Easier to explain why I said, "No," with that catch of hesitation. Because I couldn't remember, that's why. I had work upstairs, ungraded stories, the response to an exercise: "Write about a moment of extreme emotion: fear, hate, love, joy, laughter." The idea is to have them write about a true emotion and use this as a benchmark against which to compare the emotions of their fictional characters. Something by Clark might be there, if he'd done the assignment. They often didn't. And, indeed, when I look there's nothing, just a note – brief – he'd been sick, and below his own signature, another – larger, flowing. It takes me a second to realise; it's his father's.

So why was I sorry? Because I'm a writer-in-the-schools. I earn $8,000 a year ($6,000 less than my wife's bookstore job pays) and we are pregnant. I was sorry I hadn't had the nerve to say: "How much?" He might even have been bullshitting me, the reporter. CNN would never do business like that, right? But something in his voice, the shift of register, made me think he might have just slipped into freelance mode. The phone was hot where I was pressing it against my head, but for a second I could have sworn it was his warm breath in my ear. Now I wondered – $1,000, $5,000, $10,000? Who knew? I was only sure it would be more than anything I'd ever gotten for my own work. And out of this irony, of course, came this idea. *I* could write a piece by Clark. I could write it and sell it. I could. His letter was typed, printed. He was a loner, without friends. His father was dead. He was dead. Who would know?

No narrators from beyond the grave?

Have your character want something.

Ten thousand big ones.

As a plan it seemed so simple at first, at least if you separate it from the issue of morality. And separating from that issue is something I teach my students. Don't stop yourselves writing something because it might hurt someone; your family, your friends. Don't stop yourself writing it because you think it's too personal, sexual, violent. Don't censor yourselves, I tell them, at least not alone when it's just you and the paper.

Oddly, they're prudish. Reluctant to write about feelings, except in the safest, most clichéd terms. Love, sex especially, makes them sneer with embarrassment, while violence is simply comic.

"But what's the point?" I remember one of them asking (I wish I could say it was Clark, but I can't picture him any more than I can bring to mind the faces of three or four other boys who sit in the back row with their baseball caps pulled low over their eyes).

"What's the point writing it if you're not going to show it to someone?" And I have sympathy with this. I believe in writing for an audience. Writing fiction is an act of communication – not just facts or opinions like a newspaper, but emotions. I tell them this. And in truth once something is written, actually expressed, showing it to someone – the desire to do that – is hard to escape. It's the momentum of the act. So I tell myself that writing a piece as Clark isn't the same as passing it off to others as Clark's, but once you've got it – especially if it's good – what else is there to do with it? So perhaps the moral problem does lie behind this practical one: it should be easy to write this piece – it doesn't have to be *good* after all; it needs, in fact, to be bad to be good – yet, after all the mockery I've heaped on their work, I can't do it. I can't imitate my students.

God help me, I'm blocked.

Here's the trouble. If I'm to write this and overcome the lie of it, I need it to mean something. I want to offer, coded, buried, subtly perhaps, an answer, a psychological, sociological subtext, that will explain these deaths, and in explaining offer some hope or comfort to us all. It may not be *the* meaning, but surely any meaning, even a sniff of meaning, is what we want. It is the writer's instinct to offer these things and, beyond mere morality, I can't quite shrug off this duty to, of all things, art.

Which is why I find myself in my 1988 Subaru Wagon, driving out to a gun range on the interstate called the Duke's Den. I have never fired a gun before and I decide that this – everything else notwithstanding – is the problem. If I want to understand Clark, take on his voice, I should at least try to understand how he expressed himself.

And this, too, is what I teach them. Show don't tell. Write what you know. Did Clark's baseball cap bob at that one? Did he take notes? Some of them do and it still amazes me, makes me think they're making fun, when in truth they only set down what they don't understand. "Show," they write carefully, "and tell."

Write what you know is even worse. They look at me as if I've asked them to raise the dead, as if they know nothing or everything. Some I have to persuade that their lives are important enough; others that they're not quite as important as they think. But either way what most of them know is deadly – not the stories themselves, nor their lives as such, but how they live them, think about them. The best ones, they know this already. Know it like an instinct. Write what they know? Not yet. Not until they know what they know. But the worst ones? They don't even want to know what they know.

"So is that why we can't write about suicide? Because if you know it, you're, like, dead?"

"Yeah, and there're no narrators from beyond the grave, right?"

They look at me, so pleased, so earnest, like they've figured it out and I feel my heart clench. I think about explaining that the rule really ought to be "Write whatever you know just a little more about than your reader." But truly what I want to tell them is that these rules aren't after all rules for writers; they're rules for people who are trying to be writers but won't ever make it.

So I don't get any suicide stories (although as one bright spark recently pointed out: "It's ironic, don't you think? Considering how many writers kill themselves."). Instead, I get first-kiss stories, first-joint stories, the death of pets, the death of grandparents, sad fat girls, thin sad girls. The tone is always the same – life is tragic; tragically small or epicly tragic (the chasm, come to think of it, that suicide bridges).

Lighten up, I want to tell them. It's not the end of the world. You've got your whole lives before you. All the lines my father taught me when I was their age and deciding to become a writer, all the lines I've taught them to recognise as clichés. Except, as they like to remind me, that doesn't mean they can't still be true. Some people do have apple cheeks or strawberry hair or cherry lips (the fruit-salad style of physical description). Don't clichés, in fact, have to be true to become clichés? No, I tell them, we just have to want them to be true.

What else do I teach them? Certainly not how to be creative. I'm not into breathing exercises, or free writing or journalling. Sucking up to the muse. Nor even how to write correctly – I'm no grammar maven. "How to tell stories," is what I told CNN, although the line never aired, and that's closer to the truth.

I teach them what Forster says: that there are stories and there are plots. That stories are simple sequences of events (this happened and then this and then that), but that plots are about causes, motivation (this happened because of this, on account of that). Plots are what stories mean. And the truth is that life is all stories and fiction is all plots, and what we're looking for in Clark's story is the plot that makes sense of it. Which is why it has to be someone's fault – his, his father's, the NRA, Nintendo, Hollywood, all the escape goats – doesn't it? This happened because of that or that or that. Or all of them.

So I teach them how to tell stories, or (since we're all storytellers every time we open our mouths) how to tell them better, which is to say I try to teach them to make sense of their stories, to figure out what they mean if they mean anything. Because the way we tell stories explains them.

Write what they know? Mostly, I just try to help them know what they write.

So that's what I teach them; how to plot.

And if that's beyond them, what I try to leave them with is this: when in doubt, when stuck, blocked or fucked, to always ask themselves, "What if?" (Even if their instinct is to ask, "So what?")

What if I pick up a gun and fire it?

The range is quiet. It's the weekend after the shooting; we're still in shock. I show my driver's licence and join for $25, which entitles me to rent guns from behind the counter for $5 an hour. It seems so cheap – what can you get for five bucks? – but as I buy ammunition for my choice, a .38 calibre revolver (I just pointed to the first gun I recognised from TV), I realise that this is what costs. Guns are just games consoles, VCRs – it's what you put in them that costs. The man behind the counter is unfailingly polite and helpful. He reminds me of a hardware salesman, the kind of guy in a brown apron who'll show you how to use a tool, dig out exactly the right size of wrench or washer for your job. The kind of guy who loves what he does and who'll tell you all about it if you're not careful. His name is Vern, and above his head, hanging up like so many hammers and saws on a workshop wall, are all manner of guns, not just pistols but rifles, even a replica Tommy gun, the kind of thing Al Capone might have used. There's an air of fancy dress about the display; an air of the toy store, the magic trick. On a ledge at the very top of the display is a line of model-railway rolling stock. Vern is a train enthusiast, a hobbyist.

After the gun and the shells – they come in a plastic rack, not the waxed-paper box I expect – he hands over a pair of ear defenders and then asks, "Target?" I must look puzzled, because he repeats himself. "What kind of target?"

"What kinds do you have?"

He grins, glad I asked, and starts to show me. There's a simple roundel, each ring marked with a score; the "classic" silhouette; a sheet covered in playing cards for "shooting poker"; a double silhouette of a gunman and a woman, his hostage; and finally a set of caricature targets of everyone from Saddam Hussein to Barney. I take the classic silhouette and Vern rolls it for me and secures it with a rubber band. He hands me the lot – gun, shells, target, ear defenders – in an EZCarry plastic tray and points me back towards the range which is separated from the shop by double glazing. Through the glass I can see one man, broad-shouldered, greying, balding, firing. "You put your headset on in the booth," Vern tells me, indicating the double set of doors between the shop and the range. "Take lane three."

Inside, with the ear defenders pinching my skull, the shots from the other man in the range sound like a distant hammering pulse. I set up in the lane beside him. Place the gun on the counter and the shells beside it, work the toggle switch that brings the target towards me on a wire. All this is familiar from the movies. When the target board arrives I'm momentarily at a loss as to how to fix the silhouette to it. I look around and there's Vern on the other side of the glass pointing and when I look again I see a tape dispenser mounted to the wall.

I run the target back about halfway to the rear concrete wall. It's ridged, corrugated, and it takes me a slow moment to realise that this is to prevent ricochets. The concrete makes the range cooler than the shop, like a bunker, and it smells, but only faintly, of the Fourth of July, fireworks. And this creeping nostalgia, the insulation of the ear defenders, the odd underground cool, give the experience an air of unreality.

The target jumps about on the wire for a few seconds like a puppet and I wait until it's still before turning to the gun. Vern has taught me how to load it, flipping out the cylinder and dropping in the shells. It's a six shooter, but he warned me to put five shots in and leave the chamber under the hammer empty, "to save your toes". The bullets go in very easily and quickly – the whole thing feels well made in a way that very few things do these days – and I slide the cylinder back into the gun. I hold it away from me and down and then slowly raise it. Vern has shown me how to cock the hammer and fire or how to pull the trigger all the way back. He has advised me to keep my trigger finger outside the guard until I'm ready to shoot. I'm frightened of it going off before I'm ready, of seeming dangerous. But once I have it in position, cocking it is simple and when I fire my first shot I'm surprised how easy it comes. (Vern is a good teacher.) There's a crack and a small flash from the gun, but the recoil is almost playful in the way it bats my hand up. I've hit serves that jarred worse. I look last at the target and see a small neat puncture in the shoulder of my silhouette. Almost too neat, but for the slight tearing of the paper. I fire again. And again and again and again. Because after all, what else is there to do? By my fifth shot I'm not cocking, but experimenting with pulling the trigger back. Two of my shots score tens in the target's chest. With my next set I take aim at the head and put all five on target. I feel like Dirty Harry, or Steve McGarrett. Just not Clark.

Beside me as I'm loading again, the other shooter reels in his target, unrolls another and tapes it up. He's old, grandfatherly, dressed in polyester, metallic-blue Sansabelt pants and a teal polo shirt. He nods and I nod back. He looks like a bowler and I realise that's exactly what this experience is reminding me of, bowling. I'd laugh at him rather than nod back, that slightly too portentous nod, except that he has a loaded weapon on the counter before him, a tool with which he could kill me. It occurs to me that if he took that into his head the only thing stopping him would be the fact that I might shoot back.

I try to ask myself what this might have meant to Clark, but I can't guess. The experience isn't inspiring, just deadening, mechanical. I feel the panic rising again, the greed. We need the money. I think of my own son, my unborn son (I wanted to know the sex; not for me the surprise ending), for whom I'm doing this, and I wonder what might possibly ever drive him to kill me. I know I thought about killing him. We talked about it, about a termination, an abortion. We hadn't planned on this. I kept thinking something would come up; a new job, a major publication. I had a story with one of the slick magazines and they had held it for weeks, months, so long my hopes were rising day by day. A score like that – thousands of dollars – could change our lives. I found myself putting my imaginative energy not into new work, but into visualising that moment, the letter in the mail, not in my own self-addressed envelope, but the magazine's embossed one, telling me blah, blah, blah, *delighted*. I didn't say so, but I think I'd decided we'd keep the baby if I sold the story. When the rejection letter ("too familiar") finally came with that sudden rushing inevitability they all have, I couldn't stop shaking. My wife, used to rages or resignation, was speechless. But later, lying in bed, I realised, *how insane*. In the morning, we talked it through again and I told my wife I thought we should go ahead and she cried and held me and I felt saved.

So the thought that one day in some world this child might kill me, might shoot me in the face, who wants to imagine that? And yet, and yet, when I think of my own father, there have been . . . moments. If I had a gun, knew how to use one. Oh yes. But petty reasons, anger over a grounding, over using the car, disappointing him. Not worth killing for. Not worth going out and buying a gun and lying in ambush for. But if the gun were to hand? Not worth running upstairs for, perhaps, not worth crossing the hall for, but if it were on the counter (what the fuck would it be doing on the counter? but just suppose), on the table, in my hand. I did punch my father once. I'd come in late and he waited up, barred the door to my room. We yelled at each other and I raised a fist. There was a moment when I could have lowered it, merely threatened, but having made it I couldn't stop. I hit him and he took a step back, out of surprise, I think. "Do that again," he told me when he'd recovered himself, and I did – bowing to that curious complicit male desire to make a bad thing worse, to transform an accident, a mistake, into a tragedy, to render ourselves not hapless, not foolish and vain, but heroic, grand, awesome. And he took the next blow too, and then he beat me unconscious (in fact, he only raised his own fist and I took a step back, fell down the stairs and knocked myself cold – so close is tragedy to farce – but the first version makes a better story). Except if it hadn't been a fist, if it had been a gun I'd raised, he wouldn't have had the chance, would he? And all over nothing.

He's dead now, my father, and as I empty the gun I'm thinking of naming my son after him.

Shooting is actually duller than bowling, I'm finding, duller and easier. I can daydream while doing it. There's something effortless and magical in the seemingly instantaneous bang and the appearance yards away of a small hole. I fire another twenty rounds. I move the target back, forward. I shoot to kill, I shoot to wound, I shoot from the hip. I suddenly understand why someone might rent a machine gun. What I want most in the world I realise is a moving target, a more interesting target. The idea on the range is marksmanship, but there's no real challenge here. I look down the barrel of my gun, but watch the shots of the man next to me. He doesn't seem much better, and I've only been shooting for twenty minutes. I watch him cluster his shots in the high-scoring body of the target, one, two, three, four. Nothing. And something about the rhythm, my focus on his target, makes me swing my gun over and put a fifth shot into the face of his target. Perhaps because of the angle I'm firing from, the bullet makes a ragged hole, tearing loose a strip of paper that curls slightly, flaps like a tongue. I hold my breath, horrified. I keep the gun raised, keep sighting down it. I can't hear anything from my neighbour behind his screen. Perhaps he's reloading, hasn't noticed. The pause goes on and eventually, I empty my revolver, slowly and methodically into my target. When I'm done and my gun is down and I'm pushing out the shells, I feel a heavy tap on my shoulder. It's him. He's waited for me to empty.

Have some conflict.

He mouths something, and I shake my head, lift an ear cup.

"What the hell was that back there?" he asks again, gesturing towards the target, without taking his eyes off me. His hand is huge and mottled red and white where he's been gripping his gun. His other hand is out of sight.

"Sorry," I tell him, and it sounds as if I'm speaking in slow motion. "A. Mis. Fire?"

He looks at me for a long moment, waits for my eyes to meet his, the dark muzzles of his pupils behind their yellow protective goggles. It occurs to me that they are the exact same shade as my computer screen, and I imagine my precious last words drifting across them, the letters springing into existence under the beating cursor: "like a dear in the headlights." Finally, he nods and says, "All right, then," vanishes back behind his booth.

I reload, pressing the shells home, letting their snug fit steady me, and wait for him to start firing again. And wait and wait and wait until my hand begins to tremble, and finally I can't not fire. The gap between thought and action is so fine. It's like standing on a cliff, the way the fear of falling makes you want to end the tension, take control, jump before you fall. I felt the death mole, if you like. I felt it burrowing forward, undermining me.

Only when I'm empty, do I see my neighbour's target beside me jerk finally. He puts five rounds into the head of his target in a tight fist, then draws it towards him, packs up and leaves. I still have ammo left. Unfinished business, like a chore. I pick the gun back up and fire round after round after round like hammering nails.

Sometime in there – after the fear wears off and then the elation, and the boredom sets in – I realise there's nothing to learn here. This won't tell me anything about Clark. And the thought of the continuing failure fills me with sudden despair. I put the gun down for a moment, afraid of it. I have about one suicidal thought a year, but this isn't a good time to be having it. And then the moment passes, because I know with an adrenalin-fuelled clarity that killing myself won't make any kind of difference. I know my wife will go on, my son will be born. My work won't suddenly be discovered. There's no point. And it's a crushing feeling. Knowing that the ultimate gesture, the very worst thing you can do, is nothing special, a failure of imagination.

I fire five more times, reel in my target, roll it up in a tight tube.

When I return my gun and pay, Vern gives my credit card a long look.

"I thought I knew you. You're the teacher from that school. You were on TV." He shakes his head sadly, and for a second I think it's a moment of contrition, and then he says, "What are you teaching those kids, anyway?"

Have your character change.

I pass behind school on my way home and I have to stop, I'm shaking so much. It's in my bones now, the distant ringing shudder of the gun. My hands smell of powder, my hair, my shirt, and I clamber out of the car before I gag. There's an old pack of Marlboro Lights in the glove compartment from before my wife got pregnant, and I fumble for a cigarette, suck on it until all I can taste is tobacco smoke. The storm fence here has been festooned with tokens; flowers, cards, soft toys hang from the wire. Damp from the dew, a little faded already, they ripple in the breeze, fluttering and twisting against the chain-link as if caught in a net. I lean on my hood, watching the twilight seep up out of the earth towards the still-bright sky.

What do I teach them? I teach them that telling stories is the easiest and hardest thing in the world, and among the looks of disbelief and confusion there's always one who nods, who gets it, like the teenage fatalist who asked me once, "Because there are only so many stories, right? Like seven or something." Seven, or ten, or a dozen, although no one can agree what they are and there're countless ways of telling them wrong. But the theory feels right. A finite number of stories, which writers try to tell over and over again. So suicide is boring? Then how do you make it not boring? How do you make it exciting? How do you make it new? So original, so vital, that it speaks to an audience?

Before the light fades completely, I step up to the fence to read the messages. The first moves me close to tears, and I sag against the wire. It's such a relief. I read another and another, hungrily, but by the time I've read a dozen, my eyes are dry as stone. I snatch at them, plucking them down, the ribbon and coloured wool they dangle from gouging through the soft card. Taken together they're clichéd, mawkish, misspelled. There are hundreds of them stretching forty, fifty yards in each direction, as far as I can see in the gloom, like so much litter swept here by the wind. And I want to tear them all down, I want to rip them to shreds. Every awful word.

YOU'RE LISTENING TO PAUL POWER
Graham Hodge

You're listening to Paul Power on Cream FM. Good morning Vietnam. It's 8:02. If you've just joined us – try getting up earlier: you might make something of your lives. Just kidding of course listeners – but if you *have* just joined us, today's a very special show. Here's why . . .

It's almost certainly my last show ever. Last show on Cream FM; last show on any FM. FM? Jesus, I wouldn't even get a gig on medium wave after this. Yes folks, the theme of today's show is "career suicide". I'm not playing any songs – the "Cream of the Sixties, Seventies and Eighties" can fuck off. I'm just going to keep talking and talking and talking like this till they drag me talking and talking out of the studio – which could happen at any moment. As soon as anyone with any clout gets wind of the sordid goings-on in this ghost town at the end of the dial, I'm out of here.

Let's see what tune I *should* be playing for you now . . . Ha! My trusty playlist here says I am currently *not* playing *More Than A Woman* by the Bee Gees. How appropriate: if it weren't for that song, I might not be here now, burying Paul Power.

Cut to: New York. Yes: New York, New York – *that* New York. I'd landed an evening show on the legendary K-ROCK. I'm not just being a self-aggrandising wanker – for once. We literally *had* to call it "the legendary K-ROCK" at all times. You got fined if you didn't. It was like a swear box: ten dollars in the failed-to-say-"legendary" tin. K-ROCK was the dream gig, if you happened to be obsessed with getting a career in music radio, which is exactly what I was.

Only there was a teeny-weeny complication. At that stage it was still a teeny-weeny complication, but it was getting bigger every day. By the time I got the dream offer from the legendary K-ROCK, Raie, love of my life, had a baby brewing.

There was no way she was going to New York. Absolutely no way. Who can blame her? Would you go and have a baby in a big ol' place where you don't know a soul, and where the kid's dad's going to be running around like a blue-arsed brown-noser, trying to make it in radio's First Division?

She assumed she and I were of the same mind: unfortunate timing, these things happen, other dream gigs will come along, hey-ho. Only I wasn't quite of that mind. I was more of a totally infantile, cloud-cuckoo-land, *male* mind that went as follows: if I could do the K-ROCK thing for – what, a *year*, maybe two? – and Raie could bring up our little 'un, supported by family and friends, then I could return to a top-drawer gig back in Blighty and our little family would be happily reunited.

"You're out of your fucking mind," was Raie's response. Unequivocal you'd think. And yet, like the reformed alcoholic who can't resist a little stroll round the offy, I still pondered the options . . .

You know what it was? The thing that swung it? I'll tell you. It was a present. The New York thing came at the end of April. My birthday's May the fifth. Raie loved giving presents – and she was brilliant at it: always knew exactly what I wanted, even if I didn't have a clue myself. And this birthday, I knew she'd nailed it. I could tell because she had a glint in her eye when she told me she'd been shopping. She's very pleased with herself, I thought – this one's going to be a belter.

The day came. She made me breakfast in bed – nice baguette, toasted, bit of Bonne Maman, apricot. Lovely. Then came presents. I opened one or two – a book, a CD, perfectly chosen – then she said, "Now this one," and handed me this small, squishy parcel, grinning from ear to ear. I knew this was The One. I opened it. It was clothing of some kind. I glimpsed an orange pattern – not obviously my kind of pattern – are those really *shamrocks*? I'm thinking – but OK, we'll go with it. I unfolded the thing inside. Only it was not a thing – it was things. Three things. Three little, people-shaped things. Where there should have been a Paul Smith V-neck, there was a trio of headless gingerbread men. "They're bodysuits," said Raie nervously, sensing my confusion. "For the baby."

Clothes for the baby? On *my* birthday?

I didn't freak out there and then – I poker-faced it. Raie knew something was up but she didn't get it out of me. I phoned K-ROCK on the sly, said yes that day. Then, a few weeks later, I disappeared. Off to New York. Just like that. Gone.

So there's my next revelation for you listeners: I walked out on my girlfriend and her three-month-old bun in the oven. We'd just had the first scan. It wasn't looking much like a bun any more. Paul Power, careerist coward.

New Yorkers are the most passionate rock fans in the world. I was talking to thousands of them every day – and most of them talked back. They'd get on the phone and explain at length why song A was better than song B: "Paul, don't get me wrong. *Livin' On A Prayer*: it's OK. But that blue-collar angst, that Springsteen-lite stuff – that was *not* what Jovi was about. Now, *You Give Love A Bad Name*? That, my friend, is *quintessential* Jovi. Boys versus girls. 'You promise me heaven, then put me through *hell*' – I'm tellin' ya man, that's *war poetry*." And so on. Or might be something short and sweet, but no less passionate – I took a call from one guy, all he said was: "Paul Power – you ROCK man!" and hung up. It doesn't get much better than that. Paul Power couldn't get enough of it.

But after a couple of weeks, Jason, the guy who ran the station, grabbed me on the way out. "Let's go get a cuppa coffee." We went to a diner round the corner. "Paul man," he said, "this is New York City. Rock 'n' roll is what drives this place. You can *smell* it everywhere. Here, people *live* it man – twenty-four seven."

"Sure Jason," I said. "I think I'm getting that . . ."

Jason shook his head. "Paul man, you gotta find me some more *energy* buddy."

"OK Jase," I said. "I'll give it a go."

"Just get me more energy," he said.

In New York, you don't give it a go, you just *get* it.

So my next show, I really gave it some welly. Quick bit of chat – weather, traffic, blahblahblah – then boom! – into the next tune; quick bit of chat – blahblahblah – boom! – next tune, and so on. For three hours. I was practically hyperventilating. It's a good job they have so many adverts in America: I had a chance to breathe. But you know what? I felt like I was getting it, like I was really living the rock 'n' roll – even – yes, maybe – living the American Dream. Introspective boy shakes off shyness (not to mention a gift for wrecking relationships) to conquer the airwaves in the world centre of ROCK!

At the end of the show, I was folding up my lucky headphones, still gulping for air like a doggypaddling toddler, when I felt a paternal hand on my shoulder.

"That's a whole lot better Paul," Jason says.

High-fives all round? Not quite.

"But Paul man, you gotta gimme more energy buddy, more energy . . ."

I started hanging out at a place called Milady's, downtown, corner of Prince and Thompson, and that was *not* a good location then: pretty dodgy, not the "prime real estate" it is now. The artists and musicians had colonised the spot long before, but any yuppies who took a punt on a loft down there then were either very stupid or very savvy. Not like now. Not a decaf soya latte in sight. But I liked it. Some of those big warehouse blocks were built by emigrés from Manchester, and now they seemed more real than the huge skyscrapers clustered to the north and south.

Once, on my day off, I must've put twelve hours in at Milady's. I'd gone there in the afternoon and just stayed there, drinking whisky shots, lining them up like Andy Sipowicz, a total cliché, talking bollocks with the locals until chucking-out time, whenever that was. Outside it was raining of course – clichés love company don't they? Everyone's always moaning about the rain in Manchester. Everyone's always moaning about everything in Manchester to be fair, but the rain's usually up there in the list of popular gripes. I haven't seen the stats, but I don't reckon New York gets any *less* rain than Manchester – it just gets it in a few massive doses. When it rains in New York, it *buckets* it down. Within seconds, the gutters are rivers, three-foot geysers are shooting out of drains, the roads are flooded. And that was the scene as I wobbled my way out of the bar that night. Luckily for me, a cab was just passing. Even more luckily, it *stopped*. Driver must've been desperate: I wouldn't have picked me up in the state I was in. I had one foot here and one foot here – a good yard apart, my balance all over the shop. You know that thing you can do where you close one eye and if you're lucky the double vision goes single again? I was doing that. Wasn't working. And of course I was soaked from head to foot. But stop he did. He was a huge old black guy with a flat cap and sad eyes. I had to think for a second.

"Upper West Side," I said. Except I said it like this: "Upper Wesht Shide. Wesht one-o . . . one-o . . . *sheventh shtreet*."

The driver didn't say anything, didn't nod, didn't blink even. Just swung a right and headed uptown. He had the radio on. That's right: the Bee Gees – *More Than A Woman*. I'm drunk, feeling chatty – yes, chatty even by radio-DJ-verbal-diarrhoea standards.

"The Bee Gees!" I say. "You know what? A lot of people don't realise this but they're actually from Manchester! Manchester, *England*? That's where I live!"

There's no reaction from the driver.

"Or *lived* I should say. I *used* to live in Manchester. Now I live here. In New York."

Silence.

"I work in radio actually."

More silence.

I try a new angle. "You ever wondered what this song is about?" I say, still slurring away. No answer. Oh well. I carry on. "'More than a woman', right? Think about it. What does that mean? Who, or what, is 'more than a woman'? He's singing about everything that's good about a woman, but there's something *else* . . . Listen to the words: '*I never really looked before*'. He's just discovered something, right? Something *new*? Something that makes her – this woman – *more* than a woman. You with me so far? This thing that makes her more than a woman – it's got to be something that women don't have, right? And if it's something that women don't have, that's got to be something that *men* have . . . Do you see what I'm saying?"

(Still no reaction from the cab driver. But I'm on a roll . . .)

"It's pretty clear to me that there's only one possible explanation for what's going on here. 'More than a woman'? This woman has a little extra something. A little extra *apparatus*. That's got to be it: he's singing about a *transvestite*! Barry Gibb was banging a *trannie*!"

I thought that was pretty persuasive and pretty darn funny for 4 a.m. or whatever it was. But the driver didn't laugh. In fact, he didn't do anything. He just kept staring ahead, through the rain. I wondered if he'd even heard me. Or was he just ignoring the drunk in the back? I was about to tap him on the shoulder. But then he said something at last.

"You're wrong," he said. Not in an aggressive way, just like he was stating the facts.

"Oh?" I said.

"It's not about that AT ALL," he went on.

"OK," I said, surprised that this guy had a view on the subject. "Let's hear it then."

Here's what he said: "See, by '75, '76, the Bee Gees were BIG. They were a BIG, SUCCESSFUL group, you get me? And what comes with success? Money: sure. Drugs: maybe, if that's your thing. But what ELSE? That's right: WOMEN. Lemme ask you sir: how many women you had intimate relations with?"

"Me?" I said, caught off guard. How do you answer *that* one? "Oh, I dunno, twenty or so?" I said.

"Twenty? Huh. See, if you're Barry Gibb – or any of the other goddamn Gibbs – you gonna hit that number in a WEEK. You gonna be sleeping with hundreds – I mean HUNDREDS – of women. And they're gonna be a certain kind of woman, right? The EASY kind. GROUPIES. Now, groupies have their time and their place, sure they do. But one day there comes a time they all begin to look the SAME. It don't matter how beautiful, how available, how ready to do weird shit in the sack they are – it's the same GODDAMN thing, over and over again. And that is what sex, love or whatever you wanna call it means for a Bee Gee in the mid-1970s. That word 'woman''s been twisted into something else, something CHEAP. So at this point our boy Barry's on the road, touring for maybe the third time in a YEAR, and meets someone different: a woman who's not a groupie. Maybe she's an electrician working on the show, maybe she's the manager's wife, maybe she's a photographer. It don't matter what she is, but the point is THIS: she's different than all the rest. She's intelligent. She's funny. She's WISE: she understands that being a Bee Gee ain't all that – that being a Bee Gee is HARD.

"And most important of all, she loves him for WHO HE IS, even when he's being an asshole, which is a LOT, because of all the money and the groupies an' shit . . . Our boy Barry falls in love. BAM! Big time. He sees what he's been missing all this time. He's been blind. With all them groupies he 'never really looked before'. Never had no cause to. You hear me? So this woman is not just a woman – remember what that word represents for these guys – she's something else ENTIRELY.

"This woman is better than a woman – she's MORE than a woman. She's a different goddamn SPECIES. She's the real goddamn deal. Trannie my ass. THAT'S what that song's about."

I sobered up like that. Jesus, yes! He was right. One hundred per cent. He was talking about the Bee Gees in the '70s – but he was really talking about me, of course he was. Raie was more than a woman. She was the real deal. Intelligent, funny, wise. Loved me for me, despite everything.

And wasn't there another message here? Another meaning of "more than a woman"? Raie wasn't just a woman now – our child was in there too. Woman plus child equals more than a woman. The song made perfect sense: perfect, tragic sense – and this cabbie had to be some kind of angel, sent to me on a wet, drunken night in New York, to save me from a terrible, terrible mistake. Cliché? So what? I gave him a fifty-dollar tip, and the next day, soon as I woke up, I went into the station, found Jason, and told him I was quitting. He didn't seem that bothered – "Paul man, I have to respect your decision" – but I didn't care: I didn't want my big break any more. I was heading back to Manchester, back to Raie – my little family reunited.

But that's not how it worked out. That would've been a cliché too far.

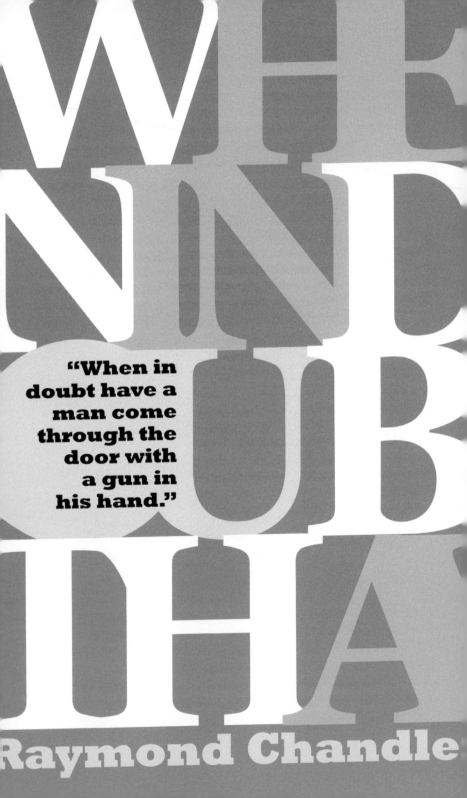

"When in doubt have a man come through the door with a gun in his hand."

Raymond Chandle

IN A DARK PLACE
Richard English

Deedee, my mum, lives in Cambridge Place, Kensington, a cobbled Victorian street that curves for two hundred yards to a dead end. The front door opens directly into the drawing room, the size of a safari park, a lot of it in semi-darkness. Black chenille curtains hang everywhere, all closed, and the air's stale and hot. Overworked radiators gurgle and splutter in tune with Deedee's dyspeptic stomach.

Swallowing a slug of peppermint water, she's lounging on a chesterfield sofa, on one side of which is a fly-leaf table with cabriole legs, on the other a Steinway piano. Nobody's allowed to play it, although it shines like a mirror, and nothing's permitted to stand on it except for the photograph of Dad during his passing out parade from Sandhurst.

I drop into an armchair that smells faintly of dog pee. Scattered around the skirting are several wicker baskets with chewed-up cushions lying in them. Over the last few years, Deedee's house has evolved into an animal crisis centre with soft furnishings.

"Sorry I'm late," I say.

"You should have been here at four, Ben."

"Traffic."

"You'll have to speak up."

My throat's deteriorated since I saw Harriet, my soon-to-be ex-wife, and so has my outlook. Hoicking a Vicks spray bottle out of my jacket, I give myself a squirt and twitch as Deedee twiddles her thumbs. She's still annoyed with me.

"Oh, Mum, don't do that."

"What?"

I grit my teeth and nod at her whirling thumbs.

"Oh, really."

Tartan trousers cling to her skinny legs while a thick white cardigan splattered with blue polka dots hangs loosely over her shoulders. Her creamy grey hair, sharp nose and paper-white skin add to her cadaverous appearance. To her credit, she occasionally bakes a cake or knits a pullover like the one she's wearing, but she spends most of her time as an avid chronicler of my misdeeds or a merciless critic of the rest of the universe. This is amazing because she has so little contact with the outside world. Once a month she shops at Harrods and attends her psychiatrist's appointment, and during the summer she visits Crufts and various cat shows. Otherwise, she stays at home, orchestrating animal management and bossing me around when she can get hold of me.

"Have you seen Michael?" she asks, referring to Dad by his full Christian name as if he were a friend of the family rather than its absent black sheep. I have to pretend that I could easily have heard from him although we haven't spoken at length for several decades.

"No. He hasn't been in touch."

She looks surprised.

"I'm sure he will. It's your birthday soon."

I don't like to contradict her on the subject of Dad. It's best to distract her.

"Do you want to see the Thorburn?" I ask, holding up the watercolour portfolio case.

"There's something wrong with your voice," she says, as her head sinks towards her chest before rising again.

When she speaks, her mouth sticks together at the edges and does not open fully. The middle area of her upper lip lifts off her teeth, up and out, as if invisible threads tied to her nose are yanking it. Then her jaw snaps shut like a Venus flytrap, the lips flattening against each other. The process repeats itself, especially if she's being critical.

"Are you eating properly?" she asks.

"Sort of."

"Time for a cup of tea. That'll perk you up." She calls behind her, "Olga, OLGA," and claps her hands. "Where is she?"

A granite-faced woman in a grey skirt and a starched blouse marches through the doorway.

"Oh, there you are. Could you serve us Assam and the cake?" Deedee turns to me. "I've baked strawberry sponge."

Olga hauls the side table between us.

"Now, what about the Thorburn?" I say, tapping the picture case with the spray bottle.

"You'll have to speak up, dear."

I shake the Vicks and give myself a long squirt that makes me blink.

"How are you?" she asks. "You don't look well."

I'm about to say, "What a surprise," but I restrain myself, crinkling my mouth into a false smile.

Olga's back with the tea things and lays out the gold-rimmed Wedgwood, a silver bowl and slices of cake on a Georgian serving dish.

"Sugar?" Olga asks me.

"Just milk, please."

She's known me for fifteen years but still goes through the ritual of enquiring if I want sugar, never referring to me by name. She's very loyal to Deedee and the animals, although she does her best to deny my existence.

I stir my tea, watching the swirl of white dilute in the tan liquid like light in the dark side of the drawing room. After blowing on the surface, I take a swig and tilt back my head and gargle to sluice out the taste of the throat spray. Deedee raises an eyebrow and sighs, her cup halfway to her lips.

Olga serves me a slice of strawberry sponge. I take a bite. It's one of Deedee's best. I've always liked her cooking, which is surprising, as I hate just about everything else about her. She can prepare the most remarkable steak and kidney pie. When I was a boy, I used to help her. A recipe out of Mrs Beeton. Page 226, I think it was. Maybe 228. She got me to look it up and read it aloud to her. First, she cut slabs of stewing steak into cubes and then peeled the white, stringy fat off some lamb's kidneys before chopping them up. She laid out the meat and offal on a wooden board with mushrooms and miniature onions that I sliced, bits flying onto the floor. I used to munch any spare as I liked the crunchiness and the way they made my eyes water. Next, she sprinkled flour over the ingredients and stuck the lot in an oval dish that was yellow on the inside and pale green underneath, and slung in a twist of rosemary. Everything was covered in fine white powder. Her fingers, cheeks, apron and even my hair. We had to wipe each other down with tea towels. Finally, she made the gravy out of Oxo cubes and boiling water, adding pepper from a wooden grinder that creaked and pinches of rock salt. She wouldn't let me watch her mix the pastry. "My little secret." She winked as she flopped it over the meat. When she opened the oven door, I could feel the rush of hot air. If I was too close, my fringe sizzled. Smiling, she bent down to put in the dish.

I finish my piece of cake, rubbing traces of icing sugar between my fingers, and stretch over to the side table to put my plate down.

Deedee's brown eyes have a soft look. "How are you?"

"Fine."

She peers at my neck.

"What are those marks?"

"Nothing. Cut myself shaving."

"With garden shears? You've got bags under your eyes and the whites are bloodshot."

"It's the Vicks. Oh, please, Mum, leave me alone."

"Are you sure you're all right?"

"Yes."

"You seem tense."

"It's all these questions."

The housekeeper looms out of the kitchen and clears away the tea things, glancing at my neck.

"Not you, too, Olga!"

Deedee sits upright.

"Here comes Roquefort," she says.

A blue Burmese slides around the corner of the chesterfield, rubbing his cheek along the leather before jumping silently onto Deedee's lap. She adjusts his red collar and polishes the identity tag, which he doesn't need as he goes out even less often than his owner.

"That's better, dear," she says.

"Better? No, it isn't. I don't even want to paint."

There's a growing pressure behind my eyes and my palms are sweaty. I wipe them on the thighs of my trousers.

"Oh, Mum . . ."

"What, dear?"

"It's weird. Everything's weird. I don't know what's happening. Can't even buy a pint of milk without worrying the shopkeeper wants to poison me. And when I walk along Westbourne Grove I keep thinking the bus will veer onto the pavement and crush me."

My throat's seizing up again. I need relief.

"How's Harriet? Doesn't she help?"

I shake the Vicks bottle, which is nearly empty.

"The divorce is driving me spare. I can't sleep, work or anything."

"You need support, dear."

"I don't know where to turn. Everything's flooding me."

Deedee picks at her cardigan and purses her lips. The upper one moves in its strange way, signalling that she's trying hard to keep control of herself.

"Have you seen Dr Thwaites?"

"Not exactly."

"What does that mean?"

"I saw the GP."

"He's not a specialist," she says.

"Wrote me a prescription for Prozac."

"That must have made things better."

"No, worse. Gave me constipation so I threw the pills away."

A growl. Deedee stares into the blacked-out area of the drawing room, tickling behind the cat's ear.

"Roquefort's going to win Best of Breed this year at Olympia."

"That's a joke. He came fourteenth last time and that was only –"

"And poor Gilbert. Disqualified."

"I'm not surprised. What a beast."

Another growl. I peer into the gloom.

"Is that him?" I ask, wondering if I can open the front door before the albino wolfhound pounces on me.

"You had an appointment to see Dr Thwaites," she says. "Several, actually. What happened?"

"Got confused. I went to Queen Mary's, Roehampton. Wrong hospital. By the time I reached St Mary's, Paddington, the psychiatric department had closed for the weekend. The other times . . . I can't remember. Anyway, I don't want to end up like you. A permanent outpatient."

"I only see him once a month for a check-up. That's all."

"Christ! It's a life sentence."

"And you think that what you've got isn't?"

"A passing phase?" I try to sound hopeful.

"I doubt it." She nods at my dirty shoes. "You need to smarten up. And to relax. Why don't you get a pet?"

"I've got one. Bobby, my parrot. How could you forget?"

Deedee and I are competitive about our animals although she easily wins the contest. Her menagerie roams freely throughout her house while my solitary bird lives in a cage with occasional flights of freedom.

She lifts Roquefort into the air, his hind legs dangling.

"You love your mummy, don't you, precious?"

The cat's liquorice lips crack into a smile before he starts purring. She lowers him onto the cushion beside her where he twists himself into a semi-circle, his tail wrapping around his paws.

"You've got to do something about yourself," she says. "I know I wasn't the perfect parent. Of course, that's no real consolation but you don't have to stay in your misery for ever. You can reach out for help."

"For God's sake, I don't know what to do."

"I've told you. See Dr Thwaites. You're having a breakdown."

"Like you had . . ."

Deedee looks hurt. So does Roquefort. I'd better shut up.

". . . all those years ago," I finish the sentence silently to myself and slump into the armchair, an old spring digging into my back.

It was the Easter hols and I was home from school. During the night I thought I'd heard Deedee downstairs. There were shouts, screams, banging. Maybe Dad was back and they were having a row. I slung on my jeans and shirt, although I couldn't find any socks.

From the top of the stairs it looked like a pool of dirty foam had leaked over the hall carpet. Perhaps there'd been a fire and Deedee had discharged the extinguisher that she kept for emergencies and she hadn't been able to switch it off. But when I got down to ground level, I waded through heaps of torn paper, the edges tickling my ankles. A scrap of tissue was floating in front of the walnut clock. I blew at the fragment. It fluttered in a circle like a feather before dropping towards the floor.

A smashed chair blocked my way into the kitchen. Others were lying on their backs. Courgettes, lettuces and broccoli had been pulled apart, the pieces tossed at the sideboard. The carcass of a roast chicken left over from Sunday lunch was in a pool of milk, a carving knife sticking out of its breast, and the place reeked of balsamic vinegar that had been sprayed over the walls, the clumsy hand of a deranged graffiti artist. Sellotaped to the fridge were slices of white bread with fuzzy lettering on them while scattered over the kitchen table and worktops lay pages from torn up *Observer*s, *Country Life*s, *Tatler*s and recipe books, all bearing scrawls in large black letters.

A whirlwind of tissue swirled around Mum, whom I could hear mutter about God, Dad, me. Then I noticed the ink blots on her fingers and the stain over her chin. She was tearing up loo rolls and writing at a frenetic pace with a laundry marker. She must've had an idea of such vital importance that if she didn't record it on everything that came to hand, it would be lost like the heavenly chord.

"Mum," I called from the doorway.

She glanced in my direction before writing her one word in capital letters.

"Mum."

She looked up again.

"You're just like your father," she said.

When she ran out of lavatory paper, she picked up *Yellow Pages* from the floor. The pen squeaked as she kept printing the same word. Some of the pages she folded in half, others she made into paper aeroplanes that she launched into the air. One landed on the electric rings of the cooker and a second on top of the fridge. A third stuck in the light fitting above the Welsh dresser. While she was busy making another paper plane, I grabbed what was left of the directory. She hurled the dart at me and then yanked the book out of my hands. Her eyes were puffy, her cheeks streaked.

I stretched for the marker pen.

"No," she screamed, shoving me in the chest.

I staggered against the sideboard, my foot slipping on some lettuce, and sprawled on the floor, banging the back of my head against the washing machine. I blinked furiously to clear my vision. Then I noticed a ball of paper close to my nose. I eased myself into a sitting position and uncrumpled it, revealing a torn page from *Country Life*. On it was written "MICHAEL".

Roquefort leaps off the sofa and rubs his whiskers along the drawing-room carpet. Rolling onto his side, he stretches his paws before he faces me, lips drawn, the tips of his incisors showing like a vampire's. I point the Vicks at him and squirt. Several drops splatter on his head. He jumps up and sprints into the gloom, hissing.

"You'll hurt him." Deedee wags a finger.

"You only care about the animals. What about *me*?"

A rancid taste washes through my mouth and I rub my tongue against my lower front teeth, dislodging cake crumbs and releasing the faint flavour of strawberry. I stare at Deedee and she stares back. I can't read her expression but her gaze makes the skin on my cheeks flare up. I lower my head between my knees and wrap my forearms around my shins. Something good has got to happen but I have no idea what.

The springs in the chesterfield creak, the soft pad of feet. A silence into which all my neediness pours. Deedee touches my shoulder in a light, nervous way. She's unsure of what to do and so am I. Her fingers comb slowly through my hair.

"Poor little Ben. It's all right, Mamma loves you."

I want to put my arms around her and give her a hug. She'd like that, I'm certain, but I can't move. I've forgotten how to hold her. How to hold anyone.

A breath on the back of my neck makes me shiver, and a pair of damp lips kiss lightly, then firmly, when I don't resist. The arm of the chair squeaks as she leans over, her bosom pressing onto my shoulder, while her face turns sideways and the ribbed part of her ear squashes against the back of my head. Staring downwards, I peer at the ridges and ruts of my brown cords, the furrows of a ploughed field. There are worn patches, creases like scars, and folds where the trousers are gloving at the groin. I wiggle my toes inside my Oxfords and notice that some of the stitches that bind the soles to the uppers have worn away and that the aglet is missing from one of the laces. Out of the corner of my eye, I catch sight of my father's photograph. There's a scowl on his face and I try to sit up.

"You're suffocating me," I gasp.

An arm slithers around my chest.

"Please, Mum. Get off."

I thrust upwards. She doesn't budge. I'm trapped and can't breathe.

"Mum!"

"I was only trying to help," she says.

She peels off like a scab from a wound and steps back to the chesterfield, picking up the portfolio and unzipping it. She sits down, balancing the Thorburn on her knees, blocking out the lower part of her face. Her eyes scan the picture with deep concentration until they stop and focus on me. They lose their clarity. A flash of old pain.

Olga stretches over the chesterfield with a silver tray, on which is a glass of water and a collection of brown bottles. Deedee nestles the picture on a cushion and grabs a bottle labelled "Valium". She unscrews the top and pops a yellow pill into her mouth, taking a drink and easing back into the sofa. She picks up the avian portrait and lays it on her lap, her head dropping forward.

"You can feel the textures of the beak and feathers," she says. "The richness of the blue sky, the detail of the claws and nest . . . A masterpiece."

I grab the Vicks spray from the floor and press the squirter. It's empty.

Deedee taps the Thorburn with the tip of her forefinger.

"Excellent," she says. "It will go well with the other pictures above Roquefort's bed."

"Can you give me cash? The bank's being uncooperative with me at the moment."

I zip up the portfolio case, eyeing the open medication bottle on the fly-leaf table.

"Olga handles all that sort of thing. See her on your way out."

The housekeeper whisks the picture away from Deedee who's sinking into the chesterfield like the Lusitania after being torpedoed. While they discuss the supper menu for the animals, I tip some Valium into my pocket.

LOVING RELATIVES
Mary Irene Masaba

The whole family had gathered together to harvest beans, when we heard screaming and wailing.

"Who can that be?" asked my mother.

"Who knows? But it sounds like someone has died," Magode my cousin-brother replied.

The wailing got closer. It seemed to be heading our way. Two of the neighbours' pot-bellied little children ran to our house.

"What is it?" My mother was fidgety.

"Your aunt is coming down the road crying. One of your relatives has died."

"Who?" Mother was almost shouting. But no one knew.

Soon, Aunt Susana, my father's sister, came round the corner in tears, followed by curious people.

"Sorrow, sorrow," she cried over and over.

"Who died?" Mother was desperate to find out.

Other people pushed closer to her.

"Annette Nambuya. Our relative is gone. She has left us." Annette was my father's relative.

It was as if she had dropped a snake in the middle of the small crowd. Everybody jumped back.

"Oh my mother!" someone screamed.

"Do the rich also die?" someone said sarcastically.

After a while, the wailing calmed down a bit and my mother

asked, "What killed our relative?"

"She died in a car accident last night at Budadiri."

"What happened?"

It was then I discovered that I liked a good story.

"She was coming home last night, when she crashed into a *matatu* minibus on the bridge over river Sironko."

"How can two cars be on the same narrow bridge?" someone asked.

"They say a man from Teso was driving the *matatu*. He was in a hurry to get to Mbale before dark. He was going too fast when he crashed into Annette. She was taken to Budadiri hospital. The medical people did everything they could. But she broke the thread of life and went to Magombe, the land of those who have already left." As soon as she uttered the words Aunt Susana began to sob once more.

People started crying all over again and cursed the driver of the *matatu*.

"So did the killer driver also die?"

"No, he did not. He drove off towards Budadiri."

"We shall look for him. We shall find him and fix him," an uncle said in a voice that frightened me.

"Our relative will not die for nothing," someone else said.

Several people agreed. I had been listening intently but then I caught my mother's disapproving look.

Six months earlier, just after I had turned eight, was when I first saw a dead person. It was my baby brother Daudi. My big brother Samwili started it all. One day, he was carried piggyback from school with a disease. All five of us children caught it. We were ill for ages before we started to get better. Except the baby. He died. Relatives and neighbours threw themselves on the ground and wailed and tore their clothes. They cried for days. I was sad Daudi died even if he used to cry a lot and give me a headache. But I was happy that many people were sad too, even if they had known him for only six months. I was sure that since they had known me for lots longer, they would be even sadder if I died.

The sadness had already gone out of Mum's voice as she started to order people about.

"Where are the boys?"

"They have already gone to the late Annette's home." This was Gagula, my mother's younger brother who lived with us.

"Gagula, you are in charge of things here while we are gone," she told him.

She phoned Father from her mobile and left a message.

"You will stay here," she said to me.

"The boys have gone already. Annette was my relative too." I had never seen what a traffic-accident victim looked like and did not want to miss this chance. Aunty Susana came to my rescue.

"Annette loved this child. She called her 'she of the beautiful legs'. Let her go and see her relative for the last time."

Annette had always called me "*mayumbu*" after Granddad's ugly *nyumbu* chairs with fat legs. They were made in England a very long time ago.

Mother changed her mind.

I chose a dress Annette had bought me from Dubai at Christmas. It was sky blue and covered in glittery dots.

"What do you think you are wearing?" Mother asked.

I looked down at the dress. It did not need ironing.

"Do you think you are going to a party?" She sucked her teeth.

I went back in and changed. But this time, I had forgotten the belt of mourners.

"You must wear the mark of mourning." She went into the house, brought out a long *kanga* cloth and trussed my belly. She tied a small cloth around my head.

Everybody had changed into clean clothes but no one wore their very best, in case they were accused of being happy with the death.

"Let us go," my mother said.

Almost like a choir, the women took up wailing and screaming and set off single file. I found myself walking in that line wailing. I was not sure how I felt. I knew I would miss Daudi more than Annette whom I had known all my life.

All along the way, people ran from their houses to find out who had died. Later, we branched off onto the uncovered road to Annette's house. The sun burned through my dress and it was only ten in the morning. The tight band of cloth around my waist made breathing difficult. Sweat ran down my back. The adults increased their speed. I ran to keep up. This was worse than running to school at seven. The journey to school was over before the sun was this hot.

I felt my ear burning with pain and gave out a little cry. My mother was holding on to it and pinching it.

"Why aren't you crying for your cousin?" She kissed her teeth.

Silent tears streamed down my face, but they were tears of anger and pain. I began to wish that I had not come.

As soon as we walked away from the built-up area, the crying and wailing stopped. Instead, there was chatter and laughter. The whole group ahead had stopped to cool off in a small stream we had come to. I stepped into the water and washed my face and dusty feet. I felt the sting of a slap on the back of my head.

"Do you or do you not know that it is traditional not to wash until the deceased is buried?" Mother yelled at the top of her voice.

"I did not know," I said weakly.

"What do you mean you don't know? Isn't it only a few months ago that your own brother died? Did you wash then?"

"No."

"So what do you mean you did not know?"

"She is a child. Maybe she has forgotten," someone with a kind voice intervened.

The mention of my brother reminded me that I missed him and I started to weep silently.

"What are you snivelling about now?"

"Nothing."

"The loss of her relative might be affecting her," said the same kind voice.

She was right there, only she had the wrong relative.

We set off again. Stories and jokes were told and everyone was carrying on as if we were taking a stroll. Suddenly, like a frightened flock of birds, the people around me erupted into wailing, running and crying as they streaked past me.

"Oh my sister, what will I do without you?"

"You have gone, and you have thrown me away."

"Oh my special friend, now you have gone who will look after me?"

I looked up to see that we were within hearing distance of the dead person's home. Everyone was putting on a good show of great sadness.

I caught my mother's angry eye and realised I was not crying. I tried to, but the cry got stuck in my throat. I rubbed my eyes vigorously with my forefingers to make some tears, but none came. I hoped that my eyes had at least gone red. I put my hands on my head, hoping I looked sad as I followed my family. The wailing grew louder as we approached Annette's home.

The track opened up into a large manicured compound swarming with people. The galvanised-iron roofing of the main house glinted in the morning sunlight with the sparkle of adverts that scream "Win!" But the largest group was at the gazebo, where the dead Annette lay. My brother Samwili was there. I pushed my way to the front. When alive, Annette had been the brown of a well-fired cooking pot and her face had been shaped like that of a cat. The face on the bed had black blotches like someone who has been in a bad fight and it was all round and puffed up like a pumpkin. A white bandage held her head together. A couple of teeth were peeping out. Annette had had perfect teeth, like a maize cob. Her nose and ears were stuffed with cotton wool.

"The cotton wool is to stop flies laying eggs in Annette to make maggots," Samwili whispered in my ear. Gross. It didn't stop the flies trying. The blue and green metallic ones buzzed around. Even the small houseflies joined in.

Kuku Jessica, Dad's mum, sat silently near the body, gently waving them away with a fly whisk made out of a cow's tail. She ate and said very little. Her eyes were fixed on a large framed studio photo of a smiling Annette. I suppose she did not want to look at the mangled Annette.

"Move. Let me see my relative," screamed someone behind me.

I was jolted sideways. Napuswa the elder, looking like a brown Michelin man, bulldozed her way forward. In her wake was her half-sister Napuswa the younger. They threw themselves on top of the body. Napuswa the elder had torn off the buttons of her *gomesi* in a moment of intense grief. She had worked her fat arms out of the sleeves which hung empty on either side of her like hollow logs. The *gomesi* was held up by several sashes at the waist. She was not wearing a bra. Her enormous breasts, big as gourds, now drooped around the dead Annette Nambuya as if she was breastfeeding. But if Annette had been alive, I think she would probably have died from those breasts squashing her to death.

A hot wave of sweaty smells hit me and I felt ill. Kuku Jessica gave me a very small smile and I felt guilty because I was not crying. I wriggled out into the sunlight. My mother was still wailing by the body, so I stood against the wall of the gazebo to wait for her.

"Girl child, do not stand over people like a soldier. Sit down." An old lady stretched out her gnarled hand and pulled me down gently. She was in a large group of women all with uncombed hair. She picked up her clay pipe, placed it in the corner of her mouth, drew on it and blew out puffs of smoke.

"You have set me off," said a lady in an orange *gomesi* with banana-sap stains on the back. She pulled a roll-up cigarette from behind her ear and lit it from the old lady's pipe.

"My sister, pass me the gourd," said a lady to my left.

She shared a papyrus mat with two other ladies who looked like her. She slurped from the gourd and passed it on to the third sister. They sat in a ladylike way, like most of the younger ladies, their feet tucked under them. The old ladies stretched out theirs.

I sat down, then remembered and knelt down like a child should in the presence of elders.

"Peace, Grandmother," I said offering my right hand. The old lady looked into my eyes, then offered both her hands turned upwards. From our Daudi's death, I remembered that greeting at a funeral was different. I placed both my hands, palms down, into hers. We then crossed hands twice saying, "Sorrows, sorrows," before lifting each others' upwards and then letting go.

"Sit, sit child," the old lady said. She moved slightly and I sat on the goat skin beside her.

"Whose child are you, my child?" the old lady wanted to know.

"Oh Grandmother, that is Magona's daughter. Don't you see the resemblance?" someone said.

"My sight is not what it used to be. I have not seen you since you were this high." She indicated the height of a toddler.

"I have grown, Grandmother." I had no idea who she was.

She caressed my hand and pressed it a bit as if she was buying an avocado.

"You are fat and beautiful. That is good," she said.

"How did our relative die?" a newly arrived mourner asked.

"They say the car crushed her to death."

"The car did not crush her to death. She died in the hospital."

"From bleeding, brought about by the car crushing her."

"You also, why are you such a clever clogs?"

The clever clogs kissed her teeth.

"It is a big death. It is a blow to me." The person who said this had a high-pitched voice which sounded fake.

"They say that a Muteso man just killed her and drove off."

"It is as if he was sent to kill her."

"Who wanted her dead?"

"There are people . . ." She trailed off.

"I hear the husband has some Munyole woman," someone else volunteered.

"And you know how these Banyole are with witchcraft . . ."

There were a few "Mmmmm"s and "Aaaahhh"s and an "Ehhh?"

"People, tell me, where are her children?"

"The husband is hiding them in the house."

"Am I wrong, or does the husband seem less than sad?"

"What do you want him to do? Cry?"

"Why not?"

"Don't be silly. Men don't cry."

"Get out of here!"

"Did I or did I not see him bawling like a baby when his mother died?"

"They say he cried so much, they thought he might be the first person in the world to cry blood."

"Ha! I thought he would go beyond blood and cry chips of wood."

A few people laughed.

"So why isn't he crying for Annette in the same way?"

"Tell me about it."

At this point, my mother came out of the gazebo. She greeted several people. When she got to me, she took me out of the others' earshot.

"I don't like the way you seem to hang about looking for stories."

"They talked. I just listened," I protested.

"Too intently. Are you planning to grow up to be a rumourmonger?"

"No. I want to grow up to be a nurse," I replied.

"Senzi," she said kissing her teeth.

I couldn't understand why she called me that. Senzi dogs are stupid and silent.

She led me to a group of men under a large gusabasi tree. Mother stopped about two metres from the men and knelt down.

"Sorrows, old men," she said.

There were all sorts of men. Granddads, uncles, dads, men who were not relatives.

"Sorrows, old lady. Sorrows, Mother. Sorrows, Aunt," they replied at the same time.

"We have suffered." Suddenly, Mother's voice was sorrowful.

The local priest sat next to Mafabi, the dead cousin's husband. I checked his face but it did not look very sad to me. Maybe the gossiping women had a point. On a coffee table beside him was a large open book the size of the school register. It had a long list of people and how much they had donated towards the funeral expenses.

Most funerals have a few people, mostly local. But this one had lots from all over the country. The Muslim caterers cooked loads of pilau rice, meat and chapattis. There was plenty of beer – bottled, canned and *busera* beer served in large pots – *waragi* the flammable local gin for those who preferred "the burning one", and plenty of soft drinks. At the other end of the compound, a log fire was going. Several squatting young men were skewering pieces of meat and chicken and sticking them in the ground by the fire to roast. A heap of green bananas lay beside the fire. The smell of roasting meat hung over the argument that was going on nearby.

"We must carry on the tradition." Moses, a red-eyed distant relative in black trousers dirty at the knees, swayed and spoke slowly, emphasising each word with his index finger. His brother squatted on the grass, plucking one of several chickens they had caught running around in the compound.

Uncle Kiwuta tried to reason with them. "But guys, the caterers have provided plenty of food."

"We don't care if the caterers have brought mountains of food. Tradition demands we eat roast bananas and meat, and we shall have it. Give us more meat," another of our cousins added. His mouth was already oily.

Ben, a teacher at Mutufu primary school, said, "Bro, we are Bagisu. We shall do what our forefathers did. Remember your roots."

The treasurer sent for more fresh meat. But they still ate the caterers' food as well.

"Why are you standing by the food fire?" Mother had followed me without me noticing. The men by the fire turned to look at us. I felt shame grinding the inside of my stomach and rising till my ears burned.

"I don't know," I replied.

"I don't like you to stand around food like a greedy person."

"I wasn't asking for food."

"Go find somewhere more ladylike to wait," she ordered and walked off.

I saw a bunch of women, colourful as a row of flowers, sitting on papyrus mats on the veranda of the main house. I walked up to them, greeted them and sat down.

"Uhmm! Tell me more," a lady in a faded-blue *gomesi* said.

"As I was telling you, they say that the Muteso man was hired to kill Nambuya. They say that he followed her from Mbale and tried to drive her car off the bridge."

"People are wicked."

"I heard that there are some people who were not happy that Nambuya was doing so well."

"People have such bad hearts."

"I tell you jealousy is at the heart of all this."

"I heard of a Muganda woman, the husband's lover, who has been seeing a witchdoctor to get the husband."

"But I heard she is a Munyole," I added.

"You child with no breasts, what business do you have knowing older people's affairs?"

That shut me up. But I was intrigued by these stories and went around the compound listening in whenever they were retold. Every version was different. The only facts that remained largely unchanged were the car accident, the Muteso man (only one version said he was a Kenyan), the bridge, and the death. The rest was salted and spiced so much that by mid-morning, when the porridge was served, I was not sure what had actually happened.

"Did they just pour in the sugar or what?" said the lady who had shut me up.

"If they had put too little in, you would have complained."

"I am eating off the effort of my relative. Leave me alone."

She ate her porridge quickly with the spoon, then with her bony calloused finger she wiped clean her own bowl and that of a fat-bellied child who sat beside her. Without blinking, she put both ceramic bowls and the spoons in the folds of her *gomesi* just under her breasts. The rest of the people acted as if they had not seen what was going on. That day, half the crockery disappeared.

My mother found me in the late afternoon.

"I want you to stay by me. We are going to gather our bedding."

As is the custom at a funeral, we all slept outdoors on dry banana leaves. Some people who lived nearby brought thin Vitafoam mattresses which they covered with token banana leaves. Some had tents. Fortunately, it was a dry night as my mother and I slept on the patio under a thin blanket.

In the middle of the night, I needed to go for a wee. Mother got up to take me.

"I can go by myself," I said.

"Oh no you don't."

My mother came with me to the banana plantation. She wrapped a *kanga* cloth around my shoulders to keep out the chill. I was surprised to find a lot of people in the plantation. Some were married women acquainted to my family. Young men I did not know seemed to be leaning against them. There was a lot of rustling and grunting in that plantation as if there were pigs rooting around. Mother covered my head with the *kanga* cloth and rushed me back to our sleeping spot.

People kept going back and forth, singing and drinking, till morning. I woke up achy all over from the hard floor I had felt through the banana leaves. I rubbed my eyes and straightened my crumpled dress. Stretching my legs, I went to look for a toothbrush tree, broke off a branch and brushed my teeth. I headed back to where my mother was seated on the veranda. There were some wailers in the gazebo. Kuku Jessica was still there. I wondered if she had moved at all during the night.

The caterers brought porridge, tea and bread. This time the porridge was served in plastic bowls and we were given disposable spoons. Still, some bowls went missing.

A huge tent was put up and filled with rows of foldaway chairs. The gravediggers were also at work. They cemented the inside of the grave so that it would be dry for the funeral the following day.

"Pass me the banana leaf," a cousin said.

He shaved off the leafy part and was left with the hard spine. He placed it alongside the body and made a notch, moved it along and made another notch. The diggers used it to measure the ground. We all knew that Annette was five foot seven. It said so in her identity card and her passport. But they did not use a tape measure which is taboo.

She was buried on the third day. Her body was put in a coffin at around midday. I could not see through all the legs surrounding her. Lots of Annette's and her husband's friends turned up in their Pajeros. Samwili, some boys and I went around to inspect the cars. Everyone agreed that the best vehicle there was the Hummer.

The body was taken to the large tent which was now a makeshift church. The real church was too far away. The priest talked about the Lord giveth and taketh away. But what reason did the good Lord have to kill off Annette? I wanted to ask somebody but decided that it was not a good idea. Last time I had asked about the Virgin Mary, I had been labelled a "troublesome child". They say the Lord works in mysterious ways. Maybe he had secret ways of killing or saving people. One of my aunts said that she was saved, though she never said what she was running from when the Lord saved her.

An uncle stood up and walked to the front.

"Ladies and gentlemen, all our visitors, relatives, and in-laws, it is good that you have come to be with us in our time of sorrow. God bless you all. I will talk a little bit about our departed daughter Annette Nambuya."

He talked about her schooldays. I began to wonder what I would have been doing at this time if it was a school day. Constant chirruping came from a flock of weaver birds in a nearby thorn tree. Smoke rose from the open fire in the compound and drifted lazily in the direction of Buhugu. I leaned against my mother.

I was jolted back into the "church" by the congregation singing "Abide with me".

Starting with Annette's children and husband, we filed singing past the body in its open coffin. Some people began wailing again, some threw themselves at the coffin or fell on the floor and had to be helped away. I just looked. The coffin was grey and polished like a marble floor. I stood on tiptoe and looked. Inside the coffin was pretty, done up in pleated white satin. I wanted to touch the body to see if she was cold. Samwili had told me that dead people are cold but I was not tall enough to stretch and touch her. Someone pushed me forward and I lost the chance.

After everybody had filed past, the body was taken to the grave to be buried. We sang "Rock of ages" and "The Lord is my Shepherd" at the graveside, which we had sung at my brother's funeral as well. Then the priest read some stuff about dust to dust, ashes to ashes, and everybody threw some soil on the coffin. The diggers began the work of closing and cementing over the grave. Three people would stay by the graveside until the concrete set to stop anyone from planting bad medicine or, worse still, stealing the body. There was a commotion with cousins and aunts rushing away.

Back in the gazebo, a relative was sitting on top of the rolled-up mattress on the bed where the dead body had lain earlier. Another aunty was trying to push her off.

"Get your filthy hands off my mattress," said the one pushing.

"Who said it was yours?" asked the sitter. "It is mine because Annette promised me a mattress for Christmas, so this one should be mine. Besides, you said the bed is yours. Take it. I am taking my mattress. No matter what."

She heaved the mattress onto her head, and turned to go. The other lady tried to wrestle the mattress from her but then noticed someone else shifting the bed. She abandoned the mattress chase and plonked herself on the bare, sprung bed, which was too heavy for her to carry. If she needed to go to the toilet, she left her three children on it. Later, her eldest son helped take it home.

I heard screaming and went to look in through the bedroom window. Dad's six sisters and some cousins were in the room.

"Give me that." Aunt Mele snatched a garment from Aunt Kasalina. Kasalina tried to get it back.

It was a bit like watching children in the nursery school fighting over toys. After a while, the sisters realised there were lots of clothes in Annette's wardrobe and became more vicious. Baba Gidudu, my dad's brother, intervened.

"Stop this fighting. There are more clothes in her town house." The women's faces lit up.

I wanted to laugh when one of the sisters grabbed three pairs of size six stiletto heels. One was a silver-and-see-through party pair that Annette used to call her "Cinderella shoes". The second was a purple pair with killer heels and the last was a green and red pair with a matching bag. My aunty was a size seven, going about barefoot in the village. I could not believe she was going to walk in ill-fitting shoes on the muddy village paths.

"Annette said that she would give me a *gomesi* to cover my old shoulders," an aunt said from the doorway. She was given a green *gomesi*, but not one of the best ones. As soon as she went out with it, others came in with various stories of what had been promised them.

The demands were not limited to women. The uncle who had spoken in church insisted that he get the bike Annette had promised him. A week earlier, two bikes had been delivered to the house but Annette had not said who they were for. He got the bike.

"I wonder what things are like back home?" Mother said to no one in particular.

She nudged me. I got on my knees again to say goodbye to the relatives near me. I extended my hand but it was ignored. Mother yanked me up as if I was a goat. I stumbled after her.

"You do not say goodbye at a funeral," she hissed at me as we walked away. "Didn't you see that at your brother's funeral?"

What I really wanted to tell her was that I had not had to say goodbye at my brother's funeral since I lived there. But I didn't say anything as I was worried about receiving a slap for backchat.

On the way home, I realised Annette had lived for thirty-five years. I wondered how many of my people would really miss her, not the shoes, money, clothes and all the other things they had got from her over the years.

EL SALVADOR DEL REY
Josh Raymond

"Things can be divided," said the man who helped me pitch my brand-new tent, "into looseners, sharpeners and straighteners. The morning smoke is your loosener, for easing you into the day. The cheeky line you have before you go out is a sharpener, and the one you have at four in the morning when you can't see straight – well now, that's a straightener."

He puffed on his joint.

"Straighteners don't always work," he admitted, "but it's still important to know."

I remembered a word Mr Lawler used in a biology lesson, running his hand through his messy black hair as he paced around the room.

"It's a taxonomy."

The man blew a fragrant cloud over my head. He was wearing tattered surf shorts and a necklace made of white stones.

"Whatever. It's just important that you know. If you know, then the spirits will take care of the rest."

I definitely *don't* know what this is, and Aaron never said it would make me need to shit. I leave him and the others by a stall selling glow sticks and make my way across the field towards the Portaloos, batteries of green plastic huts whose irregular door slams sound like gunfire.

"For Christ's sake, Dan, go before we get there," Aaron said and, obediently, I did, sitting in the tiny rocking compartment of the train from Paddington before returning to perch on my backpack in the aisle, the carriage packed with noisy brightly coloured people. Aaron and I looked at the site map as we headed west. Sarah and Julio looked at each other. Everyone in the sixth form fancies one or other of them – they're like two fishermen who can't believe what they've caught.

But that was thirty-six hours ago, and now I'm getting desperate; my gut is a snake that is heavy with eggs. Head torch on and bog roll held tight, I open the door to an evil reek of chemicals and crap. When I'm locked in, safe and invisible at last, I sit down and relax.

The business of wiping my arse feels repetitive, satisfying and somehow urgent, and I am dimly aware that I've stopped minding the smell. An antibacterial wet wipe from my pocket lets me clean palms and fingers like a surgeon, and my hands feel cool and fresh when I step out into the crowded night.

Walking fast over uneven ground, I realise that I want to talk. The snake laid her eggs – beautiful green shiny egg-laying snake. A snake in the grass, the grass beneath my feet. Beautiful green shiny . . .

"How you doing, mate?" says Aaron.

"Good, yeah, good. Wasn't that bad actually. Definitely feel better. How you guys doing?"

Aaron gives my shoulder a squeeze. It feels great, somehow, and I wonder if I can ask him to do it again.

"We're good, really good. Just let me know if you start to feel anything weird, OK?"

Julio and Sarah are swaying to beats from the glow-stick tent. He takes her hand to look at her watch, a little shared gesture they've developed since being here.

"He's on in a bit," says Julio. "Shall we get to the stage?"

We agree to meet back here if anyone gets lost; people look similar in the dark.

The crowd by the main stage looks like an encamped army, banners and flags oddly still through coloured smoke. The stage itself is a massive arcane artillery piece, its silver shell a shield from the moonlight and scuttling roadies attending its mechanisms. Julio and Sarah lead the way. She holds her free hand out to Aaron, who takes it and reaches back.

"Come on, Dan," he says. "So we don't get separated."

We string our way into the warm living darkness. I smile at strangers as we pass. Aaron's hand feels safe and strong, and when we find a space I have to force myself to let go.

Tonight, the army's general is a white-haired old man in a smart grey suit.

"Promise me," my dad had said as I was leaving. "Promise me that you'll go and see Leonard Cohen."

The songs are about towers and dancing, love and saying goodbye, and everyone seems to know every word. When each one ends he says, "Thank you, friends," in a voice like a thousand years.

Friends. Having girls in the sixth form changed the whole thing – spitballs and bullying stopped being cool. My only weakness never did get found out; I'm the shell-protected tortoise who beat Achilles to the line.

I turn my head slowly from side to side. Aaron is looking straight ahead, his face lit up in pink from the stage. It wasn't just new girls who came to school last September.

We join hands again when the crowd disperses, and are soon running light-footedly over open ground. Music is coming from a tent between some trees, and there are tables outside it shaped like mushrooms. The night air tastes sweet as we catch our breath.

"That was amazing," says Julio.

His dad is Spanish. I'm not sure I can remember my GCSE, but drumbeats and warmth make talking easy. *"Me ha divertido muy bien. Fue estupendo."*

We high-five across the spotted mushroom.

"Hablas bien," Julio replies, with more kindness than honesty.

"So he's a linguist as well," says Aaron.

His eyes look wide in the dark, and his hair flops over his forehead.

I am thinking, "As well as what?"

Sarah is rolling a joint, arranging components on the mushroom's white spots. Julio kisses her cheek.

"You're brilliant at that."

She smiles at him as she works. "It's the last thing to go, and the first thing to come back. Here for the team all night."

I look up into the trees. There are golden lanterns everywhere.

If the main-stage crowd was an army, then the dance tent is the monster it was sent to kill: a hammering pulsing blue leviathan, held down by ropes thick enough for a ship. Sweat drips from the doorways; this thing has its own *weather*. There is a DJ high up in a booth at the front – so small, so far away, so loud. A thousand people? Two thousand? Ten? We throw ourselves forward, find a space, and go.

Our dance is a circle round water bottles and bags. Conversations are fascinating and friendly; it isn't only Spanish words that come easily tonight. People with whistles and spiked neon jewels pump their fists and grin. Aaron's face is shining, and I feel like I'm watching him too much so I turn outwards to face the crowd.

A man has his shirt off and his arms raised in a great hairy-chested salute to the ceiling. Five seconds later he's looking right at me, blue eyes under messy black hair. I feel a cold slice of adrenal shock – he has read my mind, I'm sure of it. But then I realise that I *know* him. I grab Aaron's arm and pull him over. He is quicker on the uptake than me.

"Oh my God!" he shouts. "SIR!"

Mr Lawler, teacher of taxonomies, has a piece of white chewing gum in his open mouth. He stares at us for a couple of seconds, then thrusts both fists into the air, twice.

"Fucking hell. LADS!"

We shake hands hard. Mr Lawler looks like he's on his own, and we make room for him in our circle. Aaron takes his shirt off, too. Mr Lawler, who never sets detention and doesn't mind if homework's late, without question the best and finest teacher in the world, is dancing right here with us. I want tonight to be the night when secrets end.

I step forward into what feels like bright empty space and say the two short words I have never said to anyone. Aaron, very slowly, is nodding. "I know you are, Dan. I know you are."

We dance closer, and the beats seem to shift. Aaron's body smells like the energy and sex that bind the world together, and when I pull him towards me he hesitates for a second but then kisses my mouth with warmth and then strength – a glorious, triumphant melting together that fills my stomach with love and my veins with liquid fire.

And the last person I looked to before my chrysalis burst open was not my old friend Julio, and not his beautiful girl who is here for the team all night. No. The last pair of eyes that looked upon the secret-bearing me were blue. Mr Lawler had a huge smile right the way across his face. When Aaron and I pull apart to drink some water, I get someone to take a picture of the five of us on my phone.

Mr Lawler leaves us there after a while.

"Have a good one, guys."

"Take it easy, sir."

We shake his hand and wave.

"I'm danced out, too," says Sarah. "Shall we go for a wander?"

We leave the giant blue tent behind, and soon pass many things. Fairy-lit clearings with pink Day-Glo birds, a stall that plays the Beatles, herb tea. A man with a spectral face shouts a woman's name over and over into the night, and someone has made a huge iguana out of wood. The joints that Sarah rolls taste like food and send us deeper somewhere; heroes of our own adventure dreams. Aaron is a sailor and Julio a prince. Sarah glows and seems to summon hints of dawn over a field of bright white tepees.

Hours have slipped away before we sit on the ground amongst bright discarded flowers. Impossible thoughts sink like slippery ships, and tiny dots cover the sky. I have a sense I can't articulate that one of us is missing, even though we're all right here. It is time to go back to our tents.

The air feels colder now, and Aaron has let go of my hand. I want to be back in the great blue tent of warmth and truth and music. I want the strength to dance again. We trudge around the corner on a corrugated tin path, and are about to make our final climb to home.

"Stand aside," someone shouts, "for the rolling king in a can!"

I step back quickly and look up the hill to see a crowd near where we are camped. Women in sequinned dresses and men in velvet suits – a vision from Alice's looking glass but too complex not to be real. One of them has a crown and a purple cape. He bows and crawls backwards into a metal drum that has been laid on its side, so that only his head sticks out. A man in a top hat rolls him a gentle half turn to where the path slopes away. It looks . . . steep, and suddenly my energy returns, and I am running – sprinting to the top of it, waving my arms in the air.

"Your highness, stop!" I shout. "Wait!"

People turn towards me. They're dressed for long ago, but their childlike, waxy faces show that they, with us, are citizens of this strange new morning. Aaron is watching me, too. I don't have much time to explain.

"His head's sticking out," I say. "When the drum starts to turn he's going to smack it on the ground."

The king twists awkwardly to face me. "What?"

"Even if you tuck your neck in, the force will pull it back again when you pick up speed. You'll get hurt."

The king appears to be thinking hard. "Might I," he says, "perform the roll head first?"

I look across at the lords and ladies who have come to see the rolling king in a can. "Head first, I think, will be fine," I say, and Aaron throws his arms around me from behind.

"Brilliant Dan," he says, and Julio raises an imaginary glass. "*El salvador del rey!*" he cries. The saviour of the king. I am the knight who has won his favourite's heart.

The man in the top hat aligns the metal drum and lets it go. People cheer. The drum rolls slowly then gathers speed, the king's feet turning like he's in a washing machine. But the weight of the king makes it start to veer off towards the tents, a little at first but then sharply, and we can see the grey two-man it's going to hit and the cheering dies and the dull thump of metal connecting with something soft sounds clearly up the suddenly silent hill. What the fuck have we just done?

The king in the can is wedged up against the grey tent, and we falter our way down the hill towards it, uncoordinated and afraid. The tent moves. A man in boxer shorts and a vest staggers from between the flaps at the far end and stands, then looks down at the figure climbing dizzily from the drum.

"Fuck me," he says, "it's the king." He looks up at us. "It's the fucking KING!"

We roar. The king dusts himself down and bows, and then the man turns to every rainbow cocoon in the drug-eaten morning and throws his hands to the lightening sky and yells, "I'VE BEEN CHOSEN BY THE FUCKING KING!" And when we return to the top of the hill I cannot say how long we stay there – drinking fizzy wine in plastic cups, and talking to the king and his retinue.

I never thought my tent had room for two. We zip down flaps and lie beneath a spread-out sleeping bag. I think of outer space. That if Aaron and I just hold tight we'll fly to some distant star. Two salty-rich releases are our final dose. I am loose. I am sharp. I am happy.

Aaron rolls away from me, and we look up at our green polythene ceiling.

"Does anyone know about you?" he asks.

"My sister asked me once but I snogged some girl at her birthday party to put her off. How about you?"

"My mum lives with her girlfriend in LA. I think she might suspect but I've never told her. My dad would kill me and then himself. What was it like with the girl?"

"Not bad. Bit like eating too-ripe fruit."

He says, "I like your words," and then I think we sleep.

We pack up the tents early Monday after a bleary night spent spinning out small change and crumbs of weed. Our bags are heavy and there is garbage on the ground but no flowers. The army is beaten, and tired in retreat.

"What you doing for the summer?" I ask.

"Staying with my mum," says Aaron. "Eating burgers, getting tanned."

We walk on.

"Funny to see Mr Lawler, wasn't it?"

Aaron doesn't seem to want to talk about that.

The train stops in a field for cows on the line. I can't wait to be clean and back at home, but the pylons and woods outside make me miss our adventure dreams. The others are asleep. As green gives way to grey, I'm unsure if London will ever feel quite real again.

But this is the summer of shameless thoughts and repeating my two-word mantra maybe a thousand times a day. When Aaron's back I'll tell the world, but telling myself will do for now. We only speak once. The guys in LA work out, he says.

So I read books by Hemingway, and find Leonard Cohen's music in my dad's old box of records. I think about honest talk and undrugged sex and, when the first day of term comes round, spend way too long in the bathroom.

I see him through the common-room window – that slouchy walk and a carry-out coffee. Each pose I try in the armchair feels more stupid than the last, and I end up pretending to look for something in my bag.

"Hey," he says.

"Hey."

Boys hug in our school, but I feel Aaron's shoulders stiffen.

"How was your summer?" I ask.

"Cool, you know."

He doesn't ask me about mine, and, by the time we get to the science block, we're pretty much walking in silence. I tell myself it's been a while. We're early, so we sit at the back. Mr Lawler draws the reproductive organs of plants: anther, filament, stamen.

"I like the words," I whisper.

Aaron keeps looking straight ahead. I remember damp morning air in the tent, clothes kicked into a corner, sweat on the roll mat. I lower my hand very slowly under the table until it finds Aaron's leg, but he jerks it away like I've stung him and shakes his head. I can't feel him up in class, of course, but later . . . I nudge him with my elbow.

He looks at me like he's really angry, and his whisper is an almost-silent hiss. "You don't fucking get it, do you? We're not off our heads in some stupid field. I'm not doing this here. I can't *be* this *here*. It's bad enough that *he* fucking knows."

He makes a sharp gesture with his hands towards the front of the classroom, which I realise doesn't just refer to Mr Lawler, or even the school, but to something much bigger and to Aaron more frightening, something to which all the festival's magic could weave only one night's exception. I look away from him and out of the window, where a plane landing at Heathrow becomes a small green tent shot down from the stars. I imagine each wonderful thing that will now not take place. Mr Lawler is explaining the biochemistry of pollination.

We catch his eye on the way out, and he indicates without words that we should stay behind. He clicks the top on and off a board marker, and his voice is less confident than when he's teaching.

"The photos, lads. Have you uploaded the photos?"

I had done it the day I got back, one of many forgotten things. Mr Lawler bites his lip.

"Don't worry, sir," I say. "I scrubbed the one of you."

"That's good," he says. "I'll see you later."

We're halfway across the room when Mr Lawler speaks again. "Lads?"

We turn.

"I know this place isn't exactly short on pastoral care, but if you ever want to have a chat about anything . . ."

"Cheers," I say, and Aaron bends to lace a shoe. I walk away from him into the corridor, past the form lists and anatomy posters, and into the bustling chaos of the stairwell.

"If I chance to talk
a little wild, forgive me"

William
Shakespeare

REVOLUTIONARY COLOURS
Moira Sharpe

(with a nod to "Casa Tomada" by Julio Cortázar)

Eventually the big house, built with generations of children and grandchildren in mind, became too much for my sister and me, and we retreated to the servants' quarters in the annexe. Life didn't change much for us, even then, in our part of the house. Except that now there was no cleaning to do Irene knitted more than ever. Once the breakfast things were cleared away, she would sit down and bring out her wool, and the clicking of the needles would start. The only difference was that she asked me now to fetch brighter colours – blues and scarlets and sunny yellows, colours that I found somehow disturbing although I didn't know why.

We never saw them, and rarely heard them. Now and then there was a shifting of furniture, or the twang of an old floorboard. Once we heard voices raised, as if in argument, but they cut off abruptly and we heard nothing more. We didn't know how many there were, but of course we knew who. They were all over the town now, with their big dirty trucks, shouted orders, and mania for checking documentation. We gave up our house to them, preserving our own little corner, and trusting that in the end we, and the house, would outlast them.

Until one evening around nine o'clock, it all changed. The first we heard was someone trying the iron handle on the oak door that separated our passage from the rest of the house. Then someone tugged at the door, but the big bolt held. Irene stood up, spilling her knitting on the floor in a tangled skein, hand at her throat almost as if she thought she could stop the breath in her chest. Our eyes met and I lifted the lamp from the table where I had been reading, although I had no clear idea of what I was to do. Where was there for us to go?

The sound of the axe was unmistakable, as was the terrible splintering that accompanied it. I stood helpless, undecided. I am after all a scholar, not a man of action. Then Irene amazed me by seating herself again and coolly taking up her knitting as if nothing was happening. I watched fascinated as the needles took up their familiar and soothing dance through the wool, their clicking lost in the awful crescendo coming from the door.

I heard the moment they broke through, the grunt of satisfaction as the last panel gave way, the sound of the bolt being drawn back, the heavy step of boots in the corridor. Irene and I stilled into our separate stances, like a frieze of domestic life, me with my back to the table, lamp in hand; her, with needles poised now, waiting.

Then he appeared in the doorway. He was very young, and more than a little drunk. His uniform was stiff and new, but crumpled, the brass buttons undone at the throat, his hair savagely barbered in the military style. He was still holding the axe, with splinters of oak attached. He gaped at us, at this lamp-lit tableau from another world, then seemed to realise how threatening he must seem, and lowered the axe to the floor. He drew himself up and clicked his heels together, his hand fumbling at his buttons.

"Madam," he said, with a short bow. "Sir. Please forgive me. I had no idea there was anyone living here."

I returned his bow. "As you see, this is our house."

He tilted his chin and stared straight ahead.

"This house has been commandeered by the General's army. However, I see no reason why you should not continue to live here, in this annexe. I will see to it that you are not molested."

Irene rose from her seat, clasping her hands loosely at her waist.

"I thank you, sir," she said quietly.

His gaze drifted towards her, and I saw the very moment their eyes locked.

Over the next three weeks, as I came and went, it seemed to me the young soldier was more and more a visitor to our part of the house. I would come home and find Irene, seated in the parlour, pouring tea from the silver teapot that she had reclaimed from its storage space, and offering scones she had baked herself from our dwindling flour supply. The soldier sat, very stiffly at first, buttoned up, and wearing his dress sword, but as time went on I found him in more and more casual attire and in more and more animated conversation with my sister. One time I heard them laugh.

When I commented to Irene on the frequency of these visits, all she said was, "His name is Enrique. He misses his mother."

In between visits, it seemed that my sister knitted more than ever, but I never saw the results, except once when I saw her cast off one bright red sock, and start immediately on another. She no longer asked me to go and fetch wool for her.

I found myself very irritable during this period, and unable to settle to anything. The soldiers were everywhere now, their dull brown uniforms transforming our pleasant little town into a veritable barracks. The cafés were full of them, they formed in little groups on street corners, their cars and trucks blocked up the roads, and the nights were full of their rowdiness. I never heard shots myself, but I heard reports from other parts of town that weapons had been discharged in sport, and at least one person had been badly injured.

It was the following Monday that Señor Perez rang me. He had just taken delivery of a calf-bound set of the essays of Seneca, and was I interested? I said I was, and asked him to call the next evening after shop hours. I was very pleased with the Seneca, which was in excellent condition and only slightly foxed on the endpapers. We came to a mutually agreeable price, and it was mine.

Seneca is somewhat of a passion of mine, and I confess I spent more time than I should up in my study over the next few weeks. Irene brought me my meals on a tray and brushed aside my apologies for leaving her so much alone.

"I have my knitting," she said.

I am one of those people who is able to shut out the outside world when I am concentrating. I have learned, as scholars must, to study in the most adverse conditions, and when I am focused very little penetrates my private world. However, I am not superhuman, and sometimes the sounds from the main house next door forced themselves on my attention, occasionally so loud and insistent that they could have been coming from downstairs. I heard loud voices, and laughter, and the scraping of furniture, sometimes the clinking of bottles, and I could only imagine the drunken revelry they represented.

One day – it was a Sunday as I recall – there came a great crashing that seemed to be right under my feet. Alarmed for Irene, I raced down the stairs and threw open the parlour door to find just such a scene as I had imagined, but not next door – here in our own little annexe. Four or five young soldiers lounged around on the settle and in the armchairs, in various states of inebriation, uniforms unbuttoned and talking loudly. Irene sat in the corner, knitting, with a contented smile on her face. One young man was in the act of righting a kitchen chair which had either fallen over or possibly been thrown, causing the crash I had heard.

One by one they saw me in the doorway and the conversation faltered, then died. The young man who had righted the chair began to brush it off carefully with an apologetic air. Bottles were set quietly on the floor, and feet hurriedly swung off the furniture. Uniforms were buttoned, and, as boots were pulled back on to stockinged feet, it appalled me to see that every one of them was wearing a pair of bright red socks.

Irene lifted an eyebrow and said sweetly, "Hector! What a surprise. Come and join us."

Of course, I did no such thing. Without even dignifying her with an answer, I turned on my heel, took my hat and cane from by the door and left the house. I was in turmoil. Not only was Irene's behaviour utterly depraved, but she had betrayed everything we stood for, giving comfort and succour to the forces that threatened our very way of life. It was unforgivable, and I was completely at a loss to explain it. If her own moral good sense had deserted her, then I saw no way to control her.

As I made my way to my usual café I was aware of something different in the atmosphere of the town. I looked around, trying to puzzle it out. The soldiers were still there, still in their dull brown uniforms, but instead of gathering together in small, bristling groups, they were dispersed. One was here chatting to a shopkeeper, another leaned over a baby's pram, his neck red with embarrassment as the baby pulled faces at him and the mother gazed on fondly. Another sat at a pavement table, his rifle, forgotten, propped beside him against the wall. And everywhere I looked, among the dull brown, were flashes of colour – here a red sock, there a purple scarf, there a yellow balaclava. And as I looked more closely, I saw that even the rifle had, tied around its muzzle, one single strand of pure white wool.

"WRITE A LITTLE EVERY DAY, WITHOUT HOPE, WITHOUT DESPAIR."

Isak Dinesen

THE TREE OF THE DEAD
David Quéva

19 July 2006

Dear Virginia,

I am truly sorry I didn't write earlier but they wouldn't let me. Even Marc wouldn't let me but it's over now. We have finally made it. We have finally escaped. We are finally free. We left about two weeks ago. When I say we, I mean Béatrice and me of course. The poor thing has changed such a lot. She insisted on taking every single thing with her. Her toys. Her sister's toys. She insisted on taking this china doll that Bérénice loved so much. Do you remember? I didn't say a word but the doll sends shivers down my spine. It reminds me of the cold and oppressive feeling that invaded me just before I opened their bedroom door. I've never told this to anyone before, Virginia, not even Marc. I never told him. Neither before nor after our divorce.

You know what happened. You read the article in *Le Monde*, I guess. We didn't have the opportunity to talk about it afterwards, did we? You didn't ask any questions and I didn't offer any answers. It was better that way. The pain was buried deep inside of me but I can't bear it any longer now. I need to share it with someone. With you, Virginia.

As I said, I opened their bedroom door. Béatrice and Bérénice were there, face to face, like a bad B film projected in slow motion on the big screen; Bérénice had an Auchan plastic bag on her head

145

and it was tied around her neck. The knot was a double knot. I remember this detail very clearly. And then there was this dirty china doll slipping from her hands. I fell on my knees, paralysed; a thick fog invaded my head. I remained there, speechless and reactionless, for a few seconds, a few minutes, a few hours – who knows? The white china doll had this look of *rigor mortis* about her and her eyes were wide open. Her big round eyes were wide open and they were glistening like oily black marble beads.

I am not sure what happened next. My head is to this day full of spasmodic, jagged images. I must have recovered my senses; I probably untied and took off the plastic bag covering her head. She was limp like a string puppet whose strings have been cut off. Her eyes were rolling upwards, her face was purple blue and her hands were soft, warm and clammy. In the other corner of the room, Béatrice was trying to say, "Mummy, I didn't do it," between sobs. I didn't do it. Those were her last words. She hasn't spoken since. In my memories, I can hear unending silent sobs. Afterwards I used to wake up every night at 2:55 a.m. and I could hear someone sobbing in the cold darkness. The sobs sounded like they were coming from here, there, everywhere. I had continuous sobbing in my head like a Paris drizzle. No beginning and no end. I feel so much better now. Much better really.

But what about you, Virginia? What are you up to these days? Any news from *Monsieur Marc Lacan*? I don't actually know why I'm asking. I'd rather forget what happened. That's one of the reasons why I have decided to get away and start again from scratch. You will probably have noticed, thanks to the postcard accompanying this letter, that we decided to settle down in a small Burgundian village called Pisy, where every house is made of the same yellow sandstone and all rooftops are covered in the same grey slates. Don't try and find Pisy on a map though; you won't be able to. Pisy is tiny, with only 64 inhabitants. With both of us, that now makes 66. "There are more cows and sheep than human beings," said Mr Atherton, the mayor of Pisy, the first time we visited the town hall to fill in the usual paperwork. John Atherton is an Englishman from Manchester who settled in Pisy with his French wife about 5 years ago. He's got a charming accent but his bushy beard and grumpiness would trick you into believing he was a Frenchman; it's the other way round with his wife, Ginette. She is the spitting image of Petula Clark. Very funny. In the village church there is a permanent exhibition of nude paintings relating the life of a transcendental Christ, or something cast in the same mould. The artist who painted these extraordinary canvasses also lives in the village. His name is Paul Saint-Pierre.

Béatrice will start at the local school in September. She will be in Year 3, at least if I manage to convince the old spinster of a headmistress that is Mademoiselle Dellebarre. After all, Béatrice might not be able to speak but she is not retarded. Talking of which, there isn't a single child in the village apart from Béatrice.

Oh, yes! The most important thing I guess: we live in quite an amazing house *en viager*. It is the ancient residence of a country squire from Pisy who chose the village for the same reasons that we have: a greensward lost in the middle of nowhere, a haven of peace and silence where I hope we'll be able to put everything behind us.

We are sharing our opulent-looking mansion with an old lady whose name is Florimonde. A weird name. I have never heard it before. Have you? It has a wilted-flower ring to it and it is pretty accurate since she cultivates pansies and chrysanthemums in the garden, which is also ours. She lives on the ground floor and we occupy the first floor which is reached via a massive oak staircase that creaks like an old rusty prison door. Florimonde has not really been welcoming. I think she hates children. She keeps pretending not to notice Béatrice. The poor child follows her wherever she goes. Yesterday, she even untied her hair and tried to offer the old lady her favourite blue ribbon. Of course, Florimonde behaved as if she hadn't seen her, and Béatrice was left stranded on her own by the little brook we have at the back of the garden. I am so worried about her, Virginia. She looks so weak, so transparent and so vulnerable. Her big blue eyes are like a summer sky where clouds are gathering before a storm. She walks in this awkward way as if she is carrying a heavy burden on her shoulders. I am not sure what I can do to help, but Pisy's pure air, beauty and calm will undoubtedly do us some good and put both of us back on our feet.

Pisy is the highest village in Burgundy; it was built on the hills and the views are simply breathtaking. It is a bit isolated but that doesn't matter since I've decided to get back to nature and have given up my mobile phone, computer and even my watch for good. I asked Florimonde to keep them under lock and key during our stay here. I kept only my private diary and a few pens. I will write to you on a regular basis but don't feel obliged to write back. I know only too well how extremely busy you are. Just allow me to write regularly. That is the only favour I ask from you, Virginia. I cannot ask for more. You have done so much already!

See you soon in Pisy. (I have prepared the guest room for you, in case you feel like visiting us!)
Eurydice

7 August 2006
Dear Virginia,

I now realise that my last letter was a bit disjointed. I had so many things to tell you that it was probably full of incomprehensible details and digressions. This time, I will try and structure my thoughts as neatly as I possibly can. I hope you won't mind me writing again even though I haven't received anything from you yet. I forgot to tell you that in Pisy, apart from a post office, there is no shop. If we need to go shopping, we go to Montbard by coach, and if we need bread, a little van comes every morning. You just need to let the baker know that you will need one baguette a day for instance and *le tour est joué*! We don't have to do much anyway. Florimonde likes to be in charge!

We are getting used to our new house but the village of Pisy has something weird about it. I mean, not so much the actual village, but rather the people living in it. There is something weird here but I can't figure out what it is. Do you remember that television series from the 70s called *Le Prisonnier*? Well, it's just like that – it's as if there is a silent conspiracy within the community. I feel like I am being observed all the time. Do you think it's possible that Marc found out where we live and has started spreading gossip among the villagers? That would at least explain why everyone takes such a keen interest in Béatrice.

I met Paul Saint-Pierre, the painter, yesterday evening. We were introduced during one of the village *kiosques*. A *kiosque* is a kind of barbecue organised by voluntary workers from the village. They cook and sell their own products and collect money for some sort of charity. Everyone wears a T-shirt that reads, "*Je kiosque à Pisy. Et vous?*" They sell the T-shirt for a few euros and I decided to buy one for me and one for Béatrice. Christine Beugnet, who was selling homemade desserts, asked me if the second one was intended as a gift. I told her it was for my daughter, Béatrice. Madame Beugnet looked stunned but Béatrice and I moved aside without commenting any further. The village square was sort of nice, if a bit unreal. It had been decorated with multicoloured light bulbs and elderly couples were dancing as slowly as war veterans to the tired, creaky and dusty voice of Fréhel. The whole village was there. It seems to me that they are all doctors, researchers or psychotherapists and they were all asking questions about Béatrice. I felt quite uncomfortable. All the more so since none of them had children with them.

Béatrice is making progress, you know. She has started communicating via an old school slate that we found in the attic. I tied it around her neck with a rope so she doesn't lose it and she keeps pieces of white chalk in her pockets. She makes little drawings. A cake means "I am hungry" and a bottle means "I am thirsty". Little things like that. Anyway, as I was saying, Paul Saint-Pierre came up to us and Ginette introduced him. He looks like Picasso but he limps with his left leg and looks permanently dazzled by the sunshine. He has tiny black and cruel-looking eyes. He talked to us about abstract painting. I talked about Béatrice and her new way to communicate. He looked intrigued and asked me if I would mind having our portrait painted by him. I thought the question was slightly forward (after all, we hardly know him) but accepted, and he insisted on showing us around his studio straightaway. The studio has barred windows and is actually quite dark. It came as a surprise. I always thought painters' studios needed a lot of light. Do you remember how bright Cézanne's studio in Aix was? I understood better when I caught a glimpse of his work. All the canvasses were absolutely huge and extremely dark and tortured. Even Béatrice shrank back when confronted by the painting called *Noirceur Océanique*. There is something in his paintings. Something disturbing that captures pretty well Pisy's mystery. I don't know if what I am saying makes sense. The village is charming but at the same time I feel the finger being pointed at me constantly. A bit as if I was walking round the village while cradling a dead black cat in my arms. Yes, that's it. That's exactly it. You see what I mean? Anyway, I accepted Paul

Saint-Pierre's proposition after having a look at Béatrice's school slate. The idea of this painting didn't seem to upset her in the least. We'll start tomorrow.

Florimonde is weird as well. She speaks very little. She always wears a long apron and hides her grey hair under a faded sort of headdress. She uses a carved wooden cane worn out by years of walking. There are only two teeth left on her lower jaw but she doesn't seem worried about it, and she has a bearded chin. She is always muttering something but I am not too sure what it is. It sounds like an ancient dialect. Béatrice often stands next to her but Florimonde never acknowledges her presence. It's better that way I suppose. I really wouldn't want the old hag to pour hogwash into Béatrice's head.

That's all for now. You should come and visit us really soon, Virginia. I can't wait. By the way, if you were to meet Marc, please don't tell him where we are. I do trust you, Virginia. I trust you like I would my own twin sister.

Eurydice

23 August 2006

Virginia,

I wrote to you two weeks ago but didn't send the letter. I re-read it and realised it was all very self-centred. Please forgive me, Virginia, but Pisy is occupying all my thoughts at the moment. I am not sure I understand myself what is so unusual about it. There is one thing though: you know that Pisy is built on the hills and that our seigneurial dwelling place overhangs pretty much the whole village? Well, it so happens that last night, I woke up with a start. It was 2:55 in the morning. It's the first time I've done that since we settled down here. I thought I had heard someone sobbing. I felt terribly oppressed and short of breath. I went over to one of the huge windows and opened the shutters noiselessly so as not to wake Béatrice, who sleeps in the room next door. The night was cold and my breath was leaving white wisps behind like indiscreet ghosts. I realised that wherever I looked, as far as my gaze would carry, fires were burning in the night. I don't know why but it seemed to me that people were communicating – sending signals to each other. As this happened during the night, I got scared and thought it had something to do with fire worship, devil worship or God knows what else. I closed the window and went back to bed but my night was peopled with nightmares: Béatrice was rocking Bérénice in her arms and the latter was lying in a pool of her own blood.

The following morning, I felt like I had a hangover. I went downstairs and asked a few questions of Florimonde who answered that most farmers around Pisy used the burning technique to clear their fields. Apparently, it makes the earth more fertile. I then asked her why in the middle of the night and why the whole village at the same time? But she muttered something in her beard and went away.

It is an accumulation of small things, there is no doubt about it. I mean, I don't know but it's like the mice. You know, when we arrived here, our nights were as silent as a country graveyard but for the last few days, I have heard mice nibbling at the walls. I might be imagining things but even Béatrice looks nervous and ill at ease. She drags Bérénice's old white china doll everywhere around the house. I am wondering if I shouldn't take this soiled doll away from her. I wouldn't dare though. I am scared of it. It is the silent witness of what happened in their room.

And there is this thing about the children. I mean the children in the village. It's almost the end of August and there is still no trace of a living child in the whole village. Isn't that unusual? Then there's this tree as well. I almost forgot the tree. Our garden has a slightly truncated shape and spreads like a carpet towards the little brook I mentioned before. Béatrice and I follow more or less the same path each time we go down there to sit in the sun. A few days ago, Béatrice drew a tree on her slate and pulled my hand so I would follow her. She took a route I didn't know and after about half a mile we approached the same brook from a different angle. On the other side of it, there was a tree, a venerable oak tree with branches tortured as if by osteoarthritis. We crossed the stream and once we were close enough I realised that some of the leaves were not actual leaves but ribbons. Blue ribbons. Tied to the branches of the tree were hundreds and hundreds of blue ribbons. Some looked as if they were only a few weeks or a few months old; others must have been tied there years, or even decades, ago. The blue had faded; the cloth was damaged, frayed, worn out, threadbare. I looked hard at Béatrice and, shaking her in spite of myself, I asked her how she knew of the tree's existence. Very slowly and while squeaking the chalk on the surface of her slate, she drew an old lady with a cane. Florimonde.

We went back home and I demanded an explanation. Florimonde talked about a legend. The tree of the dead. In the old days, each time someone died around the village of Pisy, a blue ribbon was tied to one of the branches of the oak tree as a sign to the rest of the community, and children in particular, of divine protection. I thought I was going to be sick. I shouted at her, told her to her face what I thought of her grotesque story. I forbade Florimonde to take Béatrice to see the tree again from that day onwards. I strictly forbade her. She said she hadn't taken her there in the first place but I don't believe the crafty old madwoman. She is trying to turn Béatrice's head; she is trying to turn her against me. The woman is mad, Virginia. I have no doubt about it. She is mad.

Please, Virginia, send me a letter as soon as you can and let me know what you think about the whole thing. Is it my imagination or is this village completely unhinged?
Eurydice

5 September 2006
Virginia,

I guess you will never write back but I will keep sending letters. There are no children in the village, Virginia. There are no children any more. All excuses and all pretences, all subterfuges will not fool us any longer. Unhealthy things are happening here. Children are used in black masses and possibly tortured or even killed – I don't know, I don't know any more. I am so scared for Béatrice. She is becoming violent. She is shaking her head in every direction; she looks like she is possessed by a demon. She refuses to hold my hand, struggles like the very devil and lets out animal shrieks. I don't know what the old witch has told her about me but we need to leave this damned village as soon as we can. Will you help us, Virginia?

Paul Saint-Pierre has finished our portrait. I had the shock of my life when he unveiled the painting. It's a chiaroscuro portrait in which I don't even appear. There are two figures indeed but they are Béatrice and Bérénice. They both have some of my features but I am not there, Virginia. Bérénice is in the foreground; she looks sensible and docile. She is wearing a blue ribbon in her hair. In the background there is a malevolent-looking Béatrice; she has a shifty look in her eyes and her hands are clasping her sister's neck as if about to strangle her. I didn't say a word – I could hardly breathe. I took Béatrice by the hand and started running. She was trying to wrestle herself free but I held fast and kept running. I clutched her hand firmly – I could feel her stumbling over and I knew that she must have grazed her knees on the stones but I didn't care. I was dragging her. I was running but I had no idea where I was going.

I stopped. I was completely out of my mind and out of breath. Chance had taken us to the tree of the dead. I tried to stop Béatrice from going any closer but could not summon up the necessary strength. Béatrice had untied the blue ribbon that she normally wears in her hair and was trying to tie it to one of the lower branches. On her slate she had drawn two little girls who were holding hands. I snatched the slate from her and started shaking her violently shouting, "Stop this now! Are you going to stop this?" I don't know what went through me. I asked her for forgiveness afterwards and I rocked her in my arms.

Won't you answer my letters, Virginia? Won't you help me? Has Marc managed to convince you, too? I know everything went wrong. I know I broke something. Impossible to go back now.

I must talk to Béatrice. I found little messages, little notes rolled up and hidden under my bed or stuck between the wooden beams of my room. I know the trick, you know. They are just words, cock-and-bull sentences, prayers, magic formulas, childish scrawls. I burnt them all, those little rolled-up messages. I realise I should have kept at least one so I could have sent it to you to prove that I am not completely deranged but I was panic-stricken and I burnt them all. All of them, Virginia. They were from Béatrice. One read "Murderer" and another one "Liar". I know it's Béatrice. She reported everything she knew to Florimonde. She told her everything but why can't I get a second chance, Virginia? Why?

The plastic bag from Auchan. I knew that Béatrice wanted the same doll but it was always one of them at a time. She wanted the same doll as Bérénice but I said no. Not this time. Next time it will be your turn, Béatrice. Today it's Bérénice's turn to get something. That was the rule but I saw hatred in her eyes. She was clenching her fists but didn't say any more and when we came back home, they both went upstairs with the ugly white china doll in its Auchan plastic bag.

I know it's Béatrice who suffocated her sister but it was to teach me a lesson. She wanted to teach me a lesson for having a favourite blue-eyed girl. To teach me a lesson, do you understand, Virginia? To teach *me*, her mother. She was crying. She said: "I didn't do it, Mummy." These were her last words. I know it now. I know it, Virginia. I tiptoed downstairs to the kitchen, and for long minutes Béatrice had the horrible sight of her dead sister in front of her. I went into the kitchen and took an identical plastic bag from the cupboard, a bag with a giant red 'A' for Auchan on the front. I went back to their room and I am the one who killed Béatrice. I killed her and Marc had me locked up but I didn't learn my lesson, Virginia, I didn't. I am only learning now, in this mad prison village. I am becoming insane and we must leave straightaway. I must leave, Virginia. I must leave this very instant . . .

*

Florimonde sighed. Her shift was about to start. She put on her nurse's cap and apron and called out Eurydice's name, but there was no answer. She went upstairs and found the room completely empty apart from four letters lying on the night table. Four letters addressed to a certain Virginia but with no surname and no address. She put all of them in one of her two large apron pockets. Then she went downstairs and out into the garden to look for Eurydice. Florimonde walked very slowly towards the brook where amongst the grass she found the school slate Eurydice had been using ever since her arrival at the Village Psychiatrique de Pisy. She followed the brook and in the distance she saw Eurydice's body swinging gently from a creaking branch of the tree of the dead. Eurydice's eyes were wide open. They had the porcelain emptiness of a doll's dead eyes. When she arrived at the tree, Florimonde crossed herself quickly and tied a brand new blue ribbon to the lowest branch.

LORD OF DYFED
Russell Celyn Jones

He came back from war to find his own land had grown remote. Six months away was all it took. Now a mist was rising sluggishly from the lakes. White frost hung on branches. Fields welded with grey skies. And he felt indifferent. Viewed from horseback, the landscape reneged on him. It failed to revive his spirits. With him rode a dozen men, all paid-up hunting companions whose names he barely knew.

He was missing his time in the army, at the front line in the south-west. He'd been an officer – by privilege of birth, admittedly. Everyone understood the NCOs were his superiors really, yet never spoke of it. Older men conditioned by war, they'd taught him to control muscle-racking fear by breathing in steam; how, in hand-to-hand fighting, the best method for overpowering the enemy was to stamp on his foot. To be a good soldier you had to be a canny one.

He led the hunting party along railway sleepers laid over a hoary ground. Every now and then he caught a glimpse of the necklace of industries around the throat of the bay, producing little more than memories now, and the lamb-white beaches stretching further west. Out at sea, cargo ships were slinging in from Yokohama, Shanghai; all those places. Rio, Cape Town. Their huge white sails flopped and mooned and inhaled the wind. Clouds in the distance played upon the surface of the water, changing from white to pink and green to a rich aubergine.

Since oil ran out, warfare had become medieval again. Armies breached city barricades with battering rams, or scaled them with ladders while defenders poured boiling water upon their heads (pitch could only be dreamed of). Advanced military technology lay off rusting in the grass for want of a gallon of diesel. You could no longer call in air strikes. Ground troops charged enemy lines on horseback. Cavalry laced their steeds' feed buckets with Afghan poppy before riding like the wind into a contact, or away from a lost one. With no high tech it was hand-to-hand fighting with the Moroccans who came by sea on sail-driven frigates, and once on land were powerful by virtue of some vintage stocks of crude. Enough to run a single tank for a day at least, and a single tank, even for a day, could turn the tide of a war in your favour.

He hoped he killed some of those Moroccans himself, but couldn't bank on it. He had to be content with putting down fire from a distance, covering his platoon who rode their stoned fillies on short violent pilgrimages across enemy lines. They returned always minus someone he loved.

If truth be told he was scared of violence. That's what he learned about himself during his short stint in the military. And in that game if you didn't love violence, no one would love you. He hid it the best he could, personally slaughtering a lamb each night to feed his platoon. Cooking with the guys in a darkened field after a rout – that was what he lived for. Sitting around a roaring fire, swearing with them, hearing accounts of their kills. In the army you could say what you liked. There was no control over their statements, or his. He could be as indiscreet as they were.

He'd been removed from the front as the contacts got too hot. He was never in any real danger. Those men would have protected him with their lives. Granted they'd been ordered to, but he hoped some of them had got to love him just a little bit by the end of his tour.

The land up here was scraped clean by prevailing south-westerly winds. High enough to see the sea at all times, but not the deer. Now noon, and the temperature had soared, burning off the mists. It often reached 29°C in mid-September. Seasons were so arbitrary nowadays, as was the time of day – at least to Pwyll, who didn't work, didn't wake up until he felt like it. Another hour passed and they reached the woods and expectation grew. They dismounted to be low to the mossy floor. Above them pigeons fled the treetops in panic, rattling their bony wings against the topmost branches. A flurry of dust fell down through the shafts of light.

He began to smell a sweet scent of flowers on the air. Only good things should come from such olfactory experience. While holding this thought, he led the men into a clearing where the sun broke through and where old cars, with tyres burnt off and engines removed, had been stuffed with compost and manure – for the cultivation of hothouse flowers: the bi-coloured Soleil d'Or, Arum lilies, Mediterranean Bear's Breeches, and the Grand Monarch from China. Apache horticulturalists lived in the other cars and sold the blooms for a living.

Teirnon, his steward, who'd served under his father, moved his horse up the line to walk beside Pwyll. "How are you doing?" he asked brightly.

"To be truthful, Teirnon, fucking bored to death."

"On such a grand day as this?" His thin lips opening into a smile revealed baby-sized teeth.

Teirnon was in his late forties and that he could still enjoy a hunt confounded Pwyll, who was twenty-four. "Why are we hunting anyway, when Sainsbury's wraps it for us in clingfilm?"

Teirnon stared at him indulgently. Pwyll knew his steward would be judging now which way best to reply. His job depended on having the right hunch. And he'd been in that job a long time. In the end he said nothing and that was about right.

Earlier that day they'd ridden past isolated farmhouses and through villages. People came out onto the road to pay tribute to Lord Pwyll – but out of duty, not love; not even for a warrior back from the front. They knew he'd been sent to war as a PR exercise. The fake pride showed in their upturned faces. He sneered back at them from the saddle, staring down teenage girls' cleavages to irritate their fathers.

The gamekeepers, cooks, gardeners, stable boys, carpenters and plumbers riding with him were similarly dutiful, rounded up from off the estate by an ever-cautious Teirnon. Pwyll pulled the reins down hard to let his horse graze on clover and walked off into the woods in a strop. Soldiers – they were the best of men, the only real people in his life, who kept it honest for him.

"If you wish, my lord," Teirnon said, catching up, "we can turn back for the house."

"No, no, forget that." The hunt was all there was. "We'll get a kill first."

They moved on, but the herd was proving elusive and they reached the old slate quarry without sighting a single deer. Here the mountainside had been carved into terraces by a previous generation, exposing its blue, green and purple belly to the light for the first time in millions of years. Below these terraces was a lake pigmented a turquoise blue. The lake had been one of his regular haunts since a kid, a place where he could be alone with his thoughts. In more recent times old cookers, freezers and washing machines had been dumped there and broke the surface of the water. A dark-blue Nissan with its licence plates removed perched at the lake's edge. He could see its deep tracks in the mud. It was still in relatively good condition even without its tyres. From the back fender dangled a severed orange rope. In the windscreen were two bullet holes.

He dismounted and wandered over to the car, opened the passenger door. On the driver's side were Order of Service cards for a marriage ceremony. *Sinead and Vaughan, at Clare Vale church.* Either a bygone wedding or one the bride and groom had never reached. With these wedding cards in hand he meditated on the silent domestic appliances in the lake. This is where families came to die. Along the shore, willows had collapsed into the water. The light felt almost frail and he could hear the sound of a river fading, losing power, unable to reach its final destination of the sea.

He strayed far from the party to be alone. He allowed his horse to follow but not the men. From the edge of the lake he saw fish jumping, struggling to leave their watery prison. A single swan sat on the turquoise water. It too seemed between places, away from home, confused. A breeze skimmed the surface, making ripples. The metallic sound of leaves rustling, a smell of cut pine, a noise of animals being preyed upon. Airborne attacks on rats and voles . . .

He threw a rock into the lake to stimulate something, make something move. He watched the concentric circles expand until they reached his feet. Distant sounds of sheep and cattle, dogs barking from afar. Lots of different birds flying by: murder of crows, pairs of jays and magpies, songbirds singing their hearts out in fear of the jays and magpies.

Fifty metres away, his men waited patiently for him to give directions.

He felt the sun burn his face. He heard the fish clatter and rattle as they swam amongst the submerged fridges, cookers and tumble driers. Married couples dumped their wares here. That swan! Pearl-white with a dirty neck, head in the water, tail in the air.

On the crest of the hill appeared a stag – a glorious, grey muscle-bound alpha male etched upon the skyline. Pwyll felt his heart pull and dive. He sensed the men flinch, saw their arms reach out very slowly for holstered weapons hanging from saddles. They had a clear shot from here, but no one would go before him.

A sound of slate shards clicking; the deer turned its beautiful neck. Pwyll heard the dog before he saw it – a bark like a violently snapped branch. A brown-freckled ridgeback came off the ground at speed, drooling and snarling, and fell upon the stag, engorging itself. The stag screamed. The scream had no end and was heartbreaking to hear.

The way into this was clear in his mind. He unsheathed his Finnish bolt-action rifle from the saddle and ran along the rim of the lake. He jumped from one boulder to another. When he was high enough to see the dog's spine protruding through its skin, he braced himself with legs apart, drew the bolt, took aim and shot it through the neck. It fell upon the stag, both animals trembling. The stag scrambled from beneath the weight of the dog, got unsteadily onto its legs, briefly looked around at the world. It seemed to wait for some kind of confirmation. Then it leapt away, flying the arterial flag.

Pwyll stood with his boot on the throat of the ridgeback – a huge and frightening dog, even when dead. From over an escarpment another hunting party appeared. They had come from the east, on Arab horses, five men in black North Face jackets. One of these men broke from the group. He stemmed his mount into a slow trot as soon as he saw the dog and slid out of the saddle. Pwyll stepped away, holding his weapon across his waist parallel to the ground. Teirnon caught up and they both watched this other man fall to his knees over the dog. They heard him exhale.

He pulled the dog's limp head into his chest, kissed it and then let it crash to the ground. Rising to his full height he glowered at Pwyll, saying nothing. He had bad skin, the ravages of teenage acne. His eyes were remote and bloodshot.

Pwyll broke the silence, immediately giving the other man the advantage. "Your dog was attacking the stag."

"Well, it's called hunting. Isn't that what you're doing?"

"Not with dogs."

The stranger threw back his head in the direction of his men, who all looked sprung from the same womb, with the same buzz haircuts, square jaws. "I don't accept your apologies."

"I didn't apologise," Pwyll said.

The man caressed the neck of his horse and lowered his voice to a hiss. "You're the young bard of war, aren't you? The one they sent away because you were misspending your youth with people you shouldn't know."

"You have the advantage, sir."

Teirnon interrupted, translated the unspoken line. "This is Lord Arawn. He has the land east of the river."

"Arawn?" Pwyll repeated. He did not know the name.

The man's hand stroking the horse was covered in hair, his nails broken and dirty; an aristocrat with the hands of a gravedigger.

"How are we going to do this, son?"

"You want compensation?" Pwyll struggled to keep his voice from breaking down.

"No, son, that cock won't crow."

His remark drew a snigger from his men. Pwyll noticed their easy familiarity and envied it.

They slid off their horses and lifted the dead animal onto one of the saddles before mounting up again. Without another word they set off, riding slowly towards the escarpment from which they'd emerged.

Pwyll was shaking. He wanted to fall into someone's arms. He said to Teirnon, "Why should he be pissed off with *me* for shooting his dog?"

"Be warned. Arawn's a man of reckless determination."

"Did you see their jackets? Gortex is hard to come by."

"Arawn looks after his men – that is true." He lowered his voice gravely. "This is not over, my lord."

Their hunt was now completely ruined and everyone knew it. The party headed back to the estate as the weather changed again. They rode through the sodden woods under dripping trees onto the highway, as a way of making time. Each carriageway was lined with cars refitted for human habitation. People who lived in them had grown veronica as windbreaks, a few stiff Monterey pines from California. Pwyll liked being on this road, could sense the air of freedom everywhere. Fluttering around the cracked wing mirrors of a VW van were blue tits trying to mate with their own image.

This way back skirted the Sandfields housing estate. He knew Teirnon hailed from here and could feel the steward's dis-ease as they rode into it. At its heart was a biomass power station that burned 500,000 tons of clean woodchip each year, producing high-pressure steam to turn the turbines, generating 50 MW in renewable electricity. Pwyll could still remember a time when a petrochemical plant had stood in its place. Then a small boy, he'd been brought out here by his father to be taught about industry. A river was diverted into the plant so ships could sail right in and have their holds pumped full of benzene and vinyl chloride monomer. From anywhere on the estate in those days you could hear chemicals humming under hot recycle in the knotted steel pipes, see twenty-foot heads of flame issuing from the plant's chimney stack. That was some tough era. At night the plant was a mass of white light and steam, actually quite beautiful. But to see things in this way, in the electric green, with a metallic wind in your hair, is what it means to be young. Now his thoughts were turned to more tormenting things – the unarticulated threat posed by Arawn – and that is what it means to grow old.

They rode past weaving and embroidery factories; a John Deere tractor workshop (defunct); trailer park; units making bathroom tiles, bamboo flooring. Each street was named after a famous composer. Gangs of teenagers walked their pit bulls down Mozart Avenue towards the War Memorial and acknowledged Pwyll like they would the police. Since his father and mother died, powers had been invested in him. He was meant to rule here but didn't know how. He had yet to inspire any affection.

He asked Teirnon breezily, "You still have family here?"

"Only one brother now."

This sounded fine to Pwyll. One brother was one more than he had. Why it cost Teirnon to say so was hard to understand. He decided to do a little poaching here.

"I want to visit your bother," he announced.

"You want to visit my brother?" Teirnon repeated.

Pwyll could tell his idea didn't appeal.

"That's what I said." He did not stop to consider the consequence to Teirnon or his brother of making such an impromptu visit.

Dutifully, Teirnon led them into a row of faded grey houses. They left their horses and walked up the garden path of one of them. Pwyll could feel his resentment in the mute shuffle.

"It's no big deal," he reassured him, "just a little social visit."

The front lawn was nibbled to the stub. Something hungry had this way passed.

They reached the door, rang the bell and a shadow behind the frosted-glass panel began to move. The door swung open and standing before them was a stooped old man with fine grey hair matted with dust. There was dirt in his ears and rimming his nostrils. If he wasn't overjoyed to see his brother and his lord, he tried not to show it. He stretched his arm behind his back, gesturing them to enter.

From the street, the windows were badly smeared so Pwyll got no forewarning of what lay inside. As he stepped over the threshold the smell made him gag. Then he saw the horse in the living room. It appeared to be out on its legs, head drooping. Surrounding this world-weary nag were cabinets stuffed with bone china and silverware.

The man didn't so much as mention the horse. He repaired to the kitchen, which smelled different but not much sweeter. There was a thick layer of grease on every surface and Pwyll's shoes stuck to the floor.

"Tea?" the brother offered, dragging the syllable out like a wet rag.

As the kettle boiled, he plucked three festering mugs from the sink of dirty crockery and gave them a quick rinse. Since no one else was talking, Pwyll questioned him about the mare in the front room. "Why isn't she grazing outside?"

The brother's face soured and scrunched up. "She'll get cancer, all the carcinogens in the air."

"Do you ride her?" Pwyll asked.

"A little sideline as a rag-and-bone merchant, your lordship."

Teirnon said, "She'd make you more money as carcass for dog food. You'd earn more from her dead than alive. Either that or let her out on the moors, to eat clover and grass in her final days." He sounded bitter and angry. This was not the demonstration of brotherly love Pwyll had hoped to find.

The brother poured hot water over the tea bags and dribbled evaporated milk from a can into the mugs. Then he left the table to go feed his mare. From the kitchen Pwyll watched him lean into the horse's backside while emptying a saucepan of grain into a feed bucket. There were huge dents in the walls from where the horse had kicked back with its hind legs.

Teirnon was looking desperately humiliated. This visit was undermining the impression he liked to give off of a man from nowhere, who'd parented himself.

All that he was learning today left Pwyll feeling weightless. He rose from his chair and made their excuses, to set Teirnon free of the past. On the way out, he stalled at the bathroom door. He needed to go, but once he'd pushed open the door and looked inside, thought the better of it. Some scenes are best left undescribed.

Pwyll's own home was a thirty-five-roomed house on one thousand acres of prime farmland. Men harvesting wheat looked up as the hunting party rode in. Once maintained by a few large machines, the farm was now pecked over by teams using hand tools – men whom he rarely met. He knew nothing about farming and didn't care to learn.

In the courtyard, he wrapped the reins around a stable boy's raised arm and walked indoors via the hall. His head down he sluggishly climbed the double staircase past portraits of his dead ancestors.

From the landing he was lured into his parents' bedroom. Months after their death and it still smelled of oysters, which for some reason he always associated with nuns. His mother had been a believer and her rosary beads were draped over the corner bedpost. Pontormo's painting of the Deposition hung in a frame on the wall. Since their death he'd given orders to the cleaning staff to change nothing in this room. A few blouses hung from wire hangers on the picture rail. White jeans were folded on a chair and the last book his father had read lay open with its spine broken on the carpet. On a bedside table were a beeswax candle and a Kodak envelope of photographs.

He sat on the edge of the bed and flicked through the photographs, holding up to the sunset a picture of his mother as a young bride on a swing; his father in Royal Welch Fusiliers uniform. This was his favourite. They died six months apart.

His own bedroom had altered very little either. He kept the curtains drawn. On the wall behind his bed was a collage he'd made as an angry adolescent, from magazine pictures realigned in ways you don't see in *Vogue*. Models were burning in a city of erect penises. Men were cars from the waist down – auto centaurs. A fierce orange sun was painted into the top left-hand corner around the light switch.

With thirty-four empty rooms spanning him, he parted the curtains to take a look at the sea in the distance. He reclined in the soft single bed, on a threshold of unwelcome silence, and fell asleep. An hour later he woke, so dizzy with loneliness that he had to fix his eyes upon the horizon to steady his spinning head. A full moon shimmered over the sea like tin foil. Buoys winked their own personalised sequences. A pier was a sultry projection into the water. The sea breathed in the night like a lung.

Teirnon knocked and walked into the room, defying the protocol of waiting for an invitation to enter. Pwyll sat up in his bed. He knew this was something extraordinary.

"I've come to tender my resignation," Teirnon said.

The words passed through Pwyll like steel ghosts and he began hungering for air on that muggy, river-bottom of an evening. He mouthed, "Why?" But Teirnon did not answer. "Is it the money? I can improve your package."

"No, my lord."

"So tell me . . ."

"I'd rather not say."

Pwyll began to speculate. "Is this because we went to see your brother?"

"I'd rather not say."

"Oh for God's sake . . ." Pwyll rose from the crumpled bed. "I shot Arawn's dog, is that it?"

"I can make suggestions about my replacement."

"I don't want a replacement," he shouted, forcing Teirnon to look down at his boots. "Take some time to think about it."

"I don't need to think about it."

"Then if you must . . ." Pwyll pulled in his stomach to tighten the sound of his voice. "I'll ask the accountant to arrange your back-end payments."

Teirnon pulled the door shut behind him, leaving Pwyll listening to his own laboured breath in the dark.

By morning Teirnon had left the house. That was all the time he needed to pack up his possessions, strike his presence from the estate he'd been associated with for thirty years. Pwyll sat on a chesterfield in the lounge in front of a log fire that Teirnon had set; his last official duty before leaving. Pwyll watched it reduce to embers then ran out the house.

Through meadows he glided, beneath the hard cough of crows, the sodden grass licking at his ankles. When he'd reached his destination he opened the rusting bolt and pulled back the double doors of the barn. From out of the gloaming his father's Bentley Azure grew in brightness like an energy-saving light bulb.

What a fucking motor. He sat in it and dreamed. The smell of upholstery reminded him of his dad. He ran his hands over the steering wheel. A convertible with white kid-leather upholstery, lamb's-wool floor rugs, burr oak veneers, walnut steering wheel, digital radio, MP3 player, subwoofer and four-channel amplifier, sat nav system, refrigerated bottle cooler. All this and the keys in the ignition.

There was eleven-year-old vintage high-octane fuel in the tank. Some had been used over the years, exercising the car around the estate. More still had evaporated. There were a couple of gallons left, he reckoned. He could wait another eleven years to let that vanish into thin air, or take his father's advice and make the final journey count.

He turned the key. The battery was sluggish but the V8 engine came to life, making a sound no louder than a cat purring. He engaged the transmission. His father had been generous and solicitous. He rolled out of the barn, through the estate along the lonely potholed tarmac. Hark! What's that sound? The rumble of wrought-iron gates rolling open automatically on oiled castors. An invitation to hit the open road . . . How could he resist?

A mile from the house and already he'd smashed a wing mirror against a container dumped in the road. There were so many things to avoid, now that cars had had their day.

When he felt he'd got the hang of it he switched on the MP3 player. Violins and cymbals filled his ears. His father's music had an emotional impact on him but may not have been the most appropriate comment on the flea market he was fast approaching.

He followed the route marked out by Moroccan honeycomb lamps strung from stalls and tried not to kill anyone as he pushed the nose of the Bentley into the crowds. Boys looked down at him inside this great car and their hands came into the open cockpit to touch his hair. He felt like a celebrity. But the car was the celebrity. They didn't love him. They loved the car. Being in a convertible he heard from outside several languages crunching like gears, transporting him he knew not where, and picked up all sorts of aromas – of spices and wet dog.

He drew ever more people into the road and inhaled their dirty wind. A few recognised *him* passing through their ends. He had to drive over piles of broken porcelain and sheep carcasses to get out of this market, mounted the pavement once, corrected, and then was out of town for good.

At last he could put his foot down, climbing to 100 m.p.h. in ten seconds along the dual carriageway, past terraces of abandoned vehicles and their communities. Speed cameras, idle for a decade, were flashing behind him like the paparazzi. This was the A374 and once he veered off exit 7 he knew exactly where he was heading. He passed through housing estates where young girls walk to the playground and are never seen again, saw factories with not a single pane of glass intact. He floored the Bentley and his head kicked back into the leather headrest.

He'd been out an hour. The fuel gauge was blinking on reserve.

The music was full orchestra now, kettle drums and oily wood. He lurched around potholes and mounted grassy banks to avoid fallen trees and came within sight of a nexus of dwellings signalling Arawn's estate. He drove past farmhands tilling the soil, holding turnips in one hand, machetes in the other.

A white, beach-pebble road rang out the sound of his tyres. The house in the near distance was handsome Gothic. He circled a lake that was stocked with rainbow trout snapping at flies stuck in the meniscus. The music ebbed and flowed through the subwoofers and of all things to suddenly remember, it was his father taking him to the dentist. That's where his dad had first heard this music, playing in the dentist's surgery. Pwyll had come to have a corrective procedure under general anaesthetic. As his dad was asking the dentist about the music Pwyll felt a scratch on his arm, heard the anaesthesiologist ask where he'd like to go on holiday, replied he'd like to go on safari in South Africa and then the next thing he knew he was sitting up in the recovery bed with a swollen clutter in his mouth, spittle gurgling, blood seeping down his throat.

He heard the last gasp of gasoline. He booted his foot to the boards and plunged the Bentley into the lake.

Fish bounced to the surface with the turbulence, their frigid eyes seeking out probable cause. Ice-cold water poured into the cockpit. The engine continued to run for a moment and then fizzled out. The MP3 player kept playing that same velvety music as he swam through a spectrum cast by the spill of oil. He saw Arawn come charging out of the house along with three men he recognised from the hunting party. All were attired in military fatigues.

They brought him roughly to his feet, to stand dripping on the stone shore.

"Installation for the pond," he said. "So who's the daddy now?"

"Everywhere I go I'm asked if I think the universities stifle writers. My opinion is that they don't stifle enough of them. There's many a best-seller that could have been prevented by a good teacher."

Flannery O'Connor

HOPE AND THE STAG
Joanna Ingham

Hope kneels by the dead stag. Autumn mulch seeps slowly through her jeans, up over her cold knees. She watches her hands in their pink knitted gloves, and the way the branches shift against the sky above her head. She counts the narrow leaves dropping soundlessly, randomly, from the ash. She waits for the next harsh bark from pheasants huddled somewhere on the field through the trees, stiff furrows rimed with ice.

The stag is broken. He lies on his side with his legs folded half under him, awkward and twisted. His flank is torn, flecked scarlet. If this was all, Hope tells herself, perhaps she could bear it. There'd still be the smallest chance that he would open his eyes. But not now. Because his head is gone, the neck hacked and ragged. There is a blank where his head should be, which seems, to Hope, as wide and hungry as a hole in space. The bracken here is black with oily blood. It smells like metal, like her own blood.

The first time she saw the stag, it was winter. She traced the fields, their stony edges, then dipped into the sparse band of trees that clung to the side of the hill. The light was thin and grey, and snow fell in wet lumps that didn't settle. Mud stuck to her trainers. Panicky rabbits scattered off the path ahead and magpies squawked at her but Hope wasn't frightened. She knew that other girls would be, alone in a bare world, but that was how she felt every day, surrounded by people.

Hope almost walked right past. She was looking down at her feet trying to skirt the worst of the puddles when something, perhaps the snapping of a single twig, made her glance up and he was there, standing between the trees as if waiting for her to paint him. She had seen other deer before, little brown does skittering into the undergrowth at her approach, and even a fawn once in deep bracken. This one, though, was different. He was entirely white, entirely new. He glowed with the surprise of it. For a moment, she thought he was a trick of the light, a snow deer, the one place in the wood that the flakes had dusted, perfect and bright. But then he moved, took a couple of steps forward, and he shone against the dank black trunks.

The stag was young with a slim neck and buds where his antlers would come in the spring. His legs made Hope think of her gran's best china, the cups she still wasn't allowed to touch, but his body was strong with muscle. He held his head high as if nothing would ever scare him. His eyes were heavy-lashed and so dark against the white hide. She felt herself as motionless as he was, a statue, but she must have moved because suddenly his proud front fell away. Perhaps she raised her hands; perhaps the breath caught in her throat. He started and crashed away from her through the bushes, left an empty wood.

When Hope got home, the house was full as usual. Her mum and her sister were talking too loudly on their mobiles. Her three brothers were crowded round their enormous screen playing a game with screeching tyres and crashes. She had already decided that she wouldn't tell them about what she had seen. She wouldn't tell anyone. She didn't want to spoil it, to smear it with layers of greasy fingerprints like photos passed around. She simply had to wait for others to see what the stag had made obvious, what he knew: that she was unique.

Hope had always known she was special. No one else appeared to have noticed, but then she had always known that most people are very stupid. Her hair wasn't the blonde or red or brunette of shampoo adverts, but something in between. At school, she consistently got Bs. Since she had invariably done her homework and fed the hamster, never lingered unduly in the shower or played her music too loud, it was hardly necessary for her parents to address her at all. They were busy. They ran an Internet business together even though they seemed to hate each other. They were always around but never really there either. The dining table was covered in laptops. And then her older sister or one of their brothers was regularly up to something more attention-grabbing than she ever managed, whether flooding the bathroom or catching glandular fever, making unsuitable friends or winning science prizes.

Hope sometimes wondered if the librarian knew. Sometimes she thought she caught the white light of it reflected in the middle-aged woman's grey eyes. The public library was a concrete building with two sloping wings so that, from the top of the street, it looked like a butterfly pinned in a tray. Hope went every Saturday. She liked to work her way up and down the deep aisles of books, reading the titles on the spines until she found one she wanted to ease out in its tight plastic cover. Then she'd wait at the end of the counter until the librarian could come over and talk to her about the week's reading, stamping the book so neatly.

A new routine started in Hope's life. After her library visit she walked to the edge of town, past the rows on rows of semis with their matching cars and trimmed shrubs, to the fields and the woods beyond. She even went there in rain, taking her father's big golfing umbrella with the name of a building society faded around it. She didn't see the stag every time. Many afternoons she would just lie under a tree and read, then drift home as evening set in. But sometimes, when she looked up from the page at the end of a chapter, the stag looked back.

The bluebells were almost out when she came on him suddenly by a broken gate. She saw at once that his antlers were raw and bloody. The tender silvery skin hung off them in tatters where he'd been rubbing against a branch. When he had worried at them enough, the new horn would be bare as stone and ready for a fight. She stared but felt she shouldn't, as if he were naked. She wanted to touch, to soothe the itch. The stag gazed at her for a long time then leapt the gate and cantered across the field where she watched him run. She wished she could run like that.

In the summer holidays, the family went to Spain. They hired a huge villa by the sea with sunloungers round a pool. Hope hated it. She sat in her room peeling the burnt skin off her shoulders or reading. She couldn't wait to get home, away from the fights over beach towels and her brothers' girlfriends, from the new bikini her mum insisted on parading her round in.

When they were back, Hope spent every day in the woods where it was cool. There wasn't long before school started again. She saw the stag only once, fleetingly, when she turned a corner to find him ahead of her on the path. He turned to show himself to her, antlers spread, his coat dappled with green light. She held her breath but he sauntered away, soon lost in the deep growth. It was enough, though. She ran home singing.

Hope was waiting for her dad outside the supermarket when she heard the boys talking about it. They were kicking a football against the wall next to snaking lines of stacked shopping trolleys. There were five of them, raw-skinned, wrists and ankles sticking out of their uniforms like twigs. Hope recognised them from school, from the year above. She stared at her shoes and willed them not to look over. She couldn't help hearing what they were saying, though, in their brash new voices. They were talking about him, the stag; showing off about how they'd seen him up past the allotments and chased him with stones. They laughed and then they just started talking about something else as if it wasn't even that important. It made her want to kill them. She wanted to kick their heads against the supermarket wall hard, one after the other.

The next day Mr Peters talked about him in assembly: "the rare creature in our midst". Hope knew it couldn't have lasted for ever, her secret. Other people went walking too, out with their dogs and their kids. There were those, Mr Peters explained, who would not respect the white deer's right to "a normal life". There were those who would see it as sport. The whole town, he said, was going to work together to keep the deer "our secret". Hope looked around the hall at the lines of teenagers, almost identical with their slump and lip-gloss, the earphones dangling round their necks. She didn't want to share anything with them. She had been the first; she held onto that.

It was nearly half-term when she saw him again; at a distance, up on the hill surrounded by other deer, dark-haunched stags and a brown constellation of does. She watched them, willing him to look at her with his steady gaze. He doesn't belong with them, she thought. She sat on a log and felt the warm ooze of blood on the pad, thick and unfamiliar between her legs. All week she'd had the feeling everyone was looking at her differently, as though they knew. At night, she couldn't keep the clumsy pad in place and in the morning her sheet was stiff, spotted with rusty blood.

This was the place she had wanted to be. She'd thought that here it would be all right, that here at least she could still be herself. But the stag was with the deer and far away. The herd threw long shadows in the late sun. Then something, perhaps even her sitting quietly on the log, startled them and they cantered off over the hill as one, dissolving in the scrub. The white stag ran with them, near the centre of the group, picking up his feet so lightly. He stood out longer than the others but then even he was gone. Her eyes pricked with tears. She unthreaded her hair from its plait and set it out on her shoulders where it caught the sun like fire. She could wait.

She leans forward and places her cheek against the stag's coarse hide, letting her head rest there. He is cold and firm. Across the fields, the road into town gives off its low roar, the steady hum of people coming home to dinner and central heating and television. Normal people. Other people.

But Hope is starting to doubt. She looks at her ordinary hands on her ordinary knees with her ordinary eyes; feels her body in its old cycle of spinning and exchanging and repeating. She cannot tell if this is a miracle or the most average thing in the world. She thinks of his head, stretches her fingers into the air where it should be. It will be stuffed and mounted on a wall; one more piece of treasure in a rich man's house. Its eyes will be plastic, always open. Dust will settle on its ears, dull the dark sheen of its nose. At Christmas, they will drape tinsel on its antlers.

Stars are coming out. Hope cannot feel her feet and her face against his body is cold. She would like for them to be covered together in snow. Around them, the girl and the stag, leaves fall and trees live, disguised as dead things.

PICTURE THIS
Chris Lilly

Picture this: standing in the doorway of your kitchen, in your left hand a Tesco's plastic carrier bag. A thin bag, the handles stretched to breaking, full of tins of soup and sausages and cat food, eggs on the top. In your right hand a door key, with which you've just opened the front door, held between thumb and first finger. The other three fingers on your right hand are holding two pints of milk against your chest – with difficulty because you didn't open the door, put away your key, and then pick up the milk, you picked up the bottles first and juggled with them while you opened the door. You do things like that.

And now picture this: the kitchen table in the middle of the room, radio on one side, breakfast things – teapot, marmalade, butter, bread – in the middle of the table, because it's Saturday and you didn't get up till twelve, and then you had breakfast (on your own because everyone else is away this weekend) and then thought of doing Tesco's before the match, and rushed off, only stopping to put your plate and cup and things in the bowl in the sink.

Now, finally, picture this. Standing on the other side of the table, Sue. In her right hand, the bread knife. One of those quite expensive knives you get called Kitchen Devils, one side with wavy serrations, very sharp, good for cutting things like meat. Surgical steel, made in Sheffield. You know the sort. And in her left hand?

Nothing. Nothing at all. Just blood, because she's cut across her left wrist with the bread knife, and there's a spurt of bright-red blood, arterial blood, that happens every time her heart beats, and it goes quite a long way really, a couple of feet, and there's lots of it. Sue's standing by the sink. Sue's very tidy.

"Oh Jesus Christ," you say, and you drop the groceries and the two bottles of milk and your door key, and you start walking towards Sue, and your head is going chunkety-chunkety-chunk through all those things on health-and-safety posters, and the things you did to get your first-aider badge – how many years ago? Fifteen? Really fifteen? – fifteen years ago in the scouts. And all you can think of is the recovery position and how to do the kiss of life and how to do tracheotomies with a penknife when your boss starts choking to death on toast and paté in a restaurant, and none of those things helps at all.

"Gently, love," you say, and you sit her down, and you take the knife with your left hand and put it on the table, not looking at it, while you take the left arm – the bloody one, the sticky, wet, bloody one – in your right hand, and you try to make the spurting stop with your fingers, and it doesn't, and now your hand is wet and slippery and you still haven't looked at her face or at anything except the wrist and your right hand, which isn't your right hand any more, it's just a right hand that does almost what you tell it to do. You grip harder, just below the slash, on the other little cuts – hesitation marks they're called – how do you know this crap? – and the spurting eases because you've got your fingertips on the artery, luck not judgement, and you think, "There's a pressure point where you put tourniquets and tourniquets have to be released or they get gangrene and I don't know where the pressure point is. Oh shit why doesn't someone else come?" and you know that no one else will. And now the bleeding is less dramatic, not jetting out from her wrist, just seeping, and you still haven't looked at her, so you do. You look at her face, and she's very wide-eyed; not crying, staring at you, and she doesn't say anything, she just stares.

You're calmer now. While your right hand hangs on, you think, "Get an ambulance. Get someone who can stop her dying."

You take the tea towel from under the draining board, it's horrible and grey and greasy but you can't help that, so you let go of her wrist and the blood squirts across the room, and you whimper. Not Sue. Sue doesn't make a sound. Before it can happen again you wrap the tea towel round her wrist, and it's turning red as you do it, Sue's blood turning it red. You wrap the wrist and close your hand on the bundle, and then you get Sue to stand up, she still hasn't said anything, she stands up and you put your left arm round her shoulders and walk her across the kitchen, your right hand holding her left arm across your bodies.

You step over the groceries and into the corridor, and up to the phone by the front door, and sit her down on the stairs. She still hasn't said anything. You reach for the phone with your left hand, it's awkward, almost too far, but you get it and take the receiver in your left hand. You think, "My right hand's numb. I can't feel my fingers. I'm going to let go of her wrist," but you don't. You dial three nines, you didn't realise how much you were shaking, you can hardly find the button, then you do. Then you wait.

"Hello, Emergency. Which service do you require?"

"Ambulance," you yelp, your voice won't behave, and then another voice says, "Ambulance Service?" and you say, "There's been an accident, there's a woman losing blood fast, can you come quickly please?" and you're gibbering. Then the voice on the other end, so calm, so patient, Everymother, says, "Yes, dear. Just give me your address," and you do, and the phone number, and she says, "Thank you," and she asks if you're all right, and if you need anyone to stay on the line, and you say, "No. Thank you, no," and she goes away. Then there's just Sue sitting silent beside you, and the phone buzzing in your ear, and you're lost. You sit silent for eight minutes, because you can't think of anything to say and Sue can say nothing, and your arm is round her holding her while your right hand squeezes her wrist and the sodden tea towel drips on the carpet.

Then the ambulance men come and they take charge. They aren't kind or unkind, sympathetic or not. They do their job, throw away the tea towel, put something else round her wrist, you can't see what they do, they just do it, and Sue is sat in a wheelchair thing and they take her away.

And then the policemen who came in just behind them say: "Can you tell us what happened, sir?"

You tell them all this, which is more than they want to know, and you take them into the kitchen, which looks like an abattoir, you hadn't realised how much blood there was, and puddles of milk and broken eggs, and one of them says, "It's a bit of a mess, isn't it?" and you laugh. Why did you laugh? Then the young one says to the older one with a moustache, "She must have waited till she heard someone come in," and you think, "Yes, she must," and you wonder how long she stood there, waiting for someone, waiting for the slipping sound of a key in the lock, before drawing the knife across her wrist.

The older one says, "Can you give us some details about the young lady? What is your relationship with her?" and you have to sort out in your head just why Sue was here.

"She's a friend. She was staying here for a bit," you say finally, but it isn't true. She isn't anyone's friend, she's just someone you know, and it isn't you that knows her, it's Laura, and it's bloody unfair and you didn't want her here in the first place. Tell them she's gay, they'll like that. Tell them she wants nothing to do with men, that she brings home a succession of strange women, who all hate you for being male. Then you can talk about how they hang around in the living room so you can't watch television or play music, so you go to the pub on your own. Tell them about the time she came into the kitchen straight out of the bath, and you couldn't look at her, although she's lovely, because fancying her and disliking her was too confusing, and anyway, Laura was there. Go on, tell them. You don't though. They want to know where she comes from, and you say Bedford, then think perhaps it's Hertford, or one of those places you don't want to go to, and then think it doesn't matter much, that Sue doesn't come from any of those places in any way that counts, not in the way of going home. She just moves from place to place, using up the tolerance of acquaintances until they ask her to go, and then she moves on to the next address in her diary.

When the police have gone, you ring the hospital to find out when visiting hours are, and how she is, and what's happening to her, and they say, "Are you related to the patient?" and you say, "No, just a friend," and they say, "Well, she'll be discharged at seven o'clock, if you'd like to come and fetch her." And they hang up.

That's when you start crying, sitting on the stairs, shaking at the unfairness of it all. Why is it happening to you?

You pick your way through the mess in the kitchen, and put the kettle on. The clock says 4:15, which means it's been an hour since you got in. If it takes half an hour to get to the hospital, you've got till 6:30 to work out what you're doing. You wash away some of the blood in the sink, and pick out your cup from breakfast, and rinse the blood off it. You make yourself some coffee, then realise there's no milk because the bottles got broken. The glass is all over the floor, and the cat is lapping round the splinters to reach the milk. Then he treads delicately over the tins and starts to lick at a pool of Sue's blood drying on the floor, and you pick him up by the skin behind his neck and throw him out of the back door, as he screams at you and bites your hand.

You pick up all the tins, wipe off the milk and egg, and put them away. You sweep up all the glass and eggshells, and split paper bags and the milk-sodden loaf of bread, and the other bits you can't rescue, and put them in the bin. Then you clear off the table, very methodical, putting away the marmalade and the cornflakes. You wash the crockery and put it away wet, getting it out of the way, and then you start cleaning. You fill the washing-up bowl with water and you pour in Dettol, and you wash the blood off the kitchen table. You wash the blood off the cooker and the sink and the draining board. You sponge down the walls and the dresser and then you scrub the floor, and you put Ajax on the wet patches and scrub again, and you change the bright-red water and you rinse it again, and mop up the milk and egg, and change the water and wipe it again, until there's no more blood in the kitchen. Then you clean the hall and the passageway, and then when you're sure there isn't any blood left anywhere, you wash the bread knife very thoroughly, and take it out to the dustbin and throw it away. You feel a bit sorry about that, because, sharp as it was, it was a very good knife, and expensive. You go into the bathroom and dump your clothes in the tub, and hold the shower attachment over your head and rinse yourself clean. You take your dripping clothes out of the bath, and put them in a bucket to soak, and change. Then you go to the living room where Sue sleeps, and look through her diary, trying not to read the pages of tiny neat writing, till you find her address list. There's the number of a group of women you know she visits, so you ring it. The first time you say "Hello, could I –" the woman on the other end hangs up, because you can't stop your voice sounding male, but that's not unexpected so you try again, and finally you speak to Amanda, who you thought was a friend of Sue's. Amanda, it seems, doesn't care for Sue at all, and suggests it was a pity you found her so soon. She isn't helpful. You say thank you, and hang up, and then you ring for a taxi to take you to the hospital because now it's half past six.

You arrive at the hospital in ten minutes; the taxi came much quicker than you'd thought. You ask the man to hang on, and go in to give your name to the woman at the desk and tell her who you've come for. She doesn't respond at all, no smile, nothing. Just crisp things said into the phone while you stand there, lost. When she's finished she looks up and winces to see you still stood there, intruding on her space. She gestures to the plastic chairs round the coffee machine, and tells you to sit and wait.

For half an hour you sit there, worrying about the taxi costing more than you have in your wallet, worrying about Sue, worrying that they've forgotten you're here, and no one will ever come to find you and you'll have to sit here drinking rotten coffee until you summon up the courage to leave, probably sometime around midnight. Then they bring Sue down the corridor. She's very pale, but she's not looking manic or strange, or anything much. She has very neat cream-coloured bandages on her wrist, and other than that, normal. You stand up, and she smiles – very slight but it is a smile – and you feel a bit better. The nurse who is with her looks stern, but quite nice. She says, "Goodbye. Let's not see you in here again," to Sue, then she goes. You take Sue's arm. It's the most intimate thing you've done ever since you've known her – this touch, your hand on her arm. You held her arm this afternoon, of course, but that was different. She doesn't mind you holding her arm.

You go out to the taxi together, and you sit her in it, very solicitous. The taxi driver takes you home and charges you twenty-three pounds fifty for two ten-minute journeys and a forty-minute wait. You don't know if that's a bargain or a rip-off; you can never tell with minicabs. It's difficult to know what to tip him. You give him two tens and a five and see how long it takes him to get the change. If he's quick he can keep it; if he takes his time you'll have it back. He gets three fifty pences out without a pause, and you tell him to keep them.

Sue's standing by the door. She's holding her arm away from her body, as though it belongs to someone else. You go in, and Sue wants to take a bath, so you go upstairs to run it while she goes into her bedroom. You ask if she wants a coffee, and she says she does so you go downstairs to make it. She's in the bath when it's done, and she asks you to bring it in. She's lying in the tub with her bandaged left arm propped on the side, clear of the water. Her eyes are shut and her hair is floating round her head like seaweed, like Ophelia in that painting. Ophelia dead. She looks up. "Thanks," she says, and asks if you'll put it down on the side of the bath. You put it down and go, proud of yourself for not looking at her body at all.

You go into the living room, turn on the fire, turn down her bed. Her clothes are over the arm of the chair, her trousers with dried dark stains on them, her blouse crusted with blood. You take the blouse down to the kitchen and put it into a bucket of detergent and water. The soapsuds turn pink. Sue is out of the bath, so you go to see if she wants anything, and she doesn't. She gets into bed. "I think I'll go to sleep now," she says, so you turn off the fire and the light at the switch by the door. You feel so responsible, so depended on, standing in the doorway looking at the shrouded shape in the bed, the dark hair spread across the pillow. When you babysit, you can stand for ages listening to the tiny pops and mumbles a sleeping child makes. Little noises, while the night slows down and you focus in and in and in on the creature in the cot. Now you're doing the same for Sue, who is twenty-six. Odd. Very odd. And you didn't like her.

You go down to the kitchen to make another cup of black coffee, to look at the book you meant to read today, still sitting on the sideboard. You haven't eaten anything since breakfast. Toasted cheese? Yesterday's bread will have to do, but you can't cut it, there's no bread knife. The cat starts twining himself around your legs, prepared to forgive you for throwing him out if you'll feed him now. You give the cat his supper, then you go to the dustbin and rescue the knife, take it back into the kitchen, and wash it. While you're eating the toasted cheese, you notice a spot of blood on the top of the cooker. Leave it for the morning. Go to bed. You go to bed.

PRELUDES AND ELUSIONS
Kavita Jindal

The cold air stings my face when I step out of Walczak Tower. I stand in front of the swooping building, tapping the sole of my burgundy shoe on the pavement, as if deciding which way to go. A taxi glides by, the display strip on its body flashing at me in hot blue. *November 16, 2021*, the scrolling text informs me, *21:02 hours*. Then: *Jody Jumps Inside the Bridge Box . . . Three London shows only . . .* I miss the rest.

My foot continues to tap insistently. I am seeking control of myself. Of that beast, desire.

There are some things I am good at controlling. Contracts, computers, print on paper. People. You have to be good at dealing with people to be a successful family lawyer. Although I like to pretend that I'm a dental nurse, especially if I'm out with my mother. She disapproves of what I do. Not that she dislikes the law; it's my specialisation that is the problem.

"People drawing up contracts to control each other," she says. "I can't agree with that."

"I'm a pioneer," I tell her. "An inventor. And a millionaire."

"Look what your work has done to you," she snaps back. "What kind of life do you have?"

There we stop. She won't believe I like my set-up. She won't believe that my character is completely unlike hers. I don't argue. Arguments bore me. I am in command of myself and always have been. Until last week. That kerfuffle has left me unsteady. But at the beginning, I was in control.

It was in June last year, in a soggy marquee at my cousin Jolie's wedding reception, that I was introduced to her friend Libby Larsen. Libby didn't give me a chance to go into my dentist's assistant routine. She pinned me with her arresting blue gaze. "I've heard of you. I've seen your name in the paper. When there's a famous person brandishing a pre-conception agreement drafted by you and the poor judge has to decide whether the accused spouse is holding up their end of the bargain or not."

I grimaced. Not all publicity was good publicity. Especially now, when some former clients were ending up in the courts.

"Uh huh." I tried to change the topic, asking her, "Are you on call all hours like Jolie?" Libby worked with Jolie in Tech Support at the HQ of Stilling Environment. But the lady was not for swerving. From her clutch bag she brought out a black-and-cream duo-pho, similar to mine. "What's your number? I'm being nagged by my boyfriend. I know I'm going to need you soon."

I gave her my office number, which she input on the cream side of her duo-pho. The black side must be for work. Funny; I had chosen black to store my personal protected data and the cream casing for work.

"Were you really the first to draft pre-concepts for couples?" Libby asked.

I nodded. "The first one I produced was five years ago. I was working with Clara Redmond on pre-nups, but when I saw how difficult men were finding it to persuade their partners to have children, I thought this would ease the way. That first document was for a colleague." I smiled at the memory. "She could articulate *all* her concerns very clearly, so I had a pretty good template and then I added to it as I went along."

"So you're doing your bit to stop the birth rate plummeting further." Libby spoke as if uttering a witticism.

I heard a chuckle behind me. It was Jolie. "Ask Lena what her mother thinks."

I didn't reply and Jolie sang, "Contracts, contracts, what good do they do?"

Libby looked at me with intense interest. "And your answer?"

"If we can protect our wealth with pre-nups, why can't we safeguard something more important: the welfare of our children? And ourselves? Isn't it better to be prepared for your responsibilities than not?"

"If we are among the lucky few who can create life," added Jolie. She seemed bent on teasing me because she carried on, "Do you know that Lena forgot to congratulate me when I told her I was getting married? Instead she reminded me very seriously to bank my eggs and Paolo's sperm."

Paolo was the cherub-faced physicist who had just become her husband. I spied him at the opposite corner of the tent. I left Jolie and Libby having a fit of the champagne giggles and headed towards the groom. I may be a secret romantic but I was not going to make a girly display of cackles or tears. I needed male company to offset the bridal vibes.

It was three months later that Libby rang to make a formal appointment with me. "My boyfriend is mad keen on having a child," she said. "He insists we should just try. But really, I need a pre-concep."

I waited.

"He'll have to do many more child-hours than me," she went on. "I want it in writing. Shall I see you alone to put down my terms?"

I gave her the usual advice. "Firstly," I said, "it's better if the agreement is drawn up before you start trying. Some clauses deal with the months of pregnancy. There's even a pre-pregnancy clause about vitamin programmes and such, should you want it. And since this is an *agreement*, you should both be committed to it from the outset. My recommendation is that your boyfriend should be at the discussions."

That is how I come to have the pleasure of meeting the allegedly impatient father-to-be of Libby's to-be-conceived. Adam Gillick walks into my office and makes my heart thump. He is breathtakingly beautiful.

Libby shakes her duo-pho at me. "I told you I'd need your number. When you know who the best is, why go anywhere else? Especially when you can afford the best."

I sense Adam squirming. I hold out my hand and say something welcoming. He starts at my voice. It's husky, like it's scraped past pebbles in my throat. It always surprises people. It doesn't match my too-round cheeks and my long hair, which falls straight to my waist. If my hair doesn't get me a second look, then my voice definitely does.

Clara Redmond, the senior partner at our practice, often ribs me that I have trained my voice to be sexy. "It always cracks on an important word when you speak. You must have practised that."

"All natural," I tell her.

What we get given. Clara has the plaintive "Please, miss" voice of a shy eight-year-old, the softness of it emerging from her lips a sudden contrast to her stern bony face.

What people like Adam get given. Everything.

I sit at my aluminium desk while Libby and Adam arrange themselves in the chairs opposite. I have plenty of experience in reassuring uncomfortable men. "This first meeting," I begin smoothly, "is just me talking about fairly dull things. I'll give you a rundown of how we put together the agreement. I'll give you a list of all the suggested clauses for you to discuss between yourselves. That usually throws up any issues either of you might have. Those we'll resolve together at the next meetings."

Clara tells me that when *she* started in pre-nups, back in 1998, most men were supremely confident about what they wanted in the contract. The women tended to shrug as if they didn't really want to be there. I hadn't noticed any such difference between the sexes when I started my training in 2009. Certainly, in the pre-conception side of things, women are in control. With the current birth rate standing at four births for every thousand people, I can see why they are special, the ones who agree to have children; and even more so the ones who succeed in doing so.

Clara also tells me that human needs don't change. She may have a point. I've observed that most women do want children, but it's a good ploy to pretend they don't. Oh, how they need to be persuaded. They worry incessantly about micromanaging the future: work, childcare, parentcare, their own bodies, the cost of nappy laundry, contractual obligations to save for education, and to whom the precious ones belong, if it comes to that, as it can do.

As if you can predict anything at all. I run my eye over Libby and Adam. I suppose you can predict a few things. This document will not take too long to draft. Here are two charismatic, evenly matched specimens. The only oddness I note is Libby's habit of running her fingers down Adam's thigh to his knee, as if unconsciously stroking feathers. Feathers ruffled by discussion. By the ignominy of sitting in my office?

I see their shadowy outline through the frosted doors as they arrive for the next meeting. Adam's thumb caresses the top of mine as we shake hands. It's a fleeting sensation, like I've imagined it. I react by looking up swiftly into his face. Is that amusement lurking behind his opaque blue eyes? He's just testing, proving he's irresistible. Regaining his power on my turf. I've dealt with one or two charmers like Adam; I know better than to rise to the bait.

"As you know, this agreement sets out in detail the responsibilities and divisions of duty between yourselves, should you have a child. Once signed, these terms are legally binding and are enforceable when you're actively working towards a pregnancy." I pause. "Let's see how we're doing on the standard clauses. First question: childcare. One of you; other family; or bought services?"

"One of us," Libby answered.

"Depends on the day," said Adam.

"Huh?" Libby was surprised.

"What if I have to work?"

"But your time is flexible. You can't take on a lesson if you know you're not free."

"But I may have to. I may want to. My time is flexible not to suit me but to suit my clients."

I interject quietly. "It sounds like you need to make provision for outside help too. Let's return to this later. Let's look at . . ." I skip the question of financial responsibility for the moment, thinking I know the answer to that.

Then I declare decisively, "I need five minutes privately with each of you."

I lead Adam to the small conference room. I ask him if he wants separate representation.

"What do you advise?"

"You only need it if you feel the contract would be unfair to you. If, generally, you are both of one mind, it's not required."

We are sitting adjacent to each other at one end of the oval table. He pulls his chair forward so his knees touch mine. I can't be sure if this is deliberate. "I'll stick with you," he says. "I'm sure we'll be fine."

I know I should stay away from this type. "That's settled then," I say blandly, letting the file I'm holding brush across his knees as I stand up. He follows me back to my office, walking closer than is appropriate. I can feel him in my space. But I don't turn around to check, so I can't be too sure if he's blowing into my hair. There's mischief in his soul. It takes one to recognise one.

I lead Libby to the conference room. I look into her striking eyes, so large and clear. "You must run through these questions at home," I insist. "It's best if the first objection to any clause is aired early on. You'll both have time to think it over by the next meeting. It'll be easier then to reach a compromise."

"He's a hothead," Libby says. "He makes snap decisions. But yes, we'll thrash out some of this before we see you again."

There is something else I want to mention to the two of them once we are back in the crisp white confines of my office.

"It can be a strain drafting the pre-concep," I begin delicately. "Although we recommend it, you need to know that having a contract does not necessarily lead to having a child. With these high infertility rates . . ." I shrug. There's no legal reason for me to provide this disheartening fact, but I feel obliged to. It rarely stops anyone from proceeding.

Libby brushes aside the comment. "Oh, Lena, let's sort out the contract and then worry about whether we'll be among the lucky few or not. We've got a good chance. Adam is superfit, you know."

My desk reflects a distorted image of the superfit Adam. I sneak a look at the real thing. Tall, broad-shouldered. Wavy dark hair. Carries off a bandana. Fine-featured. Looks good in polo shirt and baggy shorts. I haven't seen him in shorts, but he's a tennis instructor, so I imagine he spends some of his working life in them. At the moment he's wearing grey casual trousers and a light-blue jumper.

"See you in a week or so," I say, watching them leave. Adam

catches my lingering eye. He gives a half smile, a satisfied "gotcha" expression on his face. We are similar animals. Except he rates higher on the scale of beauty. In my book.

I am a connoisseur of the stolen moment. I collect these, the moments focused on me, thieving from a time that is not mine, from a story that is not mine. From a man who is not mine. I daisy chain these moments to make a play to amuse myself. I call it *Preludes and Elusions*.

Sometimes I can't be sure if these delicious momentary encounters really took place or my mind converted a pencil scratch into an ink sketch. I like beginnings. Newness. The start of something. The first locked glances. The first electric touches. That's where my interest lies.

"Beauty is to be admired," Clara remarks, on the button, walking in as Libby and Adam depart.

"That one knows he's a leopard," I tell her. "He flaunts his spots without thinking about it."

She looks at me keenly, but sees I'm grinning.

"They're a sweet couple," I say. "This will be over in a few weeks. File closed."

My desk bleeps thrice: a prompt to call my mother. I click my tongue and re-set the reminder. I'm momentarily distracted from what I was explaining to Libby and Adam, who are leaning back into the white chairs in front of me.

"He's in a huge rush," Libby says, taking over confidently and talking about Adam as if he wasn't there. "You'd think the oestrogen in the water has made men develop body clocks. At thirty-six!"

Adam is examining the aluminium floor lamp with a jaded eye. I start again, diplomatically. "How did you get on with the latest draft I sent?"

"Adam's a bit sick of discussion. But as we've sorted out the financial responsibilities and the child-hours, he says to just go with the standard format for the rest."

"Right. Standard terms. Each infidelity will cost one million," I say cheerfully. I want him to sit up now, but am unprepared for his sudden vehemence.

"This isn't a pre-nup." His voice is raised. "What's infidelity got to do with conception?"

"I was joking," I reply, "but since you ask the question . . . plenty." I glance at Libby, who is suppressing laughter. "Anything can be covered in the pre-concep," I continue. "Undesirable behaviour can be curbed for the sake of the child's welfare. Any habits you dislike . . ." This is one of the ways I amuse myself.

Adam's body stiffens and puffs out. One glance at the rage on his face and I know I have made a mistake. Mentally, I scold myself.

Libby lays a calming hand on his arm. "She's teasing us," she says. "Of course, we could put in 'the child must have the Gillick cheekbones but not the temper'."

I rush headlong into being serious, hoping to deflect his glower. "There are just a few points left on which I require your feedback. You two are on a roll; let's tie it up next time."

It only takes another ten days and we are at our last meeting. There's very little to amend from the most recent drafts I'd sent out. We discuss the minutiae, because I'm paid to get that right, for half an hour. Libby excuses herself to use the washroom. I gaze at Adam's image in my desk when something makes me look up.

He's making a moue with his lips. Waiting for a reaction. I'm suddenly conscious that my lipstick is a hot pink. My Schiaparelli party pink. It strikes me that I've been applying a steadily brighter shade of pink with each visit of the Larsen-Gillick couple. I'm embarrassed, but I will brazen it out. I curl my tongue into my mouth behind closed lips, so he can make out that it's a secret smile. I won't let it break out. It will be held in; mine. He leans across the desk and puts his lips close to my right ear. I can't be sure I've heard clearly. It sounds like: "Luscious pink." My eyes look up at his, querying. He returns my look innocently. I frown into the distance, betrayed; then I turn my attention to some papers.

When Libby returns I tell them that I'll send out final copies of the document for both of them to sign. I stand up to shake hands. "Good luck," I say, and funnily enough, I mean it. I want this couple to succeed. I always do at this concluding moment. Adam squeezes my hand tight, mumbles a thank you and rushes off. He has a coaching appointment.

Libby lingers. "Care for a coffee?" she asks. "That underwater café downstairs looked so inviting."

I hesitate. It's a quarter past three. The meeting has finished earlier than I expected. I don't usually socialise like this, but I accept. "Yes, that would be nice." My legal relationship with them is almost over.

We go down to Aquascope on the ground floor. It's situated beneath the swimming pool, entry to which is on the third floor. The bottom of the swimming pool, also the ceiling of the café, is a toughened translucent glass. Hazy shapes of swimmers flutter above us. The wall to the street is clear glass and the other three walls are ultramarine blue. I feel unsteady in here, even when sitting down. It's like having an out-of-body experience. I breathe deeply and focus on the sunburst of yellow coral painted in the centre of the glass table.

Libby launches into amusing gossip from Stilling Environment, making me laugh. Then she dives into a spate of questions about my work. She is so direct and forceful, it is hard to give guarded replies and I find myself being more honest than usual.

Adam's gloss has a brooding underside, I think to myself, but Libby's brilliance is steadfast. She will be a good mother. I am about to tell her so when I realise it's after four o'clock. "I must get back now," I exclaim.

As we walk towards the door Libby asks impishly, "Is your own pre-concep drawn up ready for when you decide to have children?"

I should brush away this question. Instead I reply with rare candour. "I don't need a pre-concep."

"Would you advise that?"

"Let's not talk about what I would advise. Most people want a contract. It makes the game serious. I meant that I don't intend to have a child. So there should be no need."

Libby looked so baffled that I carried on.

"We legislate for most things, but the law can't predict human behaviour. In everyday life removed from the contract, couples have to find their own logistical and emotional solutions.

Sometimes the pre-concep worsens the situation. When it is clearly not being adhered to, one party feels wronged and bitter. Time spent in conflict would be better spent with the child."

As I speak it dawns on me that having my name bandied about in court is troubling me more than I have admitted.

Libby persists. "But why no child?"

I sigh. "I think I know too much. I get all the feedback, after. To improve the agreements, to add in clauses we didn't think about before." I force a smile. "I'm of the firm opinion that I will be a sure-shot for pre- *and* post-natal depression."

Before she can drown me with another "Why?" I press the lift button.

That was last October and I hadn't seen either of them since. I'd asked Jolie how Libby was getting on and the response was "Fine." I didn't ask about Adam. But whenever I spotted someone who looked vaguely like him, his face would come sharply into focus. His shoulders, his hands. His hair.

I hadn't thought about his voice. Until last week. I had left late from work after a drinks do for a colleague from the Macedonia office. I was standing by the lift at the car-charge depot. I had just entered my bay number and put away the swipe card when my arms were gripped from behind. For a second, I felt blind terror.

"Hello, Lena." It took me a heartbeat to recognise the voice at my neck. My scream was aborted as the voice continued, "I must speak to you. Now."

It was Adam who had seized my arms. My handbag dangled from three fingers, which I curled tightly around the strap. My wrenched wrists were held fast by my coccyx. Adam turned me around and started walking me back to Walczak Tower. "Let's go to your office."

I struggled to free myself, but was surprised at just how physically ineffectual I was. He held my wrists behind me with one hand, and walked by my side, pull-pushing me along. I hadn't managed to articulate any actual words.

"We're going to talk." The grim set of his lips gave me a sinking feeling.

"My arms . . . Let go . . ."

He replied roughly, angrily. "I'm not letting go till we get to your office."

I knew I was scared because I had an urge to giggle. It's my default setting when I really don't know what to do.

Adam got the security fob out of my handbag. We took the lift up. He marched me into my office. The lamp came on.

"My arms hurt," I protested, as he imprisoned them behind me again. He pressed me back into the metal edge of my desk. I squared my shoulders. I would not be cowed by his burning eyes. The next moment he let my left arm go free, but began rattling my body with my right arm, bruising me, swearing at me, spittle landing on my cheek. I recoiled involuntarily from his name-calling. I couldn't even think with my head being shaken off my neck.

"Stop. Please stop." I realised I was crying. "Why are you doing this?"

The slamming stopped.

"Why are you calling me a vile bitch?" My voice broke on "vile". This was the least hurtful label he'd thrown at me in the space of a minute.

"Didn't you hear me, bitch?" he said. "It's your fault. And after wasting our time and money."

"What?" I was still puzzled.

"Libby," he said, his tone even nastier and his face in a snarl, "has spent all these months *considering* whether to conceive a child. I told her, 'If anything in the pre-concep is bothering you, redraft the damn thing however you want.' But no, it's not the contract bothering her. It's the bloody lawyer."

He put both hands on my shoulders and shook me violently. "What did you say to her, bitch?"

"I didn't say anything . . ." I faltered, finding it difficult to speak. "Why do you think –"

"Yesterday I had enough of Libby's *considering*." He loosened his grip again. "We had an . . ." He paused. "I tore up the contract. But guess what Libby said. She said, 'No point in that anyway. When the expert's experience is that the agreements come to naught after the child is born, and when the expert isn't prepared to get on the child tramline . . .'"

His hand dug into my shoulder like he wanted my bone to

crumble. "Libby wonders why I begrudge her time to think. *Time to think*. That's what the woman says." Then he was shouting. "How can you be an expert when you haven't even had a child?"

"I never claimed to be an expert." My voice quavered. "I just . . . made the mistake of . . . giving my opinion."

"Who asked for your opinion?" He was still very loud. I hoped someone would hear and come in to see what was going on.

"I honestly didn't mean to put her off the idea." I felt near to tears again.

He was silent. I stuttered on. "Believe me, I wasn't giving advice . . . I was just . . . answering her questions."

"So answer this," he whispered. "What were you playing at with me?" He held my arm. My skin prickled. He was in my space, his body only two centimetres from mine. I tried to shake free my captive right arm.

"Same as you."

"You think?"

"I think."

But I wasn't sure now. I like the sudden surprise of arousal and the dispelling of it, out of necessity. I can go too far, but only for an instant, then I slide back to equilibrium. I don't want to prolong stolen moments, not even into an hour; the fleeting ephemerality is the thing. Nothing could be worse than having the object of your lightning fantasy loll around your feet all day.

Adam's game was slightly different. His rules included violence.

"No," I said. I pushed at him with my free arm, and pulled at his shoulder. "No. I don't like force."

But the man was not for swerving. "You don't like," he said. "Tell me something different, bitch."

I was squashed back against the desk; he was pressed into me, and there wasn't anywhere to go. For a few seconds, I went limp. I felt his hand on the hem of my skirt, lifting, dragging it up to the top of my thigh. He put his mouth to my ear. I heard: "Luscious pink."

I detected laughter in his whisper. Betrayed, I frowned into the middle distance before stamping my heel on his toes and poking two fingers into his eyes.

He took both hands off me to clutch at his eyes. I escaped to the door, opened it, and ran down the corridor to the next office, slipping into the darkened space. He had followed me to the door, but he wouldn't dare assault me in another office. Would he?

I waited. There was silence. I didn't care to peep out into the corridor. I smoothed down my hair with my fingers, righted my clothes, and rubbed my arms where the bruises would come up. There were clicks and little clacks, unidentifiable sounds outside. I shivered. Eventually I talked myself into running fast past my office and to the lift; a sanctuary that came for me no sooner than I had touched the button.

I took it down to the main entrance. I hobbled to the security desk with a conspicuous limp. The guard on duty was a man whom I recognised, but whose name I didn't know. I do now. His name's Izhar.

"I slipped in the washroom on the seventh floor" – I winced as I spoke – "and barely managed to get to the lift. It's so painful. I think I've sprained my ankle."

I flopped down on a chair. I think I really did look stricken and drained, because Izhar displayed the right degree of concern.

"Do you need a doctor?" he asked. "Or shall I call a cab for you?"

"A cab would be good," I said, "but I've left my handbag in my office. Will you be able to bring it down for me, please?"

"I can't leave my post, but I can ring security on the fifth. If he comes down to take my place, I could . . ."

"Whatever. Please arrange it. I don't think I can put any weight on this ankle." As an afterthought, I said, "Oh, I hope my client found his way out."

"The big guy?"

"Yes. He's gone?"

"Yeah 'bout fifteen minutes ago."

Izhar retrieved my bag while another guard manned the desk. He called me a cab and solicitously put me in it.

In a short while I was in the safety of my home but I couldn't sleep. I was too disturbed. I don't like violence. In any form. I don't like having to resort to it. I hoped I had not damaged Adam's pretty eyes.

I didn't think I could face my office the next day, but I couldn't excuse myself either. I went in to spend the day creeping about in my own space except for two meetings. I left early, just as the light was fading. I looked over my shoulder all the way to the car-charge depot. As I approached the car lift, the curly-haired youth in the cubicle, another familiar face whose name I didn't know, slid open the window to call to me. He was angry.

"Your car came down last night," he said, "and there was no one waiting to claim it." Before I could apologise, he went on. "You're lucky I knew it was yours. I could have let them tow it away. But I used my pass to send it back to your berth. There's a fine slapped on it."

I thanked him. I explained there had been a sudden emergency and I'd had to return to the office. I drove home.

Strangely, sleep is now a problem. Not in the sense of insomnia. The problem is my recurring dream. In my dream, Adam stalks me. He seizes my arms from behind. He marches me into my office and gives me an earful of abuse. I cry. He calms down. He takes hold of me again, pushes up my skirt. I yield.

In another week's time, the dream will cease; I'm sure of it. But right now, I can't help but loiter outside Walczak Tower in the dark. Straining to hear footfalls behind me. Waiting for a leopard to finish the kill. But the temper tantrum may have passed. The air around me remains unruffled. There is no heavy breathing. I fear that I am in no danger at all.

JAMES' JAM SANDWICH STAND-OFF
Richard Milward

James has the sweetest breath in Teesside. He does a burp, and smiles. He finishes off that last jam sandwich with eyes watering, then scribbles on the jar: 8/10. Chucking the crusts in the bin, James wipes his leaking brow with a bit of kitchen roll, then staggers upstairs to his bathroom. He peers into his own face for a while, eyes rolling round and round the surface of the mirror. He splashes his cheeks with cold water, and accidentally splashes his reflection as well.

"Uuuurghhhhhh," say the both of them.

They glance at each other again, though they can't really bear the sight of each other. The mirror would love to smash James' face in. James would love to smash the mirror.

Coughing, James turns his attention to that last jam sandwich again. He grins. Then, he grabs one side of the toilet seat and, with his other hand, makes himself sick. He tickles his epiglottis furiously, like a miniature boxer throwing punches at a pink, miniature speedball. If you can imagine the inside of James' mouth as a dark, miniature boxing ring with lots of rowdy enzymes and teeth for seats, now imagine the boxing ring getting suddenly flooded with green bile and red jam.

James spews ecstatically into the toilet. James spews accidentally up his nostrils. Then James snoozes sadly on the cistern.

"Uhhhh," he groans. He regrets eating the eleventh jam

sandwich, not to mention the twelfth and the thirteenth and the fourteenth and the sixteenth. The fifteenth he has no qualms about, however; it was absolutely delicious! 10/10 for Gloria and her ravishing raspberries.

Unsticking his forehead from the cistern, James blinks pukey eyelids then stands up carefully on the slippery tiles. He washes his mouth out again with cold water, while his reflection sniggers at him. It's the seventh time James has been sick this morning.

It's only 10 a.m. James' strawberry-shaped alarm clock tells him that, as he slumps back down the stairs, bent double. James hobbles back into the kitchen, where all his jam-making apparatus is set up. There's strawberries soaking in sugar; cherries bubbling and burping on the hob; jam jars sunning themselves on the draining board; plum jam settling on the worktop. James cringes. He hates plums. However, his arch nemesis – Mr Summerbottom – won the gold rosette at last year's fair for his "lovely and smooth" plum jam, and there's no chance he's seeing that old bastard picking up the honours again this year. James would love to take Mr Summerbottom's plums in his fist and twist them until they explode, then boil those manky old plums into jam and force-feed Mr Summerbottom them until he cries. The fruit, that is. Not his actual bollocks.

Stirring a knob of butter into the cherry jam (to exterminate the scum forming on top), James glances again at the plum jam, settling in the non-stick pan. Inside his belly, another shallow tide is forming. James retches thin air. He keeps thinking the plum mixture looks like the insides of a woman's pregnant belly, with floating bits of placenta, purple matter and dirty red blood cells. No amount of crushing or beating or pulverising with the fork could eliminate the plums' stubborn skins this morning. The other week James ordered an automatic hand blender from his sacred catalogue of kitchen utensils, but unfortunately he hasn't allowed the full 28 days for delivery. He bangs his fists up and down on the Formica. All he wants is lovely and smooth jam!!

James feels weak, like a car filled with out-of-date custard instead of petrol. He wants a sit-down but, on the other hand, he also wants his gold rosette.

Every August, in the run-up to the Jams, Marmalades and

Honeys competition at the summer fair, James' bathroom becomes a Roman vomitorium. However, while the Romans enjoyed sicking up their delicious din-dins just so they could squeeze in more delicious din-dins, James isn't actually that big a fan of jam. He sees it as fruity murder.

However, fruit must be murdered, if James wishes to see his arch nemesis with rosette envy. Who knows; Mr Summerbottom may even take home the infamous Booby Prize, awarded to the creator of the Year's Worst Jam. James laughs so hard, he has to steady himself on the edge of the sink, nearly baulking again. Behind him, the cherry jam burps, teasing him.

James considers charging upstairs to be sick once more in the toilet (he's not keen on being sick in kitchen sinks, especially when you're trying to sterilise jam jars in them), when suddenly there's a rapid knocka-knocka-knocka on his flat door. All groggy, James pulls himself together, and pulls himself towards the door. With one twist of the key and one twist of the handle, James lets the light of the corridor into his shady flat, then gently focuses on the postman standing there in his chubby blue uniform.

"Got these for you, pal," the postman announces, passing James a square FedEx box, with a few brown circulars on top. James says, "Cheers," or something to that effect.

Shutting the door again, James carries the package and the circulars into his living room/dining room. He chucks the circulars onto his circular coffee table, uninterested. Then, he rubs his chin, pondering what's inside the FedEx box. The parcel is a perfect cuboid, sealed tightly round each edge with matt-silver duct tape. James' address is written on the top in neat marker pen, and the postage cost £1.69.

James scratches the back of his neck. For some reason, the parcel appears to be humming. Furrowing his face, James listens closely to the FedEx box, then gradually the furrows turn upside down and he finds himself grinning wildly in the quiet of the flat. The automatic hand blender, he thinks, ravenously tearing off the duct tape with his teeth. Momentarily, all thoughts of sickness and plum placenta disperse. His hot belly acid transforms into a cool, pacific pond.

The automatic hand blender, he thinks again. Someone must've switched it on by mistake, before packaging . . .

James hopes the batteries will last the day. As he finally extracts the last of the duct tape from the edges of the FedEx box, the humming becomes more pronounced, like a sine wave getting pummelled in a liquidiser. It sounds like an almighty powerful hand blender all right, James thinks. He grins.

Pulling open the flaps of the parcel, suddenly the humming becomes a rambunctious buzzing, and James' face drops. He vomits his throbbing heart into his mouth. His breath becomes a whirlwind, and his hands become whirlpools of sweat.

Instead of an automatic hand blender, a large, fluffy honeybee pokes its head out from a crack in the cardboard. Before James can reseal the box with the crispy slivers of duct tape strewn about the flat, suddenly the crack bursts open completely and the box fires five hundred ill-tempered, claustrophobic bees into his living room/dining room. James screams. Then, he leaps head first at his settee, curls up in a ball, and hopes to God the bees find their own way out.

"The key's in the door, the key's in the door," he yelps, to no avail.

A few of the insects sniff round him, but for the most part remain locked in a tight five-hundred-strong tornado, dancing for him in the centre of the room. The bees are all startled as well, suddenly released from their cardboard jail; bashing into each other and screaming and firing their stings willy-nilly into James' carpet, like suicide bombers. James covers his head, writhing round the leather sofa, dodging the poisonous Kamikaze missiles. He's in so much shock, he can't even muster a cry for help or a teardrop, instead just clinging nervously to the leather, like the back of a friendly cow. Both James and the cow are soon drenched in sweat.

After five more minutes of clinging and perspiring, the intense hum of the bees appears to subside, and the venomous rainfall of stingers dries up. James gradually opens one eyelid, fearing a squirt of poison into his precious little peepers. He wonders if it's all just a terrible dream. Perhaps Gloria's raspberries had hallucinogenic properties, or perhaps he just hasn't been getting enough sleep.

After a further five minutes of furtiveness, finally both of James' eyes are open again. He peers gingerly from the fleshy sofa to each wall of the living room/dining room, then down to the carpet, then across into the kitchen, then he vomits his heart into his mouth again. His hands turn into swimming pools again.

The tornado of bees has taken over James' kitchen, like a dizzy dictatorship, tucking into his jam. James grunts into the crease running down the sofa arm. He pulls the odd stray stinger out of his jumper sleeves and trouser legs, then pulls himself slowly slowly from the settee, leaving behind the wet silhouette of a very frightened young man.

The silhouette watches with a pained expression as James surreptitiously rolls up his copy of yesterday's *Times*, eyeballing the bees, all of them humming together like a giant, gaseous harmonica.

Gritting his teeth, with one hand James undoes the lock on his French windows then carefully slides them open, revealing the wind and the lovely view of the car park. James glances at the back of Palladium Pets, opposite his flat – he wonders if they'd be interested in taking five hundred bees off his hands. He blows a raspberry.

In the kitchen, the rampant bee-tornado gradually shrinks, as one by one the insects realise they've entered a paradise of sweet, jammy nectar. Black-and-yellow bodies begin to line the pans of settling preserve; others do the backstroke in the boiling cherry mixture, blissfully half dead. The more ecstatic the critters get, the higher the pitch of the humming. At the moment it's a C sharp, James reckons.

James hums as well, to himself, wondering what the hell he's going to do. Raising the rolled-up newspaper aloft with one hand, he uses the other to cover his eyeballs as he charges headlong into the kitchen. He emits a girly death cry. Swinging the paper wildly, blindly, James hears the overall hum of the bees become much deeper and more menacing, especially when *The Times* makes contact with bee-flesh. Grimacing, James spins and spins and spins round and round the sticky linoleum, crashing into things, paper baton flailing. Before long, he begins to feel hot stabs in his arms and face and legs, but he carries on spinning, spinning, spinning, until eventually he spins completely out of consciousness.

Half an hour later, James wakes with his face in his living room/dining room and his legs in his kitchen, covered head to toe in bee stings. He gurgles into the millimetre-long carpet. A pleasant breeze from the French windows wobbles his floppy hairdo. He coughs out a few millimetres of fluff. Unpeeling his face from the carpet, James rolls over, groaning when he sees the army of bees again, with only a few minor casualties collapsed on the lino. Getting up, James slams shut his French windows, thinking to himself: Sacré bleu!

Hopeless tears slide down his cheeks, like ski-jumpers heading for certain death. James feels as if he's been bathing in a sea of nettles and Olbas Oil. Sniffing, he trudges up his spiral staircase, and back into the bathroom. Underneath the sink, there's a small cupboard filled with potions and elixirs and pills and anti-continence syrup and herbal Viagra, as well as a beautiful, golden can of Wasp-Eze. Uncapping the lid, James huffs and puffs through gritted teeth, as he douses himself in the wet spray. The cold antiseptic scratches into his scarlet bites, making him wince then smile, wince then smile, wince then smile.

He decides to strip off completely, piling his clothes on top of the sick-flecked cistern, then spraying up and down his naked body with the Wasp-Eze. His cock and balls shrivel up, recoiling in fear at the thought of being stung.

Frowning, James glances at his red-and-white polka-dotted flesh. Once he's completely coated in a light mist of anti-bee gas, James pulls on his clothes again and scampers back down the staircase. He cringes at the noise of flapping wings reverberating through the building, wishing he could just get on with the jam-making and vomiting, in peace.

He sighs, standing poised in the entrance to the kitchen, Wasp-Eze aloft. He feels like Robert De Niro or Al Pacino, with a .44 Magnum. He feels like a complete fucking idiot.

In the kitchen, the bees are still greedily devouring his fruit preserves. The hot cherry jam has not only a layer of frothy scum bubbling on top again, but also a layer of fluffy bees, chomping and caramelising and congealing into some kind of sweet, filthy death orgy. Over on the worktop, the brainier bees are blissfully tucking into the strawberries soaking in sugar and the plums settling in the non-stick pan, miniscule grins elongating their little faces. Elsewhere, the demented ones carry on whizzing through the air, crashing into each other and laughing, completely drunk on sucrose. They're up to about E flat now.

James bares his gnashers, then lets out another almighty death cry, firing Wasp-Eze into the kitchen. At first it works quite well, dispersing the bee-tornado, all the little critters dive-bombing into the tiled corners of the room, shitting themselves. However, it's only a 125 ml canister of Wasp-Eze and, before long, the nozzle splutters and spits out its final pathetic, dying breaths.

Yet again, it's James' turn to shit himself. As you'd expect, the bees aren't very happy with him. After regrouping, about one hundred of the black-and-yellow bastards charge bums first at James' head, giving him a sort of impromptu lobotomy with their stingers. James' forehead expands to twice its normal size, and cracks open, leaking pus. His eyes nearly fall out, so lubricated they are with tears and fear.

James falls to the ground again. He falls head first, hammering the stings further into his face and forehead. Above him, all the bees appear to be laughing, wings clapping hysterically. It's a chord this time: D Major 7.

James clambers gingerly back to his feet, wishing he had a white flag or white tea towel, to surrender to the bees. He can hardly see the bee-tornado any more, so swollen are his eyelids. He splutters a few more panicky breaths. He reaches half blind for his kitchen cupboards, in one last-ditch attempt to dispose of the little rotters.

Over on the worktops, James' precious preserves are almost completely demolished; however, he still has a few pots of Robertson's ready-mixed fruit jams in his cupboard. Removing a few jars, James softly bats away the odd bee with his forearm, flinching. He's aware his dreams will be plagued with plagues of bees for years to come. He sulks as best he can with his tight, tender face.

With hands the size of purple boxing gloves, James carries the jam jars through to his living room/dining room, and painfully unscrews the lids. Then, as discreetly as possible, he scoops out handfuls of sticky strawberry and gooey gooseberry, and smothers himself from head to toe, turning his skin and clothes into a thick landscape of jam. He creates delicious hillocks in place of his buttocks, sweet seascapes down his legs, and marmalade moors round and round his midriff.

He feels like a knight, smothered in gloopy armour. Only James' tear-stained eyeballs peer out from the mixture, wary and exposed. He takes a deep breath – accidentally filling his lungs with jam – then slithers back into the kitchen. At first the bees ignore him, so occupied they are with the bubbling and sizzling pots and pans. James stamps his foot, impatiently, leaving behind a sticky footprint.

The bees prick their ears up. One by one, then twenty by twenty, they catch a whiff of James' jammy body, the fresh coating glistening with blissful deliciousness! The bees lick their lips and bat their wings together, high-fiveing each other. James smirks, shutting his eyes, feeling his jam-armour getting heavier and furrier under the weight of four hundred-odd insects. Then he cringes, listening to the greedy bastards slurping and masticating and burping all over his flesh and precious sweater. Wriggle, wriggle, wriggle. Flap, land, flap, land, flap, land. Slurp slurp burp!

Once all the bees are safely nestled in his armpits and chin and groin etc., James surreptitiously begins to walk backwards, out of the kitchen. Taking care not to disturb the bees, he treads slowly slowly slooooooooooowly towards the front door. He twists the key anticlockwise again, and the handle. On opening the door, the air displacement rattles the bees momentarily, but luckily they stay fixed to his gluey red, black and purple flesh. James hobbles down the corridor, to the sound of Chopin's *Funeral March*, orchestrated by the bees' wings.

As James makes his way through the estate, passers-by stop passing by to stand and stare at him and his overcoat of bees.

"Are you all right?"

"Ha ha ha ha ha. Look at you!"

"What the fuck are you doing?" they say.

James doesn't reply though, so scared he is of opening his mouth and allowing the black-and-yellow pests into his digestive system. He's aware he's got quite a bit of tantalising jam down there, as well.

James can hardly breathe. There's a tiny gap in the jam to allow the odd inhalation through the left corner of his mouth, but more often than not he ends up having to spit out a stray bee with the following exhalation. He trundles slowly round the edge of the houses, with soft elephant steps.

Arms outstretched, James bumbles past the row of parked cars on Aspen Drive, feeling red hot and humiliated. As if it wasn't bad enough wearing a boiling boiler suit of angry insects, James notices all the cars are laughing at him as he treads past. Or rather, there's one Sierra in particular that's absolutely killing itself, rocking back and forth on the side of the pavement. Through one of the eye-gaps, James spots that bastard Mr Summerbottom sat behind the wheel, absolutely creased up. Next to Summerbottom, there's a telescope on a tripod, trained directly on James' distant living room/dining room window.

Mr Summerbottom holds a handkerchief to his mouth, firing hilarious spit and bogies at it. James furrows his brow, furrowing the bees as well. As he stands there, James' sad outline shimmers silver, all the little wings catching the daylight.

"Lovely *outfit*," Mr Summerbottom sniggers behind the handkerchief, behind the wheel, behind the windscreen, behind James.

James decides to remain silent. He's always admired himself for his passive-aggressiveness in situations involving horrible, threatening people and, in any case, speaking would only result in a colon full of honeybees. So, he just stands and glares at Mr Summerbottom, shakes his head softly from side to side, and walks on. As James trudges forwards, Summerbottom continues grinning into his hanky, but with a bit less conviction this time. He watches James retreat in his rear-view mirror, treading ever so carefully towards the edge of the meandering beck. For a few seconds, he watches James standing by the battered stone wall, the bees and jam all mingled like a filthy woolly jumper. Mr Summerbottom sniggers again, though it's not half as fun when the butt of your joke is all the way over there, out of earshot. He bites his lip. Putting away his handkerchief, Summerbottom keeps his eyes fixed on the miniature James standing by the miniature beck in his rear-view mirror. He watches James gently clamber on top of the stone wall, arms held out like a fat, hairy tightrope walker.

It was worth it, after all, he thinks, coaxing all those bees into the FedEx box!

James looks like an absolute wally. Mr Summerbottom is just about to reach for his camera, when all of a sudden he stops sniggering, watching – with some dismay – James hurtling head first into the murky, stagnant beck below. Miniature James disappears completely from the rear-view mirror.

Mr Summerbottom panics, heart punishing his arteries. Quickly disassembling his telescope, Summerbottom shudders in his mahogany chinos. He misses the ignition a few times with his Ferrari key ring, then finally manages to set off, away away away from the bubbling beck. As he drives, he hopes to God he left no fingerprints on the FedEx box, or on any of those bees. At no point does he hope young James is all right.

The estate falls quiet. As the Ford Sierra fades to a bee-sized speck on the horizon, ever so slowly, two crimson, human hands re-emerge from the depths of the grubby beck.

Finally free of the bees, James clambers up his staircase, leaving behind less and less wet footprints on every step. He's absolutely drenched, but somehow the sickly cold feels fresh on his prickly stings. James unpeels his sodden clothes and chucks them in a pile next to his bed, making a soggy cotton octopus on the carpet. As he shakes a few droplets from his fingers, James watches a cloud of bees whizz past the window, and he sighs.

With only a day to go until the summer fair, James wraps himself in a huge towelling dressing gown, then plods back downstairs to set to work on the jam again. He rubs his oversized head.

Rolling up the fluffy sleeves, James tries his best to salvage the remnants of the cherry jam, picking out bits of lost wings and stings, and shovelling it into a fresh jar, teaspoon by teaspoon. It certainly smells delectable, James thinks, though he's not in the mood to lick the spoon. He's had more than enough jam for one day.

Sniffing, James hobbles painfully over to the opposite worktop, where the hot, sterilised lids are draining. He screws one tightly onto his jar of molten cherries, then puts it to rest in the cool dark of his cupboard. He wishes he could climb into that cupboard too, and drift off into a sweet, cherry-flavoured dream. Instead though, he decides to tuck himself up in his own bed, in his own cupboard-sized bedroom, in the cool dark of his duvet. His whole body feels like he's just emerged from an iron maiden, and he groans with half achyness and pleasure. As James sinks softly softly into the mattress and shuts the bedcovers over the top of his body, he is just about to drop off safely to Nod when the front door wakes him, screaming, "Knocka-knocka-knocka!"

James hides beneath his duvet, fearing another visit from the bees. He waits for the knocking to stop, before lurching downstairs. Clinging to his trembling banister, James sees on the carpet a Delivery Notification note from FedEx:

SORRY YOU WERE OUT. WE TRIED TO DELIVER
YOUR *automatic hand blender*

James frowns, tearing the note into 1,021 tiny pieces.

The next day, James sits scowling at the back of Mr Summerbottom's bald spot, waiting anxiously for the result of the Jams, Marmalades and Honeys competition. The summer fair is in full swing, and so is summer. Kids with daisy chains and farmers and farmers' wives in frocks and wellies are all congregated under the giant circus marquee, with faces ranging from well done to medium rare and bloody.

Despite the sun making all the pretty flowers and cows and gigantic freak-show vegetables shine that bit more colourfully, James feels distinctly downtrodden. His face has swollen to the size of a red hot-air balloon, hidden crudely behind a brown Paisley headscarf. He vibrates on his chair, staring through oversized sunglasses as the fat, hog-faced compère hands over a trophy to a woman with a pair of massive melons.

Slumping in his chair, James crosses his chubby fingers as the master of ceremonies finally comes to the Jams, Marmalades and Honeys result. The compère holds the 24-carat-gold rosette between forefinger and thumb as he speaks into the microphone. James trembles, crossing his fingers, toes, legs, arms, and eyes. He feels sick with anticipation.

"And the winner is . . ." the compère begins, the shiny rosette burning a hole through James' sunglasses, ". . . Mr Summerbottom! For his delicious honey, ingeniously crafted using the honey of bees infused with – what does it say here? – strawberry, cherry and plum preserves. Truly wonderful! Well done, well done . . ."

James' heart lands with a thump on the bottom floor of his belly. He weeps silently behind his headscarf, blurring Mr Summerbottom as he strides arrogantly onto the makeshift stage, to accept his blurry rosette. James keeps his limbs crossed, hoping the stage collapses under the weight of Summerbottom's ego, although unfortunately it's been reinforced with steel scaffolding.

"And now for the Booby Prize," says the compère, once Summerbottom has safely left the stage. James gulps. With a smirk, the hog-faced master of ceremonies bellows into the microphone, "The *winner* of this year's worst jam goes to . . . wait for it . . . James McGunnell, for his putrid cherry jam! Haw haw haw. Come on up, James. Be a good sport now . . ."

James' heart hits the nylon floor of the marquee. He wishes he could shrink to the size of a bee, and surreptitiously fly off back to his bedroom, to cry sticky viscous tears and hum *Ave Maria*. However, goaded and prodded by the farmers and farmers' wives, James rises awkwardly from his plastic seat. As he reaches the stage to collect his prize – a plaster-of-Paris female bosom – he again prays for the stage to collapse. Mr Summerbottom sits in Row G, cackling hysterically, the peal of his laughter gently shaking the nuts and bolts out of the scaffolding.

"Why didn't you like the jam?" James whimpers to the compère, eyes all swollen and gloomy.

"It tasted of bloody Wasp-Eze, James," is the reply, just as the stage gives way beneath them.

FOUR CORNERS
Margi Williams

T. Blue leaned back against the bar with one long leg resting on the rail. A dark-skinned girl in tight jeans and a pearl-button shirt tied up at her waist was shimmying between the cowboys, bucking her hips to the jukebox music. He pushed the wide brim of his Resistol hat up off his brow with the top of his beer bottle and whistled under his breath. He hadn't noticed Hank standing next to him.

"That little gal is courtin' herself a mess a trouble, don't you think?" Hank sipped his beer.

"Trouble is a two-lane road. I expect she'd be bringin' just as good as she'd be gettin'."

"I don't suppose I'd mind some of that trouble, just for one night."

"Yep." T. Blue nodded thoughtfully. "Problem is it ain't never for just one night. Women bring the kinda trouble that is damn hard to shake."

They weighed the truth of this and fell silent.

T. Blue was eight years past forty. He had chased a ranching life across the desert borders of Arizona and New Mexico, occasionally even up into Wyoming and Montana, but it was the desert landscape that had suited him best. In 1997 he started buying up hardscrabble acreage in the New Mexico desert, a landscape that supported only bitterness and despair. He had four thousand acres now, enough ground and water to run upwards of a thousand head and keep his own head above water – just. T. Blue and Hank first met at an outfit up in northern Arizona in 1992. Hank had rodeoed for almost seven years, about a year too long in actual fact, and when T. Blue started buying up land Hank signed on. T. Blue had been married at the time. Hank was not the type and as it turned out T. Blue wasn't either but it took him at least two tries to get that straight.

The girl made her way to the bar and snaked herself up to T. Blue. Hank saw it coming and walked out front for a smoke.

"Well, are you a long tall Texan?" She sang the words, her body still moving to the music.

"Nope, I ain't from Texas." He could see her ribcage expand when she breathed and the swell of her breasts under the shirt.

"Well, I'm from round here, right over in Manuelito." She looked him up and down. "Where you from?"

"I got a place in the Bisti Badlands about an hour up north, near Four Corners and the reservation."

She stopped her dancing. "You don't live out there unless you got either part Indian or part Mexican. Which are you?"

"I suppose I probably got some a both."

"Then where'd them blue eyes come from?" She ran her fingers up his arm. She had long pink nails and smelled like cotton candy.

"I got some other thrown in." He watched her hand sliding over his starched white sleeve and thought he ought to stop it.

"So what are you doing in a big city like Gallup on a hot Saturday night?"

"'Bout the same as you and everybody else I expect."

She gave him a smooth white smile and leaned back against the bar, her long hair shining blue-black in the light.

"My name is Cherine."

"T. Blue," he said and chose not to think where this was headed.

Women fell fast and hard for T. Blue; it was just a fact, even with his hair turning grey. He was on the high side of six feet, all bone and sinew with a leathery hide and desert-blue eyes. He had a long, disjointed gait and was known to have a gentle hand. In the Bisti Badlands it was a short walk between life and death and T. Blue was a man who knew to watch his step.

Under the full moon T. Blue backed the old pick-up out of the gravel parking lot and fishtailed onto the highway, hitting about ninety before he relaxed into the drive up to the Badlands. Cherine sat between Hank and T. Blue with her hand on T. Blue's thigh. The alkaline desert soil glowed, incandescent under the moonlight; underneath lay the bones of a thousand dead Indians. A jackrabbit, its long ears flat back, zigzagged wildly across the highway and a coyote loped along next to the road, its eyes turned fluorescent in the headlights. Cherine looked out the window past T. Blue.

"You know this is where they finally captured Geronimo, out here. Five thousand cavalry soldiers and the Mexican army hunted him for a year. They had these big Presidios down in Chihuahua and Fronteras. Geronimo just had a cave and about thirty-five men. Once, all five thousand waited for days at the entrance to the cave. Figured they had 'em, then a scout spotted Geronimo and his men over at Skeleton Canyon in Arizona. All these years later and no one has ever found that other way out. It's called Geronimo's Cave."

"How 'bout that . . . You Apache?" asked Hank who had some Apache himself.

"Just my grandpa, long way back, but I s'pose I might have some of Geronimo's blood."

T. Blue looked over at the low mountains and thought he'd like to head out there someday and have a see.

Cherine started to nod off on his shoulder and she was snoring lightly when they pulled into the ranch. Hank climbed out of the cab, leaving the door open in case Cherine decided to come out his side, and said, "'Night." He walked out to the trailer he kept by the barn and T. Blue smiled hearing him cursing his own short legs and bad luck.

Cherine stretched and seemed to take a minute to register where she was, then she remembered and leaned her weight into T. Blue's side and lifted his arm around her shoulder.

"So this your ranch, huh. Are you gonna take me inside?"

He was suddenly very tired. He didn't mind her company, but that was all he wanted now.

"Yeah, this is it. Not the Ponderosa, but we do all right. I tell you what, girl. We just had a long drive – I know you're tired and I sure as hell am. Let's just git on inside and say we call it a night."

"Sure, life is full of surprises," she said as she wrapped her arms around his waist and walked inside.

In the early light he could see that she was older than he had thought – maybe thirty – and that put his mind at ease. She was small and lithe; she looked like a milk-chocolate wafer, delicate against the white of his sheets. Last night she had run her long nails up and down his spine and told him desert stories. He fell asleep listening to the story of the Painted Woman, mother of the Apaches, and he dreamed about the woman he had sent away, the woman who, long ago, had carried his child.

T. Blue never liked waking up with a woman; he preferred to be up and out before their morning talk started. But this morning he sat on his bed and waited for her. When she woke she stretched and smiled.

"Hey you, how come you're already dressed?" She sat up in bed.

T. Blue was surprised to see that she made no move to cover her bare breasts and gave some thought to climbing back into the bed with her. In this case his habit of early rising may have been ill advised but he figured Hank was already getting to it and the morning feed on the ranch was a two-man job. He handed her one of his shirts from behind the door.

"Here. You hungry?"

"What have you got? I'm pretty good in the kitchen if you like spicy."

He smiled for the first time that morning. "Yeah, I bet."

She got out of bed, went into the bathroom and peed with the door open, still talking about breakfast.

In the kitchen he poured himself a cup of coffee and looked out to see Hank, with the dogs, loading up the Cushman with hay.

"Uh, you OK here? I gotta get some things done."

"Sure. You mind if I shower? Then I'll make somethin' for us all to eat. I figure I got at least a day out here I might as well be useful. I'm gonna need a ride back into town, you know."

He hadn't thought about this. Already things were more complicated than he liked and it was more than he wanted to think about just then.

"Let's just cross that bridge a little later, all right?" He reached for the doorknob.

She smiled again. "OK."

He thought about her smile and bare breasts as he walked toward Hank. Hank stopped loading as T. Blue walked up.

"So how is it that I was the one looking for trouble and it's trouble that found you?"

"I just dunno." He really didn't. "She's all right though – she ain't what I thought. She told some good stories, and she's gonna cook us breakfast." He leaned down and scratched the dog's anvil head and it thumped its back leg in the dirt.

"My grandmother can tell stories and make breakfast. You tellin' me you brought that little gal all the way out for a bedtime story and some pancakes? What's the matter with you? You ain't that old."

"I dunno. It just wasn't like that, that's all."

Hank shook his head and went to feed the horses.

T. Blue was relieved to see Cherine was fully dressed when she called them in for breakfast. She laid out a platter of scrambled eggs, bacon, ham and toast; T. Blue saw jam and salsa he didn't know he had. Hank propped both elbows up on the table and started to eat, telling her about his rodeo days, spitting bits of egg while he talked. She put her hand on T. Blue's leg under the table while she listened to Hank. T. Blue listened too. It wasn't anything he hadn't heard before; still Hank told a story true and they held up over time. The food was good and T. Blue liked her hand on his leg. She was making little circles with her fingers and he slid his chair toward her just a bit. Hank stopped talking long enough for T. Blue to speak.

"Tell Hank that story you was telling me last night, 'bout that Apache Painted Woman and her babies."

Cherine's eyes grew serious; she straightened in her chair and began her story.

"White Painted Woman was one of the first Apaches. Children were born to the Apaches but a Giant would come and eat them. Women went around weepin' and wailin', 'How can people be created on this earth?' Then White Painted Woman started prayin' and it started rainin'. She lay down, real still, her face toward the water comin' down from Heaven. Her children was born from that water, so they called them Children of the Water. Then she looked up at God – or I guess she called him Ussen, being Apache – and prayed for the safety of her children. Her prayers were answered and the Giant was gone for ever after. Now the Indians say White Painted woman is the mother of all Apache."

They all three sat in silence and looked out at the stillness of the desert until Cherine spoke again.

"Imagine all this out there – everything west of the Rio Grande was Apache, either Mescalero or Chiricahua, and this one woman was the mother of it all."

T. Blue got lost in his imagining of cowboys, Indians, and the mighty Rio Grande. He felt he'd missed the best of this country by about a hundred years.

Hank looked her over and broke the silence. "Where you from anyway?"

"Right now in Manuelito, but I've been all around Arizona and New Mexico, even Colorado some. All the Four Corners except Utah – Mormons give me the creeps, especially the ones they got out around here. These got a whole bunch of wives and spooky little kids. I'm a one-man woman, that ain't for me. I can take a lot but that's just past the limit."

T. Blue had never really paid the Mormons too much mind but he liked a woman who had opinions and she had put some thought into this.

"What kind work you do?" Hank asked.

T. Blue knew that Hank's question was real; he loved hearing about different jobs, weighing his options, thinking if he'd like to do that. They'd met some oil workers once in Albuquerque. They were shit-faced drunk, happy to talk about their jobs until some women showed up and Hank never got to hear the end. Hank still liked to wonder about the oil rigs.

"Oh, I done all kinds of things. I managed a trailer park in Wupatki, Arizona – they were real nice people but mostly old and I hated to see 'em dying out there all alone. I spent some time up at Cortez – they got some good people there. I lived on the reservation over to Jicarilla but you know Indians. So I came back over here. I do bookkeeping for a couple of auto-supply stores. I'm real good at math. You wouldn't believe the mark-ups. Ask me if you need to buy something and I can tell you what it should cost. Things are kind a slow right now, so I got some time on my hands."

"Whooee, you really have been all over. I should have been listening to your stories, not the other way around." Hank was impressed; T. Blue knew he did admire diversity, Hank having somewhat of a singular focus himself.

They started to clean the dishes but she sent them out.

"I got nothing else to do today. You two got territory to cover."

They whistled the dogs up into the truck and while they were driving out to the fence line Hank asked, "You drivin' her back down tonight?"

"It's a long drive," T. Blue said.

"Well I ain't going. I got *CSI Miami* tonight."

"I guess it's a wait see."

T. Blue saw Hank smile out the window.

They spent the day mending fences; the snap of wire and the dogs panting in the high desert heat were the only sounds for hours. T. Blue thought about Cherine, and wondered if she was given to fits of tears or broken-bottle rages; it was always hard to tell. Hank started humming to himself. T. Blue was annoyed at the interruption but didn't say anything and Hank hummed all the way back to the ranch.

Cherine had defrosted a roast and was cooking it with some potatoes. When she watched the two men walk their dusty boots across the clean linoleum she put her hands on her hips and furrowed her brow at them. T. Blue met her gaze.

"You don't got much that ain't frozen or turnin' green in this kitchen," Cherine said.

As he washed his hands T. Blue thought of all the good reasons he wasn't married and didn't respond. Hank wanted to watch *CSI* so Cherine made up a plate for him to take back to his trailer and T. Blue started thinking about the drive down to Manuelito. He was sitting on the sofa mapping a plan when Cherine came in and sat beside him and started to rub his neck and shoulders. He hung his head down.

"That feels good."

"Yeah," Cherine said kneading her hands into his shoulders. "I think we got some promises made that ain't been delivered."

She unbuttoned his shirt and he felt her head against the wiry grey hair on his chest; the slow beat of her heart pulsed through him as she moved her hands down his long body. He leaned back on the sofa and closed his eyes, thinking about places both soft and hard. He pulled her up on him; her hair swung down across his face and he forgot about the drive to Manuelito.

In the morning his fingers were tracing the line of her belly when she opened her eyes. She looked at him for a minute, like a little girl, then laid back and watched his hand.

"I'm pregnant."

He jerked his hand away. "What! We just . . ."

"No, about three months. I just thought . . . Well, I am."

T. Blue sat up and regarded her seriously. "You got a husband?"

"Nope. The daddy – he's a Indian from over at the Jicarilla reservation. He don't know. I ain't raisin' my kid out there with a bunch of drunk Indians."

T. Blue crossed his hands behind his head and looked up at the ceiling, thinking about all the uninhabited wombs he'd visited over the years, and believed this was a first.

"I didn't hurt it did I . . . ? You?"

"Naw, it's just like a little lima bean swishing around in there right now."

T. Blue put his hand back on her belly as if to keep the baby safe.

"So you got a baby growin' in there."

"Yeah." She looked scared. "You got kids?"

"No, I got some ex-wives but no kids." He thought again about the woman he had sent away all those years ago.

Cherine rolled over on her side away from him. "You're the first person that knows."

He reached his hand back to her abdomen and she didn't pull away. This was as close as T. Blue had ever been to a baby; he'd seen lots of calves and foals, but never a baby. He ran his eyes over the rise and fall of her bare hip, and thought he was lying in bed next to a goddamn miracle.

216

"You got family?" he asked.

"Everybody's got family."

"Uh, I guess that's a fact."

He wanted to turn her toward him, to feel her body against his own, but she pulled her knees up, made herself smaller and moved further away.

T. Blue got out of bed and went to the bathroom. When he came back into the room he stood above her and thought she might be back asleep. She looked like a tiny bird and he had an urge to scoop her up and put her into a nest. He sat down on the side of the bed, pulled on yesterday's jeans, then with his elbows on his knees he bowed his head and ran his fingers through his hair. Cherine rolled over and looked at the arc of his bare back. She wanted to reach out her arm but she stopped herself.

Without turning T. Blue spoke.

"I've been thinkin' I'd like to have a ride out, see some of the country, maybe have a look-see at ol' Geronimo's Cave. You think you could find it?"

"Yeah, I been there lots. It's a ways out there y' know."

"I know. Hank can take on here for today. He won't like it but it won't kill him neither."

He turned his face to her and Cherine pulled the sheets up under her chin.

"I'd like to take you out there. You'll like it." She smiled at him.

"Yeah," said T. Blue. "Where do you suppose that Painted Lady laid down out there?"

"I dunno," said Cherine, "but they got a prayer place for her out on the reservation at Jicarilla."

"That right?"

"Yep, I've been thinkin' 'bout that prayer lately. Wanna hear it?"

He was surprised. "You know it?"

"Sure I know it else I wouldn't a asked."

"OK then, let's hear it."

Cherine closed her eyes and began to recite:

We come to White Painted Woman,
We come to her in hope of blessing.
We come to her in hope of all her different fruits.

In hope of the long life she bestows, we come to her.
In hope of this holy truth.

T. Blue felt an unfamiliar confusion, then the weight of the sadness of all of his years came down upon him. He lay back down across the bed. Cherine's eyes were still closed from the recitation of her prayer. He reached for her; she opened her eyes at his touch and then lay down beside him. Wordlessly, they lay together and watched the clouds gathering in the desert sky.

THE OTHER SIDE OF ANYTHING
Jon Elsom

William looks from Maya to the grime-streaked window. He walks to it and peers through a twice-cracked pane. Below, barely discernible through the murk, a boat passes heading upriver. An Enforcement boat, two huge spotlights turning on its deck like great socketless eyeballs, playing illuminated shafts onto north and south banks in turn. Across the vast dark grey of the Thames the lights gash the high concrete wall that runs the length of the north bank, obscuring everything beyond. William wonders how many tonight on that other side of the city will be bringing new life into this world. If they will be glad to be doing it.

Maya gasps and William turns to look. The back of her head, hair tied back with twine from a potato sack, hoops of ebony through her ear lobes, blued sea-horse tattoo behind the right ear. She has sat up a little higher in the bathwater and is feeling her lower abdomen.

Stronger? William asks. The sea horse bobs up and down. He returns to the side of the bath and kneels. He places the back of his hand on Maya's cheek. He feels suddenly self-conscious, wondering why this is considered a tender gesture – using the hard impersonal back of the hand – thinking it is a gesture that belongs to someone else. He moves his hand to cup the slick nape of Maya's neck, looks down across her half-submerged body. The vast alien hump of her stomach is obscene against the soft white familiarity of everything else: the welcoming flat hips, the silken thighs, slender arms. He looks below the colossal mound at the clump of pubic hair sprouting into the bathwater, a mutant sea anemone clamped around the entrance of a subterranean cave, waving gently in the current.

Maya inclines her head back and draws in a lungful of damp air, readying herself. William is humbled. She lowers her chin and stares ahead, concentrating. Then her neck goes rigid, her carotid artery straining against the flesh containing it. She grasps the rusty bath rails with both hands, tiny ferrous flakes cascading into the water below. William plucks something from the floor. A length of brown cloth torn from an old skirt, a sponge sewn into its middle. He offers it to Maya. She does not look. William is attuned to her signals, and returns it to the floor. A faint grunt issues from deep inside Maya's throat. Are you sure? asks William. She nods once. Her knuckles pop out as her fists clench around the rails. Her whole frame tautens and her eyes snap shut. She sometimes comes like this, thinks William. He banishes the thought as a new, cold anxiety fills his veins.

The contraction takes hold. It builds quickly, surprising them both. Oh God, Maya gasps. William, watching, prays for the pain to come and go swiftly. For the sake of Maya, yes. But also for the sake of silence. Most importantly, for that.

She stays tensed, eyes sewn together. William checks his watch: two and a half minutes since the previous one. Christ. They've been at this for only an hour and a half, since the first contraction came, gripping them both with anguish. This is even quicker, William thinks, than last time. Then, Maya told him, the entire process lasted little beyond three hours. But this is no time to think of before. With the fruits of that labour desiccated and in the ground, there will never be a time to think of it.

Maya opens her eyes and exhales through barely open lips. Coming out of it, he thinks. Good girl, hardly a sound. But it will be more difficult now.

As Maya leans back against the chipped porcelain, William regards her tenderly. He knows how hard this is – at least, he knows as well as a man these days can know. After the first time, she told it to him in forensic detail. She recounted every twinge, stab and push in a manner almost venomous, as if briefly loathing him for never being obliged to experience it – to make him feel something of it. How it was laughable that a pamphlet she had read could describe a contraction as a rolling wave that swells and breaks onto a beach. These words are written, she said, by shamans intent on the preservation at all costs of the human race. For Maya, each contraction had felt as though someone had inserted both hands into her and was manually ripping her uterus in two. She felt the pulling, burning, tearing as surely as if it were happening. Not for her a tranquil, wave-fringed beach but an Omaha of violent assault. This is how it was then, and is now, William knows. He will not do her the disservice of asking her about it; he can tell it is the same pain.

This time, though, the baby will probably come even more quickly than the last. They both know, from clandestine research, it used to be the way when women bore their first rapidly that the second would be quicker still. When women were allowed to bear a second. Quickly is not the Holy Grail expectant women should seek, William knows. Quickly means fewer analgesic hormones are released. Quickly means more pain. And more noise.

Maya's breathing is slowing now. There will be only a couple of minutes or so until the next one. William rises and goes to a low oil-drum table, on which is an old wind-up radio. He cranks the handle and turns the dial. The static hisses as though the radio despises being awoken from its slumber. William eventually finds the State radio station, which has shifted frequency inexplicably again. Poorly tuned Prokofiev pours from the dented black box. William turns it up, overloud. Maya looks across at him. He can see she is terrified. Immediately, Feeney bangs on the stud wall from next door. Little fucking weasel, William thinks. If we banged every time you masturbated we'd have no skin on our knuckles. William thumps back. It goes quiet next door. Privacy is not what it used to be. Compared to when these units in the old warehouse used to belong to solvent citizens who owned twenty thousand square feet each instead of nearer two hundred, privacy is now almost an obsolete term.

William resumes his place on the floor by the bath. He feels the cold draining into his knees and shifts onto his right haunch.

As he settles into place another contraction begins. This time

Maya jerks forward as though at the whim of an irritable puppet master. She rises out of the water onto her knees and leans forward, grasping the far end of the bath. William looks at her heavy, hanging belly. What are you in there? he thinks.

This one comes like a freight train. Maya's features distort into an unrecognisable arrangement. He can see she is trying to keep it in, but a scream is surely building in her larynx, gathering strength, ready to burst through. A scream would end everything here and now, William knows. With so many of them packed tight in this building, as in all other buildings on this forsaken side of the river, and with so many on the payroll – in one way or another – of the Enforcement, a scream is sure to be investigated. They both know this. He picks up the length of brown cloth again and, this time without asking, wraps it around Maya's head, positioning the sponge tight across her mouth, knotting the fabric twice at the back below her crown.

The gag in place, Maya allows herself a mid-pitch moan. It is not quite a scream, and all on one perfect note of D. It sounds to William like one of the fork-lift trucks at the Base. He glances at both partition walls, but no protest is made. Prokofiev has given way to an old-time folk song, a group of lilting Irishmen promising, "All around my hat, I will wear the green willow". Just loudly enough, William hopes. Maya's perfect D fades and becomes a loud exhalation of air which ends with a protracted grunt. Her body releases its tension and she lowers her arms to her knees, panting. William removes the gag.

I can't, Maya whispers. Can't do this.

Yes, you can, William replies softly, moving a sodden strand of hair back behind her ear. You'll do this, he says, and we'll do what we planned. Everything will work just like we said.

It is not just the pain that is exhausting her, William knows, though that is, clearly, almost unbearable as each searing paroxysm grips her insides. No, it is the non-expression of it. Like trying to internalise an earthquake. She doesn't need to tell him. He sees it in her face now as if it has been written there with a piece of jagged glass.

I felt it move down, she whispers. It came down, but I was frightened. I sent it back. I'm sorry. I sent it back.

It's OK. It'll come now.

I'm sorry.

No.

William strokes Maya's hair and looks down. Pieces of her uterus wall are swirling in the bath. The water, as clean as they could get it, is now losing what translucency it had, tinged with pink and clouding with mucus.

William feels a fresh wave of panic. What are they doing? What have they been thinking? This plan of theirs, they'll never get away with it. Never get away. No one leaves the city limits, no one crosses from south to north, north to south. The days of that are long gone. And if they manage to cross the city borders, what then? A diseased land, unfit for habitation. Mile upon mile of infected, infested non-England. They are insane to be considering it. And even if the air they breathe is kind to them – how far, for how long, will they be pursued?

Not for the first time William wishes for an end to it. For the five months he has known of this pregnancy he has returned to this terrible desire time and again. In his waking hours he has daydreamed of miscarriage, of stillbirth. The anguish and grief sugared by liberty – such as liberty is in this changed world. By nightfall often he has been filled with remorse. How can he wish for another dead child? And then sleep has restored him with hope, his dreams bringing glory days of new life, renewed love, another beginning in a far-off place.

And now, again, right at the end of it, William prays to a God he has never acknowledged for a lifeless child, a folded cipher slipping silently, eyes closed, from the womb. The perfect life already lived.

A splash brings him back. Maya has shifted her weight forward again and grasps the bath-end. William leans in and wraps the gag around her head, tying it in place once more. He pulls a folded towel from under the bath and sets it beside him.

This time the contraction is different, William can see. Swift and brutal, still. But with new purpose. Maya's body goes rigid as an ancient groan issues from behind the sponge. Some German techno-pop from a vanished decade has usurped the Irish folk singers. It is a fuller, louder sound, William is relieved to note.

Her body slackens off for a second. Then it stiffens again as another massive downward thrust takes over. There is nothing either of them can do now. It is out of their hands. Another guttural moan, another seismic shift. The water is filling now with physical matter. A chunk of something bloody bobs out from under Maya's rear.

Suddenly, she is on the move. Maya leans back, her hands on the bath's sides taking her weight. She flips her legs out in front of her, aided by her buoyancy. From her new position she glances up at William.

So it is now, he thinks.

Maya's body stiffens once more, the sinews in her forearms raised as she grasps the bath-sides, her legs pivoting open, knees lifting, calves resting on cold porcelain. A growl comes from behind the sponge, inhuman, drawn out. William looks down. She is opening. He looks at her face to offer encouragement but she is lost to him now. Under the water her flesh parts further. Maya's growl turns into a high-pitched squeal that reminds him of cattle being slaughtered at the city market. The flesh parts further still, obscenely wide.

And then he can see it, a smooth livid dome, smeared with gore, both slick and encrusted. The dome grows, pushing fantastically through the opening ill-designed for its purpose. At the point of highest tension, just when it seems this labial collar will simply burst and shred, the head clears the opening and the traumatised flesh snaps in around the baby's neck. William is struck dumb. He has not seen this before. The last time was different, valid, State-run. He had been present at the clinic, but like all male partners had not been permitted to witness the delivery; if a child was born handicapped through disease or malnourishment it would not be seen by its parents. It would not, either, see the day out.

William, frozen in fascinated terror, watches as the head pauses there, face down, immobile. This is a freak show, he thinks. It can't be supposed to happen like this. He wants to laugh out loud, nearly does, at the absurdity of it.

It's dead, he knows. It's not moving. I killed it. With my prayers. I willed it dead.

The head turns through ninety degrees away from him, as though driven by a clockwork mechanism. Far off in the distance, William hears Maya give a long, muffled sigh. Two arms spring out of her, followed by a torso, hips, two legs. The baby slides from her and into the water, accompanied by a firestorm of internal matter. My dead baby, William thinks. My perfect, tiny corpse. I am so sorry. I am so, so sorry. You could never have known but, believe me, you are better off this way.

Then the arms begin to flail about. The legs, too. Underwater, the creature propels itself away from Maya. Swimming, William thinks. A corpse swimming. A white rope of muscle trails behind it.

And then the creature turns its face towards William for the first time. His turn to gasp now. Impossibly tiny features, all in place, eyes still closed but mouth opening, closing, opening. He looks at Maya. She has sat back, spent, panting, no energy to lift her arms to remove her gag. William looks into the water again. He is paralysed. All he can do is kneel there, mute, unmoving. Then some synapse sparks off another and he knows what he must do. He plunges both hands into the water and takes hold of the creature within. Pulling it out he marvels at its strength, its warmth. He holds it up in front of him. A daughter. My daughter. Our daughter.

As the water drips from this girl-creature, she opens her eyes a little; the brightness of the blue startles William. The baby's mouth opens, quivers spastically. A squawk is forced from her by insistent lungs. She begins to cry. William reaches at once for the towel next to his feet and wraps it around the baby, right around, so as to muffle the mewling. It works a little, after a fashion.

William looks at Maya. She has managed to slide the gag down around her neck but lies immobile, devastated. Her mouth hangs open, saliva dangling from her lower lip. Her eyes meet his. There will be no smiles, he knows. Not in these circumstances. Not done this way. But, before the terror sets in, just for this moment, this is what they have, the two of them. This exchanged glance. This, and the bewildered whimpers coming from beneath the towel.

"If you do not breathe through writing, if you do not cry out in writing, or sing in writing, then don't write, because our culture has no use for it."

Anaïs Nin

THE COUSINS
Carol Wong

My mother is cleaning the house a day early. She's turned on the heavy vacuum cleaner, drowning out the sound of the TV with an unbearable whirr, manoeuvring it around me while I try to watch music videos, a *Seventeen* magazine on my lap. Usually cleaning the house is an all-day chore saved for Sundays, when she hands me the furniture polish with a stern look, pointing wordlessly at the coffee table, dining table and chairs. No TV, no phone, no going out until the chores are complete. I dread Sundays more than anything.

"Mom! It's Saturday," I yell over the noise. "What are you *doing*?"

She pushes the vacuum cleaner between the coffee table and couch, under the bridge formed by my legs. I reluctantly move them off the table. "The cousins. They coming tomorrow," she yells. "House need to look nice. Go clean up you room. You going to sleep in Gran'ma's room with Gran'ma."

"What? That is so not fair! Why doesn't Annie have to?"

"Lots things not fair. Go clean you room."

My grandmother on my father's side has lived with us for the past year. I've never lived with anyone so old before, seen them up close. Her white hair, the age spots dotting her face and neck, her milky eyes which she wipes vigorously with a handkerchief every morning were a shock to me when she arrived. She doesn't speak a word of English.

My grandmother doesn't do much with her days. She sleeps a lot, snoring so loudly you can hear her through the whole house. She walks around the neighbourhood sometimes, hands clasped behind her back, or reads a Chinese book in the backyard, smoking cigarettes. She has a constant hacking cough, like something is caught in her throat that she can't dislodge, and once in a while she spits in the backyard or on the street, disgusting blobs of snot, not caring if our neighbours see. It repulses me, but my parents never say anything. "That is *so* gross," I say every time, hoping she'll hear disapproval in my intonation.

Sometimes she says things to me in Chinese at the kitchen table, things I don't fully understand, but that I know are instructions to eat more rice or soup, use my chopsticks, sit up straight. She chews loudly with a slack jaw, so that you can see the food lolling around in her mouth, her dentures clicking against each other. Sometimes she tries to help in the kitchen, washing vegetables or stirring soups with a ladle, but my mother often shoos her away.

When she arrived a year ago, we watched from the living-room window as my father pulled into the driveway. She slowly got out of the car, stood beside it for a while, shifting from one foot to the other as if testing the ground. My father hauled a suitcase from the trunk and she stood there motionless, a duffle bag in her hand, a sheen of sweat on her forehead. It was a hot day in August and she was wearing a wool pants suit in a murky brown colour. She gazed at the house, her new home, with her curious family lined up at the window staring back at her.

My father told us to call her Poh Poh, Chinese for grandmother.

I didn't even know we had these cousins until last week, when my father told us at dinner. "We have family come to stay next week," he declared. "From California. My sister. And you cousins."

Annie and I stared at my parents. "What cousins?" I asked. "In California?"

My father nodded, continued to shovel rice in his mouth. "My sister have two boys," he said in between mouthfuls. "Alex and Sam."

My friends at school always talked about cousins, who would come over for birthdays or family dinners, as if they were siblings, but cooler versions of siblings. They tended to be older, perhaps in high school or university, could drink, went to parties. My friend Kathleen's cousins were good-looking older guys whom we not-so-secretly had crushes on. Her cousin Curtis had long hair, a black Trans Am, a bevy of girlfriends. I had always wanted cousins.

"How old are they?" I asked.

"Alex is thirteen, maybe fourteen. Younger one, nine or ten."

My father had spoken about a sister who lived in California, whom he'd not seen in years, but not of her kids. We got Christmas cards every year postmarked from California but the Chinese characters written inside were incomprehensible to me. When I explained to Kathleen how we didn't have any extended family around, how my parents immigrated here, leaving most of their families behind, she scrunched up her nose and looked simply confused.

I took a small comfort in knowing that we had these cousins; we were not the strange, rootless, marooned family I thought we were. My concept of relatives had been limited to curled black-and-white photos pasted in my parents' old photo albums – people I would never meet because they lived so far away, or were long dead. But now I had real ones.

On Sunday, my mother gets up early and takes a shower, blow-dries her hair, puts on a little make-up. I haven't seen her wear make-up in a long time, not since the Chinese Benevolent Association's annual Chinese New Year banquet, the one night a year she and my father would treat themselves to an evening out and a taxi ride home. She puts on black dress pants with a crease down the front, and a blue cotton blouse she ironed last night. I've never seen these clothes before; she must have bought them new. She opens all the windows in the house to let in some air. When she opens the window of my grandmother's room, she makes big waving motions for my grandmother to see. But my grandmother ignores them.

We wait in the living room, the news blaring on the TV, and I feel a nervousness come over me. The extent of our entertaining is when my father's friends from the restaurant come over for a meal, then play mah-jong at the kitchen table for hours into the night, the smell of stale cigarette smoke lingering in the house for days afterwards.

I stare blankly at the TV while Annie flips through her latest Nancy Drew. My mother fusses with her sleeves, unbuttoning the cuffs to roll them up, then deciding against it and rolling them down. She readjusts the bobby pin holding her hair back on one side, tightening it until it's smooth and taut behind her ear.

My grandmother is at the window, standing in her usual way: hands clasped behind her back, feet turned slightly out. Her face is expressionless. But I can hear her breathing heavily through her nose, the nervous clicking of her dentures.

We wait.

I must have fallen asleep on the couch. I wake up to the sound of the huge rattling Buick pulling into the driveway. My mother rushes to the front door, Annie and I trailing behind. My grandmother stays where she is, though. She lets out a big sigh as the car doors open and out step our new-found family.

Alex is the older one. He is thin and gangly, has thick eyebrows that nearly meet above his nose and jet-black hair that hangs in his eyes. Sam is younger, shorter and a bit heavier, with the same black hair. He has a big mole on his upper lip.

They peer at us as we stand in a row on the front doorstep. They don't look very Chinese, I think. They look Hawaiian, or something; their skin seems darker, less sallow, their eyes more round and creased than ours. I can't believe they are family.

My mother and aunt exchange a few Chinese words and awkward hugs. My father then introduces us, saying our names in turn, and our ages. "This is Lisa," he says, putting a hand on my shoulder. "She's twelve, almost as old as you, Alex."

"I'm thirteen," he says back to my father, as if it's a very important distinction. "I'll be fourteen in September."

"This is Annie. She's nine," my father continues, pointing at my sister.

Annie doesn't know where to look. Her Nancy Drew is still in her hand.

"Girls, this my sister. Aunty Susan."

I know her Chinese name is Soo Yung, but she must have changed it when she moved to California – just like my parents' names are now Richard and Linda, a far cry from the names they were born and grew up with. She looks about the same age as my mother, but she has stylish upswept hair, a polka-dot blouse, a silk scarf tied at her neck, eyebrows faint as shadows.

"Hi, girls," she says to us, bundling us in a hug. Her accent doesn't have the same Chinese twang that my mother's has, as if it has been smoothed away, a rough stone polished by her years in California. She sounds like someone who should be on TV.

My grandmother emerges from behind us. Aunty Susan takes a deep breath, then hugs her silently. My grandmother places stiff arms around her. There are no tears, no exclamations of joy.

We go into the house and my parents show them around, which doesn't take long. The boys will sleep in Annie's room and Aunty Susan in my bed. I've been moved into my grandmother's room on a newly bought air mattress and Annie will sleep in the living room. "Shouldn't they all be in Annie's room together?" I suggest to my mother quietly, hoping my tone sounds helpful.

"*Ai*, they be guest! Can't make them sleep on floor," she hisses.

We assemble on the couches and chairs in the living room.

"Aunty Susan and I not seen each other since you mom and I get married!" my father tells us.

"Yes," says Aunty Susan. "Almost fifteen years ago."

My mother puts a tray of Chinese tea and pound cake on the coffee table.

"Your house is lovely," Aunty Susan says.

"Ah, too messy at the moment," my mother says, waving apologetically. "We be fixing up the kitchen when we have time." What she means is, when we have money.

I survey the room, see it as our cousins might. The painted ceramic Buddha smiles at us from the mantel. A few peacock feathers sit in a vase, a large silk fan with luck symbols painted on it hangs on one wall. Chinese newspapers and magazines are piled under the coffee table. All the furniture is arranged to face our huge television, my father's leather recliner in prime viewing position. Everything still smells of Pledge and Windex, the tracks from the vacuum cleaner still fresh on the thick beige carpet. The room feels crowded, small and hot with all of us in it.

I settle into bed, on the air mattress on the floor of my grandmother's room. Annie's excited to be sleeping in the living room; it's as if we are all camping out in our own house. But I lie restless and cold under a sheet and the itchy wool blankets, thinking of Aunty Susan lying in my bed with its soft floral comforter.

I can smell the menthol of the greasy cream my grandmother rubs into her knees and knuckles every night. I don't want to be lying so close to her, don't want to see her this way, as if it's inappropriate somehow, as if I am seeing her in her underwear. Her pyjamas are a simple flannel version of her daytime clothes – a buttoned-up top and straight up-and-down slacks. I don't bother trying to read; I just want her to turn out the light and for sleep to come. I watch her comb her hair and can't help staring at her, just as my cousins did over dinner. Through the thin fabric of her pyjama top, I can see her braless breasts hanging down almost to her stomach.

I watch in disgust as she pops her dentures out, first the top set, then the bottom, dropping them in a glass of water by her bed. They are more like my aunt's perfect Hollywood teeth than my father's yellowed teeth, which have never seen a dentist. My disgust gives way to fascination as she taps some white powder into the glass, making it fizz; the fizz grows thicker, cloudier, obscuring the teeth for a moment, then dissipates, revealing the teeth again as if in a grin. Despite myself, I laugh. My grandmother just looks over at me sternly, unamused.

She closes her lips over her toothless gums, slips out of her slippers and swivels into bed. She reaches out without looking and switches off the bedside lamp. Within minutes she is snoring so loudly I have to put my pillow over my head to muffle the noise.

Aunty Susan, my grandmother and my mother are making won tons at the kitchen table, placing dollops of the pork mixture in rice-flour wrappers, dabbing the edges with egg before they twist them into their little parcels, putting them on a tray for cooking later. I hear their emphatic voices, the "Wah!"s rising up from time to time. There is a bit of laughter, which is reassuring, though it is not raucous laughter. It sounds polite, tentative.

My mother has gone back to her usual outfits of jogging-suit bottoms and fleece tops, hair pulled back in a stubby low ponytail. For her, first impressions are now over. Aunty Susan still looks immaculate, wearing a full face of make-up and a burgundy print dress. She looks dressed up as if she's going out somewhere fancy. Her hair has a slight curl to it which I envy; I've often asked my mother if I can get a perm but she always says I'm too young.

Aunty Susan comes in to check on the four of us as we sit in the living room, none of us talking.

"Why don't you guys go out and play, or something?" she asks us. Alex and I look at her in horror. We are not nine; we do not play.

"No thanks, Mom," Alex says to her.

I turn back to my well-worn *Seventeen*, while Annie writes in one of her notebooks. Sam is watching a re-run of *Happy Days*.

"All right," she says. She leaves a trail of perfume in her wake.

We sit around the dinner table, slurping our won ton soup from china spoons. Alex makes a joke under his breath to Sam, something about the won tons looking like horse's balls.

"How would *you* know," I say to Alex sharply, wanting to draw attention to his rudeness.

He shoots me a look that says *Shut up*. His dark eyes glare at me so intensely it catches me by surprise and I almost gasp. A flush comes to my cheeks, and a confusion rises up, like when the boys from school are at the mall, the boys who used to call me names, who I hate but somehow long for in equal measure.

"So where do you live in California?" I ask Aunty Susan, trying to join the adult conversation, to prove that I belong in it and not in Alex's jokes about horse balls.

"Well, we live in a city called Oakland. Kind of near San Francisco," she says to me. "My husband – your uncle – he's a doctor. Do you know what you might want to be when you grow up?" she asks me. I feel as if she's talking to a five-year-old.

"I don't know yet. Maybe an actress," I say. "I was in the school play last year."

"*Ai*," says my mother. "Why not be doctor? Make lots of money. And helping people."

"I want to be a writer," my sister pipes up. "I've already written a mystery story."

"Oh, I'd love to read that sometime!" says Aunty Susan in her perky voice.

"Aunty Susan have nice big house," my father says proudly. "Five bedrooms. And a swimming pool."

"Wah!" my mother says. "Must be very rich!"

"And two cars," my father continues. "Yeah!" he says with enthusiasm. He looks over at my grandmother, who doesn't lift her gaze from her soup bowl.

"That's right," says Aunty Susan. "We have a van, and a regular car too."

"Cool," says Annie.

In our neighbourhood no one has two cars. We were the first family we knew of that had a VCR, and that was a big coup.

My grandmother says something in Chinese that causes the parents to exchange glances. They say something back to her, something like, *It's for the best*, but I don't understand. I am too distracted by Alex across the table and how he is elbowing Sam. I feel Alex glance at me from time to time, but can't decide if I like it or not. Suddenly I wish I'd brushed my hair before dinner, put my lip-gloss on, worn a nicer top, the purple one that my friend Kathleen says really suits me.

The adults have cleared the dinner dishes and have brought up the card table from the basement to play mah-jong. As they lay the piece of green felt on the table that softens the noise, I tug at my father's sleeve. "Can I play?" I ask, wanting to escape having to hang out with my sister and the cousins.

"Can't play with five!" he says to me, as if I'm being silly. "Go play in the living room," he says. "Get to know you cousins. They leave in a few days, you know. Not much time left." He says this as if it's a warning.

The adults take their seats and four pairs of hands proceed to shuffle the pink-and-white tiles, making a loud noise. I slope back into the living room. Sam and Annie have got the Monopoly board out. Alex is sitting in my father's recliner, listening to his Walkman. I sit down in a huff and turn on the TV.

Soon Alex is bored. He takes off his headphones and starts riffling through the Chinese newspapers and magazines piled up underneath the coffee table. His look of scorn is clear. He picks up the open bag of salted dried plums that my grandmother likes, takes a whiff.

"Eww," he says. "What are these?"

I don't answer, focusing intently on my show. From the kitchen I can hear the adults talking while they play, the tossing of discarded tiles, the occasional "Pung" scattered in their conversation. I turn up the volume on the TV.

He gets up to inspect the ceramic Buddha on the mantel. It's a cheap one, bought in Chinatown years ago, its painted face almost lady-like with its rosy cheeks and lips. I realise it looks garish, naughty almost: Buddha in his reclining position, his breasts hanging over the rolls of his stomach, his face full of glee.

"Hey look," he says, seemingly to Sam. "He's got boobs!"

He fingers one of Buddha's nipples with his thumb and forefinger as if tuning a radio, making a squeaking sound as he does this. He laughs and Sam laughs and even Annie laughs too. Part of me wants to laugh, but I stare straight at the TV.

"Your house is weird," Alex tells me.

Just then we hear voices raised in the kitchen. My grandmother is yelling; my mother yells back. I hear my father and Aunty Susan say something in a calm voice, trying to be reasonable. I hear my grandmother's voice, louder than I've ever heard it: *What if I don't want to go?* I think she says. We all look in the direction of the living-room door, holding our breath. In our house, fights and arguments are a regular occurrence, but they would never take place in front of company.

We hear footsteps and my grandmother's door slam. My parents and Aunty Susan continue to talk in low voices. Then we hear them packing up the mah-jong set, putting it back in its zippered case. It dawns on me then, without explanation. Aunty Susan is taking my grandmother with her, back to California. That's why they're here.

The next day, my mother tells me to take Annie and the cousins to the local mall. "Do I have to?" I whine. She gives me five dollars so we can buy malts, paying me off. Before I can protest Annie is putting on her shoes and Aunty Susan is getting the boys' jackets. As we stand at the door, Aunty Susan covertly reaches into her leather purse and hands me a ten-dollar bill. "Get yourself some lunch if you want. Just make sure you don't all spoil your dinner. OK? I'm trusting you," she whispers. But I don't want to be trusted. I call my friend Kathleen before we leave, ask her to meet us at the food court. A friend will make this bearable, and Kathleen is my best friend. We walk to the mall, Alex kicking rocks ahead of him the whole way like soccer balls.

I lead us straight to the food court. As soon as I see Kathleen standing poised against the Orange Julius counter, twirling her blonde ponytail, fair legs bare in a miniskirt, I regret my invitation. When I introduce her to the cousins I can see her eyes widen slightly, taking in Alex's tall frame, his Nirvana T-shirt, the headphones around his neck. Even worse, I see Alex's eyes linger on her, stealing glances as we slurp milkshakes and munch on cheeseburgers.

"So . . ." Kathleen says to us both, looking from me to him and back again. "You two don't look much alike."

Alex and I glance at each other.

"My dad's white," he says. "I'm only half Chinese."

This possibility had never occurred to me.

"Actually . . ." He leans in close as if about to tell us a secret. "I'm a banana! Get it?"

I feel eyes on me, expecting me to know what this means. I want to pretend that I know; I don't want him to be one up on me, yet again. Luckily Annie swoops in.

"What do you mean, a banana?"

"You don't know what that *means*?" he asks, as if this is unbelievable. "Everyone at my school knows."

"What is it then?" Kathleen says. She can get away with it, asking these questions without fear of sounding stupid.

"You know. Yellow on the outside, white on the inside!"

Alex looks around, waiting for us to marvel at the concept. And it's true, the term seems an apt one; it unites us. I let myself smile. But then he says, "I mean, you guys aren't," indicating Annie and me. "You're Chinese through and through."

Annie and I look at each other. It sounds like a scornful

suggestion, cloaked in harmless words.

"I mean, look at you!" he says. "Your family is so much more . . . traditional. Than ours. That's all. That's all I'm saying."

Annie looks to me for guidance, to help her understand. Kathleen, too, is looking at me, for my judgement, whether she can laugh at this or not, whose side she should be on.

"We only eat Chinese food, like, once or twice a week, if that," Alex continues, as if bragging.

"I wish I was a banana," Annie says.

"No you don't!" I reproach her.

I feel something begin to crumble in me, and a lump forming in my throat. I will not cry in front of them, I think. I will not cry. I want to stand up and walk away from them all. But instead I continue to feign mild boredom, slurp on my milkshake, and hope for the conversation to end. But he won't stop talking.

"I suppose we'll be eating a lot more Chinese food once Grandma moves in with us. God." He rolls his eyes in dread. "Yum, more of Grandma's horse balls!" He winks at Sam.

"Shut *up*!" I say to him, louder than I thought it would come out. My sharp voice surprises everyone. Sam and Annie look up from their cheeseburgers. A few faces in the food court turn to look at us.

"Jeez, relax," Alex says to me, glancing around. "I'm only kidding."

"It's not funny. OK? So just shut up. She's our grandmother for God's sake."

When we get back to the house, I walk into my grandmother's room. She's packing her suitcase, folding her various pairs of brown or black slacks, her plain tops. She doesn't have many things; we never took her shopping, never really took her anywhere. She turns to look at me, and I see the milkiness in her eyes and something else – resignation. Maybe it's always been there.

I stand in the doorway not knowing what to say. She calls me over. From her nightstand she hands me a red lucky-money envelope; inside it is twenty dollars. I shake my head. She says something in Cantonese, closes my hand around the envelope, and turns back to her suitcase. I try to help her with the folding, but she shoos me away.

For dinner that night we have steamed fish, soup and rice. As we tear apart the fish with our chopsticks, I think of the time I accidentally swallowed a fish bone at dinner a few months ago and how it got stuck in my throat, how the stabbing pain brought tears to my eyes, and panic; and how my grandmother calmly told me to eat more rice to make it shift, to wash it down with some soup, how she rubbed my back in comforting circles. I never thanked her afterwards, but instead silently blamed her for making the fish for dinner in the first place.

On the cousins' last night with us, I help my mother chop the vegetables. A soup simmers on the stove, the rice cooker bubbles away. Aunty Susan sits with the boys at the kitchen table, playing cards. I can sense a shift in the room; my mother is feeling imminent relief, a weight about to be lifted. And now it's Aunty Susan whose perkiness seems to be waning, knowing her departure looms and that they are travelling back with one more person than they came with.

"Why does Grandma have to go?" I ask my mother in a low voice so they can't hear.

"Ah, is so much better for her," she whispers. "They have much bigger house. Lot more money. Can take better care." She turns to look at me. "Is much better for her. You understand?"

"Yeah," I say. "I know." But then I hear myself saying, "Doesn't she want to stay with us?"

"No matter. Is much better for her there." She says this firmly, a cue that she doesn't want to discuss it further. I think of the arguments in low voices that were just out of my reach all week and begin to understand: neither family really wanted her. I feel a twinge of guilt, that I was an unknowing party to it all.

My father enters the kitchen, back from his trip to Chinatown. The boys look up from their place at the table. He's carrying a rustling plastic bag, and as he comes closer, we can see its contents moving. I know then that my father has spared no expense on this final meal, as inside the bag, wrapped in newspaper, are three live crabs bought from the fish shop, chosen by my father and desperately trying to crawl out. Alex looks transfixed, Sam a little bit scared.

He puts the bag on the counter and my mother fearlessly reaches into it, pulling out one of the crabs, holding it by the back of its shell while the long spindly legs move frantically, pincers groping at air. I catch Alex's eye and even his gaze betrays a hint of horror, horror at what he knows is to come.

My father smiles. "King crab, on special!" he exclaims. "This good quality, real nice."

My mother runs the crab under the cold-water tap for a moment. Then she calmly places it on the heavy chopping board. Its legs scrabble at the wood, clawing, scratching. She holds the crab with one hand, and with the freshly sharpened cleaver in the other, whacks the legs of one side clean off in a quick, startling move that makes the counter shake. Sam and Aunty Susan gasp. The legs on the other side shoot straight out, horribly, and continue to grope, though more slowly now. I realise I'm staring too; I've seen my mother do this before, but now the violence of it seems excessive, ruthless. My mother whacks the legs off the other side, quickly, then scrapes all the contents of the chopping board into the sink. As she reaches into the bag for the next crab, I leave the room. I can't watch this time.

My father packs the suitcases into the trunk of the car while we say our goodbyes. Aunty Susan and my mother make us hug the cousins before they get in the car.

"Now say thank you to Aunty Linda, for letting us come to stay," Aunty Susan says to the boys.

"Thank you," they obediently repeat. Then, "See ya," they say to us, and they clamber into the back seat.

Aunty Susan turns to Annie and me. "Don't worry. We'll take care of your grandmother. She'll be all right." She bundles us into one of her perfume hugs. "We'll see you again real soon."

My grandmother is already in the front seat. I walk up to her rolled-down window. She pats me on the head, says something in her gravelly Chinese, smiles her denture smile. From my pocket I pull out the bag of salted dried plums and hand it to her. "Don't forget these," I say. "For the plane." She says thank you in Cantonese. That much I understand. *Do jeh.*

"Bye Poh Poh," I say.

I watch the car drive away; none of them looks back to wave.

That night the air mattresses are deflated and put away and I get to move back into my room. It feels bigger somehow, and a little bit empty. I fall asleep under my floral comforter, Aunty Susan's perfume still lingering in the air. I dream of my grandmother's dentures grinning at me in a fizzing glass, of her standing on the driveway of another new home, in her wool suit, blinking in the California sunshine.

PEARLS OF WISDOM
Lesley Saunders

There's a new key hanging on the hook by the front door. It's a little silver Yale on a plain silver ring. I don't know what it's for and I don't dare ask, but it wasn't there when we moved in two months ago.

I noticed it one evening. Mum was out cleaning, and I was sitting at the kitchen table doing my homework. There was a smash outside on the landing, then I heard some bloke shouting, and Kath next door screeching, "Get the *fuck* away from me!"

I tiptoed to the front door and peered through the spyhole. This bloke had hold of Kath. She was jackknifed over his knee, and he was wrenching her hair by the roots. His head was shaved and you could see the shelf where his brain ended. I thought he was strangling her. She was making this weird noise, like a dog whimpering. He'd knocked Mum's daffodils flying, and he was grinding dirt and dead flowers into the concrete with his boot. I didn't know what to do. I was thinking, "Call the police. Call the police." I was just about to run to the phone when they swung round. Then I could see they weren't fighting. They were kissing. Kath had her eyes shut, kissing him really hard, like she was chewing his face. Like she hated him.

I jerked away from the door. A dog was barking on the square in front of the flats. Then Kath's door slammed. When I looked through the spyhole again, the landing was empty. It was then I noticed the key. The sun was going down through the kitchen window and the light flickered over it. It looked like a little dying fish.

I didn't think any more about the key until I saw Mum slip it in her coat pocket before she went out for her prayer meeting last week. She thinks I didn't notice, but I notice everything.

Today, for instance, when I get home from school, I can tell she's been boiling rags again. For one thing the big aluminium pot she uses for the job is upside down on the draining board. Secondly, even though she's cooking some disgusting meaty thing in the oven, the kitchen still stinks like a swimming pool.

There's a pan of potatoes bubbling on the stove. The white transistor on the worktop is blaring, "*She loves you, yeah, yeah, yeah!*" She's wearing a polka-dot pinny, and scrubbing the worktop with Vim, the red knob of her elbow circling the air. She's scouring so hard she's going to wear it away. She must hear me come in because she glances over her shoulder.

"You're back," she says. "How was school?"

She gives me this fake little smile and turns back to her scrubbing.

"All right," I say.

"What lessons d'you have today?"

"French."

I don't know why I bother, because she never listens, but I start telling her how we had to imagine we were in Paris buying fruit from a market stall, when she turns round.

"What you doing?" she says.

She's not smiling now.

"Nothing. Just getting my homework books out."

"Put them away."

Her voice is like pelting stones.

"But –"

"Just do it."

The saucepan hisses and she runs to the stove and snatches it up. She takes it to the sink and empties the potatoes into a colander. Steam puffs up round her face. She looks like an evil genie escaping from a bottle. Her hair's pinned up in a pleat, and she's wearing a tight black skirt and stockings with seams. And while I'm shoving my books back in my bag, wondering why she's done up like Dracula's Bride, I knock the table. There's an almighty crash. Her crystal jug has fallen over and water is seeping across her white lace tablecloth.

"Look what you've done!" she shouts.

"It's only water."

"It's ruined."

She runs to the table and snatches up the knives and forks.

"Don't just stand there like a moron!" she shouts. "Fetch a cloth!"

"What are you making it posh for, anyway?" I say.

"Because."

"Because what?"

"Because Father Fergal's coming for tea."

My heart starts pounding. No one ever comes to tea. We always eat on our own. It's always just me and her. She's never invited a man to the flat.

"Why the hell does *he* have to come?"

I don't mean to shout but the words just fly out. Mum's leaning flat across the table, mopping up the water, but as soon as I say that, she stops dead. Her elbows jut into the air, her shoulder blades are sharp ridges under her blouse.

"What did you say?"

She turns and moves towards me. From the corner of my eye I see her take a fresh rag from her apron pocket and screw it into a ball.

"Sorry," I say.

"I *won't* have blasphemy in this house," she says.

"I didn't mean it."

"What do you think we are? Garbage? Like that Jezebel next door with her filthy mouth? Is that how I brought you up?"

I'm moving backwards across the kitchen. I crash into a chair.

"Answer me! Is it?"

The chair falls to the floor but I don't look down.

"Please," I say. "Don't."

My back thuds against the wall. Her face is close to mine. There are jazz-singer wings painted on her eyelids, her eyebrows are thick with kohl, and I realise she's got herself painted up for him. Her eyes are drilling into me. She lifts her hand towards my face. I can smell the bleach - it's really strong - and she's chanting

243

under her breath: "Forgive her, Lord, she knows not what she says." I swallow hard. My heart is banging. I close my eyes. Everything inside my head is black. My stomach is retching before she's even prised my mouth open.

There's a knock at the door.

I open my eyes in time to see Mum flinch. She narrows her eyes, and her lips go thin and hard. For a minute I think she's going to do it anyway. The cloth in her fist is so close that the stench of chlorine pricks my nose. But then she drops her arm, and turns away.

"Clear that table. Get a move on," she says, walking across the kitchen. She takes off her pinny. She runs her hand over the back of her skirt, and pats her hair. Then, as she walks towards the door, she says, "And don't embarrass me in front of him. Make sure you eat your food."

There's an order of nuns in the south of France called the Carthiginians. Sister Aloysius told us about them in French class. They're not allowed to talk. They're not even allowed to open their mouths in front of anyone. "The mouth is one of the filthiest parts of the body," says Sister Aloysius, "full of germs and slime. That's why we keep our mouths shut when we're eating. No one wants to see inside your mouth. It's God's reminder to us of our proximity to animals." At dinner time the Carthiginian nuns sit at long tables with partitions, so every sister is in her own private cubicle. No one can see her eating. I wish we could eat like that.

The front door whines open, and I hear Mum say, "Come in, Father. How are you?" with a pathetic little giggle.

She's never invited a man round since my dad left. I was only four then. I remember sitting on his knee and laughing while he traced his finger round my palm, saying, "Tickly round the garden, like a teddy bear." I can't remember what he looks like, only that he had really big hands, and that when he cuddled me he smelt of aftershave, and something else; a man smell I can't describe. I don't even know his name, or why he left. I asked her but she wouldn't tell me. She only said he never wanted to see either of us again.

The kitchen door opens and Father Fergal comes in. He's so tall he has to duck his head under the doorframe. His chin is rough and black where he hasn't shaved.

"So here's our little prodigy," he says, rubbing his hands together. "How's Theresa?"

"Fine, thank you."

He raises his eyebrows. I turn away to lay the fresh tablecloth so he won't see me blush. I don't know what she's been saying about me, or why he's calling me a prodigy. It's not like I'm bloody Mozart or something. I can feel his eyes on my back and it makes my stomach feel strange.

He's always looking at me weird. I've only ever seen him at Mass, and twice when he's visited my new school. All the other girls say he looks like a film star. He's always laughing and joking; even Sister Aloysius laughs at his jokes. Last time, he read a passage from the Bible, and told us a ghost story, but he kept looking over at me. I looked out the window, at the bluebells growing under the trees, but all the time I knew he was watching me. It was like he was telling the story just for me. When I looked back, he was staring straight at me. I kind of liked it, but my face started burning, and it felt like a tidal wave was crashing over my brain.

He sits down at the table opposite me. I try to make myself look up while he's talking but I can't because my head will start shaking and he will see. Mum puts a plate in front of him.

"Lovely, Denise," he says. "You can't beat home cooking."

He picks up his fork.

"How d'you like your new school, Theresa?"

He spikes a kidney and lifts it to his lips.

"Theresa's doing ever so well," says Mum, sliding into the chair beside him. "She's taking German, as well as French."

"That's grand," says the priest. "And a little bird tells me you're quite the musician."

I can't believe she's told him all this stuff, especially when she hates me playing the piano. I'm about to tell him about my grade five pieces, but she gets her oar in first.

"She's *very* talented," says Mum, "but she needs to concentrate on her studies. You can't make a living out of dreams."

Father Fergal is lifting the fork to his mouth. His lips open in a long, thin slit. The inside of his mouth is dark, almost purple, like the inside of a cave. He balances his knife and fork on the edge of his plate and makes a pyramid with his hands. His Adam's apple slides up and down his throat as he swallows.

"Well, Denise," he says, "you're never closer to God than when you're playing or listening to music."

Mum looks down at her dinner.

"Where do you practise, Theresa?"

"At school," I say.

He lifts his chin and runs a finger under his dog collar. His beard rubs against his fingernail with a little rasping sound.

"I've a smashing piano in the presbytery," he says.

"Really?" I say.

"I used to play myself, classical and jazz. In fact, I would've joined a band, if I hadn't had my vocation."

Mum glances at him sideways, like he's a traitor or something.

"Anyway," he says. "It's a sin to see such a fine instrument going to waste. Why don't you come and play after school?"

"I've got homework," I say.

My stomach feels like liquid. I can't imagine going to his house, being on my own with him. I wouldn't know what to do, what to say. I glance at Mum. She's looking at my plate, where all the food is untouched. I know if I don't start eating she's going to say something. Then they'll both be watching me.

I cut the pie into twelve equal little cubes, and arrange the potatoes in a circle. I have to eat. I *have* to eat, but I never know whose eyes are where. I slide the prongs into a chunk of meat. There's a roar in my ears like the sound of the ocean. Mum is telling him something about school, and his eyes are flickering over the gap in her blouse where the button's undone. She picks up her St Christopher medal, and slides it up and down on the chain. While they're talking I lift the fork real quick and open my mouth. But as I slide the meat between my lips he suddenly turns and stares right at me.

"Wouldn't you like that, Theresa?"

I drop the fork. It clatters on the plate. Gravy splatters over the white tablecloth.

"Theresa!" shouts Mum.

My fingers are fluttering. I don't know whether to pick up the fork or put my hands in my lap, or get up and fetch a cloth. Mum leaps from her chair, but Father Fergal grabs her arm.

"Sure, it was only an accident."

"The tablecloth," says Mum.

"Sit down, Denise."

His voice is deep and dark. Mum sits. There's silence round the table, and then Father Fergal says, "So, Theresa, will you come play for me?"

My hands are shaking. I want to say yes, but if I do she'll be raving mad.

"That would be putting you out," snaps Mum.

"It'd be a pleasure," he says. "In fact, I'll take Theresa back with me tonight. She can play to her heart's content."

"I should come," begins Mum.

"Why don't you pick her up at, say, nine?"

Mum presses her lips together and narrows her eyes.

"Grand," he says. "That's settled."

The only time the Carthiginian sisters open their mouths in public is when they sing. "You've never heard a beautiful voice until you've heard Mass sung at the chapel," says Sister Aloysius. "So mellifluous, girls. Like honey sliding from the tongue."

When she talks about it her eyes slip to the ceiling, like she's looking at God. I want to ask Sister Aloysius if the Carthiginian sisters have to be purified. Because if they never speak, if they never eat in front of anyone, if they never say anything sinful, then surely their mouths are as pure as they can be. But Mum told me never to talk about purification. She never talked about it when she was a girl. It's something everyone does, she says, but no one talks about.

Father Fergal doesn't say anything in the car. There's a box of prayer books on the back seat, with his green priest's gown draped over it, Coke cans and old newspapers all over the floor. We pull up under a street lamp in front of the church. It's really quiet here, not like our estate where there's always a dog barking, or a telly blaring, or Kath next door screaming at her kids. When we get out of the car it's starting to spit and I run to the church door, but Father Fergal laughs.

"I don't *live* in the church, child," he says. He turns the key in the front door of the house next to it. "Where d'you think I sleep? In the tabernacle?"

Inside it smells of boiled cabbage. He turns the light on in the passage and pushes open a door.

"This is where we stash the old lady."

The front room is little and square. It feels really lonely, and cold. There's three old armchairs, all different colours, an empty mantelpiece over a gas fire, and a wooden cross hanging on the wall. The piano is old and scratched, and the keys are yellow at the edges so they look thin, like old fingers, not fat and white like the keys on the school piano.

"There now," he says. "Let's make it cosy."

He moves around the room, snapping on lamps. As he lifts his arm to draw the curtains his jacket rides up over his waist. I look away.

"Sit down and have a tinkle," he says, clicking the button on the gas fire. There's a little puffing sound as it ignites. "She needs a good tune, but a talented girl like you could extract music from any old jalopy, eh?"

He walks towards me and stops behind the piano stool.

"What are you going to play? Chopin? Lovely."

He smells of cigarettes, but something else, too. Damp earth and bluebells and fungus, walking in the woods behind the school after it's been raining.

"Have a warm-up," he says. "I'll go make us a cuppa."

He goes out. My fingers are wobbly. I know he can hear me from the other room. Sometimes, when someone is listening to me play, especially a man, it feels like I'm naked.

I start playing the nocturne, and once I get going I don't think of anything but the music. There's a lake at night. Lights from a castle spark from the dark surface. A man rows a boat away from the shore, and the oars leave silver trails across the black water. On the shore is a girl in a long dress, holding her arms towards him and calling. But he doesn't stop, and the girl lifts her skirt and wades into the water up to her knees. I reach up to top C, and as my fingers come down the keys, the notes of the arpeggio are like pearls from a broken necklace; they fall and bounce away, one by one. The water seeps up to the girl's neck and closes over her head, until all you can see is a silver circle of ripples where she's disappeared.

I hold the last chord until the music fades.

"Beautiful."

Father Fergal is sitting in the chair next to the piano, his fingers clutching the arms.

"Come here, child," he says.

I look down at my hands.

"Are you afraid?" he says.

"No," I say. But I'm lying.

"Look at me."

The wave rises from the back of my head. My face starts to burn. My head shakes. I grip the sides of the piano stool. I look up. I lift my chin and look him in the eye. His face is blurry, everything shimmers, but I don't look away.

"Come here, child."

"I'm not a child," I say.

"No," he says. "Of course not. You're all grown up."

He cups his chin in his hand and looks across the room. He stares at the cross on the wall. It's just a plain wooden cross – there's no figure of Jesus on it – but a long shadow rises up the wall behind it, tall and black and lonely. For some reason I think that Father Fergal is going to cry, but then he says, in a soft voice, "Theresa. Come here, Theresa."

His voice sounds like music. His eyes are green. I've never noticed how green they are before. I stand up and walk over to him because I can't stop myself. It's like he's a magnet pulling me towards him. He reaches for my hand and pulls me down, so that I'm sitting next to him on the arm of the chair. I think about Kath kissing the man with the shaved head.

"Is there something you want to tell me?"

"No."

"You can trust me."

He strokes my hand. His wrist is covered in wiry black hair. It's strange how his arm could be so hairy while the palm of his hand is so warm and soft.

"You're a very special young lady," he says, gripping my hand. "You've a great talent. But there's something troubling you."

I think suddenly of the purifying rag, the smell of bleach, the cloth scouring my tongue, and think that if my dad hadn't left she would never have done it to me. He wouldn't let her. He would have stopped her.

"What is it?" he says.

"Nothing."

"Quite sure, now?"

My mouth is filthy. My mouth is disgusting. The rag is inside my mouth and I can't breathe. I'm gagging, I'm choking, and Mum is saying, "Mary, Mother of God, purge her of her sins," as she pushes it deeper inside, and presses her fingers over my lips. The bleach cuts into my skin. My tongue burns. The convulsion starts from my stomach, rises up my throat into my head. I try to breathe through my nose but there are only tiny wisps of chlorinated air.

When I come round, she is already running the water for the purging bath. She's kneeling beside me on the floor, praying. She helps me take off my clothes. She unbuttons my blouse, pulls it over my head, unzips the skirt, saying, "Clean at last, my angel, clean at last." She leads me into the dark bathroom and closes the door so I can take off my knickers in private. I sit in hot, clean water and hug my knees into my chest. I look at the window. The moon is a ragged pale circle in the dimpled glass.

Father Fergal is looking at me.

"Tell me, Theresa," he says.

It's raining outside. I can hear it drumming against the window. Father Fergal squeezes my hand.

"You can trust me," he says.

I open my mouth. I hesitate.

"Yes," he says.

"It's my mum," I say.

Then there's the sound of a key in a lock, and footsteps, but it sounds like it's not real, like the sounds are echoes in a nightmare, and I don't dare look at the door, I just look at Father Fergal's face, at the stubble on his chin, and feel the warmth of his strong hand in mine. But he's not looking at me; he's staring at the door, and all the sinews in his neck are straining.

The living-room door opens and Mum is there. Her car keys are bunched in one hand, and in the other she's clutching a single silver key. It's the little silver Yale I noticed hanging by the front door. The lamp light glints off it in sharp little spangles. She sees me looking at it, and shoves it in her coat pocket. Her eyes dart over to the arm of the chair, and Father Fergal snatches his hand away from mine. He leaps up.

"Denise," he says. "You're early."

He runs a hand through his hair. Mum looks at me.

"Go and get in the car," she says.

Father Fergal says, "Go, child."

The car is locked. I stand on the pavement. Raindrops prick my head. Water gushes down the gutter into the drain. It smells like the river.

Mum and Father Fergal are shouting inside the presbytery, and Mum is sobbing. Their silhouettes are black against the curtain. Then she moves away and there are footsteps coming down the hallway. The front door opens, and Mum says, "You've told her, haven't you?"

"No," he says. "Of course not."

Then she's dashing down the path and across the pavement towards me. Father Fergal appears on the doorstep.

"Denise!" he calls. "Come back!" But he doesn't come after her. The rain falls in front of his face like a crystal curtain. When I catch his eye, he looks away. Mum unlocks the car door.

"Get in!" she says.

Her eyes are wide, like they are when she does it to me: she puts her hand on my forehead and pushes my head back. She says, "Remember. I don't do this for myself. I do it for you. Because you were born of sin, and in sin you will always remain." I open my mouth and she pushes the rag inside, inch by inch. The fibres are rough against my tongue. She pushes until the rag is halfway down my throat. Everything is dry, rasping, my breath comes in moans and gasps. I can't control it. She holds her fingers over my lips and says, "Mary, Mother of God. Purify her. Purify her." I close my eyes. Everything is black. I am the girl in the nocturne, sinking towards the bottom of the lake.

"Get in!" she says again.

She grabs my arm and she's trying to push me down, but this time I snap my shoulder round and her hand flies away.

"Theresa!" she says, shocked.

She pulls me towards her. Her face is only an inch from mine, and I don't know what she will do, when suddenly her face is washed in yellow light. There's a car in the road behind me. Its tyres slush in the rain. Its engine purrs louder, louder, and then the brakes whine as it pulls up alongside us. I turn around. There's a man sitting in the driving seat, looking at us. He rolls down the window. I've seen him before, in church. A radio is playing inside his car, the lazy jangle of a saxophone, and the rough bulldog voice of a black singer. Mum drops my wrist. The man glances at the presbytery. I follow his gaze, just in time to see the door close and Father Fergal disappear inside.

"Everything all right, love?" says the man.

"Fine," says Mum.

"I was talking to *you*, love," he says, looking at me.

The man is balding on top and there are three thin strands of grey hair pasted across his scalp. He's got puffy eyes with big bags underneath. He looks about fifty, and I'm wondering how come he's listening to funky jazz music when he's that old. And then he raises his eyebrows at me, and his eyes look really kind, as if he does care if I'm all right or not.

"Yes," I say. "I'm all right."

"You're getting wet."

"It's OK," I say. "We're just going home."

We drive in silence. Her shoulders are wired all the way up to her ears. She snatches at the gear stick like she's strangling a snake. She doesn't say anything, so I look out at the rain and think about the Carthiginian sisters in the south of France. It rains there in spring and autumn, and sometimes in the summer there are showers, but it wouldn't smell of the river, it would smell of lavender. There would be no need for purification, because the only time you'd open your mouth would be to sing, and the sound would be so beautiful that your tongue, your teeth, your throat, everything would be pure. There would be no men, except for a priest to say Mass. Maybe he would be good-looking like Father

Fergal, and maybe he would care about me. Then suddenly, without thinking, I turn to Mum and say, "Is that why you made us move back here? So you could be near him?"

Her fingers clamp tight on the steering wheel.

"You know why we moved back," she says. "So you could go to a decent school."

I laugh. I know my laugh is cruel, but I don't care.

The rain dashes against the windscreen in long fingers, soothing and clean. I will go back to the presbytery after school next week and play for him again. I won't tell her, I'll just go. She can't stop me. Maybe he'll play something for me. I picture his long white fingers on the piano keys, stroking them like he's in love with them. I picture the Carthiginian sisters standing in the choir stalls every morning before breakfast, singing their psalms. They open their mouths wide so that you can see teeth, and red skin and tongues, but they don't look ugly. They look beautiful and pure. They open their mouths so that music comes flooding out like honey. And each note is pure and sweet, like a pearl dropping from the sky.

"
That's all we have, finally,
the words,
and they had better be
the right
ones.
"

Raymond Carver

EMBER
Thea Bennett

Winter is almost over. A bank of fog sits just off the shore. Nothing moves, save the grey sea sucking at the sand, and a long skein of geese above my head, speeding inland. They flail the air with their pointed wings and their cries float down to me.

When the tide turns, I will be leaving. Wherever it is that the geese have come from, flying up from the South, that is where I am going.

Behind me, Skard the cockerel gives his shrill stammering crow, calling me back to the village where I have lived almost as long as I have been a woman. Five boat-shaped wooden houses with turf roofs, standing in a circle, which sheltered my family and our thralls, and, through the frozen months, our beasts too. Beyond the village, the mean fields and the orchard from which we have scraped our living.

Our land is a strip between the bay and the mountains. The soil is thin and salty. Everything that grows must be tended carefully. Some years, for every grain of barley we planted, we harvested just one in return.

After the last two long winters as cold and hard as iron, and a wet summer without sun, the livestock perished, and the crops rotted in the soil. The other family members left. Now nothing lives and breathes in the village except myself, the old man, and Skard the cockerel. My livelihood has unravelled, like a cloak with a loose thread that pulls and pulls until the cloak is gone.

I do not have far to seek for the snag, the thorn that caught the thread. I only need remember the midsummer day that my husband Vigi set sail for the South West.

I could have gone with him. Many of the village women had already closed up their homes and sailed with their men. But the harvest was due, the cows in calf were near their time, and I did not want to leave them.

Vigi had not glanced at me for weeks, his blue eyes already glazing over with the wide horizon of the voyage to come. His days were spent at the wharf, with ropes and tar and hammers. Why would I leave my own hearth, to sit in a cold corner of the boat for days on days, not knowing what we would find at the other end?

When Vigi leaned in the door, blocking the light, his eyes not meeting mine, and asked me to go with them, I told him no. He went away, without another word, and daylight flooded back in to the house. Something shifted inside me, a belt unbuckling around my heart. I felt light and free. But now, I think refusing to follow my husband was the first mistake I made.

After they had gone, and the bay was quiet again, I walked around the boundary of our farm, looking at the young barley in the fields, the peas ready for picking, the white onions gleaming through the sandy soil.

Ember followed me. The little red mare Ember. Other husbands came back from the South and decked their wives with brooches and bangles and necklets, giving them fine carved chests with iron locks to keep these treasures safe. The only trinket I possess is the rope of polished amber beads that came to me when my mother died. And the only gift Vigi brought me was the mare, trussed by the legs like a chicken in the bottom of the ship.

When they heaved her overboard and untied her she lay on the beach for half a day, sometimes lifting her head to look around and then dropping it again. I sat by her, after the men had eaten, and fed her grains of barley and handfuls of water from the stream. She licked my hands and as evening came she stood up and took a few faltering steps, weaker than a foal from the long voyage.

Her body was deep red, like the hot ashes when a fire dies down, or the harvest moon when it hangs low in the sky. Her long tail, and the coarse hair that fell over her neck and into her eyes were pale, like the bleached grass on the dunes.

That is the colour of my hair, too. Perhaps that is why I loved her, and felt her to be almost as a sister.

The five strong foals Ember bore, Vigi took as soon as they were grown, including the first of them, the iron-grey colt Sleipnir, named for Odin's eight-legged steed, the best of all horses. I mourned for them when they were gone, trussed like their mother in the bottom of the boat. Carried off to fight and perhaps die on a foreign shore. How would I have felt if it was my sons Vigi took with him? I shall not ever know, since the two of them did not live beyond a month.

I did not begrudge Ember her fecundity. She knew that she was mine. Whenever I left the house, she saw me from the fields and called to me. As I worked on the farm, if she was not with me, carrying my baskets slung across her back, I knew that every time I looked up from my digging or hoeing she would be watching me through the long pale hair that fell around her face as she cropped the grass.

I saved her life, in the first year after she came. I found her one day lying in the long grass, her sides wet with sweat and a single long foreleg of her foal hanging out of her body. Its fellow was trapped inside her, bent back against itself, and she was fighting in vain to push it out.

A cow may labour for hours without harm, but a mare will die if she is left to struggle. I had to get the foal laid right. It is easy, with a ewe, to get your hand in and turn the lamb to where it needs to be. Ember was tight and dry inside, and her body contracted, trapping my hand and arm. She groaned and rolled her eye at me, and I knew that I was causing her pain.

I lay in the grass with her and slowly I forced the leg back, and pushed my hand in after it, seeking for the second small hoof to pull it forward, so that her foal could come into the world nose on knees, as every foal should.

I did it, in the end. The black-coated foal fell out of her and lay in a puddle of long limbs beside us. Ember, despite her weariness, was on her feet and licking the small one dry within moments. They both lived, he to grow tall, and become Sleipnir, Vigi's mount, and she to be my companion.

That was when we still had times of plenty, before the weather turned bleak and cruel.

The winter after Vigi left brought cold like I had never known. We survived, because we had grain and other food in store, milk from the cows and sheep that we kept alive, and salted meat from the old and feeble animals that we killed. Two other households stayed through that winter, but when the summer came with dark skies and lashing rain, and they saw the sheep sicken and die, and the crops wilting with blackened stems, they left for the Southern lands across the sea, taking the starving thralls with them.

This last winter, with the cold gnawing at our bones like a wolf, it was just myself and the father of my sister's husband. He sat by the fire all day, talking of the good times past through one side of his mouth, hobbling to the door to piss with his bad leg dragging on the earth floor.

So it was I that had to find wood for the fire, and break the ice so that we had water to drink. We killed the last cow, and she kept us for a while, and then one by one we killed the scrawny hens, which no longer laid because there was no grain for them to eat. And then there was nothing except limpet stew and berries.

The red and purple berries that grow over the mountain shock the mouth with tartness. Sometimes they are sweet, but they do not fill the stomach. And there are always limpets on the shore, but they are not good to eat. However long you boil them, they are hard, like gristle. My jaws ached from the chewing. Day after day, I added more tiny limpet shells to the crusted pile on the dunghill, and as the snow fell we grew hungrier.

The shortest day passed. The evenings began to lighten and turn blue. We waited for the spring to come, for the stream to flow, for the icicles that bound the edges of the roof to let go. But the ice of the far North had crept down to visit us. The cold grew deeper and we grew weaker. I looked at my body and saw that I had become lean and flat as a girl again. My monthly bleeding ceased, and my skin grew dry and loose.

Each day I crept to the foot of the mountain to look for wood. For small pieces, that I could carry easily, that I did not have to chop. My arms could scarcely lift the axe. Each day I beat the stream with a stone to break the ice, my fingers burnt purple with cold. The old man grew quiet, his head drooping, and he needed my shoulder now, to get him to the door. How much longer? I thought, as I watched the steam from his piss rising against the star-studded sky. I have never seen the stars so bright, as that winter.

I kept Ember in the house with us, for her warmth, and for company. She was old now and I feared she might freeze to death outside. She did not like to be shut in, and stood always by the door, smelling the cold air through the gaps in the wood, and waiting for me to let her out.

One afternoon, after a night of strong wind, I went into the orchard to look for fallen branches, and she followed me slowly, her ribs like the timbers of a wreck. As I walked under the apple trees, I heard a sound that stopped my heart.

Men's voices shouting and the crunch of a ship's prow hitting the beach. At first I thought it was strangers, and then I was afraid that Vigi had returned. I crouched behind a tree. Ember came and stood over me, her head hanging. Tiny snowflakes fell, drifting between the bare branches and catching in the long hairs of her coat. I breathed in her smell – horse dust and sweet hay.

The men were laughing and talking, and I heard the thud of their feet as they walked to the village. They seemed to know their way. One man came into the orchard. A tall man, wrapped in a heavy fur, over which his face glowed like the last apple left on the top branch of a winter tree, the one that no one can reach.

"Aunt!" he shouted. "Why are you hiding from me?"

Hardrada, my sister's firstborn. I saw him pulled from her, wrinkled and dark as a dried plum, his hair a cluster of red flames springing from his scalp.

He ran up the track and hugged me as if he were still a child, and not a man with limbs like seasoned wood from long months at sea, and fair skin burned scarlet by the salt spray and the slash of the North wind.

"Aunt!" he laughed, and I caught the dark smell of hunger on his breath, and felt the bleached rough hair of his beard graze my face.

He grabbed me by the shoulders, and felt the bones of my arms.

"I came by for some of your good broth," he said, "but from the lack of flesh on you I'm not sure the fare will be worth having."

I told him of the cows and sheep, all killed and eaten, and the hens that had stopped laying, and found their way, too, into the pot. I spoke of the wet crops ruined in the fields. I felt the shame of the host who has nothing to give the guest, the family member returned to the fold.

He frowned, and I saw again the angry red-haired child screaming on the mud floor of the house, while my sister covered her ears with her cloak. *Hardrada* – the hard ruler – my sister's husband named him; the tyrant of the family, whose cries rang from one end of the village to the other.

Ember pushed her head between us, and Hardrada grinned. I remembered the child's quick change from tempest to sunshine. His wide smile and the soft skin of his fat limbs when I carried him on my hip. My sister's secondborn came quickly, and as I was still unmarried I took over the care of Hardrada. I loved him like my own child, for all his rages.

Hardrada clapped his hand down on Ember's rump. His eyes were as blue as a summer afternoon on the bay. "Here is plenty for all of us, today," he said.

As the crescent moon crept up the dark-blue winter sky, Hardrada spoke, whispering words that made me shiver with desire. "Roast . . . meat . . . blood . . . marrow . . ." he said, his breath and the hair of his beard teasing my ear.

My frozen body ached for food, and for the first time in many days saliva flowed into my mouth. I remembered the day I pulled Sleipnir from Ember and how she lay and let me hurt her to save her life. I looked at her drooping head and half-closed eyes and the great sagging dip in her bony back. Did she know that I planned her death?

"She will not last the week," said Hardrada, stepping back from me. "Let's eat her now, while she still has an ounce of flesh to feed us."

"Do it," I said, and stumbled back to the house. Though I think it saved my life, I felt that I had betrayed my dearest friend, the second mistake I made.

The fire the men built that night leaped higher than the house roofs. I sat in my doorway. There was nothing for me to do; no meal to grind for barley bread, no green thing to put in the pot. The men, who had roasted a thousand stolen beasts on a thousand distant beaches, were more skilled than I at the job. From my perch on the step I saw Ember's body carried to the fire, slung by the hooves from a thick pole. They peeled back the soft red hide from her flesh, hacked at her limbs with cleavers. I was glad I did not see the moment of her death.

As I crammed hot crisp meat into my mouth, I blessed Ember for the life flooding back into my veins. My head felt light and I wanted to get up and dance around the fire. I saw Hardrada's eyes on me through the smoke and I knew I must go back to the house.

I might be the head of the village, being the only able-bodied person left, but these were men who had been a long time at sea, without a woman. I should leave before they grew unruly.

I lay on the bed and watched the red ashes on the hearth. Hardrada had told the men to carry his grandfather out to share in the feast, and I had the house to myself. A shield lay by the hearth, and on its metal boss I saw two dragons, their slim necks and long limbs twisted together so that I could not tell one from the other.

My body felt heavy from the meat. I fell into sleep, dreaming of the twining dragons, until I woke in darkness and felt someone holding my ankle.

"You are hiding from me again," said Hardrada.

"The old man . . ." I said, blinking against the dark.

"He is sleeping with the others, minding his business like a good grandfather."

Hardrada's fingers moved up to grasp the tight muscle of my calf.

"I am Vigi's wife . . ."

"Vigi!" said Hardrada, and I heard his lips click in disdain.

I sat up to push him away and his hair brushed against my cheek. It smelt of smoke. Not the familiar smoke of our hearth, but other smoke. Of beach fires and burning thatch. The smoke of many days and many sea miles travelled. I felt the heat from his body, though I did not touch him.

"Be good to me," said Hardrada.

I was filled with meat, and yet still hungry. I had been cold for so long, and he was so warm. I lay back again.

At the first I clenched tight with shock. I thought of the ship's sharp wooden prow driving into the pebbles of the beach. Hardrada sighed a long sigh, his breath soft on my face, and then he fastened his teeth in my shoulder and my body loosed itself to join with him.

The voyage of our pleasure was a long one, wild waves rising and falling through the night until we washed up on the shores of sleep, knotted together like the beasts on the shield.

In the morning, he was gone. I lay warm in the bed and felt his heat and his weight still on and in my body. I knew that I had made my third mistake, though how I could have turned aside from it I did not know.

Bright sunlight came through the chink at the edge of the door. I could hear Skard the cockerel crowing on the dunghill, and the drip of water falling from the roof. The icicles were melting.

Later, I went up to the stream with my jar. I knelt down and pressed the jar against the melting ice, so that the water could seep in.

The men slept for most of the day. They had drunk ale from the ship all through the night. I heard their snores from the house doors as I passed by, turning my eyes away from the pile of red hide and flaxen horsehair that lay by the smoking ashes of the bonfire.

Hardrada was nowhere about. Then as the light began to fade and the clear sky turned from blue to lavender, I saw him in the orchard. All day I had felt strong and well from the food, but at the sight of his red hair my legs turned weak again.

I wanted to speak to him, but what could I say? I wanted to cancel out the night, to go back to being the head of the village, Aunt, safe and unreachable. I wanted to forget, but I could still smell his hair, feel his teeth on the bruises that were darkening on my skin.

He saw me, and began to walk down to the houses. The men were stirring now, swearing and grunting, and I went to meet him, not wanting them to see us together. We stood by the stream, its gurgling flow filling the air. His eyes were full of evening light, blue grey, warning of the chill to come.

"Sail with us," he said. "We are two men short on the ship. You have ploughed these fields enough years, why shouldn't you pull an oar for us when we are tired?"

"Where are you going?" I said, my voice thick in my throat.

"I go my own way, as you should know. I am not one to stick

with the fleet," he said.

"Take me to Kaupang," I said. "I will find some family among the traders there, who will take me and feed me."

"I could do that. And waste a week in chatter and nonsense." He shook his head, frowning. "The weather is turning, the wind will be with us. I am going South."

"With just one ship?" I said.

He laughed. "Why not? I'll find a place where none has gone before, and make it my own."

I looked around at the bleached dead grass, with patches of snow still lying. I thought of the long months before any crops could grow, and I knew that I had no choice. I must leave.

There is nothing left alive in the village now except the cockerel Skard. There is no meat on the bird, he is all legs and ragged green and brown feathers, but he still has plenty of voice. He crows and crows, striding up and down on top of the dunghill. Maybe he misses his women, long since boiled in the pot, or maybe the bustle of our departure has excited him.

"For sure, I would like some hot soup before I go!" Hardrada shouts, and runs up the side of the midden. His cloak catches under his foot and he falls on his face in the limpet shells and cow dung. Skard, king of the castle, looks at him with a beady brown eye, scarlet wattles falling to the side of his sharp little beak.

Should I tell Hardrada not to waste his time? Should I regale him with the many sagas of pursuit and escape that Skard and I have enacted in the last two years? There is a good reason the bird still lives to crow and lord it over all of us. He was always the fastest creature in the village, on two legs or four.

Hardrada is up again and running across the top of the midden. Skard dodges in front of him, and just as Hardrada reaches for his tail, he jumps in the air, long legs waving, and flies clumsily up into the willow trees. Yes, Skard has the advantage over us earthbound ones.

One of the men shouts from the jetty: "Save your breath. Take a net and catch him!"

Hardrada is bent double, up on the dunghill. Is he hurt from his fall? And then I see that he is laughing, long red hair dipping and shaking. "Outdone!" he says. "Defeated! By a mangy bag-of-bones bird! Forget the net – let him live! He deserves it – he has beaten me in unarmed combat. There are many who are not so lucky. And the tide is right for us now. We cannot wait!"

Down at the jetty, the men are loading a bundle of red hide and bones, all that is left of Ember. The scraps will feed us on our journey.

The long ship Freyja shifts in the water as they step aboard, and Hardrada lays a hand tenderly on her rounded wooden side, as if to still and reassure her. I see that his fingers sense every plank, every wooden nail of her body, every rise and fall of her long dragon's neck.

I take only my clothes with me. Let my cooking pots, my hand plough, my rake and hoe, stay by the old hearth where they belong. There is no one left to steal them. So I have little to carry, as I climb aboard.

I have never been on a long ship before, only the small boats that travel up and down the coast. I am not prepared for the thrill of Freyja moving under me. Her readiness to respond to the wavelets in the creek. Her desire for the expanse of ocean stretching before us. My feet are singing beneath me. It is like taking a first breath.

They are carrying the old man down to the jetty. He weeps and begs to stay and die in the place where he was born. Hardrada tells him no. "We need you. You know the sea like no one else. Where we are going there are no sea marks set on the cliffs to guide us. You must help us to find a safe path." They lift him over the high wooden side of the ship and stow him in the prow.

And then we are cast off, and we slip with the tide away from the shore until Freyja's jaunty dragon's eye is veiled in the mist of the fog bank.

Behind me, I hear the lonely cockerel Skard calling, the stuttering jewel-bright crow that circled my days in the village like the amber beads that hang around my neck.

THE FAREWELL TOUR
K. K. Dayal

They make me smile. The matriarchs wobbling in full saris further into the sea, their petticoats drawn up to their knees as they battle the muscular waves and their waiting sons' abashed sighs. My fingers skirt the urn beside me and I'm thinking of her.

Where would Mum be in this crowd here, in Kanyakumari? In a *salwar kameez*, naturally, the trousers folded above the reach of the surf, green-purple veins clambering up her calves. She would be laughing as she tries to keep her balance, her arms outstretched as she tightropes to safety. It's not imagination but a memory regained: a chilled Blackpool when I was ten. I remember that day for its disappointment. The beach was unforgivingly hard and refused to submit to our dreams of sandcastles. The vast twin greys of sky and sea united to make me feel smaller than I'd thought possible.

"Chai, coffee, kappi. Chai, coffee, kappi," shouts the clinking-blinking chai man over and over with breaths so slyly squeezed in that they are barely there at all. He sways through the crowds so the smell of cardamom can waft on to entice new customers.

"Such small coffees?" the woman sitting further down-wall from me complains. Chai man doesn't answer but continues shouting off his chorus – "Chai, coffee, kappi" – as he waits for her to drink up and return his glass.

There's a different crowd here every day. They come to watch the sea swallow the sun, only to be disgorged the next morning. Prepubescents in frilled pink dresses, mothers' saris in the sharpest of concertina folds, boys wriggling out of chequered shirts to rush into the sea – they all stop their laughter and play for the ten-minute extravaganza. They hold their breath and watch the sun softening to a chalky pill dissolving into the clouds, into the sea.

I conjure my mother.

I can see her navigating away from the daredevil South Indian boys performing sea-somersaults for ripening women. I hear her tutting at these girls as they guard their younger siblings from mischief they themselves court while playing demure – slowly lowering their heavy petal-lids before boldly raising them until eyes meet and their noses stand proud in the sea spray.

Mum wouldn't register the men's underwear being outed: vests, *lunghis*, *kischae* and briefs with big jelly bellies. Being Indian, even one gone foreign, she accepts the spectacle, leaving only me to draw my eyes away from where thin cotton *dhotis* are wetted to transparency. She tries to impress her betters and to Ma everyone is better. I see her homing in, unembarrassed, on the smattering of Hindi spoken by tourist-pilgrims from further north, their fairer skin attracting her like a beacon. I see myself attempting to dissuade her, trying to tell her that they're middle-class Indians, we're working-class foreigns; we're not the same sort at all.

"Ma, let's check out that museum." I see her refusing to be distracted from her target but grudgingly following me inside when she realises I'm not waiting for her. In the twenty-five years since arriving in England as a young bride, Mum sent us kids off on numerous school trips in our best tracksuits or ribboned dresses and carrying packed lunches, never once wondering where we went. Here in this new India, where Ma's norms were skewed, I could remedy the situation with an excursion of her own. "So which one do you like, Ma? OK, how about portraits? Do you like people? How about these landscapes? You like doing the garden – it's the same thing, kind of . . ." I say before she walks out, agitated by the pointlessness of it all. The waste of time, the waste of doing, when the painters could have been, should have been, building families instead of colouring in. When I should have, could have, built my own family too.

The couple to the left of me leave with the setting sun and I'm exposed; alone amidst these jostling parcels of day-tripping families and friends. I begin to walk back to the guest house, shaking off the pedlar swinging his yo-yo back and forth to the rhythm of "Mad-am. Mad-am."

I am slower than usual. My ankle is swollen, poisoned by mosquitoes who swill my blood with that of the common junk-tourists. At a distance, I take a final look back. Yo-yo man has found a real foreigner, with more foreign skin than mine.

In the morning I get up at 5:30 to try again. I've been in Kanyakumari for a week; seven sunrises and seven sunsets, seen but not embraced. I decide this has to stop today. No more procrastination. No more purgatorial drama. I take my mother's urn and put it in my shoulder bag, the one with a smiling baby-blue Krishna, the perfect disguise for Ma.

I grab a place on the easten sea wall. The sun, when it rises, emerges not from the sea but from a mass of dark flat cloud, two thumb-widths deep, which sits on the water. The solemnity of the moment is broken by a camera man's persistence. "Cam-ra, cam-ra, cam-ra. Cam-ra, cam-ra, cam-ra," he shouts, flashing the flashbulb with each cry. Finally a balding city-pilgrim snaps, "How many cameras do I need, yaar?" and pulls the camera hanging round his neck, driving it into the camera man's face. I can see this is not going to end peacefully and, clutching my bag, stand as far away as possible.

I feel myself tensing up again, my jaw bolting shut. The morning shows are always so serious that I think sunset would be a better time to launch Mum into her sea travels. Yet come dusk I know I'll be so swallowed by the local flavour, I'll forget she's in my bag at all.

I'm not sure how I ended up in this polarised rut – no one said sunrise or sundown. Certainly no one mentioned the sea at all. I didn't set out wanting to rescue Mum from her landlocked Punjabi beginning to this place with a choice of three oceans. It just feels so poetic, or it did. Now all it gives me is sweaty hands and a squirming stomach. I have to let her go. She has to go, and if I can't do it here I should take her back to Punjab, where she'd want to be.

Mum had always wanted to go back to where she had begun. "India," she had summoned in her final thin voice. I did try Punjab first, Mum tucked in my hand luggage on the Amritsar-bound flight. I stayed where my mother had grown up, in the house of the grandmother I had never met. Beebeeji, as I had been taught to call her, had died years ago when I was a teenager. Mum wasn't able to come out for the funeral – it was a busy time at the factory, or bakery as Mum and the other cake-packers loyally called it.

I had met my mum's brothers and their wives five years ago, when Mum last had some sick leave. There were only two brothers left in India now, sharing the house with their seven children. The wives devotedly maintained the home front, milking their cattle and picking vegetables for dinner. My uncles, meanwhile, drank whisky in the sugarcane fields, chewing over their fears of dismal harvests and falling rice prices.

My mother's sisters, my *massia*, lived in villages close to where my mother's marriage had been settled. They came in one collective swoop to visit me, vocally disappointed by my thin plait and healthy girth. They were used to Mum turning up with a suitcase of presents and a belly full of gossip. I did not try to compete and sat there meekly drinking my sugar-rock tea while my dirty rucksack slumped in the corner. They cried the respectable amount for the loss of their sister before allowing their tears to turn bitter, despairing at how little they heard from my youngest uncle and his family, who had recently gone foreign by moving to San Jose.

Walking around the narrow cobbled streets and dusty roads, I discovered the once familiar houses had grown bloated with needless features like tall peacock-coloured gates and additional terraces; the whole village breathed the brittle cement-scent of change. Proud residents ushered me inside homes built on the sweat of their sons waiting tables in Hounslow and husbands tending oranges in California. Drinking sweet tea, they shared their dry biscuits and dreams of soon joining their men overseas.

I could not leave Mum there. With so many people eager to abandon those territories. I felt that even the "expired", as they tactfully call the dead in India, still deserved to know life was close by.

When Ma had gone, we argued that she wasn't all that sentimental. But in the end I couldn't just dump her in the River Severn, even though my brother tried to convince me it might be what she really wanted. It was hard to know where she belonged, especially since, if she was with me, all she'd say was: "Stupid girl. Stop wasting your time with me. Go to Punjab, meet a tall Sikh husband . . . Your aunts can introduce you."

Dad didn't give me any procedural advice. He didn't say anything at all when I took her from their red-brick semi. He just sat at the plastic-covered dining table staring at his untouched sausages and the ice cream melting in its dish.

My brother resisted, said it was his job as the only son. I didn't know if he was right or wrong but didn't want to fight. Then as my hands became butter-soft around the brassy curves of the urn, his became tense claws. The last time he had left Britain was for a school trip to France – he'd come back with a broken heart. I hadn't known him to leave the Midlands since. So it was, Mum finally belonged to just me.

I could only manage to stay a week in Punjab before I got on the first internal flight. It disturbed me, looking at the list of destinations – Mumbai, Lucknow, Bangalore – that they could be India too. The first flight happened to be to Chennai, in India's southernmost state of Tamil Nadu. It felt like kismet. All I knew in that waiting room was that I wanted to get the furthest away I could from what Mum had been, while still keeping to her wishes of an Indian farewell.

This morning I sat at the Kanyakumari bus stand for an hour, letting the hands of my watch glide on; and still further on past my departure time. Given in to heaviness, I was unable to board the bus let alone respond to the intrusive questions that pass for small talk on the sub-continent. "What is your good name?" and "Why are you so fatty?" and "Why are you not in air-con?" I had no choice; repulsed by the future, defeated by the past, I had to stay here until it was done.

Ma has begun to interrupt my conversations with others. I am not allowed to forget my disloyalty. "Are you single?" "Just you, madam, in double room?" When I confirm their suspicions it always sounds like a confession and I can hear Mum laughing at me. Shutting me up. Sending me back to my room. I'm tired of it. Of her. I'm beginning to hate her. Her need to be released so far from us. Her constant disapproval from over my shoulder.

I need to leave my room and get back to the shore. I need to get back to the peninsula where India recedes to a pinpoint, her breadth surrendered to the sea. I wipe the sweat pooled in the crevices of my neck, and lie back on my cot. I try to turn the whirr of the fan into the gushing of the ocean with its power to lull us into serenity. I must sleep; she must let me sleep if she doesn't want me to hold her hostage.

In my dreams I climb over the sea wall on the east, careful not to slip on the sheen of the rocks. There is no clue that light is going to be reborn; it's so dark and final, even the sea is afraid. Ma slips free, grains of her sticking to my fingers, but mostly free. The sea inhales her until her grey is the grey of the three seas. Now she will go to places she didn't even know she wanted to. My eyes are not on the sun when it rises, but on the foam, watching fragments of my mother trying to scramble back to her precious India. A small piece of her, I hope, trying to make its way back to us.

I wake up in the morning darkness. Today I will walk to the east wall. Today I will return alone.

NOTES ON CONTRIBUTORS

Anna Ackland grew up in north Essex. She taught English as a foreign language in Spain and Japan. While teaching creative writing, she started to write herself. Since then, she has performed a comic piece at the Greenbelt Arts Festival, and is now working on a collection of poems and stories about trees.

Chimamanda Ngozi Adichie was born in Nigeria. She is the author of two novels, *Purple Hibiscus* and *Half of a Yellow Sun*, and is the recipient of a 2008 MacArthur Foundation Fellowship. Her story collection *The Thing Around Your Neck* was published in April 2009 by Fourth Estate.

Anna Baggaley graduated from Bristol University with a BA in English and Drama. After a brief stint of globetrotting, she began a career in publishing. Currently working in the editorial department of a world-famous romance publisher, Anna lives in South London and enjoys reading, eating cake and being right.

Thea Bennett is a writer and actress, and divides her time between Northamptonshire and London. She has published two novelisations of children's TV serials, and enjoys reading her short stories at writLOUD. "Ember" forms part of the novel she is currently working on.

Emily Cleaver has had work published in *Smoke* and *One Eye Grey* magazines, performed at the live fiction events Liars' League, Tales of the DeCongested and writLOUD, and is working on a collection of stories set in Victorian London. She works in a second-hand bookshop on Charing Cross Road.

Peter Ho Davies is the author of a novel, *The Welsh Girl*, longlisted for the Man Booker Prize, and two story collections, *The Ugliest House in the World* and *Equal Love*. One of Granta's Best of Young British Novelists, he currently teaches in the US.

K. K. Dayal lives in London. Her work has featured in the 2003 Serpent's Tail anthology *Kin*. She is currently working on a novel.

Jon Elsom was born in Southampton and lives in London. He is a creative director in a large advertising agency. "The Other Side of Anything" is his third piece of published fiction and is an extract from the novel of the same name, on which he is currently working.

Richard English is a British Academy Award-winning researcher who writes for *Rocks Backpages*. His publications include *Living with Hepatitis C* (1997) and *Coping Successfully with Hepatitis C* (2000). For 2009, he is the recipient of a grant from Arts Council England (Literature) to complete his novel *Sunrise with Sea Monsters*.

Sue Gedge has twice read at writLOUD. Her first novel, *The Practical Woman's Guide to Living with the Undead*, can be read on www.authonomy.com. She has contributed a short story to the Romantic Novelists' Association anthology *Loves Me, Loves Me Not*, published in autumn 2009 by Mira Books.

"You're Listening to Paul Power" is an extract from the novel of the same name, **Graham Hodge**'s first book about a primetime radio DJ who wants to make amends – on air. Graham has a BA in Modern Languages from Merton College, Oxford and an MA in Creative Writing from Birkbeck, University of London. He is thirty-five and has a family, a mortgage and a day-job in the music industry.

Joanna Ingham writes fiction, poetry and drama. She was a runner-up in the BBC Wildlife Poet of the Year Competition 2008. Joanna works part time at The Women's Library running education projects, primarily with young women. She also facilitates poetry and scriptwriting workshops in a range of settings including schools and day centres for older people.

Kavita Jindal's short stories, poems and articles have been widely published in literary journals, anthologies and newspapers. Her poetry collection *Raincheck Renewed* was published to critical acclaim by Chameleon Press in 2004. Kavita was born in India and currently lives in London. Selected work can be read on www.kavitajindal.com.

Russell Celyn Jones is the author of *Soldiers and Innocents*, which won the David Higham Prize, *Small Times*, *An Interference of Light*, *The Eros Hunter*, *Surface Tension* and *Ten Seconds from the Sun*. He has taught at the universities of Iowa, East Anglia and the Western Cape, South Africa, and currently runs the Creative Writing Programme at Birkbeck, University of London. His retelling of one of the stories in the Welsh folktale collection *The Mabinogion*, from which "Lord of Dyfed" is an extract, will be published by Seren in October 2009.

Chris Lilly was born in 1953, and moved to East London in 1977. He teaches in Tower Hamlets and lives on the Isle of Dogs. He started writing again after a twenty-year break for children. He is currently in the second year of the Birkbeck Creative Writing Certificate course.

Mary Irene Masaba writes children's stories. A teacher and a newsreader for Radio Uganda/Uganda Television, she relocated to the UK in the 80s and worked as an outreach worker. She was a runner-up in the T. S. Eliot International Short Story Competition 2007. "Loving Relatives" is from a novel in progress.

Jean McNeil is originally from Nova Scotia, Canada. She is the author of *Hunting Down Home*, *Nights in a Foreign Country*, *Private View* and

The Interpreter of Silences. A novel set in Antarctica, *The Ice Lovers*, will be published in September 2009. She lives in London.

Richard Milward was born in Middlesbrough in 1984. He is the author of two novels, *Apples* (2007) and *Ten Storey Love Song* (2009), both published by Faber, receiving accolades from such folk as Irvine Welsh and Lauren Laverne. He is currently working on the screenplay for *Apples*, as well as a new novel. A recent Fine Art graduate of Byam Shaw School of Art, Richard has been known to read from his novels with a hand-painted mask on his bonce.

Born in northern France in the 70s, **David Quéva** has been teaching modern foreign languages for the last seven years. He started learning English at the age of twelve and moved to London in 1998. His writing reflects his French background and his interests include the supernatural and world literature. He is currently working on a collection of short stories.

Josh Raymond is a rowing coach. His short stories have appeared in *The Mechanics' Institute Review* Issue 5 and *Tales of the DeCongested* Volume 2, and he sometimes writes book reviews for the *TLS*.

Lesley Saunders was born in south-east London. She has worked as a journalist on the *Mail on Sunday*, the *Evening Standard*, and a national newspaper in Ghana, West Africa. Her other passion is music, and she currently writes classical reviews, in between working on her second novel.

David Savill lived and worked in Hungary, Bosnia and Georgia before joining the BBC as a documentary programme maker. His short stories "Death in the Family" and "Table Rock Lake" are published by Tindal Street Press. He works as a visiting lecturer in creative writing at the University of East London. David is completing his first novel, *The Last Days of David Hasselhoff*, from which "Free Country" is an extract.

Moira Sharpe works as a student adviser in a big adult education college in central London. She was born in York but has lived in

Hackney long enough to feel like a Londoner. She is currently studying on Birkbeck's Creative Writing Certificate course and is working on a collection of short stories.

Originally from Western Australia, **M. L. Stedman** lives in London. Her stories have been published in the anthologies *Desperate Remedies* and *Tales of the DeCongested* Volume 1. "Notes of Experiments on Mice and Other Mammals" is from her collection *Outsiders Within*. She is now writing a novel.

Margi Williams is a southern California native who spent 2008-09 in London, writing and learning about life on the other side of the pond. She hopes to return to the UK permanently some day, but for now she is working on her first novel back under the California sun.

Maggie Womersley completed the Birkbeck MA in Creative Writing in 2007. Her first novel, *Eddie Bain's House of Horrors*, tells the story of a young family who discover a human skeleton under their garden shed. Maggie lives in London with her husband and son.

Carol Wong grew up in Victoria, Canada, and lived and worked in Vancouver before relocating to London in 2003. She completed the Birkbeck MA in Creative Writing in 2009. "The Cousins" is from a work in progress, a collection of linked short stories.